Christine Coleman spent her childhood in the Sussex countryside, and her late teens and early twenties in Dublin, where she learned to enjoy Guinness and climb mountains while gaining a degree in English. She now works as manager of an Adult Education Centre in Birmingham, and devotes most of her spare time to writing fiction and poetry.

The Dangerous Sports Euthanasia Society is the first of her novels to be published. The initial germ of the idea for this took hold while she was dangling from a paraglider 3,000 feet above a lagoon on an island in the Indian Ocean. She believes that the saying 'Life begins at forty', doesn't go far enough, and feels that as we get older we can gain inspiration from seeing people in their seventies or eighties rise to the challenge of new ventures.

THE DANGEROUS SPORTS EUTHANASIA SOCIETY

After her escape from an old people's home where her son, Jack, and his new partner have placed her, Agnes's quest to find her grandchildren is complicated by unexpected encounters. These new friends include: Joe, the helpful lorry driver; Molly, the garrulous hotel-owner; Gazza, the student; and Felix, the retired barrister's clerk, whom Agnes pulls back from attempted suicide. Hoping to rekindle Felix's desire to live, she invents the Dangerous Sports Euthanasia Society, but soon fears that this falsehood, having acquired a momentum of its own, will end in tragedy.

CHRISTINE COLEMAN

THE DANGEROUS SPORTS EUTHANASIA SOCIETY

Complete and Unabridged

ULVERSCROFT
Leicester

First published in Great Britain in 2005 by
Transita
Oxford

First Large Print Edition
published 2008
by arrangement with
Transita
Oxford

British Library CIP Data

Coleman, Christine
    The dangerous sports euthanasia society.—
    Large print ed.—
    Ulverscroft large print series: general fiction
    1. Older women—Psychology—Fiction
    2. Older women—Family relationships—Fiction
    3. Large type books
    I. Title
    823.9′2 [F]

    ISBN 978–1–84782–209–3

Published by
F. A. Thorpe (Publishing)
Anstey, Leicestershire

Set by Words & Graphics Ltd.
Anstey, Leicestershire
Printed and bound in Great Britain by
T. J. International Ltd., Padstow, Cornwall

This book is printed on acid-free paper

DEDICATION

For my mother, and for Douglas,
Sara and David.

Acknowledgements

With thanks to Helen Purcell, Andy Oldfield and Paul Lathrope for their encouragement and helpful comments throughout the long process of bringing Agnes to life; to Helen Carey for her guidance in the early stages; and to Clarissa Dickson Wright for sowing the first seeds of the idea for this novel during our discussions about writing a TV script.

1

Agnes Borrowdale, seventy-five years old a
week on Tuesday, hoisted herself onto the
window sill and perched astride it, gripping
the wooden frame. So far, so good, she
murmured, still buoyed up by the surge of
excitement. Then she turned her head from
the safety of the room and peered down over
the edge. Far below her dangling foot, blobs
of yellow floated on a blur of green. She
screwed her eyes tight shut, but it was too
late: every muscle was quivering like snapped
elastic. With a huge effort of will, she tilted
her body towards the room and collapsed
onto the pale pink carpet.

When her head stopped spinning she
hauled herself up again and took a dozen
faltering steps across to the bed. Without
removing her trainers, she lay flat on her back
and closed her eyes. 'In, two, three, four, five,
hold your breath, and — out, two, three, four,
five.' The bracing voice of that keep fit tutor
had left its mark. After a few more deep
breaths her heart resumed its normal,
imperceptible beat.

Agnes stared up at the high ceiling. Strange

that she'd not noticed this similarity to the bedroom she'd shared for half a century with Henry: the map of hair-line cracks in the grey-white plaster.

Sitting upright with her legs straight in front of her on the bed she contemplated her feet in their almost brand-new trainers, and became aware again of her quickening heart. Adrenalin, she reassured herself. It'll help me think straight.

One: she must not be seen by anyone in these clothes. Phyllis Mapperley, or some other member of staff was bound to be hovering near reception in the hall, and if she tried the back stairs she risked bumping into one of the cooks or cleaners. If she really was going to carry out her plan that day, the window was the only answer.

Two: The Harmony Home For The Young At Heart was built on a slope, so the first-floor windows at the back were in fact much closer to the ground than the ones at the front. Anyway, didn't heights always appear more daunting from above?

Three: this attack of vertigo had taken her by surprise. Once she'd prepared herself mentally, she'd be better able to cope. 'Mind over Matter', Henry always said.

'Now then, Lambkin . . . ' His voice again. His idea of a joke: Agnus Dei — Lamb of

God. She could almost feel warm air stirring like breath against her ear and cheek . . . 'More haste, less speed.'

Extraordinary, the way Henry's words still challenged her unspoken thoughts, after all these months: 'Is your journey really necessary?'

Agnes sighed, and wriggled down until she was staring at the ceiling again. Old habits . . . From the moment they'd met, Henry had taken over responsibility for decision-making. He'd seemed to listen to her suggestions, but somehow his arguments were always more persuasive. It had quickly become as natural to her as breathing to defer to his judgement.

Now, he was not here. She'd had to work out this plan unaided. Was that sudden attack of vertigo a warning sign from her own subconscious? Her mouth twisted into a wry smile. 'Subconscious! Just another word for conscience,' Henry would say.

Agnes sighed again. Her legs still felt as floppy as dough but her mind was racing. That series of phone calls — for days she had played them over and over in her head: Lucy, Monica, then at last, Jack.

She still found it hard to remember that Lucy was no longer 'daughter-in-law' — that she'd cut herself off with that deadly little prefix, ex. Even more ex now that she'd moved so far away with her new man. But Emily and Sam could never be ex. Though Agnes hadn't seen them for almost a year, they would always be her grandchildren.

She'd been gazing at the ceiling unblinking for so long that her eyes were beginning to sting. Closing the lids made the gathered water spill out and trickle down towards her ears. She found herself unclasping tight fists as she raised her hands to wipe away the slithers of liquid. Not tears, as such. Of course not.

A dull humming started up in her right ear, like the echo of a dialling tone. The pay phone in the hall downstairs . . .

★ ★ ★

Monday. She'd finally plucked up courage to dial the Nottingham number. Early morning, but never mind how many coins the phone gobbled up. What else would she be spending money on now?

'Lucy? Is that you? Agnes here.'

'Who?'

'Agnes. Your children's . . . '

'Of course! Agnes! I'm so sorry. How're you doing?'

'I wondered if I could just have a little chat

4

with Emily before she goes to school. It's so long since we've . . . '

'Agnes, it's ten to nine. We're late already.'

'Sammy, then. Perhaps I could talk to . . . '

'He's got nursery now, Agnes, remember? Mornings are not a good time, I'm afraid.'

But the evening had been no better:

'What a shame! I've just managed to settle them down. They'll be up all night if I disturb them now. I'll get them to ring you.'

'But I haven't actually got my own phone in this place, Lucy, and they don't really like taking messages here, so perhaps . . . '

'Sorry, Agnes. That's Sean — just got home, speak to you soon. No! It's only Agnes! Yes. I'm COMING!'

⋆ ⋆ ⋆

The following evening was the real start of it, the uneasy realisation that things were not right, that something had to be done.

'Oh! Sean! Er . . . good evening. Are the children . . . ?'

'You deaf, or what? Who else would be making that bloody racket?'

'Good gracious, what a commotion! Perhaps if I could just talk to . . . ?'

'Chrissake, Luce. Can't you get your kids to shut the fuck up?'

5

'Hello? Hello? Sean? Are you there still? Lucy?'

Agnes felt her stomach knot itself again, as she remembered how she'd listened, dry-mouthed, to the dead sound of the handset. What a two-edged sword the telephone was, the way it hurtled you into the middle of other people's lives, gave you a sudden, shocking glimpse, then shut you off in an instant. Like trains passing at high speed. Violence witnessed, with no possibility of intervention.

She'd made herself calm down. People used those words all the time nowadays. Sean's angry voice didn't have to mean . . . She could hardly expect Jack to go chasing off on a three hour drive and bundle his children into the car and . . . And what? Take them back to the house he shared with Monica? Apart from anything Monica might say, what actual rights did Jack have now? And how would Emmy and Sam react?

So she'd restrained herself from immediately dialling her son's number. She had to sound rational. In full possession of her wits. Anyway, better to wait an hour or so, just to make sure that he'd be home from work.

But later had not been late enough. Her heart sank when she heard Monica's voice. It galled her to remember how relieved she'd felt for Jack, finding just the person to restore his self esteem after Lucy's desertion. It hadn't taken Agnes long to see below the sweetly sensitive exterior to the bedrock of selfishness.

'Jack? In? Chance'd be a fine thing! Try tomorrow, Agnes.'

'This is urgent, Monica.'

'Urgent! What d'you-think it's like for me, then? I mean, it's nine o'clock already and the girls are both out but I'm left here on my tod, as usual, pouring my own drinks — '

'I'm sorry about that, Monica. He really is working too hard at the moment, isn't he? Could you ask him to ring me as soon as he gets in?'

'I'll tell him, but don't hold your breath. Anyway, surely there's someone there who can sort things out for you? That place is costing us enough.'

'This is something private.'

'What sort of private? Jackie doesn't keep any secrets from me, you know.'

'Actually, I really do want to have a word with my own son.'

'Have to join the queue, then, Agnes.'

It wasn't till the following day that she'd finally managed to speak to Jack.

'Ma, For God's sake! Not at work, please!'

'But I have to talk to you, Jack. I'm worried sick about — '

'Can't it wait till Sunday, Ma? I'm coming over to see you then, remember?'

'I am still in full possession of all my faculties, thank you, in spite of what you might think. It's the children. That man of Lucy's. He's — '

'Look, there's nothing for you to worry about. Can't talk now. Ring me at home later.'

Then yet one more call in this frustrating series of attempts at communication.

'Of course it's me. Who else would it be? The girls are never in these days. No, Agnes, not home yet. Yes, I will remember to tell him you called.'

Now it was Saturday and still no word from Jack. Here she was, to all intents and purposes a prisoner in this so-called Harmony Home. Young at Heart? She'd never felt her age more than at this moment — weak-kneed and feeble. But there was no getting away from it, she must pull herself together and try again. She simply had to reach Nottingham today, check on Emily and Sam with her own eyes before Jack came to visit her.

It wasn't as though he didn't care. In his own way he was truly fond of his children. More demonstrative than Henry had ever been to him. Certainly more approachable than her own father. But would Jack take any notice of her fears, based only on that brief phone call to Sean, those few angry words? After all, he was already convinced she was losing her marbles. Wasn't that why he'd put her here in the first place?

Jack. Barely a trace of him left. Not her Jack. If she'd been told that DNA tests had proved he wasn't her son after all, that some time during his early twenties a switch had been made, and the real Jack, enquiring mind and spirit of fun intact, was out there, roaming the world, it would have made more sense. How can a man of forty-three be older than his seventy-five-year-old mother?

When did it happen, this estrangement? It must have started a long time before the breakdown of his marriage to Lucy. But it wasn't till that terrible Sunday almost two years ago that she'd finally become aware of quite how unbridgeable the gap between them had grown.

⋆　⋆　⋆

Sunday lunch with her family had been the highlight of the week for Agnes, since she'd become a grandmother. Recently though, these occasions had been less regular. This time it was just the three of them, Henry and

9

Agnes and Jack, wedged apart by the solid edges of the kitchen table. Jack arrived late, and without Lucy or the children, but he'd given no proper explanation for their absence.

'Delicious, my dear. Gravy perhaps not quite up to your usual standards, though. What do you think, son? Is it your mother that's slipping, or is your ageing father losing his taste buds?'

At least he's broken this wooden silence, Agnes thought, glancing from Henry to Jack, and back at her own plate. She suddenly felt as though she were outside her own body, gazing down at herself, her husband and her son, the three of them locked into their own private thoughts. And though she knew she would be able to make some light-hearted comment that would re-establish the habitual link with Henry, she was almost afraid to speak directly to Jack in case her words should echo back at her from his closed face, their meaning distorted.

His eyes, darting from side to side, had never seemed so dark — the brownish-black of a glacial lake. At last, barely moving his lips, he blurted out, 'Lucy wants a divorce.'

The right words, silences, gestures, how different things could have been. But Henry had switched into automatic preacher mode, the sanctity of matrimony, the possibility of reconciliation. Then Agnes's own words, like spilt milk. 'Jack, dear, do try to look at things from Lucy's point of view. You have to admit you've been rather neglectful recently, such long hours at work. Perhaps if you could just . . . '

By the time she'd risen from her seat and walked round the table to stand behind him and place her arms around his neck, the damage was done. It was like embracing stone.

'You've always been kind to me, and lovely with the kids, Agnes,' Lucy said when she'd phoned that evening, 'and of course, it's not that I've got anything against Jack himself, but . . . '

'But you only live once,' said Agnes, and Lucy had been totally oblivious of the irony in her tone and responded gratefully, 'Oh! You *do* understand! I'm so glad!'

The final blow had been delayed until Agnes was left to bear it alone. Two weeks after Henry's funeral, Lucy phoned with the announcement that Sean had got a new job in Nottingham. 'Head of Art. A really good school, ex-grammar. Just the break he's been looking for. We've managed to find a lovely house to rent till we've sold his. We will keep in touch though, I promise. Once we've settled in properly, you must come and stay.'

At the time, Agnes was too numbed by her own grief to take in the full implications of this news. Nights were the worst. More often than not, she'd pull down Henry's heavy coat from the cupboard in the hall, and curl up on the sofa with the tapestry cushion rough against her cheek, rather than haul herself up the stairs and climb alone into the bed they'd shared. Waking, stiff and cold at three in the morning. Wondering how many sleeping pills it would take. Thinking, no, not yet. I can't go like this. Turning on all the lights. And the wireless in the kitchen. Dance music. World news. Cleaning the oven again.

★   ★   ★

A few weeks later, when Jack had finally managed to sort out the tangled mess of his father's estate, there was more bad news. Sitting in the vicarage kitchen, sheaves of papers spread all over the table, he tried to explain the details of what had happened.

Agnes feigned interest in the rows of columns, the 'not-withstandings', the 'where-to-fors', but it was all a meaningless mass of words and numbers until Jack finished off, 'I'm sorry, Ma. You'll have the basic pension, and that's it. Lord knows what Dad was think-ing of, trusting that old crook, Naughton. Just because he played the organ nicely. I told him often enough. You can't say I didn't warn him.'

She still hadn't fully grasped the extent of the disaster. 'No, dear, I know you tried. Still, what can't be helped must be shouldered. Other people manage, so I'm sure I can.'

'I mean,' went on Jack, 'even Dad should've realised there's no such thing as a free lunch. Honestly! Fancy believing in moral investments that not only guarantee a comfortable income for life but can somehow bring untold benefits to starving children in Africa! And to tie up the house in that way, after the church had let him buy it for such a bargain price! I'm sorry to have to say this, but it was downright irresponsible. Not fair on you at all, having to cope with all this at your age.'

'I'm not senile yet. I'm sure I can manage my own affairs. And your father did what he believed was right at the time,' she added, a trifle sharply.

'Of course. I'm not saying . . . It's just, well. We have to think about what this will mean for you. No house. Virtually no money. You'll have to come and live with us.'

There was a long silence as Agnes began to absorb the implications of what Jack had told her. 'Us' meant Monica and her two teenage daughters in Jack's recently acquired house in Haywards Heath. They wouldn't want her, even if Jack did.

She glanced across the table at her son. He was examining the grain of the wood, tracing his forefinger along one of the straighter lines until it curved into a spiral, round and round and round, then back again. She'd not seen him do that since — oh — since he'd left home.

Home. Even without Henry, this was still home. Every room throbbed with his . . . not absence, exactly, more like *non-presence*. The way you can deliberately push the tip of your tongue hard into a new, raw gap between your molars, keeping alive the lost tooth for a little longer.

Worse still, this place seemed like her only remaining link with Emily and Sam. They'd not spent any time here since before Henry's death, but she still kept their beds aired, and their favourite toys and books displayed on their own shelves of the bookcase in the morning room. Just in case.

She pushed back her chair, walked across to the Aga and picked up the empty kettle. 'More tea, dear?' she asked, keeping her voice as light as she could.

She found herself smiling at the relief on his face. Poor Jack. Just like his father. Never did know how to cope with any form of emotional upset.

What choice had she got? And would it really matter where she lived, now that she had to leave this house? Looking on the bright side, moving in with Jack might well be the best way of getting to know him again. What was that expression they used these days? Bonding, that was it. And he might agree to drive her up to Nottingham, or even bring the children back down with him for the occasional weekend.

'What can't be helped must be shouldered,' she repeated. Then, hearing how those words might sound to him, continued gently, 'That's a very kind offer, Jack. I shall certainly give it some thought.'

2

The wide front lawn of number 11, Saxon Meadow was separated from the pavement by a silver chain fence looped between foot-high white posts. A small weeping willow brushed the grass, neatly striped after its final cut of the season. As soon as Jack had closed the front door behind them with one foot, nearly losing his balance before resting her two suitcases on the cream carpet, Agnes knew that she had made a terrible mistake. Since their first meeting, her initial liking for Monica had rapidly diminished into tolerance. Jack is happy with her, that's the important thing, she'd repeated to herself each time their paths crossed. But now, as Monica strolled across the hall towards her, the contrast between the wide smile on her lips and the coldness in her eyes made Agnes shudder.

She quickly realised that this wasn't really Jack's house in anything but name. It was Monica's. And Donna and Hailey's. Even the balding, overweight Corgi, Queenie, appeared to have priority over Jack when it came to choice of chair in the living room. In spite of all her efforts to be understanding and patient with them all — Yes, Henry, she had tried her best, she honestly had — it seemed that the only way of avoiding exhausting misunderstandings was to spend more and more time alone in the ground-floor study-bedroom that a previous owner had built on at the back of the garage. Agnes had only caught the occasional glimpse of Donna and Hailey before she'd moved into their home and she knew that her arrival wasn't likely to be easy for them. No doubt they'd both had their own plans for the extra space that she was occupying, though Donna did have the grace to mumble, 'No sweat. Honest. I can use my bedroom for my art stuff. Least I can keep it safe from Hailey there.'

When Jack was little, Agnes had found it much easier to relate to other children of his age than to their parents, who seemed to prefer to keep the vicar's wife at arm's length. But young people these days were allowed to grow up so quickly, and at fourteen and sixteen she found Hailey and Donna rather daunting, particularly Hailey. Not so much the rings and studs in her earlobes and even her eyebrows, and her hair a different colour each week — it was her sulky expression and her sharp tongue. Not rude, exactly, but enough to make Agnes wary of starting up a conversation.

Donna was a little easier. At least she would smile occasionally, but she always seemed too busy with her painting and drawing to have any time to chat. She'd once casually suggested that Agnes might sit for her 'one of these days', but nothing ever came of it.

Agnes was beginning to lose hope of ever seeing Emily and Sam again. During her first few weeks in Haywards Heath she'd sent letters and cards almost weekly, but nothing ever came back to her from them, not even crayoned stick-people or smiley faces. She'd tried phoning, too, but Lucy was always ready with some excuse about bedtime or play-school, or a special television programme and they'd ring back later. They never did.

'Obviously I talk to them about you and Dad,' Jack would insist, returning from his fortnightly visit. 'And they send their love.' But he was always too exhausted or too busy or too upset to give her any details about them. As for taking her with him on one of those Sundays, well, yes, of course he would, but he'd have to arrange somewhere to stay the night, as she'd find the return journey too tiring. Er, no, not this time, it could be a bit awkward for Lucy. And no, he was sorry, but this Sunday he'd promised to take them to a funfair with a couple of their friends. Then it was: why not wait till the school holidays, when he could bring them down here for a few days? Of course Monica and the girls would be happy about that. No, it most certainly wasn't a question of them allowing or not allowing. Whatever gave her that idea?

The days and weeks blurred into each other and as the nights grew longer, Agnes spent more and more time slumped in front of her flickering TV screen. Christmas came and went, bringing nothing but a brief, stilted phone conversation with Lucy, followed by two slightly puzzled-sounding children's voices saying 'Happy Christmas Grandma,' and rattling off lists of what Santa had brought them.

'Yes, Agnes, of course they know who you are. They're just over-excited right now. Yes, we'll arrange something in the New Year. Speak to you again soon.'

The boundaries of Agnes's physical existence had begun to shrink in on her, closer and closer each day. Her room was cut off from the rest of the house, and the garden was rarely used by anyone during the winter months. Monica was out most of the day at her part-time job in the building society, or shopping, or having lunch with other women of leisure. Donna and Hailey, when not at school, would be in their separate bedrooms with their own friends, playing music that didn't seem so very different from the racket the teenage Jack used to enjoy, except in the level of decibels.

On days when it wasn't pouring with rain, Agnes would force herself out for a walk around the sprawling new housing estate with its almost identical 'executive dwellings'. She'd make a sandwich or a bowl of soup at lunch-time and Monica would bring her an early supper on a tray, before Jack arrived home from work.

'Please don't go to all this trouble again, Monica,' Agnes had said, the first time. 'I'm quite happy to cook my own meal, or better still, wait till the rest of you are ready to eat.'

'No bother, Agnes,' said Monica sweetly. 'Evenings are chaos in the kitchen, what with Donna and Hailey always wanting something different, and never at the same time, and Jack late so often. And it's much better for the elderly to keep to a routine, isn't it?'

Elderly! What an unerring instinct the woman had for selecting words with the greatest potential to annoy. Agnes widened her eyes and smiled. 'I certainly wouldn't want to upset your routine, dear,' she said, and scored herself a mental point as Monica tightened her lips. But when she was alone with her chicken-burger, peas and half-cooked oven chips, she saw her minor victory for what it was, childish and rather mean. It would be more of a challenge not to let herself become so easily irritated. Monica probably had no idea of the effect of her words, and after all, this was her home. Agnes was the intruder, and she must do her best to fit in.

So she kept to her own room, except on evenings when she was invited to join Monica and Jack in the living room, where they sat entwined on the cream-leather sofa sipping whisky from each other's crystal tumblers in front of the enormous TV screen. Jack did seem to be making an effort to include her in desultory conversation about the particular game-show host or the characters in the latest police drama or comedy series. Perhaps that was the problem — the obvious effort. She just couldn't summon up the energy to pretend an interest.

Most of her time was spent perched in the high-seated Parker Knoll armchair in her over-heated room, her slippered feet resting on the footstool, an unopened copy of *Barchester Towers* on her lap. 'You'll enjoy Trollope, my dear. You really will, if you can just make that little bit of effort to get into it.' But every time she picked it up and looked at the spine, she found her eyelids growing heavier.

The garden beyond the window was sludge-green and greyish-brown, the curtains were oatmeal, the wallpaper mushroom. The walls themselves seemed to be drawing in a little closer each time she raised her eyes towards them, till she began to feel as though she were at the bottom of a mineshaft or a well that was becoming deeper every day. But it wasn't in the least claustrophobic — quite the opposite, once she'd discovered that she only had to reach out and touch one of the sides for it to dissolve in front of her.

Sometimes, it was like watching a film from sixty or even seventy years ago, strangely familiar events that she had not been aware of remembering. But more and more often she was actually the child, Agnes Rutherford again, rambling over Bodmin Moor with her twin, Sebastian, or climbing the scratchy apple trees in the orchard.

When she looks at Seb, she feels as proud as if she's peering at her own reflection. It's like seeing the secret, sturdy self that lives inside her: the daring one that only comes out to play when she's alone with him. He has Mother's red-gold curls. Her own hair is mousy and straight. Even when Mother dampens it and binds it into all those little plaits until it's dry, the wavy bits don't last. Seb is only twenty minutes older than her, but Mother says that's what gave him a head start. Father says, 'Tosh! He's a proper little man,' and his eyes go kind of sparkly as he thumps him on the shoulders, and he hardly glances at spindly, wispy little Agnes.

One Saturday morning in early January, when Jack's voice from somewhere far above her had wrenched her back into the body of seventy-four-year-old Agnes Borrowdale, she had cried out in such a tone of pain that he'd rushed into the room instead of waiting for her usual, 'Who *is* it?'

'Are you all right, Ma?' he'd asked in concern, as she looked at him in a daze.

After this, it seemed that either Monica or Jack or even one of the girls was constantly popping a head around her door on one pretext or another. Then Monica's doctor, who was also a family friend, just happened to be passing and dropped in on a visit. Agnes had found her patronising, but managed to tap into reserves of politeness and make some responses. When this same woman called back again a day or two later, bringing a stocky, bearded man whom she introduced as 'my good friend, Dr Morgan', Agnes found it harder to remain civil. Not only were his questions more intrusive, but their visit had wrenched her away from a particularly vivid episode with Sebastian. This time, they were

23

about ten years old, and she was still convalescing from the rheumatic fever that had made her so ill for months and months, her normal zest for adventure not yet fully restored.

Her legs begin to feel a bit wobbly as she clambers over the gate at the end of the orchard and starts to follow Seb down the steep slope. It's cooler here. There're fat clumps of moss on the knobbly roots of the trees. The earth's so dry it's coughed up lots of flinty stones. She could easily slip. Seb looks back and notices her hesitation. 'Hang on a tick,' he calls, and scrambles back up. He's standing just below her, gripping her hand. He clamps a strand of bramble under his foot, then guides her down to a thin sapling trunk, which she clings to for a moment, giggling.

At last they push their way out from the shade, into the bright June sunshine of the meadow. She flops down onto the grass. The crushed stems smell like a mixture of dandelions and line-dried sheets. She stretches out flat on her stomach, dangling her arms over the edge of the bank, splashing a long, leafy twig up and down in the stream. Seb is winding a rope round the overhanging branch that he's sitting on . . .

Never mind, I'll be able to get back there

soon, the adult Agnes told herself, as Monica, home from work unexpectedly early, ushered in the two visitors and then muttered something about 'things to get on with', and left the room.

'So, Agnes, I may call you Agnes, I hope?' said the man, bending towards her and smothering her small hand in both of his. 'I feel I know you so well already.'

The man's impossible! thought Agnes, barely repressing a shudder. If Monica was expecting her to entertain her tiresome visitors for her, she was going to be sadly disappointed. For the next ten minutes or so Agnes kept her face as blank as she could, and merely nodded or shook her head by way of response. Dr Morgan had taken one of these nods as encouragement to draw up a chair in front of hers. She was beginning to find it hard to keep a straight face while watching what she could see of his mouth shaping the words as they emerged from a gap in his thick brown beard. She found that this helped her to block out the sounds the words made. It was more amusing to guess from the man's expression what the appropriate response should be, and even more amusing when his look of bewilderment informed her that she had guessed wrong.

Just when she had begun to tire of this game, and decided that perhaps she really ought to behave more kindly towards her visitors, the woman doctor leaned across and said something to the man. They both stood up, made their goodbyes, and left the room.

Later that evening, Agnes was about to step through from the garage into the kitchen when she heard Monica's voice, and froze. 'Poor Jack. What a shame for you to have to see your mum going, you know, mental.'

Jack's voice, interrupting sharply, 'He didn't say that at all, just that she's depressed and needs to get out more, before she does get seriously ill.'

Agnes put a hand on the door jamb to steady herself. Too late, she understood the purpose of that visit.

'Yes, yes of course, depressed. Ever so sad, isn't it? Shouldn't be left on her own so much, he said. I know my little Queenie's only a dog, but p'rhaps I should encourage her to sit with your poor mum when we're all out.' Agnes winced and shuddered, but leant her head nearer to the door. 'You know I'd do anything, anything I can. But the trouble is . . . ' There was a prolonged pause.

'The trouble is?'

'Look Jack, I don't like to say this. I am actually rather fond of the dear old thing, and

26

after all, she is your mother, but — '

'Fond of me!' whispered Agnes, feeling suddenly afraid.

'The trouble is, I just don't think she'd listen to me. You wouldn't believe how difficult she is when you're not here. I mean, she virtually ignores me when I bring in her tea. Never invites me to stay and chat. She should be with people more her own age. She'd find it easier to be nice to them, wouldn't she? Look at the way she's for ever picking on the girls.' Monica's voice was quavering now. 'Honestly, Jack, I just don't know how much longer I can . . . ' A loud sniff was followed by a sob.

Agnes clamped her mouth in a tight line and scurried back to her room before she had to listen to Jack murmuring sweet nothings into those blonde stripes in Monica's hair.

This episode had startled her back into the present. Ill? She was not going to give that woman the satisfaction of making her ill. But her recent vivid memories of childhood could not be shaken off altogether. As she straightened her shoulders and drew in a deep breath, she could almost hear Seb's voice:

'That's more like it, Sis.'

*   *   *

27

Over the next few weeks, Agnes was secretly working at rebuilding her own strength. At the same time she quickly overcame her earlier scruples about eavesdropping. Monica had a wider range of voices than she'd first realised: not just the patronising tone she reserved for Agnes, and the refined 'telephone' voice for use with strangers. There was the honey-sweet, caring one, the petulant, if-you-really-loved-me one, the steely, my-mind-is-made-up one, and then, very occasionally, the hysterical sobs that could be sustained for as long as Jack could endure them.

Agnes found a compelling fascination in overhearing Monica working her poison on Jack. It had been a shock at first, though. There was no denying the stab of pain she'd felt when she became aware of just how gullible her son was. *Oh Jack!* How she longed to sit him next to her on the sofa-bed and draw his head onto her lap. She'd stroke his shoulder and run her fingers through his thinning hair and remind him of the fun they used to have together in those happy days before Henry had insisted that at nearly eleven, Jack was more than old enough to be sent away to boarding school.

She wouldn't, of course. He'd take it as another sign of senile dementia. Nothing she could say would make any difference. He was forty-three and in love with Monica.

In a way, this was not so very surprising. When she'd first met her, Agnes herself had been taken in by Monica's soft voice and apparent kindness. It had been Jack's turn to have Emily and Sam for the night. He was still living in the house in Lewes then, and Agnes had driven over early on the Sunday morning so Jack could have a lie-in. The children rarely spent the night in the vicarage, now that their time with their father was rationed, so this was one of her few opportunities to have Emily and Sam to herself. They were snuggling up with her on the sofa in front of their video of *The Lion King* — Agnes's seventh time in as many weeks — when a sleepy voice from the doorway behind them said, 'Is this a private viewing, or can anyone join in?'

Sam pulled the ribbon-edged fragment of cot blanket from his mouth and wriggled off Agnes's lap to jump up and down against the back of the sofa, calling out, 'Minca, Minca!'

'He can't pernounce it properly,' said Emily. 'She's called Mon-i-ker. She looks after me and Sammy and Daddy sometimes.'

Agnes felt a stab of disappointment at the intrusion, quickly followed by curiosity. This youthful looking woman seemed completely unabashed at being seen by Jack's mother in his navy towelling bathrobe. She knelt down in front of Agnes, smiling, and held out her hand. 'I'm so pleased to meet you at last, Mrs Borrowdale. Jack's told me so much about you.'

'Call me Agnes,' she said, taking the proffered hand and looking quizzically at Monica. What kind of things would Jack have been saying?

Monica's round face beamed in apparent delight. 'You must be so proud of him,' she went on, reaching for a cushion and settling herself at Agnes's feet like a child. 'The way he's coped with, you know . . . And he's such a wonderful father.'

Jack had mentioned, a couple of weeks previously, that he'd started 'seeing' another woman. Whatever Henry's views might be, she would have given her blessing to anyone who could banish that lost expression from Jack's face. It was an unexpected bonus to find herself warming towards this woman. She seemed open and unaffected — pretty too, but not in any flashy kind of a way. Her plump face was saved from blandness by broad cheek bones and rather striking slanted eyes with dark, curling lashes.

What had really impressed Agnes was the tactful way Monica reacted when Sam slid himself off the sofa into her lap and reached up to plant his slobbery kisses on the edge of her mouth. She had gently placed her hands on either side of his head, looked at him with a loving smile, then bent towards him and murmured something in his ear that had made him shriek with laughter. A moment later she was handing him to Agnes, saying, 'You look after Granny now, Sampam, while I take Daddy up a mug of tea.'

It was only after further acquaintance that Agnes had realised there could be other ways of interpreting this behaviour. Monica was probably too self-absorbed to imagine that anyone could disapprove of anything she did. Her apparently tactful withdrawal from the room, so that Agnes could enjoy her grandchildren on her own, was more likely to have been an excuse to get back into bed with Jack.

Monica might not be clever in an academic way like Lucy, but if there'd been such a thing as a practical degree course on manipulation techniques, she would have graduated with distinction. Overt confrontation would be worse than useless, so Agnes meekly agreed to go each Thursday afternoon to the Senior Citizens' Social Club for bingo or ballroom dancing with tea and biscuits. Monica dropped her off and collected her the first couple of times, but after that she was trusted to make her own way there and back by bus. It didn't take Agnes long to discover that on the same afternoon, in a church hall five minutes brisk walk away, the local Adult Education Service was running a Keep Fit class.

Some deep-rooted survival instinct had, months ago, prompted her to start hoarding her pension, and by this time she'd accumulated quite a nice little wad of twenty-pound notes that were wrapped in plastic at the bottom of her wash bag. No point in spending any of that too freely, with her future still so uncertain. As a vicar's wife, she'd sorted through enough cast-off clothes for jumble sales and charity gift shops to know where to look for a suitable outfit. After rummaging in vain through the Ladies' Casual Wear section of the Oxfam shop beyond the Post Office in search of something that wouldn't swamp her small frame, she'd selected a shiny turquoise tracksuit from the larger end of the children's clothing rail.

'Ever so popular, those, a few years ago,' the woman had told her. 'It'll wash and dry like a dream.' The glaringly white, size four trainers with citrus yellow flashes had come from the sports shop in the precinct. It was staffed by youngsters who swayed and jerked across the floor to the same thudding music favoured by Donna and Hailey.

So far, so good. But what if she was too old for those classes, if there was an upper age limit of say, sixty-five or seventy? Or what if one of Monica's friends happened to see her there? Ridiculous! She had every right to go wherever she chose. It was more a case of retaining some privacy, really. She knew Monica was succeeding in convincing Jack that she'd be much better off in a nice, genteel Home. And Number 11 Saxon Meadow was not a place she would ever be able to think of as home for herself. But meanwhile, the less that Monica knew of her activities, the better.

There was no shortage of other charity shops to browse through nearby, and it seemed fitting that it should be the Help the Aged one that provided the answer. She'd spotted the wig first, on a stand in the window. It was a thick, orangey-gold tangle of long hair with a wide, wavy fringe. 'Ooh, that's lovely!' giggled the plump woman behind the counter, 'Fancy dress, is it?'

Agnes smiled and nodded. 'Mutton dressed as Lamb. That's what I'm going as,' she answered, then turned back almost shyly to study the strange effect of this wig that fitted so snugly over the top of her own neat grey

French pleat. The coarse, rust-coloured hair tumbled below her collar bone, the fringe covered her forehead and eyebrows, and some longer curling strands hugged the edges of her cheeks, altering the whole shape of her face.

'Try these with it,' said the woman, handing her a navy baseball cap and bright pink, padded elastic band. 'See, if you tie back the long bits into this, like so, and then pull this whole ponytail out through this elastic strap here at the back, like so. There!' and she laughed in triumph. 'You could pass for a teenager now! And look, here's a nice bright little back-pack to store everything in. Only nylon, see. Ever so light. Just six quid, the lot.'

Agnes barely heard her as she gazed in silence at the stranger in the mirror: something cold seemed to brush the nape of her neck and tickle down her spine. It was like one of those dreams where you know that you're dead because someone else has stepped into the place where your own reflection should be.

This was not a youthful face, certainly, but it would have been difficult for anyone who did not know Agnes to guess her true age. There were fine lines around the pale blue eyes and the wide mouth, with deeper diagonals etched from the sides of the small snub nose to the corners of the upper lip, but the centre of the cheeks, with their ghosts of freckles, were almost unwrinkled. The deepest furrows were now hidden by the fringe. Her own son would find it hard to recognise her like this, especially once she'd put on that tracksuit! Agnes felt her mouth break into a smile and she was almost relieved to see the familiar small chip on the edge of the front tooth as the orange-haired woman smiled back.

3

The harmony home was turning out worse than Agnes had expected. 'Out of the frying pan' was the phrase that sprang to mind, a few hours after her arrival. The brochure had extolled the beautiful surroundings and the modern comforts that had been 'so tastefully incorporated into the faded grandeur of this Georgian mansion.' As far as that side of things went, it had been reasonably accurate, apart from the long delay in installing telephones in all the rooms. This was probably deliberate: many of the Young at Heart were now making do with mobiles. The name Harmony Home had only recently taken the place of Rest Home for Retired Gentlefolk, but there were few other signs of admitting to technological and social changes of the past fifty years. The most misleading aspect of the brochure was its references to the level of independence enjoyed by the residents.

After more than two weeks she had only once been able to visit the small nearby town of Horsham and that was in the Home's own mini-bus. 'Local buses are so unreliable, dear,' she'd been told, each time she'd asked. 'Only two or three a day. Anyway, the library van calls round every Monday, and there's that nice little general store in the village. Every month or so we have a trip to Guildford, too.' Agnes was beginning to suspect that Jack, or perhaps that Dr What's-his-name, had placed some kind of extra security order on her: every time she strolled out into the garden a member of staff, or one of the more established residents, appeared as if from nowhere and tried to engage her in conversation. The only place where her privacy could be guaranteed was behind her own locked bedroom door. One of the few television programmes from years ago that had made any impact on her was one with that actor, Patrick McSome-thing, who spent each episode trying to escape from an idyllic seeming village, where everyone was so nice to him, but he could never get away. The other possibility, that she herself might be suffering from paranoia, was almost as disturbing as the idea of being under constant surveillance.

Her actual arrival at the Harmony Home, slumped in the passenger seat of Jack's Volvo, had seemed like a reversal of the natural order of things. As the car had turned onto the driveway between the stone gateposts and swished along the curve of gravel under the still-leafless, stumpy branches of pollarded lime trees, Agnes had found herself re-living the feelings of more than thirty years ago — the same fluttering creatures jostling in her stomach, the same tightening of her chest and throat, the same determination not to let the stinging in her eyes become tears. It was even the same day of the week: a new term usually started on a Tuesday. But the man beside her was not Henry, and there was no eleven-year-old boy, stony-faced, on the seat behind her.

What had Jack felt as he stooped to kiss his mother's cheek, saying cheerily, 'Bye, then, Ma. I'll pick you up about eleven on Sunday?'

Once a week was going to be the routine, Sunday one weekend, Saturday the next. If she wanted to retain her sanity, she'd have to practise counting her blessings: some of the Young-at-Hearts appeared to have no visitors at all. Jack would alternate his Sundays between his children and his mother. 'Yes, yes. Once things have settled down a bit, of course I'll take you with me, Ma. Make a weekend of it.'

It wasn't till the Monday morning at the start of her third week that Agnes had first attempted to phone the children. It was the day following Jack's 'Nottingham' Sunday, and she'd given him two small packages to take with him — crayons, colouring books and a few sweets from the village store. These small gifts could make an opening for her to start a conversation with Emily and Sam, help them to remember who she was. She should have realised that Lucy would be about to take them to school, and that eight in the evening would be too late to call. It seemed that Time was already beginning to lose its public meaning for her.

Then came the disturbing conversation with Sean, or rather, his words to Lucy, words that she could not banish from her mind: 'Can't you get your kids to shut the fuck up?'

No more attempts at evening phone calls, then. She wasn't going to risk Sean picking up the phone again.

So it was Thursday, the morning after she'd phoned Jack at work, and failed to have a conversation with him, that she'd tried Lucy once more.

'Oh, Lucy! Thank goodness it's you.'

'Agnes? Look, I don't want to sound unfriendly, but it's really not helping matters, you ringing all the time. Could you just stay out of things for the moment? If you don't mind.'

'What is it? What's happening, Lucy? Are the children . . . ?'

'The kids are fine. Absolutely fine. And

please, don't go worrying Jack. He's got enough on his plate right now, and it'd just make matters worse if he . . . I mean, you know what Jack's like. Look, I've got go.'

'No, wait, Lucy. Please. Can't I do anything? Perhaps I could come up for a bit — help look after . . . '

'No! No! That's the last thing I'd — ! I mean, no. Thank you, Agnes. You're very kind. This is something purely personal. Just stop worrying. I promise I'll be in touch soon.'

'Don't go worrying Jack!' muttered Agnes, hauling herself slowly up the stairs. Fine chance of doing that, when she couldn't even get hold of him.

She locked the bedroom door behind her and sank into the small armchair by the window. Sunday seemed a long way off. Anything could have happened by then. And Jack wouldn't be visiting Nottingham for a whole week after that. What could she say to him anyway? She had nothing really concrete to go by. So, Sean had shouted at Lucy because the children were making a noise. That sort of thing was not exactly unusual in families. He and Lucy could be going through a bad patch. It didn't mean he would harm the children in any way. That had always been the one thing Henry had managed to find in his favour, the fact that he liked children.

'Come off it, Dad,' Jack had scoffed, still raw from the blow of Lucy's desertion. 'In my experience, most teachers are bloody sadists.'

'Listen, Son, I quite understand your feelings about this man, and I have to say that I'm finding it very hard to think at all kindly of him in the circumstances, but surely, someone who dedicates his life to children . . . '

But sitting in her room alone, remembering this conversation, and with Sean's crude and angry words still reverberating in her head, Agnes was becoming more convinced that Jack, and her own initial instincts, had been right. Sean was one of the smooth-tongued brand: charming to colleagues and parents, disdainful of any but the brightest pupils. He would have no reserves of patience for anything less than perfect behaviour from another man's children in his own home.

'Henry, what would you be doing now, if you were me?' Useless question. If Henry were still in a position to be doing anything she wouldn't be in this place.

Agnes slumped forward in her chair, her head in her hands, rocking herself gently. After a few moments she gradually became aware that she was humming and then

41

crooning the words of *Rockaby Baby.*

'Cry baby,' Seb used to say on the rare occasions that he saw her in tears. 'No good sitting there with a face like a week of wet Mondays.' Not unkind — just his way of trying to cheer her up.

At the thought of Seb, she rose to her feet, smiling. He had always encouraged her adventurous self: daring her to follow him up to the swaying, top-most branches of the huge copper beech on the windiest of days; building two rackety go-carts so they could race each other down the steepest of the narrow roads that snaked over the moors.

Mother hadn't liked that. 'You should take better care of your sister, Sebastian. She's too frail for such rough games.' Though Agnes had sensed a slight softening in Father's face when he'd seen her grazed knees and elbows, he'd supported Mother's ruling: no dangerous sports for little Agnes.

Well, there was no one to hold her back now. She must go on a recce to get the facts. No point wasting time in wondering precisely how the idea had entered her head. She'd go and ask about trains to Nottingham that very minute.

'Oh no, Alice. That won't do at all! Oh dear me, no!' Phyllis Mapperley gave a high pitched little laugh and patted her manicured hand on Agnes's forearm.

'Agnes. My name is Agnes,' she said coldly, shifting her arm.

'Yes, dear, as I said, Agnes. I'm afraid that residents here don't just take themselves off for the night without due notice.'

Agnes froze, staring at the woman in disbelief.

'Now then, why don't we step into my little den for a moment? That's right, dear,' she cooed as Agnes, still in a state of shocked surprise, let herself be led towards a high-backed chair beside a large desk that was almost obscured by heaps of papers and piles of glossy magazines. 'I'm sure we can sort things out in a jiffy,' she continued, 'but it is so important to keep lines of communication open at all times, don't you think? So, shall we telephone your son right now? Or should we wait till he gets back from work?'

Agnes gripped one hand on the edge of the desk and forced herself to breathe more deeply, quelling the rising panic. After a moment or two she said in a steady voice, 'Oh, I don't want to cause any inconvenience. There is no particular urgency. My son is coming to see me on Sunday afternoon. I shall speak to him then.' She stood up and made for the door, pausing to turn and say,

'Sorry to have bothered you, Mrs Mapperley. Please don't give it another thought.'

'Phyllis, dear. We're all friends here, I hope.'

'Yes, quite so. Phyllis. Such a pleasure to speak to you. Good day.'

Back in her room she flung herself face down on the bed beating against the pillow with her fists like a child. Insufferable woman! How dare she interfere like that! How *dare* she!

Any residual doubts and fears that Agnes had at the prospect of finding her own way to Lucy's house were scorched away in the heat of her indignation. No one, nothing, was going to prevent her now. She would wait till tomorrow morning, and stroll calmly into the garden. Most of the women here seemed welded to their own enormous handbags, so there would be nothing strange about her, clutching her own. It was large enough for a toothbrush, spare underwear, and a tightly rolled up nightie. She would make a few sedate rounds of the croquet lawn then gradually prise herself away from the usual hangers-on and wander past the herbaceous borders, through the shrubbery at the side of the house, into the kitchen garden and out through the small gate in the back wall. The bus stop was no more than a quarter of a mile up the road, and she should be able to catch the 11.30 to Horsham. There were bound to be reasonably regular trains from there that would get her to Victoria, even if she had to change, and it shouldn't be too difficult to find her way across London to Euston. She'd travelled on the underground a few times, years ago, though never on her own. It couldn't have changed all that much. And it was Euston she needed, wasn't it? Well, someone would put her straight about that.

Things were a little more vague about what she'd do when she eventually arrived in Nottingham, but too much forward planning could be counterproductive. One could end up doing nothing at all. What was there to worry about? She had money. There were such things as taxis. A small, clean, inexpensive hotel somewhere near enough to Lucy's house should be reasonably easy to find. This was an investigation, after all. Private detectives did that sort of thing all the time. They wouldn't make much of a living if they refused to set foot from their office before knowing precisely where each step of the journey would be leading them.

As she fell asleep that night, it wasn't Henry she was thinking of but Seb.

★ ★ ★

The next day she woke to the sound of gurgling water. She lay with her eyes closed for a while, wondering about the plumbing before she realised with a jolt that this was the noise of rain gushing down drainpipes. The kind of rain that was likely to last all day. In fact, it began to ease off a little by late morning, and at half-past one Agnes was standing by her window looking out at an almost cloudless sky, wondering if there would still be time to catch the two o'clock bus. Most of the residents retired to their own rooms for an hour's nap after lunch, or sat watching quiz shows in the main lounge, digesting their food before venturing out for a walk. This was the quietest time of day, a time when she had the best chance of avoiding all company. She clenched her fists, trying to summon up enough energy to make the first move, then rubbed her clammy palms against the soft tweed of her skirt, as she pictured herself descending from the train at Victoria station. Crowds of hurrying people jostling and shoving, gabbling and shouting. The journey was going to be enough of an ordeal as it was, but rush hour? Friday afternoon? A small sigh of relief escaped her as she allowed herself to submit to the voice of reason.

So it was Saturday before she could venture out into the garden hugging her bulging handbag, and forcing herself to stroll across the lawn without looking too purposeful. There were a couple of women not far away, chatting on a bench set into an alcove in a low wall of moss-covered stone. One of the women turned towards Agnes and waved, calling out, 'Come and join us, dear. It's such a lovely sunny spot.'

'Thank you!' she called back with a smile. 'I'd love to. But first, I'm just . . . ' and she gestured vaguely towards the herbaceous border at the far end of the lawn, letting her voice trail away into an indistinct murmur. Once she'd sauntered round the side of the house, she'd be able to quicken her pace and make for the shrubbery.

In the course of the next hour and a half, Agnes had to accept that she had made a big mistake the previous day in being so cowardly about facing rush hour crowds. There probably weren't such things as rush hours in London on a Saturday, but it was beginning to look as though she would not have the chance to confirm this. She hadn't even got as far as the shrubbery because her nonchalant saunter round the corner of the house brought her face to face with Phyllis Mapperley.

'Ah, Agnes, the very person! I wanted you to meet a new friend. This is Sheila. Just

47

arrived this morning. I know you two will have a lot in common.'

In spite of herself Agnes felt a twinge of admiration for Phyllis. The woman couldn't have found a better way of trapping her. Agnes was aware that she could be a little brusque with people at times, but never deliberately unkind, and certainly not to someone like this, a thin, stooping woman with a tight little smile on her lips, and bulging, watery eyes.

Switching in to listening mode with vulnerable strangers came as naturally as breathing to Agnes. It was an ability that had surprised her in the early days of her marriage to Henry; she had never considered herself to be 'good with people'. Quite the opposite. She'd been so shy and awkward as a child in any company but Seb's. The first time she'd found herself having to entertain a visitor to the vicarage, she'd glanced up at the clock on the mantelpiece and registered the passage of every creeping minute until Henry had returned. The following day the hesitant knock had been at the kitchen door, not the front. The man standing there, shuffling from foot to foot, had been reluctant to enter, and she had focussed on putting him at his ease as she made them both a mug of tea. Half an hour had passed before she'd even noticed.

By the time Henry returned it felt as though she'd known the man for years.

After that, entering into personal conversations with needy strangers had seemed to her like opening a door in her mind and stepping through into a private place where she would hold herself as still and quiet as a woodland creature, waiting. She'd tried to discuss these experiences with Henry, but he had so clearly misunderstood her, talking of souls and God, that she had merely smiled and nodded and dropped the subject. After a while she'd stopped trying to analyse it. It was simply something that she did. But only with mere acquaintances or strangers. Or little children.

So Agnes had smiled at Sheila, and sat down with her on a bench overlooking a bed of fiercely pruned rose stalks. She found herself automatically tuning in to the frightened, sad person behind the stiff smile and barrage of words about the wonderful husband, a man of the cloth, recently laid to rest, and the invalid daughter, also, now, one of the dear departed, and how Sheila enjoyed making tapestry kneelers, and perhaps the two of them could start a little sewing group here?

Too late, Agnes remembered the two women chatting on a different bench, round the other side of the house. Now there was no chance of catching the eleven-thirty bus. Even so, it would be better to slip away as soon as the coast was clear. Perhaps she could walk on along the main road till she found the next bus stop, or the one beyond that.

Agnes was about to suggest to Sheila that she might like to meet some of the other Young at Hearts, when Phyllis and another member of staff approached. Agnes sprang to her feet. 'Well, I'll say goodbye for now, Sheila. It's been so nice talking to you.'

As she began to walk away Phyllis fell into step beside her. 'I do appreciate you looking after Sheila like that, Agnes. It's so important that new residents feel at home as quickly as possible, isn't it? In fact, I've been meaning to have a little word with you for some time.'

Agnes felt a tight knot forming in her stomach. Was she never going to escape from this woman? 'Er, Phyllis, I'm afraid — look, I'm awfully sorry, but I need the loo. I'll see you later.'

But Phyllis was not to be deflected, 'I could do with spending a quick penny myself. I'll come in with you.' seeing Agnes's face she laughed. 'Oh no, dear! I meant in to the *house*. There's three toilets in the cloakroom off the hall.'

As they stood washing their hands, Agnes caught Phyllis's eye in the mirror. 'Like being at school, isn't it,' she smiled.

'Is that a good thing, Agnes? I mean, you are happy here, aren't you?'

'As happy as one can hope to be. This is a very . . . ' Agnes struggled to find a suitable word, 'a very *elegant* place.'

For a moment Phyllis became a genuine person for Agnes. Her face lit up as she said, 'Oh yes! Elegant! That's exactly what I wanted it to be.'

Agnes turned off the tap and moved across to the drier. 'Never see the whites of their eyes, that's the trick,' Seb used to say.

But the moment of danger had passed. Phyllis continued in her usual, careful voice, 'Sad to say, there's little enough elegance in the world today. Which is why we pride ourselves on keeping this as a little oasis of gracious living, where everyone can enjoy just being themselves, away from all the vulgar hustle and bustle of modern life.'

Agnes stepped aside to make room for Phyllis at the drier. 'I'll see you later,' she said, and began to walk towards the door, but Phyllis was striding after her, shaking the last drops from her hands. 'What about joining me for a nice dry sherry before lunch? Or I have Bristol Cream, if you prefer.'

'That's very kind. Thank you. But . . . ' Agnes racked her brain. If she said she was going for a walk, Phyllis would insist on accompanying her. 'I have the beginnings of a headache coming on. I think I'll just take myself off to my room and lie down for a bit. Perhaps later? Or another day?'

⋆ ⋆ ⋆

In her own room, alone at last, she sat down by the window and reviewed her situation. It was now twenty past twelve. Lunch would be ready at half-past. The next bus for Horsham would leave at two o'clock. Another day was in danger of just drifting past, with nothing achieved. And meanwhile two small children, in the privacy of their mother's lover's home . . . 'Agnes, my dear. You have done all you possibly can. Surely, if there were any real danger, Jack would already have . . . And anyway, you'll be seeing him tomorrow.'

Yes, they'd be going out for a little drive, find somewhere for afternoon tea. But Jack would be more likely to take some notice of her concerns if she'd managed to catch sight of the children herself first, talked to the neighbours, perhaps, something, anything, rather than this terrible blank. The way Jack was at the moment, so preoccupied with work, and the way her words seemed to come out all wrong whenever she tried to hold a serious conversation with him — that look on his face, a shutter coming down — a kind of Venetian blind that filtered out the real meaning of what she was trying to express, so that only a distorted version could reach his brain.

It was more than likely that Phyllis had phoned him on Thursday evening to inform him of the request for information about trains to Nottingham. She might even have spoken to Monica. Either way, she would probably have been advised to keep an eye on Agnes's movements. 'The old dear gets very confused these days. Lord only knows what's going through that poor head of hers.' Agnes could just imagine Monica's caring tone, reserved for 'those less fortunate' so long as they weren't anywhere near her own door-step. It was only natural that Phyllis should take her orders from the ones who'd be paying the bulk of the bill. Although the other residents were unlikely to be wandering around outside for the next hour or so, Agnes would have to get past Phyllis and her henchmen in order to leave the building in the first place. She had a choice: admit defeat, and give up now, or — or *what*, exactly?

She rose slowly to her feet and stood by the window again, looking up at the sky. It seemed like years since she had seen it such a bright, unbroken blue. The sun's rays were beating through glass that magnified their heat against her body. Only a two-inch strip at the top of the wide sash window was open. She pushed it shut, then bent and heaved the bottom half up as high as it would go. A wispy breeze floated in, bringing a mixture of chill and warmth. Agnes leant forward over the sill and looked down.

'Possible,' she murmured, 'but not in these clothes.' She fingered the interweaving knots of ivy stems that almost obscured the mellow brickwork. They looked thick enough to bear her weight, but the tendrils clinging to the crumbling mortar seemed flimsy as centipedes. The drainpipe on her left looked more promising.

She opened the wardrobe and pulled out the almost-empty suitcases. From one she retrieved the tracksuit and trainers, and from the other the orange wig, the baseball cap and the black and pink nylon back-pack. Far better to be wearing these in any case, even if she hadn't got the drainpipe to contend with. She'd not had enough practice at this kind of escapade, or she'd have realised that already. Private investigator, indeed! What had she been thinking of, imagining she could spy on Lucy and the children without being observed? So, what else should she bring? Clearly she must pack what she was currently wearing. She wasn't exactly going to be popular here when she arrived back the next morning, but she probably wouldn't be allowed to even set foot over the elegant threshold in this tracksuit.

'If I do come back,' she said aloud.

Now then, what else? Apart from the handbag, of course. A spare jersey or two. It would turn colder by evening, but her winter coat would be far too bulky. The folding umbrella. The charity shop carrier bags. Plastic bags always came in handy.

As Agnes slipped off her tweed jacket and stepped out of the skirt, her heart gave a series of little skips and jumps. Feeling like a naughty child, she gathered up all her belongings and crammed everything in on top of the clothes and shoes, fastened the zip, then lifted the back-pack, testing its weight. Not too bad. Once she'd wriggled her arms through the shoulder straps, she would barely notice it.

When she checked the wig and cap in the mirror, she felt again the momentary chill that she'd experienced in the shop. Then she raised her hands to her face, patted the cheeks and stretched her lips into a smile that quickly turned into a genuine laugh as she walked across to the window and hoisted herself up onto the sill.

★ ★ ★

The attack of vertigo had come as a complete surprise. Perhaps she'd been too confident in her ability to reach across to the drainpipe and gradually lower herself to the ground, with the added assistance of the sturdy ivy stems. Pride before a fall — only she hadn't dared risk falling further than back onto the carpeted floor of the room. And then having to sit there, sick with disappointment as well as vertigo, until she'd recovered enough to stagger over to the bed.

But she was not going to give up now, after all this preparation. The last half hour or so lying flat on the bed had calmed her, as well as re-fuelling her determination. I've done much trickier climbs than this with Seb. Piece of cake, he'd call it.

She swung her legs over the side of the bed and sat up. The back-pack was still lying under the window where she had let it fall. She picked it up and rested it on the sill as she looked down at the narrow flower-bed below and scanned the lawn and the edge of the trees beyond it. The place was deserted.

Leaning to her left she pushed her fingers

into the dusty tangle of leaves and pliant stalks near the almost smothered drainpipe, reaching for a thicker stem to test how securely it was held in place by its intertwining neighbours. Something plummeted past her peripheral vision and she glanced in dismay at the empty sill, then down at the pink and black bag on the edge of the lawn. No going back now. For the second time that day, Agnes hoisted herself up onto the window ledge.

This time, she did not hesitate. It was as though her body had been taken over by some instinctual creature undistracted by thoughts or feelings. Before she knew it, one hand was clenched around a twisted ivy branch, the other slowly slipping away from the edge of the sill, and her feet were below her, scrabbling ankle deep into the foliage. The left hand found something secure and knobbly to cling to as her right palm felt the cool metal of the drainpipe. How dark and shiny the outer leaves were, inches from her face. How deep the musty tangle of hairy stalks, mantling the almost invisible bricks. The lining of her nostrils itched. A huge sneeze exploded from her with such force she that lost her footing. Her hand jerked loose from the smooth metal. Her palms and wrists were scratched as she grabbed for something to break her fall. A split second later the ground jumped up and thudded into the soles of her feet, making her tumble backwards onto the lawn.

She sat for a moment, until her breathing steadied, then turned round onto her knees and slowly rose to her feet. Nothing broken. A few mere scratches. She brushed herself down, picked up the bag again and scurried across the lawn, not daring to glance back over her shoulder until she reached the safety of the shrubbery.

4

Amazing, the way footwear could affect your mood. Agnes had initially been horrified at the price of her trainers, such lightweight items, barely any leather visible in spite of the label on the box. Nylon mesh covered most of the upper part of the shoes, and the ridiculously thick white soles were made of moulded plastic poly-something. But as soon as she had pushed open the heavy, creaking gate in the wall of the vegetable garden, and stepped across the grass verge onto the faded tarmac surface of the narrow road, the soles of her feet felt as though they were bouncing on cushioned springs. After a few moments she paused and looked behind her. There was no sign of the Harmony Home, even the chimneys were obscured from view behind trees and high hedgerows: it could have been a hundred miles away. As the road began to slope gently downhill the muscles in her calves seemed charged with an electric current, her heels refused to touch the ground, and she found herself skipping along like a six-year-old.

After a few paces, with the bag jolting up

and down between her shoulder blades, and bubbles of laughter mixing with snatched gasps of breath, she managed to regain control of her legs and slowed to a walk.

Still smiling, she rounded a bend and there was the STOP sign at the T-junction ahead, and the bus stop on the other side of the main road. She pushed back her cuff and raised her angled wrist: ten minutes to spare. Look left, look right. A car approached; a sudden blast of air flung dust in her face with a swish and roar. Agnes blinked. What speed was that one travelling? Oh, and which side of the road should she be waiting on for the Horsham bus?

Her first instinct had been correct. She did need to cross the road. There was a wooden bench on the strip of grass at the edge of the lay-by, and behind that a small copse with tangled undergrowth. Agnes looked at her watch again. Eight more minutes. Might as well sit down; she had a clear view of the road in both directions and would have ample time to step forward and stretch out her arm to stop the bus when it approached. It was cooler here in the shade of the trees, though still warmer than might be expected for early April. Apart from the occasional whiff of hot engine as another car flashed past, the air was alive with earthy smells of last year's leaves and this year's new sap rising. The chattering and trilling of the birds matched the unaccustomed feeling of exhilaration that welled behind her breastbone as she replayed over and over in her mind the details of her ungainly scramble down the ivy-covered drainpipe.

Agnes suddenly became aware of her hands and feet and upper arms. They were becoming distinctly chilly. Her stomach lurched. How long had she been sitting here? What had happened to the bus?

Calm down. It's only five minutes late, she told herself, rising a little stiffly to her feet. There was a notice attached to the pole: a mass of tiny print. Her reading glasses were in her handbag in the back-pack. She sat down on the bench again and fumbled with the zip. It got stuck in the fabric, half-way along. She glanced up at the road. Nothing in sight yet. She tugged, and let out her breath as the zipper worked its way free. Now the handbag, and the little pocket in the lining. A noise in the distance. Only a car. Take out the spectacles, shove the handbag back down. Fasten the zip. Carefully, now! More haste, less —

With the back-pack on her shoulders again, she peered through her glasses at the timetable. Monday to Friday. Then, Saturday,

Sunday. Oh, stupid woman! Why didn't you think of that? Things are often different at a weekend. The first bus this afternoon had left at one o'clock. The next wouldn't arrive till four.

Her legs felt weak as she lowered herself onto the bench. Think, now. *Think!* Can't stay here much longer. At any minute Phyllis could be tapping on the door of her deserted bedroom. She'd stoop and try to peer through the keyhole. Knock again. Draw out her own set of keys.

So, what were the options? Scrambling through the undergrowth into the wood and changing into her normal clothes. Sneaking back in through the gate of the vegetable garden and emerging from the shrubbery onto the lawn, as though nothing had happened? No, Henry. Absolutely not! Agnes was surprised at her own feelings of revulsion at the thought. It would be like agreeing to lie down again meekly in your own coffin after you'd escaped from being buried alive.

She could walk on towards Horsham, and still get there well before the next bus was due. A car appeared in the distance, approaching more slowly than usual. The shape looked familiar; it was dark green, like Jack's. Like *Jack's!* Agnes froze then lowered her head so that the peak of the cap would obscure her face. She held her breath until she heard the sound of its engine fade away. Then she remembered the sight of her reflection in the mirror, and laughed. Even if that had been Jack, he would not have connected this strange looking, orange-haired woman in her shiny turquoise tracksuit, with his own aged mama, demurely dressed in tweed suit and thick tights with dark brown Hush Puppies.

As she breathed out with a sigh, relaxing her stiff shoulders and neck, she found herself thinking of Seb again, that time they'd gone to Launceston without asking Mother, and they'd missed the bus back and hitched a lift home in a little black Ford.

Hitch-hiking! Years ago, perfectly respectable young people would think nothing of it, though at only thirteen, she and Seb had been in deep trouble when their driver turned out to be the district midwife and she'd insisted on taking them all the way to their own front door. Things were very different these days, but still, she really should put as much distance, as quickly as possible, between herself and any potential search party from the Home.

Popping into the trees for a moment first wasn't a bad idea though. There was no telling how long it would be before she could get to a loo.

She found a narrow track through the brambles and scrubby bushes to a small space between a tight cluster of silver birch and a huge, gnarled oak. Before squatting down on a level patch of dead leaves beside the oak, she wriggled the back-pack off her shoulders. As she pulled her trousers up again and straightened the tracksuit jacket, she noticed a hole in the trunk of the tree. She and Seb once had a hollow tree where they used to accumulate a store of provisions for their secret expeditions. There was that time when they'd hidden blankets and spare jerseys for the big adventure of sleeping in the cave they'd discovered on the moor, and then it had rained all afternoon but even the plastic sack that everything was wrapped in had remained bone dry.

Agnes bent down to pick up the bag; it seemed to have increased in weight. Did she really need to lug all this stuff with her to Nottingham and back?

When she emerged onto the lay-by a few minutes later, the tweed suit, shoes and thick tights, as well as the bulky handbag, emptied of all its necessary contents, were securely wrapped up in two plastic carriers and wedged into the dry, slightly musty-smelling hole half-way up the trunk of the oak.

She was standing by the bus stop,

wondering if it would be better to wait here till the next car came along, or to start walking, when she heard the distant noise of an engine and tentatively raised her right arm. She quickly lowered it again as a bright red open-topped car came into view, driven by a young man in sunglasses and reversed baseball cap, with another, almost identical, in the passenger seat, and a third in the back. But the car had slowed to a halt and the one in the rear seat leant across and called out, 'Jump in, darling.'

Agnes took a step back and said, with a steadiness that surprised her, 'That's very kind, thank you, but I'm waiting for the bus.'

'La di da! That's *very kind*!' mimicked the one in the front passenger seat, feet propped on the dashboard.

'What you stick your thumb out for, then?' growled the driver, tugging on the handbrake, and reaching for the door handle.

'Leave it, Gav,' said the first one, taking off his sunglasses and peering more closely at Agnes's face. She forced herself to meet his eyes with an unblinking stare. He turned away, muttering something incomprehensible and tapped the driver on the shoulder. Masking his mouth with a cupped hand he whispered loudly, 'She's got to be fifty at least! Well past it, anyways.'

'Never past it. What about, y'know, that old bird in — ?'

'Fuckssake, Gav. Stop arsing about,' said the one in front.

'Anyways, we got company,' added the other, glancing behind them.

The car screeched away in a cloud of exhaust, and Agnes collapsed back onto the bench before her knees could give way beneath her. She was reluctantly wondering whether she might not have to follow Henry's advice after all when a man's voice called across to her from the open window of his car at the far end of the lay-by.

'Er . . . I wouldn't want to intrude, dear lady, but could I be of any help, at all?'

Agnes blinked away a prickle of tears. Relief, that those horrible young men had gone. Relief, and disappointment that the driver of this dark green Volvo was not Jack.

★ ★ ★

Leaning back against the seat, her head not even reaching the level of the head-rest, Agnes found herself explaining that she was heading for Nottingham to visit her grand-children.

'You don't look old enough to have grandchildren,' said the man.

Perhaps it was her recent shocking experience, or perhaps there was something in the way the man's eyes seemed to glint behind his glasses, that compelled Agnes to say, 'Don't be ridiculous. I'm old enough to have great-grandchildren.' Then she added with a laugh, 'And you're old enough to know better.'

'I stand corrected, ma'am,' he smiled. 'So, you're heading for Nottingham. Now, that is an extraordinary coincidence, because so am I. May I ask what part of Nottingham?'

'West Bridgford. Do you know it?'

'I do. And very nice it is too.'

There was a moment's silence as he manoeuvred a roundabout, and then he said, 'I wonder if I might venture to make a suggestion?'

'Of course.'

'You were intending to catch a train from Horsham, right?'

'That was the plan, yes,' said Agnes slowly, realising what was coming and trying to work out whether she should accept an offer of a lift all the way there. It would certainly be a relief not to have to brave the London Underground. But there was something about the man's voice, something she couldn't quite . . . Nonsense, she told herself. It's just his accent, the way it slips from time

67

to time. *Perfectly harmless.*

'Well, that really is most kind of you,' she said, when he proposed what she'd expected.

'Not at all. I'd be glad of the company. Gets pretty lonely, driving around the country all week, staying away in hotels. I could be changing to more of a desk job next year. Cut down on my time away during the week. It'd be a mixed blessing, though. The wife doesn't like the idea much either.'

'Oh?'

'Says she's used to living her own life during the week. I wouldn't put it past Sandra to have someone else warming my half of the bed when I'm not there.'

'Oh dear! That's, that's not very nice,' faltered Agnes, beginning to wonder about the wisdom of having accepted this lift. How long did it take Jack to drive up on a Sunday? Two and a half hours? Three, even? Plenty of time for over-intimate confidences from a stranger, and she didn't have the vicarage kitchen as a way of establishing boundaries. 'And, erm. Have you got any children, Mr er? I didn't catch your name, I'm afraid.'

'Not surprising. We didn't introduce ourselves. Derek Thatcher, at your service. Before you ask, *not* Dennis. No relation at all to the Iron Lady. And you are?'

'Er . . . Alice. Alice Dale.'

'Alice. Nice name, that. Course, I couldn't really blame Sandra if she has been, you know, playing around a bit. Fair's fair. Have to admit, I take the opportunity myself, whenever it crops up. You'd be surprised, the number of women ready and willing for a bit of rumpty tumpty with a total stranger. You married, are you, Alice?'

Agnes knew she would have to contribute a certain amount of information about herself. A good thing for him to know that her late husband was a vicar. Might help to keep the conversation running on more acceptable lines.

'Vicar, eh? Whoops, better watch what I say, then,' he laughed. 'Though I bet your hubby would have had some tales to tell, when all's said and done. Men of the cloth have to listen to it all, don't they?'

'Henry never discussed that side of his work with me,' she said in her most chilling tones. She was feeling distinctly uneasy now with this man at her side, his flabby lower lip glistening with spittle.

Her rebuff seemed to have the desired effect: the next twenty minutes or so passed comfortably enough as she encouraged Derek Thatcher to talk about his two grown-up sons by his first wife, and his ten-year-old daughter by his second.

'M25, the motorway we all love to hate,' said Derek as they approached the slip road. 'No stopping now till we hit the M1.'

Once he'd manoeuvred his way onto the outside lane, Derek resumed his attempts to confide in her about his 'little adventures', as he called them. When she politely but coldly declined to show any interest, he continued, 'So, how about your young days, then, Alice, before you settled down to married life? You're still a good-looking woman now. Bet you had more than a few admirers in your heyday. A real goer, if you take my drift.'

Agnes abruptly turned her head and looked out of the window, seeing nothing but a blur. Her cheeks and neck were hot, but the rest of her body felt like ice. What had she let herself in for? What did she have to say to quell this flow, without being downright rude? She was a passenger in his car after all, and they were on a motorway. She couldn't demand to be let out here and now.

'Whoops! Done it again! Me and my big mouth!' said the man, 'Take no notice, dear lady. Got carried away. Have to say, you don't look like a typical vicar's wife. Meet all sorts on my travels. You wouldn't believe! From henceforth, I will be the perfect gentleman. Upon my honour!'

Agnes remained silent, trying to focus her

attention on the cars and lorries they were overtaking.

'I could kick myself, I really could. And we were getting on like a house on fire. Me and my big mouth. I apologise most sincerely, Alice. No offence meant.'

Oh dear. She would have to make some acknowledgement. 'None taken,' she said quietly. 'I'm a little fatigued, though. Would you mind if I just close my eyes for a few minutes?'

'Feel free,' he said, sounding so relieved that she almost felt sorry for him. 'I could put on a bit of music if you like. Got a nice *Best of Classical* here somewhere.'

'Thank you. That would be lovely.'

★   ★   ★

The first tune on the disc was the overture from *William Tell*. She hadn't intended to close her eyes fully, but it was the only way of preventing tears from spilling out. It had been Henry's favourite. It had irritated her so much after hearing it at least once a day during the first few weeks of their marriage that one evening she had finally burst out, 'I am sick and tired of listening to that darned thing! When are you going to finally get it out of your system?'

Henry had lowered his book, removed his reading glasses and stared at her in astonishment. 'My dear Lambkin! Why ever did you not say so earlier!'

She'd immediately felt ashamed of herself. Fancy swearing like that! And Henry, so patient and understanding.

For a while after that he would only play it when he thought she was out of earshot, but she could not bear the idea of anything coming between them. When, a few days before Christmas, she found the two halves of vinyl wedged into the rubbish bin, she knew what she was going to give him as an extra present.

He had been so delighted that she'd insisted on listening to it with him as they sat hand in hand on the sofa. From then on it became part of their Sunday evening ritual.

Agnes clasped one hand firmly over the other. It was the one on the driver's side, the right hand, that used to reach out for Henry's. She clenched her jaw, using muscles she'd not been aware of to prevent her lips from quivering.

Piano music. *Midnight Sonata*. The moment passed . . .

★　★　★

Now she is at the wheel, foot jammed against the accelerator pedal. 'I never knew I could drive,' she murmurs. Mild surprise switches to blind panic as the racing car screeches round a hairpin bend. Below her open window, the mountainside has become a sheer cliff. The car hurtles over the edge and drops away from her like a stone. As she plummets down, down through the swirling white clouds, a winged Henry floats beside her, scolding her about dangerous sports. 'Highly irresponsible. Should know better. Positively suicidal.' Just as the ground comes into view she tugs at the loose safety belt across her chest, and a parachute billows above her, breaking her fall.

Agnes opened her eyes with a start as the rhythm of the engine changed. The car was easing its way around a crowded car-park. 'Time for a pit-stop,' said the stranger beside her. 'Hope you don't mind.'

Agnes gave a little gasp and raised her hand to her mouth. Dreaming! She hadn't meant to fall asleep. 'Are we there yet?'

Derek Thatcher laughed, 'My kids always used to say that! Nowhere near, I'm afraid. Just at the start of the M1. I need a quick slash and then I'll grab a bite of something. Had no dinner yet. How about you? Would you like anything?'

Her mind was slowly re-adjusting to the situation. This was a motorway service station. No public transport from here. She had experienced a few embarrassing minutes, shut up alone in the car with this man, but, in reality, what had she to fear? He was a rather sad and lonely person, and he had seemed truly upset by the way his conversation had embarrassed her.

He was no different from many of the callers who'd dropped in at the vicarage over the past fifty years, hoping for a private word with the vicar. The only danger she was facing now was that of being too obsessed with herself and her own dignity. Like Phyllis Mapperley! She felt a twinge of shame and gave a wry smile.

'I wouldn't mind a little something,' she answered, remembering that she, too, had missed lunch. 'But you must let me pay for yours,' she added tentatively, wanting to make amends for her ungenerous thoughts, but wary of offending him.

She chose a plate of mixed salad, but Derek Thatcher refused to let her pay for his cod and chips. 'Comes off expenses. Not that I'd ever let a lady foot the bill.'

She had slung her back-pack across one shoulder when she'd left the car, and was about to rummage in it for her money when she remembered that she'd separated out her store of cash and had placed three twenties and a few pound coins in a little purse, zipped securely into the pocket of her tracksuit top.

The place was nearly full, and they found a spare table with difficulty. Agnes had noticed a tall, round-faced young man next to her at the salad bar as she'd looked around for a price list. 'Up there, bab,' he'd said, pointing to the card on top of the drinks machine. His smile was open and friendly, reminding her of a cornflakes advertisement, with his blue-green eyes and his mass of freckles reaching up to the receding hairline of sandy curls. A few moments after she had settled herself onto the plastic chair opposite Derek she saw the same man wandering between the tables scanning the room for an empty space. She caught his eye and indicated the vacant chair at her side.

'Joe Geraghty,' he said, as he sat down. Agnes felt more relaxed now, and was able to tackle the variety of cold pastas and grated vegetables with more enthusiasm. She had been hungrier than she'd realised. Derek and Joe were exchanging experiences of long distance travelling jobs; it turned out that Joe was a lorry driver, working for a haulage firm in Birmingham.

Agnes shifted in her seat, 'I think I'll just pay a quick visit to the ladies,' she said, but the two men hardly seemed to notice her.

★　★　★

Standing at the long row of hand basins, she straightened the peak of the cap and smoothed back the bushy orange ponytail. It didn't seem possible that only this morning such a different reflection had been staring back at her as she and Phyllis Mapperley stood side by side, washing their hands. Perhaps she had been too harsh in her judgement of Phyllis as well, too enveloped in her own misery to allow herself to give any thought to others. 'Mmm. Save that till later,' she muttered to the almost-stranger in the mirror. 'This isn't the time or place for soul-searching.'

Joe was mopping up the salad juices with the final piece of soft white roll when Agnes sat down again. There was no sign of Derek.

'I'll be off, then,' said Joe, wiping his mouth with the back of his hand. 'Nice meeting you.'

He disappeared in the direction of the toilets, and Agnes glanced that way a few times, expecting to see Derek emerging. She caught sight of Joe's freckled head as he wove his way through the milling crowds towards the car park, and suddenly understood that Derek Thatcher was not going to arrive back at the table. The entire service station was seething with total strangers, every one of them attached to someone else. She felt conspicuously alone.

'Better the devil you know,' said Henry, prompting her to dash out and see if the green Volvo was still parked where she had last seen it.

After minutes of pacing up and down the rows of unfamiliar cars, her chest so tight she could feel each shallow breath, Agnes had to accept that she was now stranded. For a second or two she almost laughed: she had spent the whole morning trying to avoid Phyllis, yet an hour ago would have welcomed her with open arms in order to get away from Derek Thatcher, and now, if he'd suddenly re-appeared he'd have seemed like a knight on a white charger. Then the wave of panic broke over her: all she could think of was how quickly she could scurry off to the ladies again and shut herself into a cubicle and let the tears flow.

But before she could turn and run, words that she could not ignore pushed their way up from somewhere deep below her conscious mind: the lorry park is over there. If you hurry, you could still catch that nice Joe Geraghty.

5

In the breakfast-kitchen of number 11, Saxon Meadow, the usual Saturday feeding rituals were taking place.

Jack was scraping the spoon around the plastic container of his low-fat mandarin yoghurt. He wondered if Monica was going to issue her normal warnings about his waistline when he livened his caffeine-free coffee with a little of the double cream that he'd sneaked into the Sainsbury's shopping trolley that morning. Monica was standing by the fridge, refreshing her tall glass of tonic water with another lump of ice and a quick shot of clear liquid from the green bottle behind the packet of Frosties. Hailey, still in her Donald Duck nightshirt was reaching for the same cereal box, and mouthing, in a stage whisper, 'At it already, Mum?' while Donna, in a shapeless sweatshirt and baggy combat trousers, was emptying a tin of baked beans into a pan on the hob and staring dreamily at the wisps of smoke curling up from the toaster.

Monica frowned at Hailey but Jack was saying, 'For goodness sake, wake up, Donna. Toast's burning.'

' 'S'OK. No need to shout.'

'I am *not* shouting,' said Jack. 'But I would like to be able to enjoy my lunch without the smell of burning breakfast all around me. What time of day d'you call this anyway?' Then, as Hailey poured a torrent of milk into her bowl, scattering Frosties in white puddles over the table and onto the floor, he exclaimed, 'God give me patience! Can't you girls ever leave us in peace for a moment?'

He regretted these words as soon as they'd left his mouth. He really should try to be more patient with them both. It wasn't their fault that they came as part of the package with Monica. Still less that they were not six and four years old. Not Emily and Sam.

'Fuss, fuss, fuss. You're worse than poor old Ags,' said Hailey, snatching up her cereal bowl and making for the door. 'I was going to watch tele, anyway. Don't like the smell in here,' she said, glaring at Donna. 'An' I don't mean the toast.'

'*Poor* old!' said Donna, ignoring the last comment. 'Don't remember ever catching you spending any time with her. Bet she's only too glad to be rid of you miserable lot.'

'What d'you mean, miserable?' demanded Monica, taking a large gulp from her glass. 'There's just no pleasing some people. Worked myself to the bone for her. She won't

79

leave me alone even now, forever on the phone about one thing or another.'

'What's that?' asked Jack, looking up from his careful trickling of cream over the back of a teaspoon into his coffee.

'Agnes, always phoning,' said Monica. 'Rang again, Wednesday night.'

'Wednesday! I wish you'd told me, Monica. What did she want?'

'Didn't say, did she? Never does. And she knows very well you'll be taking her out tomorrow.'

'Poor old bat's prob'ly bored out of her skull,' muttered Donna.

'Oh Lord!' exclaimed Jack. 'She rang me at work on Wednesday morning. There was a bit of a panic on about one of the big accounts — went clean out of my head.' He thrust out his jaw and tapped a finger against his lower front teeth. After a moment he said, 'Think I'll just pop over for a bit now. Check she's OK.'

'Surely it can wait till tomorrow, Jackie, can't it?' asked Monica. She swallowed another mouthful and put down her glass before sauntering across to stand behind him and rest her palms on his shoulders, massaging him lightly through his Polo teeshirt. She bent forward and placed her cheek against his, murmuring, 'You did *promise* we'd take the girls to choose paper and curtains for the back room.'

Donna glanced up from her beans, watching Jack's hesitant expression.

'Er, you wouldn't mind too much, would you, Donna? Only, well, she does tend to work herself into a panic these days.'

'Na,' said Donna through a mouthful of beans. 'Meeting me mates, later. Anyway, not bothered about curtains, an' I want to paint the walls black.'

Monica withdrew her hands. 'Don't worry about me, Jack. Why should anything change, just because your mother's not living here any more? I'll take Hailey on my own, if Donna's busy. Black! I don't think Hailey would like that.'

★　★　★

Jack was surprised to find himself humming as he set out on the half-hour journey to the Harmony Home and made his way through the overspill suburbs. Not that he liked disappointing Monica, but at least on this occasion he had stuck to his guns and was following his conscience. He really should have phoned Ma back on Wednesday: she'd sounded genuinely worried, and even though there was bound to be a perfectly simple explanation for whatever it was that was bothering her, a quick phone call could have put her mind at rest. Fancy just forgetting!

But as he cruised along the quiet country lanes he began to wonder if he'd over-reacted to Donna's mutterings. Perhaps Monica had been right, 'a rod for your own back, dashing over there all the time!' Wouldn't a quick phone conversation have been just as effective? Settling in, that's what she was doing. Early days, yet. Wasn't that what Dad had said, when Jack had managed to have a turn at the telephone, after his first ten days at that school. 'Buck up, Jack, my boy. Everyone's a bit down, first couple of weeks. Soon knuckle under and start to enjoy it. You mark my words. Just don't go bothering your mama, there's a good chap.'

But he had bothered her. 'Make him let me come home, Ma,' he'd pleaded in a whisper, as the queue behind him for the phone grew longer. 'It's not getting any better. It's worse, if anything.'

He'd felt a flush of triumph when he heard her voice go shaky. But she hadn't brought him home. He'd survived it, of course. Not done too badly, in fact. Probably had all turned out for the best, in the end.

It just went to show, though, didn't it? Shouldn't trust a woman.

'Ah! Yes. Good afternoon, Miss Mapperley. Is my mother about?'

'Mr Borrowdale! How nice! We weren't expecting you till tomorrow. Your mother? Yes, I took a turn around the grounds with her just a while back. I do believe she may be still in her room. Would you like to pop up?'

After knocking and calling at the locked door, Jack suppressed a sudden surge of irritation. Of course his mother had every right to be somewhere else! Sitting in the garden, perhaps, chatting to a new friend. It was certainly warm enough, almost like summer; he'd like to have been out walking on the downs himself, somewhere near enough to the coast to smell the sea. Not that he got much chance of doing that these days. If he'd not been here now, he'd be traipsing round some department store or D.I.Y. place with Monica and the girls.

When, after twenty minutes of searching the entire house and grounds, there was still no sign of Agnes, Phyllis agreed to use her own keys to open the bedroom door for Jack. He burst into the room ahead of her, not daring to let himself think what he might find, but the room was empty. He dashed across to the wide-open window. As soon as he'd looked down, he gave himself a mental shake. If by some extraordinary misfortune she had managed to tumble out, someone would already have seen her crumpled body sprawled on the flower-bed below. Ridiculous to be so worried. Must be the strain he was under at work just now. That bastard, Burrows. Just looking for an excuse to get rid of him.

'Well, I don't know where she could be, I'm sure,' said Phyllis, a little defensively. 'I was taking particular care to keep an eye on her, after what you'd said.'

'What I'd said?'

'You remember, that she was getting strange ideas about her grandchildren, might attempt to take herself off to Nottingham, that she's really not up to travelling anywhere on her own.'

A quick search of the room revealed no clues. Nothing appeared to be missing.

'Perhaps she's just popped down to the village,' suggested Jack.

'Most unusual,' said Phyllis. 'She does know that we don't encourage residents to wander out on their own without informing us first. But you may well be right.'

The village was no more than a few houses, a pub and a small Happy Shopper, about a quarter of a mile from the front gates in the opposite direction to the main road. It did not take Jack long to question every inhabitant of the place. No one had seen a grey-haired old woman in a three-quarter length tweed jacket with matching skirt, woolly tights and lace up shoes.

★ ★ ★

'What do you mean, not there?' demanded Monica, enunciating each word with exaggerated patience as Jack walked in through the front door, his shoulders drooping. 'Are you *quite* sure you looked everywhere?'

Before he could reply she carried on, 'Anyway, I did say you should ring first. That's the whole afternoon wasted now. Hailey was so disappointed.'

'Mum! Muuum!' came a petulant voice from upstairs. 'If that's Jack, can we go now? You did promise, and I don't see why we couldn't have gone without him in the first place.'

'It was supposed to be a little outing for the whole family.'

'Yeah, yeah. I get it. You mean you needed Jack's plastic.'

'Not at all. As I said — '

Jack felt as though his nerves were branching out into a hundred raw endings.

'Don't you understand anything, Monica? My mother has completely and utterly vanished off the face of the earth, and all you and your spoilt daughter can think about is how quickly you can refurnish that bedroom.'

'I hate him. He's not my dad. An' I hate you for making us live in this dump,' shrieked the girl's voice. Footsteps stamped along the landing and a door slammed shut.

'Now look what you've done,' Monica began, then stopped herself and drew a deep breath. 'I'm sorry about Hailey, Jack. I don't know what's got into her recently, Look, we both need a good stiff drink, and then we can talk things over sensibly. I'm sure there'll be a perfectly simple explanation.' She raised a hand to touch him on the arm, saw his face, and moved towards the lounge door.

Jack followed, as though on an invisible lead, and halted on the edge of the deep-pile cream carpet, watching her. He hadn't noticed any sound from the television when he'd first stepped into the house. Now, the brassy blare of theme music from one of those American *Bare Your Soul* chat shows seemed to be heralding Monica's entrance as she undulated down the room towards the bar by the patio windows. Oh God! That arse in those tight black jeans . . .

'Still boozing, Mum?' Donna's voice.

'What's going on?'

Jack gave a start, and the bulge in the crotch of his trousers subsided. How could he let himself think of sex at a time like this?

Donna was sprawled on the leather sofa, and Jack was struck by the incongruity of her fluffy pink rabbit slippers, the only frivolous thing about her. Everything else was beige or sludge brown, even her straggly hair, and the fat snuffling Corgi, Queenie, lying across her stomach. Must take after her father, Jack had thought when he'd first met her, three weeks after he'd fallen for Monica. Donna was stocky and plain faced, but even so, at sixteen, she could be making a bit more of herself. She seemed determined not to try.

'I said, what's going on?' repeated Donna. 'Can't a person watch TV in peace?'

Those girls were always around the place. No privacy. Even the bedroom he shared with Monica wasn't guaranteed against invasion by one or other of them, except late at night. He and Monica sometimes had to take his car out and try to find a suitable parking place down a country lane. Like bloody teenagers. Things had got even more difficult with Ma living there too.

Ma. Where on earth was she?

Monica handed him a cut glass tumbler of whisky. 'You've had a shock, Jackie. Get this down you, love.' She caught Donna's eye and held a finger to her lips. 'Tell you in a minute,' she whispered.

Jack gulped a mouthful, spluttered, then drained the glass and allowed Monica to lead him to the large chair near the marble fireplace. She put her own glass down on the coffee table, fetched the bottle of Bells, and poured Jack another large drink before perching herself on the arm of his chair. She placed one hand on his shoulder and announced as though speaking for a small child, 'Jack says that Agnes has disappeared from the Home.'

'Run away, I guess. Thought she might,' said Donna, and turned back to the TV, one hand absently stroking Queenie's head. 'You wouldn't believe what some people will do for five minutes of fame!'

'Run away!' exclaimed Jack.

'Agnes? Fame?' said Monica.

'Na, that silly cow, there,' Donna pointed at the screen.

'Donna!' came Hailey's voice from the top of the stairs. 'You been messing with my things again? Can't find my new hair stuff anywhere.'

Jack leaped out of his chair, strode over to the TV and switched it off. 'What did you mean, Donna? Run away?'

As Jack took a step towards her she added, 'Nothing. I didn't mean anything really. Just . . .'

'Just what, dear?' asked Monica, positioning herself next to Jack. 'If you know anything, anything at all, you must tell us. Jack was about to call the police.'

'Police?' said Hailey, entering the room. 'It's only cheap stuff from Boots, wouldn't want even Donna arrested for that. Something else she went and did to me last night, though, I'd see her locked up and throw away the key, given half a chance.'

'Ta very much,' said Donna. 'I wouldn't touch your fucking stuff. An I don't know what you're on at me for, neither — only let on about your age for your own sake, stupid.' Before Hailey could respond, she went on, 'Aggie's done a runner.'

'Don't use that language, dear,' said Monica automatically, and then turned to Hailey. 'Agnes has disappeared. Donna seems to think she's run away.'

'I only meant that I wouldn't put anything past Agnes,' Donna went on. 'She was a crafty old bird, acting dumb. I just got a kind of feeling, you know, that there was something up. You and Jack couldn't wait to get rid of her. Hailey made it damn clear she wanted her bedroom. Stood out a mile she didn't want to be stuck in a home with lots of other boring old farts. So what d'you expect?'

'P'raps she's been kidnapped,' said Hailey. 'Any minute now some creepy bloke'll ring up and demand a million pounds. Next thing we know, you'll be getting an ear in the post.'

'Hailey, dear! That's not very helpful,' said Monica. 'I'm sure there's a very simple explanation. She probably just went out for a little walk and took a wrong turning somewhere. Why don't you ring them, Jack, and see if she's turned up yet?'

'They promised they'd phone me if there was the slightest news. I should've insisted they called in the police straight away. Just thinking of their precious good name, and I was too bloody stupid to realise. Oh God!' He bent down to pick up the bottle and refilled his glass with a shaking hand. 'She's been knocked down by a hit and run driver. I know it. She'll be lying injured in a ditch, bleeding to death. My mother. What harm did she ever do any of you? Donna's right. She didn't really want to go to live in that place. I should never have listened to you, Monica.'

'Don't you try and dump that on me. It was your idea, not mine. And anyway, it was me who had to do all the looking after. No one can say I didn't do my utmost. You're the one who chased off looking for suitable homes. You told me she was perfectly happy there.'

'Haven't you called the police yet, then?' asked Hailey. 'I mean, isn't that what you're supposed to do when a person disappears? Bet you wouldn't even bother if I didn't come home one night. Fat lot you care about anything, 'cept making money.'

'That's enough, Hailey,' said Monica. 'People can't just go bothering the police the minute they don't know where somebody's got to. It's different with a teenager, of course. But an old woman of seventy-five . . . Jack'd look pretty silly if she's been sitting in the local teashop all this time. Or caught a bus to the nearest town.'

'Bus!' exclaimed Jack. 'Of course! Why didn't I think of that!' He gulped down the rest of his drink, put the glass on the table, and turned towards Monica. 'You're brilliant, darling,' he said, kissing her on the lips before he dashed from the room.

The front door slammed and the three of them watched through the window as Jack got into his car and began reversing it off the drive.

'How much whisky does it take before you're over the limit?' asked Donna.

6

'M6 at last,' said Joe. 'Not long now.'

'How does your wife know what time you'll get to the depot, though, if she's meant to be picking you up?' asked Agnes. 'I mean, the way the traffic is these days.'

He lifted one hand off the wheel and patted the pocket of his denim jacket. 'Mobile. I'll be ringing in a few minutes. Look,' he continued, 'I'm really sorry I can't take you all the way to your daughter-in-law's in the truck. The boss always checks on the mileage. You sure you'll be OK, taking the train to Nottingham?'

'I'll be fine, thank you, Joe,' said Agnes more cheerfully than she felt, suddenly realising how sorry she would be to say goodbye to this kind-hearted man. It had been lovely to hear him talk with such affection about his family — his wife Sally-Ann expecting their second child, his little boy, Scott's third birthday party last Sunday.

'I can't tell you how much I'm looking forward to seeing my grandchildren again,' she went on.

'It's nice your son's ex-wife has kept in touch,' Joe said 'When was it you said they'd be expecting you?'

Now was the time to say, 'actually, she's not expecting me.' It was clear that Joe would not feel obliged to interfere if he knew her true circumstances. But how could she explain to this nice young man that her ex-daughter-in-law was actually trying to sever all contact? It was even more shaming that her only son . . .

So Agnes let herself be overtaken by a sudden coughing fit, and the conversation shifted to childhood ailments which led on quite naturally to difficulties with schools.

'I had a terrible time with Jack,' she said. 'Henry insisted on sending him to his own old school. I couldn't bear the idea of him boarding, but . . . Oh, I often wonder if I shouldn't have held my ground. He just didn't seem able to settle. He was still ringing me at the end of his first year, and sounding so forlorn. It nearly broke my heart when he had to go back that following September.'

Agnes gave a little shudder, and Joe looked at her in bewilderment. 'Weren't there any proper schools near you, then?'

'It's hard to justify these days, Joe. I know it must sound terribly cruel to you, but then, well, for people who were accustomed to that way of life . . . So anyway, Jack. He just wasn't academic at all. But he did well enough in the end, university and so on. He has a good job now, though he does seem to have to work such extraordinarily long hours.' Agnes gave a little laugh. 'Look at me, going on about my family, when you've got such an important event around the corner! When exactly is the baby due?'

Joe was keeping his eye on his rear mirror, and didn't answer. Agnes craned her neck round at the lorry behind them. 'Isn't he rather close?' she asked.

'Too right he is. I can't go any faster with that clapped out Fiesta hogging the road. Oh, that's better!' After a moment he pulled onto the inside lane and let the other lorry past. 'Rather have him in front than up my arse, bloody Frog,' he muttered. 'Begging your pardon,' he said to Agnes.

'Don't mind me!' she laughed. 'Now then, where were we?'

''Bout five miles south of Brum,' said Joe, then, 'Oh! I see. The baby. Another three weeks yet. And it'll be late, more'n likely, if it's anything like Scottie. Too comfortable where he was,' he laughed. 'Makes it a bit difficult to get the timing right when it comes to planning days off work.'

'Of course. You'll have to be looking after

Scott. Haven't you any neighbours or family who can lend a hand?'

'Sally-Ann's mum'll stop with us for a bit, after she comes home with the babbie. She's OK, Pauline is. Not one of those Mother-In-Law types always sticking their nose in. She's — '

Agnes was startled by a sudden tinny blast of the *William Tell* overture. That tune! Twice in one day! But this time she smiled, imagining Henry muttering about distractions to drivers as Joe removed the phone from his pocket and the lorry swerved a fraction to the left.

'What d'you mean, just fell over? You *sure* she's all right? Yeah. Yeah, coming up to Junction 5. Be right home. Someone'll have to pick the truck up later. Pass her on to me, will you.' Agnes looked at his tense face. It was clear that he'd forgotten her presence. 'Don't worry, love. You'll be fine. Everything'll be OK. Just hang on in there. I'll be with you before they arrive. See you in five minutes, pet. Love you, too. Bye, now.'

He glanced in Agnes's direction and his eyes re-focussed. 'Sorry. That was a neighbour. Sally-Ann tripped over the back step. She's not hurt, just shaken, but it seems that the waters, y'know. There's an ambulance on its way.'

95

'Three weeks, you said. If labour's started now, that's not so early. There shouldn't be any cause for worry.'

Joe was slowing down on the slip road that led to a huge roundabout. 'Look, I meant to drop you at the station after Sally-Ann met us with the car. But now — '

'I won't have you worrying about me,' said Agnes firmly. 'I'm perfectly capable of finding my own way to the station. But if you'd like me to stay around for a bit, till you've had time to sort things out . . . '

'I, er. That's very kind, I'm sure. But . . . '

'But I'm a total stranger. That's perfectly understandable,' she said calmly.

'It's not that. No. You, er, you don't feel like a stranger, it's just, your daughter-in-law. She'll be expecting you.'

'My ex-daughter-in-law. No. She . . . Actually, I didn't make it clear exactly when I'd be arriving.'

'Well, if you're sure. Just till I find out what's happening.'

'So that's settled then,' said Agnes.

★ ★ ★

Joe navigated a few more roundabouts, and then turned off the busy dual carriageway onto a street lined with 1950s semi-detached

96

houses, most of which were boarded up. 'No, this isn't it, thank goodness. Just a short cut,' he said. 'They're meant to be rebuilding this whole estate. But nothing ever seems to be happening. The council are fucking useless. Oh! Sorry! That slipped out.'

'No, really, don't bother about me. Don't forget, I've been living in a house with two teenage girls!'

'Terrible, isn't it. I hate hearing women using bad language.'

'I'll try not to shock you, then,' laughed Agnes. 'I shock myself sometimes, these days!'

There was silence for a while, and Agnes shuddered at the desolate scene as Joe steered the lorry through a maze of short roads and crescents. As they'd travelled further north, a grey haze had spread across the sky. Now a few drops of rain were splattering onto smeared bodies of insects on the windscreen. Crisp packets, chip papers and empty drinks cans were tossed into erratic dance by sudden gusts of wind along the cracked, uneven pavements. Election posters trailed and flapped from lamp-posts, broken fences, wheel-less cars. VOTE GREEN For a Greener City. Your Future Lies with LABOUR. Red and blue graffiti assaulted her eyes with crude messages from boarded doors and windows.

Joe slowed down at a T-junction and Agnes exclaimed, 'Look, people are still living in some of these! Little children! How terrible to be surrounded by derelict buildings like this.'

'Nearly there,' said Joe. They were off the estate now. These were terraced houses, older, Edwardian or late Victorian, and their front doors opened directly onto the pavement. The lorry was taking up the entire centre of the road. Agnes found herself looking down onto the roofs of parked cars which seemed uncomfortably close to the lorry's huge wheels.

He was approaching another T-junction, where he turned left. These terraced houses had small front gardens, most of which looked well cared for, with low brick walls and neat hedges, and narrow beds of daffodils and multicoloured primulas. The cab window on her side was being tapped by twigs of horse chestnut trees, about to burst into leaf.

Almost before Joe had switched off the engine, he was jumping down onto the road and racing round the front of the cab to reach the pavement. At the same time, a door opened and a frail looking woman with tight grey curls and a stooped back hovered in the doorway, staring up at Agnes, who was still sitting in the cab.

Agnes looked at her watch. Nearly six

o'clock already. If it turned out that she wasn't needed at Joe's, she could ask him for directions to the station. Nottingham wasn't all that far away. Or perhaps it would be wiser to find a cheap hotel somewhere near here, and get an early train in the morning. Once she'd got some facts under her belt, she could phone Jack and get him to postpone his visit till she got back to the Home.

Thinking of Jack made her heart beat a little faster. He was sure to be angry with her, especially if what she witnessed was a scene of domestic harmony. But at least she would have set her mind at rest.

★   ★   ★

Joe's front door was flung open again and he stepped onto the pavement, closely followed by a small boy screaming, 'Lemme go! Lemme go!' as he struggled to free his hand from the grasp of the grey-haired woman.

Agnes opened the cab door and swung herself round, holding onto the seat as she lowered herself to the ground. By this time, Scott had managed to loose his hand and had flung both arms around his father's knees. Even more like the cornflakes advertisement, she smiled to herself, as she squatted down and held out her right hand to the child.

'Hello, Scott. I'm Agnes. Let's take your Daddy into the house and then you can tell us what's been happening.'

The child allowed Agnes to take one hand, while he clung to Joe's trouser leg with the other. Agnes found herself leading them into the house as the older woman stepped to one side of the tiny porch to let them pass into the neat front room where a wood-effect gas fire was flickering behind a large mesh fireguard.

Once inside Joe stooped down and picked up the child, holding him close, cradling his son's head against his shoulder. The boy put his thumb in his mouth and looked sideways at Agnes. 'Sally-Ann's already gone,' said Joe. 'Edie says we've only just missed her.'

'That's right,' said the woman, who was taking small steps backwards and forwards in front of the window, glancing out every now and then, as though the ambulance might reappear at any moment. Her hands were clasped in front of her chest and she rubbed her palms together as she spoke. 'That poor young girl. That poor young girl. In agony, she was. Babbie's on its way and no mistake, ready or not. Still, them amberlance men seemed to think it would be all right. Though if you ask me they looked not much more 'an kiddies their selves.'

Joe threw a desperate look at Agnes, before

burying his face in Scott's hair.

'You'll be wanting to get off to the hospital right away, then, won't you Joe?' she said. 'So if you just scribble down your work's number, I can let them know what's happening. Edie and I will look after Scott till you get back, won't we, Edie? I'm in no hurry to go anywhere just yet.'

'I . . . I . . . Are you really sure you can cope, Agnes?'

'Well, if you prefer your new friend to me, I don't mind, I'm sure,' sniffed Edie. 'I suppose you think I'm too old to handle Scott now. Though I don't know as Sally-Ann would be too pleased, you letting a stranger into the house.'

'Oh, Edie. I didn't mean to offend you,' said Agnes gently. 'Of course you're not too old. It's just that I know what a handful a three-year-old can be, and I thought you might like someone else around.'

'That's right,' put in Joe. 'And Agnes isn't a stranger. We've been friends for ages. So if you don't mind, I'll just run upstairs and grab a few things for Sal.' Joe placed his hands round Scott's waist to lower him to the ground, but the child clung on with his legs and tightened his grip around Joe's neck.

When the pair of them had gone upstairs Edie took a step towards Agnes and peered more closely at her face. 'Funny hair, if you don't mind me saying. And as for wearing a kiddie's cap! Well, I mean, young people these days, enough to give a blind man a headache. But someone old enough to know better!' She sniffed and turned away towards the window. 'Still, if you're a friend of Joe's. From work, was it?'

'In a manner of speaking.'

'And what manner might that be when it's at home? Bit la di da that's what. Though from the look of you I thought you was one of them social workers at first.'

Agnes laughed. She'd not given any thought to her appearance since Joe had helped her clamber up into the cab of his lorry a couple of hours earlier. 'You're right, it is a mess isn't it? To be perfectly honest, my own hair hasn't grown back yet after chemotherapy. I chose this because I wanted to cheer myself up, after what I'd been through. Bit childish, I know. But then, when you've found that you're alive and reasonably healthy, after being told you've got only a few months to live . . . I suppose it just went to my head!' She gave another peal of laughter, but at the same time a tremor of surprise ran through her. How easily that lie had slipped out! Worse still, how she was enjoying it: Edie's wary face, not sure whether to laugh with her, or to express concern for her health!

After a moment Edie said slowly, 'Went to your head! That's good, that is,' and she punched Agnes lightly on the shoulder, opening her mouth in a grin that revealed pink, almost toothless gums.

They were both still laughing when Joe and Scott stepped down into the room. Joe, looking relieved to see the two women on more friendly terms, said, 'This kind lady is going to help Edie look after you, Scottie. That's right, isn't it, Edie?'

'Course it is, Joe. Now get along with you. That wife of yours'll be wondering where you are.' She turned to Scott, 'You tire me out, you do. I'm getting a bit old to be dealing with noisy little boys all day. Auntie Agnes can run around after you quicker'n what I can. Three score years and ten, that's what the bible says. I'm nearly five years past that.'

'Nanny-Edie is very, very old,' said Scott, looking across at Agnes as he clutched Edie's flowered skirt. 'You're only old a little bit, Auntie Ness. Can you still run? Nanny-Edie can't run.'

★ ★ ★

Hours later — was it really that same day? — Agnes was climbing the steep narrow stairs up to the spare bedroom in Joe's converted loft. She was alone in the house with a three-year-old stranger who had happily let her feed him, bath him, tuck him into bed, and read to him until he fell asleep.

She lowered herself onto the narrow bed under the skylight and unlaced her trainers. Her clothes were loose fitting and comfortable. Better remain fully dressed. Scott might wake up crying at any time.

She pulled the light-cord and snuggled down under the quilt, lying flat on her back so that she could look up at the stars. No matter that they shone less clearly here than in the black of the countryside. I wish I could believe that you were up there, somewhere, Henry.

She pushed her lips into the semblance of a smile. What *would* he say if he could have seen her in that wig? Even when she'd pulled out her first few grey hairs, years ago, he hadn't liked it. 'My dear Lambkin, we all have to accept the ageing process with as much good grace as we can muster.' Lambkin! Typical of his awful puns. And then, before a cross word could pass her lips, he'd bent to kiss the top of her head and sung that song that irritated her so much, about silver threads and growing old, but she could never tell him because she knew it was his way of saying he loved her.

When she'd looked in the bathroom mirror after Scott had finally fallen asleep she had been shocked at the sight of this woman with orange hair. But when she'd removed the cap and wig, it felt for one uncanny moment as though the real Agnes was missing, hovering somewhere between the new Agnes and the old.

There was no doubt that wearing the wig and cap took a good ten years off her. Joe and Edie, and even Scott seemed to think she was a lot younger. And that was another thing she hadn't really acknowledged before, how women of sixty or so begin to vanish like the Cheshire Cat, so that by the time they're over seventy they're virtually invisible. No one even notices the grin. She had done it herself today, just assumed that Edie was older than her, and not up to much, when in fact there was a lot more to Edie than met the eye. And it was Parkinson's that had given her that stoop and the tremor in her hands.

Yes, Henry, to my shame, I did feel superior to her, and proud of my accomplishments. Proud of my ability to deceive people! Jack and Monica, blissfully unaware of the keep fit classes. That patronising Phyllis Mapperley, thinking she'd got me safely imprisoned in the Harmony Home. 'Good riddance to bad rubbish,' is what she'll be saying, now that she's found out that the bird has flown.

At this thought, a wide smile spread across her face. Perhaps I won't be able to go back. Ever!

7

If Felix Biddle had been given prior warning that Agnes Borrowdale would be at New Street Station that Sunday morning, he would have selected a more appropriate time for his attempted suicide.

Sitting in the almost deserted food bar devouring his second chocolate croissant under Agnes's penetrating gaze, he realised that for the immediate future he was going to have some difficulty in shaking off his mortal coil.

He was not quite sure yet about the precise nature of his feelings on the matter. They included pleasure at the way the sudden nuggets of chocolate emerged through the bland layers of warm pastry; irritation that he would now have to face a week's accumulation of washing up piled in and around his kitchen sink; curiosity about this odd-looking woman who had so forcefully accosted him as he had stepped forwards to peer down at the gleaming, inviting rails; and eagerness to learn more about this Dangerous Sports Euthanasia Society she was inviting him to join.

Agnes, too, was experiencing a conflicting range of emotions as she watched a flaky crumb flutter onto the man's jutting chin before sliding down to join remnants of other meals on the blue and beige patterned jumper. Her day was not turning out in the least as she had expected.

But what had she expected? And when had 'yesterday' become 'today'? It was before midnight, surely, that she'd woken from the early stages of sleep to hear a child's voice calling, 'Mummy! Mummy!' No, she wasn't dreaming, nor had she been transported back forty years to the time of Jack's feverish bout of chicken pox. As soon as she had recollected where she was, she'd turned on the light and made her way carefully down the steep stairs to Scott's bedroom.

After fetching him a glass of water to sip, and stroking his hair, whispering in a low monotone, 'There's a good boy. Go to sleep. Go-o to slee-eep,' she tried to return to her own bed. But each time she started to withdraw her hand, he opened his eyes and whimpered again. Eventually she lifted his quilt and curled up beside him, drawing his small, warm body against her, and breathing in the soapy scent of his soft curls.

When she woke again pale light was filtering through Scott's Disney Pooh Bear curtains. Scott was lying half-way down the bed, flat on his back on top of the quilt, one arm loosely curved above his head, the other bent across his gently rising chest. Agnes raised herself onto her elbow and gazed for a moment at the sandy lashes on the flushed, freckled cheeks, and the little dribble of saliva at the corner of his half open mouth. Oh, Emmy! Sam! Then she sat up with a start as she heard a clatter of crockery from downstairs.

Joe was in the kitchen, pouring steaming water into a couple of mugs. He turned an exhausted face towards her, and his mouth dropped open.

Agnes raised her hands to her hair, pushing back long loose grey strands and retrieving a dangling hairpin to clamp them back into the matted bun. 'Yes, it is me, Joe,' she laughed. 'Sorry to startle you. I forgot about the wig!'

''S'all right,' he muttered. 'I was jus' gonna wake you. Hope Scottie didn't disturb you too much. Got back about two and you were both out for the count.'

'Oh my goodness! I'm not much of a babysitter, am I? You could've been a burglar,' exclaimed Agnes. 'But what am I thinking of? Is the baby . . . ? How's Sally Ann?'

'Fine. Everything's fine.' His face belied his words. Agnes held her breath. 'Girl,' he went on, as though reciting a lesson he'd had to learn by heart. 'Two minutes past one. Six pounds five ounces.'

Another long pause. 'And Sally Ann?' prompted Agnes.

He bit his lip and turned his face away from her. 'Not so good. They had to cut her open to get the baby out in time.'

'Oh, Joe. A Caesarean! I am sorry! But she's all right though? Sally Ann's all right?'

'She'll be OK. They said . . . ' His voice was shaky. 'She lost a lot of blood. But they said it's not unusual. They said — '

Agnes waited a moment, then murmured, 'Come and sit down, Joe.' She drew out a chair for him and fetched the mugs of tea.

After a few sips, he said with a weak smile, 'Sorry, Agnes. Bit of a shock, that's all. I'll be off to the hospital again, soon as I've got Scottie out of bed. I'll take him along to Edie's then drop you off at the station after.'

'But couldn't I — ?'

She was interrupted by a light tapping on the front door. 'You in there, Joe?' came Edie's loud whisper through the letter box.

Agnes felt a twinge of disappointment as Edie bustled in. She would have liked to be the one to wake Scott up. Feel his chubby little arms reach up around her neck. Stop it, Agnes. You're not needed here any more.

Anyway, what was she thinking of? Why had she set out on this journey in the first place, exposing herself to all those risks? Hitch-hiking was not the harmless sport it might have seemed to her and Seb all those years ago. It was positively dangerous. 'Thoroughly irresponsible, engaging in dangerous sports,' Henry used to say. 'Causes no end of trouble to others.' She shivered as she remembered her dream, just the day before, in that man's car, plunging over a cliff edge —

'I'd drive you in to New Street Station, Agnes,' Joe was saying, 'but I'm afraid it's in the wrong direction, and I want to get back to the hospital quick as I can. I'll drop you off at Erdington. There'll be plenty of trains.'

'That's very kind of you, Joe,' she answered. 'Unless there's anything else I can be doing here till Sally-Ann's mother arrives?'

'We'll be OK, thanks. Pauline'll be here dinner time. Stopping for a few days. And now that Edie's here, we can leave Scottie to sleep for a while longer.'

How quickly things can change, thought Agnes. Though Joe appeared on the surface to be as friendly as ever, he didn't really need her in his life. He had Edie, living just a street or two away, and his mother-in-law arriving later to take care of everything. Agnes wasn't likely ever to see him or Scott or Edie again. Really, she must stop this habit of getting close to people she had no reason to be connected with. Do her more good if she could learn to make her nearest act more like her dearest.

★   ★   ★

Surprising how a station in the middle of this huge urban sprawl could look as though it had been transported from a country village or small market town. The platform was deserted. Hardly surprising, at ten to nine on a grey April Sunday. Agnes sat on a red metal bench and her hands felt clammy as she tried to imagine herself walking along Lucy's street and stopping outside her house. What would she do then? March up to the front door and say, 'I've come to check that my grandchildren are being looked after properly!'

No point trying to make a detailed plan. She would have to assess the situation when she got there. Meanwhile, she must relax. Go with the flow was a phrase she'd always liked the sound of. She looked up at the row of soaring poplars on the opposite embankment. She left her seat and strolled over to the edge of the platform, peering at the rails, first one way and then the other. Vanishing points always seemed so mysterious, the way the eye could join together two rigid objects that were destined never to touch.

The approaching train broke through her reverie. She experienced the slight churning in her stomach that always seemed to be activated by the sight of the gap between platform and doors when a train slowed to a halt. As she placed first one foot, and then the other on the floor of the carriage she found herself remembering how she had accosted Joe as he was starting up the engine of his enormous lorry at that motorway service station. He was a virtual stranger; she'd met him less than half an hour earlier, but there she was, bold as brass, asking him to give her a lift to Birmingham. There'd been no hint of even a flutter of apprehension as she'd allowed him to help her clamber into the cab, whereas now she was struggling hard to quell a rising panic. If the doors had not hissed closed behind her and the train lurched into movement, she might have changed her mind and stepped back onto the platform. And then what would you have done, you daft woman? Gone back to Joe's? Said, 'Please can I stay and play at grandmother again?'

She took a few deep breaths and forced herself to become interested in the back gardens of little houses, and then a snaking complex of roads on concrete pillars, followed by scrap-yards piled with rusty, dented cars, then derelict warehouses along a choked canal. There was nothing to be afraid of in train journeys. They were absolutely safe, compared to hitch-hiking, and she'd barely given that a second thought.

The approach to New Street Station seemed to go on for miles — a long, long tunnel followed by towering walls like black cliffs, splattered with pigeon droppings. Miniature bright green ferns clung to gaps in the mortar between the bricks. The sloping ends of the numerous platforms came into view long before the train showed any real sign of stopping. Agnes noticed a man with a shock of white hair standing by himself on the neighbouring platform, well beyond the sheltering roof. The train had slowed enough for her to get a good view of his face, and she drew in a sharp breath. He was staring blankly down the track and his whole body conveyed an unmistakable message.

When Agnes had descended from her carriage she hoisted the back-pack onto her shoulder and followed the small stream of passengers up the stairs to the main concourse. She turned left towards the sign for Information to find out about the platform for the Nottingham train, but after a moment she stopped and looked at her watch. Twenty minutes to go. Old habits die hard, she thought, smiling wryly, as she turned and made her way back in the opposite direction.

The man was still there. Agnes walked the full length of the platform towards him, as briskly as she could without appearing too purposeful, then stopped about six feet away. It was like trying to approach a wounded bird. Or that sick fox cub, years ago, under the hedge in the neighbouring field. She leant against a pillar and became absorbed in watching a pair of pigeons strutting up and down on the opposite platform. The man was aware of her presence. She could sense it in the stiffening of his posture, though he did not look round.

This part of railway-land was a kind of limbo: exposed to the open sky, and almost out of earshot of the occasional crackling tannoy announcements. Every few minutes a crescendoing rumble was followed by a train clattering and swaying out of the darkness of one of the tunnels.

Each time the first hint of sound rolled towards them the man would tilt his head a

115

little, as though trying to detect its direction. Five trains had clanked to a halt beside other platforms before one burst from the tunnel along the track that led directly to where he was standing. As he took a step closer to the edge, Agnes realised in a flash that this train was not slowing down. She darted towards him and grabbed his left wrist with both her hands, tugging at him and shouting 'No! No!' Noise and motion blurred together for an instant as the roar of the train enveloped them both in darkness and the man stumbled back, knocking her to the ground before he, too, lost his footing. Buffeted by the noise of the train, Agnes felt as though her own voice was locked inside her head, futile as in a nightmare. When quiet was restored in the wake of the din, she found that she was yelling at the top of her voice and quickly shut her mouth. Embarrassing enough to have a strange man sprawled across her legs! He struggled to his knees beside her as she sat up and regained her breath. They looked at each other in silence and then both spoke at once,

'What the devil d'you think you're playing at?'

'I do beg your pardon,' she began, then winced as she placed her left hand on the ground and attempted to lever herself up from the cold and dirty floor.

'I hope you're not going to blame me if you've managed to hurt yourself,' he said curtly.

Agnes subdued a surge of irritation. A potential suicide is hardly likely to be full of the joys of spring. 'Of course not. And it's only a little sprain. It's entirely my own fault. I shouldn't have startled you like that, only . . . ' Oh dear! What if she'd been wrong? What if he was merely a harmless train spotter? 'Look, let me make amends by buying you a coffee or something.' She held out her right hand. 'Allow me introduce myself. I'm Agnes Borrowdale.'

'Felix Biddle,' he muttered, extending his hand and helping her to her feet. 'Better let me carry that,' he went on, as she bent to pick up the back-pack. Agnes found to her annoyance that her knees were trembling a little and she made no protest.

They walked in silence, and as they approached a straggle of waiting passengers it felt to Agnes as though they were rejoining the world of the living. She wondered if Felix was having similar thoughts, and if so, whether he was feeling relief or disappointment.

* * *

117

Felix was the first to draw out a chair and slump down at the shiny white plastic table in the station food bar. Agnes drew a deep breath and lowered herself onto the seat opposite.

She had nothing to lose by telling him why she had pulled him back from the edge of the platform. If it turned out she'd been mistaken, she could apologise, laugh, and still be in time to catch the next train to Nottingham. If she was right, then it would, of course, be harder to extricate herself. A person can't interfere with someone's suicide attempt without shouldering some responsibility for the next few minutes, at least, of that extended life.

Before she could speak, though, Felix surprised her by asking quietly, 'What was it that made you — ? I mean, erm, how did you know?'

She explained how she'd seen him as her train drew in to the station, and how her role as a vicar's wife had brought her into contact with many people in a similar state. When she finished talking, he kept his head bent over the crumbs on his plate.

That thick mass of white hair! Would it feel as dry and wiry as it looked? Or soft to the touch, like Henry's? What was it about the top of a man's head that made him seem so vulnerable?

At last, without raising his eyes, Felix said, 'I know you meant well, and I suppose I ought to thank you, but — ' Another silence.

Agnes waited.

'But I wish you'd bloody well left me alone. You've got no idea how hard it was to pluck up the courage to — I'd got there! I'd actually managed to virtually — And now I'll have to go through it all again.'

No! she raged inwardly. No, you most certainly won't! Although she had guessed what Felix would say, Agnes was stunned by the force of her anger at his words. Life! This man still had Life pulsing through him. He was flesh and blood, not a bundle of dry bones, six feet down in the cold earth. She wasn't going to let him just throw it away.

Pulling him back from the platform had been a physical act — a temporary measure. Now she had to think of some way to change his mind. Direct opposition to the idea would be worse than useless, so . . .

If you can't beat them, join them. Another one of Henry's aphorisms.

But the words emerging from her mouth a moment later were certainly not Henry's. Agnes found herself taken over by the inventive storyteller who'd responded so gleefully to Edie's comments on her hair. One part of her brain seemed to be dictating the

119

words, while the other part was spellbound at her own audacity. 'If you're really determined to go through with it, then you'd better be my first recruit to — to the Birmingham branch of my society for — '

'If that's a bunch of do-gooders, trying to keep people alive when they'd be better off dead, forget it,' interrupted Felix, pushing back his chair and beginning to rise to his feet.

'Far from it,' retorted Agnes. 'My Society is committed to assisting older people to end their own lives when and how they choose to do so.' She smiled as Felix collapsed back onto his chair and stared at her, open-mouthed.

What next, though? What kind of Society? Agnes lowered her eyes and coughed discreetly into her hand. Think, woman, think! Suicide? No. Too crude. And it has to hint at something positive, or at least, exciting. 'We at the Dangerous Sports . . . ' Agnes began, then coughed again. 'So sorry! Tickle in my throat. Where was I? Yes, we at The Dangerous Sports Euthanasia Society wholeheartedly support the notion of suicide for the over sixty-fives. Are you over sixty-five, by the way?' she asked, injecting a note of concern into her voice as she leant forward to peer more closely at his face. 'I find ages so difficult to judge, don't you?'

Felix stared back at her, mesmerised, 'I'll be sixty-seven tomorrow. Thanks to your interference. What I mean is — '

'I know, I know. You didn't want to face another birthday,' Agnes interrupted breezily. She put the remaining small piece of croissant in her mouth and carried on speaking as she chewed. 'Anyway, our only objection to traditional methods is the fact that they're so sordid and unimaginative.'

Felix gave a loud sniff, but he was still listening.

Agnes became aware of her heart: pitta pat, pitta pat, pitta pat. Would she really be able to sustain this preposterous idea? 'Once people discover that they're not unique in their misery, that in fact there are thousands like them, it puts a whole new slant on life. And death, of course,' she added hastily.

'Yes, death. That was the point of the exercise.'

'Well,' she continued, 'we prefer to look at death a little more positively in its own right.'

'If you mean God and all that stuff, forget it.'

'No. I didn't mean that at all. We're totally nonprescriptive about anything except the range of methods available. And even that's being extended all the time as people find new ways of having fun.'

'Fun!' exclaimed Felix. 'That just goes to show how much you know about it. Fun, indeed!'

'Felix,' said Agnes gently. The change in her tone seemed to take him by surprise. He blinked rapidly to clear the sudden film of moisture from his eyes.

'Felix,' she continued, noticing the effect with satisfaction. 'I do know about it. I've had first hand experience myself. It was the founder-member of the Society who found me. Particularly unimaginative, I fear: a bottle of pills.'

'And now you're glad to be alive! Well, you won't catch me like that. I want to die! Get it? I — WANT — TO — DIE! And now,' he went on, succeeding this time in rising to his feet, 'if you don't mind, I'll be on my way.'

'You're a very arrogant man, aren't you?' said Agnes, outwardly calm. 'What's so special about you that gives you the right to think you know what's going on in my head?'

'Why did you stop me from falling under that train? You'd have jumped with me, if you really wanted to be dead yourself.'

'You haven't listened to a word I've told you about my Society. I haven't even got to the Dangerous Sports yet. Still, you probably wouldn't have the guts to join us. You're obviously set on your own rather common-place way of quitting this life, and I'm sorry I went to the trouble of preventing you.' Agnes let her voice tremble a little. 'Especially as I'll now have to wait at least another hour for the next train.'

She allowed her words to hang in the air for a full minute before she turned her head away from Felix and bent down to pick up the back-pack from the floor beside her seat. Then she slowly rose to her feet and began to wriggle her arm through one of the shoulder straps.

Agnes was leaning sideways from the waist in an awkward attempt to reach behind her back for the other strap, when the bag swung away from her, causing her to stumble and lose her footing.

A moment later, for the second time that morning, she was lying in a heap on the floor. Through half-closed eyes she watched a pair of feet slowly draw nearer. Cracked brown leather. Trouser cuffs, somewhat frayed, thick corduroy, brownish green, flecked with mud. The feet were replaced by knees, and a large hand was hovering awkwardly an inch or two above her arm.

Another tentative cough, then, 'Are you all right, emm, Agnes?'

She moaned softly.

'Agnes?' he repeated.

She opened her eyes and made a feeble attempt to rise. 'How stupid of me,' she said in a weak, brave voice. 'I'll be perfectly all right in a moment. Now, if I can just ... ' Her right arm was pinned beneath her body, and she twisted round till she could place her left hand on the floor to lever herself to a sitting position. She drew in a short breath and winced in genuine pain.

'That's better. Thank you so much,' she said, as Felix placed a hand under her elbow and helped her struggle to her feet. 'Now, perhaps, if you could help me get this bag onto my — Oh dear! Ooh,' Agnes raised her hand to her forehead and let her voice trail into another moan. 'I think I'd better just sit quietly for a moment. No please,' she went on as Felix slumped onto his chair again, 'don't let me detain you. I've caused you quite enough trouble already.'

'Not at all.' The words came out in monotone, an automatic response.

'No, really. If I feel the need of any further assistance, I can ask that nice young man behind the counter. I do assure you, I shall be quite all right.'

'For goodness sake, woman!' Felix burst out. 'You know perfectly well that I have no plans at all for the rest of this morning. Nor any other morning. The least you can do is entertain me for a bit, while I try to adjust to the fact that I'm still bloody *here*. Go on, give me a laugh, tell me something about this Euthanasia Society of yours. Then you can toddle off and catch your train. Not that I've the least intention of taking any notice of what you might say,' he went on.

Had he glimpsed the involuntary twitch at the corners of her mouth before she had managed to suppress the sudden smile?

'Well, since you ask. Now then, where was I? Oh yes, the Dangerous Sports,' Agnes scanned her mind for ideas. 'Before I start, I wonder — may I impose on your kindness a little further? I could do with a cold drink. A sip of water, perhaps?'

'Of course,' said Felix, appearing to welcome a concrete activity.

By the time he returned with a bottle of Malvern Spring water and a tall glass, clinking with ice cubes, Agnes had regained her confidence in her own inventiveness.

'I believe I was explaining that our society is in whole-hearted support of an individual's right to choose his own time to withdraw from the Stage of Life.' She paused, and picked up the bottle of water, then glanced across the table at Felix. Was his posture a little more relaxed now, his shoulders less rigid?

'Mmmm. OK. And?'

'It's just that we aim to inject as much pleasure as possible into the method of exit.'

'Piffle!' he exclaimed, folding his arms across his chest.

'I beg your pardon!'

'Pleasure, my foot! Absolute piffle!' he repeated.

Agnes recovered her composure. This was only to be expected, after what he'd been through. She lowered the unopened bottle back onto the table and clasped it between clenched fingers.

'What I mean is,' she went on, 'there will always be those somewhat timorous folk whose imagination is limited to a desire for a peaceful death, asleep in their own bed. You know, close their eyes one night, drift off, never wake up.'

She paused and looked Felix full in the eyes — deep-set, dark blue, almost navy under the bushy white eyebrows. 'Not you, though. You clearly have a need to retain awareness right up to the edge of that mysterious boundary between Life, and whatever lies beyond.'

'Nothing at all,' put in Felix abruptly,

'Quite so,' said Agnes. 'But not everyone would agree, and the DSES is a broad church.'

'There! I knew it! Church!' Felix almost spat the word. 'You people are all the same.'

Agnes smiled and continued smoothly, 'I use the word metaphorically, of course. We are totally non-prescriptive about the beliefs of our members. Buddhists, Hindus, Christians of all sorts. Died-in-the-wool Atheists. But I digress. The nub of it all is this: we believe that fear is the greatest enemy of mankind, the most effective brake to our natural creative impulses.' The words were emerging from her lips almost without direction from her conscious mind. She noticed the way his head was tilted slightly to one side in a listening posture. She had regained his attention — for the moment.

'Of course,' she went on, 'fear must have an evolutionary purpose — our species would not have survived for long without the instinct for self preservation. But equally, we would not have progressed very far without the explorations of a few more adventurous members of those early tribes.'

She unclasped her fingers, lifted the bottle and unscrewed the lid, stealing another glance at Felix as she poured a small amount onto the melting cubes and raised the glass. She was still managing to hold him. How quickly this new talent of storytelling was developing! As the cool water slipped down her throat, she felt a surge of adrenalin pulse through her veins.

'Yes, fear,' she continued, still not sure about precisely where her train of thought was heading, and still less, whether Felix would remain on board. 'You may well think that suicide is the ultimate way of conquering fear. It does, of course, require unparalleled strength of purpose, not to say courage. And there lies the heart of the matter.'

Felix was leaning forward now, elbow on the table, slowly rubbing his forefinger along his large, unshaven chin. So far, so good, she thought.

'Such courage should not be wasted in one sudden fireburst, like a Roman candle. Properly directed, it can provide a source of energy that could light the whole sky for weeks!'

She stopped, noticing his sudden frown. 'Oh very poetic, I'm sure,' he sneered. 'But where's it all leading?'

Agnes realised that she was in danger of being written off as a crackpot. 'Oh dear! I'm really not very good at explaining, am I? You're being very patient with a foolish old woman.'

Felix shifted in his seat and sighed heavily. 'I'm sure you're doing your best. Can't be easy, explaining that load of twaddle.'

Not a very pleasant man, thought Agnes, composing her face into a warm smile.

'What I mean is, throughout our life, the demon, fear, prevents most of us from undertaking a whole range of exciting activities — especially people with a responsibility towards family members. How often have you heard people say, 'I'd love to jump out of an aeroplane, but I know I'd never dare?'

'Never,' snapped Felix.

Anything else he might have said was muffled by a sudden tannoy announcement: 'The train arriving at platform six is the . . . ' There followed an indecipherable succession of crackles, hisses and nasal mutterings.

'Perhaps not,' continued Agnes when the noise ceased. 'But that doesn't mean they haven't thought it. Chances are, they've managed to block out their desire to dangle from a parachute at fifteen thousand feet, or take up rock-climbing. Deep sea diving. Lion taming. You name it, and there'll be somebody in your street who's dying to do it.'

Felix pursed his lips and shook his head. 'Weird kind of company you must keep!'

'All right, then,' said Agnes, straightening her back and raising her chin. 'Tell me this: when you were a boy, did you ever have dreams about flying?'

Felix flinched. 'What's that supposed to prove?' he growled.

'In strictly scientific terms, nothing at all, as an isolated fact. But have you never let caution and common sense get in the way of something that one half of you was longing to do?'

'Not . . . not exactly,' he muttered, averting his eyes.

'Well, I have to accept that you may be one of the exceptions, but that doesn't alter the facts. Eighty-one percent of the people in our survey allowed fear to suppress their urge for adventure at some time or other in their lives.' Nice touch, that, always something compelling about statistics.

Felix gripped the edge of the table and leant back against his chair, arms stiffly extended. 'And the point of all this is?'

Agnes gave a little laugh, 'Oh my goodness. There I go again. Rambling round the houses. I don't know why they chose me to start up a new branch! The point! Of course! The point is, once death is seen as a goal to be welcomed, rather than a threat, fear loses its hold. The individual can now safely embark on whatever activity — or Dangerous Sport — they've been afraid to take up in the past.'

'Safely? You're not exactly consistent, are

you?' put in Felix.

'Safely. Because they can be sure of the eventual outcome, the fulfilment of their dearest wish, Death.'

'I still don't see — '

'People do find the concept a little hard to accept at first,' she responded, while her brain went into overdrive. 'One has to put aside conventional thinking, of course. But conventional thinking is against suicide in the first place.'

Felix relaxed his arms and leant forward a little. 'So?'

'Only those who have truly been to the brink can understand that,' she continued triumphantly. 'What our Society does is help with the logistics, the actual nuts and bolts of getting hold of the right equipment, instructors, travel arrangements, wills, life insurance, that sort of thing. We're in the middle of producing an alphabetical list of possible activities. A lot of people prefer to start off fairly gently — with the letter 'a', as it happens — abseiling is a popular starter — and work their way up to things that take a little more planning and organisation, like climbing the North face of the Eiger, or trekking through the Amazon using nothing that a nineteenth century explorer could not have possessed. The one rule is, no cheating.'

'What d'you mean, cheating?'

Agnes savoured the moment: she had won his full attention now. 'Members must not deliberately set out to fail. For instance, they can't tamper with the abseiling equipment, or loosen the wheel nuts on their Formula 1 racing car. Dicing with death is all about having the proper gambling mentality. That means there has to be at least a minimal chance of losing, in other words, of surviving. It makes the activity so much more exciting. And of course, death always does win, eventually.'

'Well, I don't know. It sounds like a pretty rum show to me,' said Felix, but with less hostility.

'Precisely!' replied Agnes, nodding her head and smiling, 'We're more than happy to let the rest of the world think we're a crowd of harmless cranks. That way they leave us alone. If they actually believed we mean what we say, they probably wouldn't even let us cross a road on our own without first bringing all the traffic to a standstill. It's iniquitous, the way older people are dictated to by spineless do-gooders young enough to be their grandchildren. I shudder whenever I hear their paralysing catch phrase, it's for your own good!'

He was nodding at this in apparent

agreement when the tannoy crackled again. Agnes looked at her watch. 'I'd better be getting along now. That could be my train,' she mouthed as the torrent of unintelligible syllables drowned the clink of cups and murmur of voices around them.

Felix remained seated while she stood up and reached for her bag again. 'But — you still haven't explained,' he muttered. 'I mean, I know it's utterly crazy, but — '

'Oh dear! I'm really sorry, and I have so enjoyed talking to you. But I can't risk missing this train too. I never wanted to take on a huge city like this, it's so daunting. And now I've got this meeting in Nottingham that I simply have to go to. Our Founder is running a series of briefing sessions for all the new Northern sector Trail Blazers.'

'So you'll be coming back?'

'Oh yes,' Agnes crossed her fingers under the table. White lies are necessary sometimes, Henry. Then she smiled at her sudden scruples. She'd done nothing but lie for the last half hour or more. 'I'll be stationed here for as long as it takes to set up a new Branch. I'll only be gone a couple of days or so. Should be Wednesday, Friday at the latest.' Agnes paused, frowning as she tapped her fingertips against her closed lips. At the very least she must phone to check on his state of mind. And who was to say she might not indeed return if it seemed necessary?

'I know!' she exclaimed, smiling again. 'Why don't I have your phone number, then we can arrange to meet up later in the week.'

Felix hesitated.

Agnes lowered her eyes and attempted a coy giggle. 'Hark at me! That's one of the penalties of joining this Society, a girl can lose all sense of shame! Seriously though, I don't mean to intrude on your privacy. But you've been so kind, considering how you must have felt about my interference. And I would find it such a comfort to know that there was at least one familiar face among these teeming crowds when I get back.'

'Could do, I suppose,' he muttered. He picked up her bag and slowly followed her as she wove her way between the tables without looking back. 'If I'm still here, that is,' he added.

The train was almost empty. When Felix had passed her the back-pack she bent forward from the doorway and held out her hand to him.

'Take care, now,' she said. 'I mean, well, of course, if you do find yourself unable to remain till I get back, then, I, er, I wish you luck. But it would be nice to see you again, if at all possible.'

Felix grunted, and looked down towards her trainers. Her hand was being so tightly squeezed that she began to fear it would be crushed. She wriggled it slightly and he abruptly let go.

'Think I'll just go back home to bed,' he said morosely. 'I'm all in. Could be ages before I manage to summon up enough courage to try again, so go on then, give me a ring, if you must. Please yourself. It's all the same to me.'

'Goodbye for now, then,' she called along the platform to his retreating shoulders and bowed neck.

As soon as she had taken a few steps into the carriage, the adrenalin that had supported her all morning ebbed away. With knees like jelly, she collapsed onto the nearest seat and closed her eyes.

8

Jack was slumped on the hard blue plastic mattress of the police cell, waiting for his solicitor to arrange for his release. He looked at his watch. Only two minutes since he'd last done so. Twenty-five past ten. Why did everything grind to a halt on Sundays?

Humiliation. That seemed to be the main purpose of these places. Of the whole process. Waiting. 'Name and address? Occupation? Date of birth?' Waiting. Clank and rattle of keys. Blank corridor, fluorescent light on sickly yellow walls, concrete floor, stale air. 'Date of birth? Occupation?' Don't these people communicate with each other? 'Just checking. Have to get it right, don't we?' Then the cage — bars from floor to ceiling like in some cowboy Western. As if he wasn't already on the wrong side of at least two locked doors. Bored looking youths bolstered by their uniforms. 'Disappeared, eh? And why did you not report this at the time?' More waiting. Repeating the same story. Again. Exchange of glances. Raised eyebrows. Lowered voices. 'Very agitated. Bit wild, like. If the old girl's been . . . Best keep him in for the night.'

Drunk and disorderly! That was a lie. He'd been driving with the utmost care, merely slowed down a bit while watching out for the entrance to the Harmony Home. No law against driving at fifteen miles per hour, was there? Weren't the bastards always ready enough to pull you over for speeding? The crystals had barely changed colour. Only the merest fraction over the limit, proved by the way he'd kept his cool. If he'd been under the influence, he'd not have managed to restrain himself from shoving his open hand into the copper's smirking, baby face, and jamming his foot against the cell door before it was slammed shut.

Once he'd accepted that he'd have to wait till morning before he could do anything he'd made himself calm down. How often had he moaned to himself about having no time to think? That'd been one of Lucy's main gripes. 'You'll never manage to make time for me and the kids as long as you breathe and sleep your damned job. You've got to step back from it long enough to sort your head out.'

Lucy.

Monica had been coming out with stuff along the same lines during these last few months. What is it with women that they expect you to be thinking about them day and night? They'd change their tune soon enough if you let work take a back seat and the money supply started to dry up.

Lucy was the lucky one. She'd been able to give up her teaching when Emily was born. Lounge around the house all day while he was slaving his guts out to support them. Not that he'd wanted his wife to work, of course. But a bit of appreciation would've been nice. And it wasn't as if he neglected her in the physical department. That was always on standby, day or night, ready to leap to attention at the slightest hint. Time! *She* could talk. What time did she have for him, once she'd got a baby to fuss over? After Sam it'd been even worse. And she hadn't needed stitches then, so it was quite reasonable to expect things to get back to normal a bit sooner. What was a man supposed to do?

What he was not going to do here, now, with God-knows what perverts spying on him through CCTVs, as he conjured up the Lucy of those early days, tall and slim, with glossy dark hair that swayed between her shoulder blades as she walked. Or tumbled in strands over her breasts as she gazed down at him. Dreamy brown eyes. Straight, narrow nose and little nostrils that quivered whenever she got aroused.

He'd not done more than glance at any other woman after first setting eyes on Lucy, that Saturday lunchtime in Gino's. He'd only gone in there to get out of the rain. Been planning to spend most of the afternoon in bed with Marie, his Brighton stop-gap for weekends when he was visiting Ma and Pa. But this time, when Marie had eventually answered his persistent ringing on her bell, she'd opened the door as far as the chain would allow and hissed, 'Piss off, will you. I'm fed up of being at your beck and call,' before saying loudly, 'No, sorry. No one of that name living here. Try next door.'

Brighton seafront in November was not the cosiest of places, but he didn't feel like going back to his parents' house yet. Anyway, the wind was hurling rain and spray across the promenade at such an angle he'd have been soaked before he was half-way to the car park. Gino's would be warm and dry at least.

It was Lucy's hands he'd noticed first. She'd come up beside him so quietly he hadn't heard her. He was sitting by the window watching separate little cataracts careering down the other side of the misted pane, and wondering what he was going to do with the rest of the afternoon. Not to mention the next forty-odd of his three-score years and ten. Suddenly a small hand with long, tapering fingers and blunt nails was holding out a menu. Then the voice, dark and low, intimate.

'Did you want something to eat, Sir? Or was it just a drink?' He swivelled round and let his gaze travel from the narrow waist, accentuated by the sash of the apron, and rest for a moment on the angle of the white bib front before continuing up to meet those huge inviting eyes.

'A drink, was it? Or were you wanting a meal?'

By the time he'd found out that she wasn't a regular waitress but a student at Sussex University trying to supplement her grant, it was too late. He was in love. Anyway, she was so much younger than he was that he could feel more at ease than he usually did in the presence of a clever woman.

'Where did things go wrong?' he muttered, rolling onto his side to face the wall. He lay still for a while, staring at the regular outline of bricks under paintwork the colour of rancid cream. Some patches of grainy reddish-brown were visible just above the edge of the mattress, a few inches from his face. He reached out his hand and eased a fingernail under a loose fragment of paint. A small shard plopped onto the mattress. The area of exposed brick grew larger. *Fuck!* A sharp sliver was stabbing into the tender flesh under the nail. He managed to pull it out in one piece, then thrust his throbbing finger into his mouth, soothing it with saliva, sucking at it like a dummy and moaning softly.

After a few moments he became aware that his knees were drawn up against his chest, and a small voice in his head was calling 'Mum, Mum'.

He opened his eyes, withdrew his hand and sat up, swinging his legs round and onto the floor. He blinked a few times, shook his head vigorously, winced and stood up. Forty-three years old and collapsing like a baby! Now that was something to be ashamed of. OK, so Monica hadn't sounded exactly sympathetic when he'd phoned her on his arrival at the police station.

'Wanker,' was her first word. Then, 'Oh, Jack, love! I am sorry! It's not really your fault. But look, if I came now, I'd only end up in the next door cell. I had another drink or two myself, after you'd gone. And there's absolutely nothing I could do, anyway.'

Cow. Not really his fault. Too fucking right. If she'd been able to control her kids a bit better . . . bloody Hailey . . . none of this would have — What if he lost his licence? No. Get a grip. Reach the office by train easy enough. Owed holiday anyway. About time he had a break. Find Ma. Yes. Bring her home. If Monica didn't like that she could — well, she'd just have to put up with it, if she wanted to stay. Never had been a patch on Lucy, though. Oh God! Lucy, the way she used to be, before the kids came along. Not that he didn't adore them, of course. Sam, Sam, my Little Man. Emmy. Sugar Plum Princess.

All gone wrong since then. Why? He'd been patient with Lucy. Women can get like that after babies. Perfectly normal. And if he's not needed at home, he might as well take on that bit extra at work. After all, family man now. Can't risk being side stepped. Have to watch out for that weasel, Stenlack. Stab him in the back soon as look at him. Step into his shoes and kick him down the stairs. And if Lucy's asleep in the spare room by the time he gets in, it's what she wants, isn't it? Not as if he was the one to stray.

How was he to know about that shit, Sean. Shorn! Fucking loser. Teachers. Arty farty. Those who can, do, those who can't . . . 'Do me good, night school,' Lucy said. 'Develop my creative side a bit. One evening a week I can call my own. You've no idea what it's like, stuck here all day with the kids.'

Seemed like only the next week she was saying 'So you see, I had to make a choice.

Couldn't keep it up any longer, all the lies, the double life. No hard feelings, Jack. It just didn't work out for us.' And then only a year later, 'Sean's got the job in Nottingham. Head of Art. Of course you'll still be able to see the kids!'

★   ★   ★

As usual, Ma hadn't been exactly supportive. 'Jack dear, you have to look at your own part in this, too. You must try to keep on good terms with Lucy, if only for the children's sake. Don't think too harshly of her. You have been so very occupied with your work these last few years. Henry was only saying — '

'Oh, so you and Dad could see it coming and didn't think fit to warn me?'

'Of course not! One never imagines such things could happen in one's own family, and of course I'm not blaming you.'

Funny how negatives make a positive. Not your fault. Not blaming you. No disgrace in being near the bottom of the class. Your reading isn't at all bad for your age. You're not bad at football, at running, at spelling.

What would she say if she could see him now? No disgrace in being locked up like a criminal?

Hey, come on, Jack. It's Ma you should be

worrying about right now. Isn't that what's put you here in the first place?

His sudden flare of anger died away, leaving his mouth dry and his palms moist. Ma. What have I done to you?

★ ★ ★

'What's all this about your mother, then, Jack?' said Piers Lackland, fiddling with the code on the slim-line briefcase that he'd positioned like a games compendium on the scratched wooden table between them. Chess, or Snakes and Ladders? thought Jack, glancing around the tiny windowless room. Even smaller than last night's sleeping quarters. No space to swing a cockroach, let alone a cat.

'It's all right,' Piers assured him. 'They don't tend to bug these interview rooms. If I'm going to do my best for you, I have to know precisely what they might be trying to pin on you.'

Before Jack could reply with more than a shrug, Piers exclaimed, 'Got it!' as the lid of his case flew open. 'Present from the wife,' he said, and drew out a notebook. 'Go on, Jack. Your mother?'

'Vanished,' muttered Jack morosely. 'Damned cops, fat lot they care. More interested in

144

grilling me about a couple of small whiskies. God, Piers, anything could have happened to her,' and he went on to describe the events of the previous afternoon.

'Stop worrying yourself, Jack. From what I remember of your mother, she's a formidable woman. Well able to take care of herself. Wasn't going senile, was she?'

'Not as such. No. I mean, she didn't go wandering round the streets in her bedroom slippers at two in the morning. Nothing like that. Just . . . '

'Mmm?' prompted Piers, steepling his finger tips. 'Just?'

'Well. I suppose it's been since Dad died, really. Seemed to sort of, I dunno, close in on herself. Shrink. And then, since she moved in with me and Monica. Well. It was just impossible.'

'Always hard, having an elderly parent living in the same house. Causes no end of problems, especially when there's a second family involved. Any particular reason why she couldn't have just carried on living on her own?'

'Apart from the money side — as you know, Dad really messed up, left her nothing. Well, apart from that, I didn't like the thought of my mother ending up alone in some poky little flat. Not that I wouldn't have rented somewhere nice enough for her. Bought a place, even. But I wanted to look after her. She'd been so close to Dad. He'd always done everything, house arrangements, budgeting, bills and so on. I thought it'd be nicer for her.'

'And she agreed?'

'Once I'd explained it all to her. She could see it would make sense financially, make life easier for everyone.'

'And then?'

'Trouble was, well, she was getting so difficult. Didn't get on with Monica or her kids, you know how it is. Looking more and more frail every day. Hardly saying a word to me. I went to a lot of trouble to find a really nice place. More or less her own little flat. Well, sort of bedsit, anyway — en suite bathroom, own kettle and all that. As independent as she could want. And be with people more from the same generation, you know, sharing interests, making friends. Cost a fortune, but she'd have been able to settle there without needing to be moved again in a couple of years. Would have been a good deal cheaper to let her get a council flat like she said she wanted. But she hasn't a clue about these places. She just wouldn't have coped on her own. I kept telling her.'

'So. She had no money to leave you. But

on the other hand, you could have been paying out a substantial sum for several years.'

'What are you saying, Piers?

'I'm not saying anything, Jack. Merely considering what tracks the police might go down. Have to be prepared. It's a tough old world out there, you know.'

'For Christ sake! If you think I — !'

'Calm down, Jack. Look, there's bound to be a perfectly simple explanation. People go missing all the time. Nobody's thinking anything at all at the moment. They'll need to find out where she's got to, considering her age. They'll just be wanting you to answer a few routine questions, sort out this drink-drive charge and then you'll be able to get back home. Have a shower and shave. Collect your thoughts. What friends does she have? Or other relatives?'

Jack rubbed his fingers along his jaw line. 'None that I know of,' he said. 'Except the children. And Lucy, of course. That was the first place I tried. No reply from there. Must've been out for the day. I'll try her again, soon as you get me out of here.'

★ ★ ★

Ten minutes after leaving the police station — escaping, was what it felt like — Jack

147

pulled into a layby, switched off the engine and leant back against the headrest, closing his eyes. He was torn between yearning for a shower, shave and strong fresh coffee, and a reluctance to face Monica and her kids. On second thoughts, Hailey and Donna never surfaced on a Sunday till at least one o'clock. Perhaps Monica would be feeling suitably contrite by now. She had some very — comforting ways of demonstrating contrition. He opened his eyes, rubbed the corners with his fingertips, shook his head and blinked. Need to focus, old man. Ma. That's who you're meant to be thinking of. Got to find Ma.

He leant forward and rummaged in the glove compartment for his mobile phone. Glad he hadn't had that on him last night. Bloody cops would have made a note of every number in the address book. He scrolled down to L and pressed for Lucy's number, then waited for the ringing tone. He counted eleven rings and for a split second thought he had connected to Lucy's voice in real time before he realised that she was not there.

Bloody ansaphones. He'd try again once he got back to the house. What message could he leave? 'Sorry to bother you, Lucy, but I was just wondering if you've seen . . . ?' 'Hello, Lucy, Jack here. Could I have a quick word with . . . ?'

9

After a while Agnes felt the muscles in her neck and shoulders relax, soothed by the rhythmic noise and motion of the train. The new Agnes was taking control again. No wonder she'd felt exhausted! Who wouldn't, after what she'd been through in the previous twenty-four hours: her escape from the Harmony Home; her brief and frightening encounter with those youths; her rescue and subsequent desertion by Derek Thatcher; then Joe Geraghty, and the worry about his wife, followed by the drama with Felix. More than most people would have to cope with in a year, let alone a couple of days. Not bad going for a seventy-five-year-old.

A new Agnes? Yes, and no. In fact, this Agnes was someone she had first encountered years ago. Before Jack. Before Henry, even. She closed her eyes again and for a moment the train was rattling across France on the start of her great adventure. Twenty years old and life about to begin. Not just life-after-Seb that must somehow be endured. This would be Life with a capital L. Switzerland. A house party. The luxury of proper food at last.

Chocolate! She'd almost forgotten the taste. Champagne, too, a taste she'd never sampled, and dancing. With men. Young *men*, not children or grandfathers. Some of her old schoolfriends had been propelled into premature adulthood by the war. She felt in many ways as though she'd been frozen in time as an awkward fourteen-year-old, cooped up as she was in the depth of the countryside, her greatest contribution to the war effort looking after the hens, learning to milk the newly acquired cow and managing the vegetable garden after the gardener joined up.

Nearly twenty-one, and never been kissed! The mirror told her she was almost pretty. No feature so dreadful that it could cause her shame. Even the snub nose was just about acceptable. Her figure, too, a little short, but neither too fat nor too thin. Her skin was smooth and firm. Her inner wrists showed a hint of the blue veins that carried the blood to and from her quickening heart.

Agnes held her hands out in front of her, palms down. These brown-spotted objects did not belong to her. They were like a grotesque costume, applied to a young actress by the make-up department on a film set where the heroine appears as an old woman in the final scene.

'But I am an old woman!' she murmured,

shaking her head. Henry's voice sounded in her ears, with his silver threads song. 'Thank you, Henry. For the time being, my silver threads are hidden under bright orange. I'm as young as I feel, and right now I feel — well, in fact, age doesn't really come into it at all.'

★ ★ ★

Finding her way to West Bridgford seemed a less daunting prospect, now that she had completed her second train journey of the day. She smiled to herself, resisting the temptation of jumping into one of the taxis lined up outside the station, making her way instead to the bus stop recommended by the helpful woman at Enquiries.

'That's right, duck. West Bridgford,' said the driver. 'I'll tell you when we reach your stop.'

As she swung herself onto a seat near the front, something began to thud behind her rib cage and she noticed that her palm had left a film of moisture on the metal pole.

She still had no proper plan of action. What was she actually going to do, once she'd located Lucy's house? Easy enough in theory to say get the lie of the land, make sure the children are being well cared for. But what if

151

she was recognised by Sean or Lucy? What would she say to them?

Would Jack yet know about her disappearance? Would anyone at the Harmony Home have noticed her absence? If Lucy did recognise her, she'd feel duty bound to tell Jack.

'It's for your own good, Agnes,' Lucy would say.

Oh no she wouldn't. Agnes was not going to give her the opportunity, yet. First things first. Locate the children, and then decide.

As the bus lurched to a halt just past a row of small, shuttered-up shops, the sun finally managed to burst through the last layer of grey cloud. Agnes stepped down onto the glistening pavement and stood for a moment watching the bus disappear up the tree-lined road. The upper twigs and branches were losing their winter-clear definition under smudges of opening buds. The sky had that bright, newly-washed look of a recently restored Renaissance painting. Fra Angelico blue, Henry called it.

Agnes felt her spirits lift. The street was almost deserted and the only sound was the twitter of birds, testing their voices after the mid-day rain. She drew out the scrap of paper on which the Enquiries woman had scribbled a rough sketch map. Cross the road, then first on the left. As she turned into Lucy's road her heart gave a sudden leap. Two small children, one on a pink bike with stabilising wheels, the other wobbling precariously on a more grown-up model, were making slow progress away from her up the steep incline. She quickened her pace, and called out, hesitantly, 'Emily! Sam!'

Perhaps they hadn't heard her. She called again, more loudly. The younger one stopped pedalling and turned to stare. It was not Sam, on his sister's outgrown bike. It was not even a little boy. The older child glanced back, wobbled more violently and tumbled onto the pavement, shrieking even before she hit the ground.

Agnes hurried towards them. The younger one was crying as well, now. Agnes was lifting the bike and about to help the girl to her feet when a woman's voice called out, 'Hey! What's going on? Jodie, you all right, sweetheart?'

Agnes stepped back as a large woman in over-tight jeans bent down to examine Jodie's knee, then scooped her up against her purple sweatshirt while the younger child clutched at her legs. Noticing Agnes's worried look she said cheerfully, 'No real harm done. Jodie always screams blue murder. That bike's on the big side, really, but they grow so quick at this age, you have to get the next size up, don't you?'

Agnes smiled and murmured in agreement, then strode on up the road. She was trying to look purposeful, and made no attempt to peer at the house numbers until she had almost reached the brow of the hill. When she glanced back, the street was empty.

A black enamel '56' was screwed to the middle of one of the pair of mustard-yellow gates. There was no car on the short driveway. Funny, the way a house could give away its secrets with almost imperceptible clues. Something about the hang of the curtains — not closed, but not dragged open as far as they could be to let in the maximum amount of spring light, the lack of empty milk bottles in the porch, the neatness of the gravel, unscuffed by recent footfalls. No trace of toys, left out in response to a call to wash hands for tea.

They've gone away, thought Agnes, fingering the bolt on the gates. How quickly a mood could change. For a minute or so she felt weak and tired again, and clutched at the wooden struts to steady herself. Then the positive part of her brain kicked into action. It's Sunday, the whole street is virtually deserted, they're probably out for the day. Now pull yourself together and work out what to do next.

She walked slowly back down the road,

eyes on the pavement, considering the options. It was now far too late to get back to the Harmony Home in time for Jack's afternoon visit. Phyllis and Gwen and Sheila and all the rest of them would be finishing off the stodgy apple crumble and melting ice-cream by now. Her absence couldn't have remained unnoticed for this long. So what would Phyllis have done first, after searching everywhere for her? She was hardly likely to wait till Jack turned up this afternoon and then say, 'Oh my goodness! Wherever can Agnes have got to?' Or perhaps she was hoping that Agnes would arrive back in the nick of time.

There was no getting away from it. She had to phone Jack as soon as possible, stop him setting out on a fruitless journey. It would be up to him then to decide what to tell Phyllis.

When Agnes reached the T-junction at the end of the road she paused and looked around her. A few yards away on the opposite side was a phone box. Once inside it, with the heavy door closed behind her, Agnes unzipped her pocket and drew out the small leather purse, her heart thudding audibly in this confined space. As she placed the coins on the metal ledge she tried to work out what she was going to say to Jack and, even more daunting, what he was likely to say to her. One thing was certain, he would not take happily to the idea of his mother wandering around West Bridgford trying to spy on her own grandchildren. And if he caught sight of her now, dressed like this!

If she spoke to Jack now, she'd be strengthening his opinion of her as a senile old woman, getting steadily battier each day. Worse still, she'd have undertaken this whole adventure for nothing. He'd be up here like a shot, insisting on taking her back before she'd had the chance to put her mind at rest about the children's safety, or to confirm her recent fears.

The fact that she'd never liked Sean did not automatically make him a monster, and Lucy, for all her faults, would never deliberately endanger her own children. Nonetheless, people do change, and it's often those closest to them who are the last to see it. Look at Jack, hardly recognisable now as the son she had loved so dearly. She couldn't rest easy until she had somehow managed to make her own assessment of the situation. Unfortunately, but unavoidably, Jack was going to have to wait till she had something more concrete to report.

Agnes scooped up the coins and returned them to her purse. She had been scarcely aware of the slightly musty smell of old phone books and stale cigarette smoke until she pushed open the door and stepped back onto the pavement.

Now that she had made that decision, she'd be able to put all thoughts of Jack to one side, and focus on the task ahead. The sudden sense of relief was as tangible as the fresh air filling her lungs.

The next physical sensation was the pangs in her stomach. She'd eaten nothing at Joe's that morning, and it was several hours since the chocolate croissant at New Street Station. Where would she find anywhere open on a Sunday afternoon? She hadn't noticed anything in that row of shops by the bus stop, except a pub on the opposite side of the road. No. That's one thing I won't do on my own.

Agnes decided that she might as well walk back up Lucy's road. There could be something at the top end, and, who knows, Lucy herself could have returned by now from the other direction. Agnes might even see Emily and Sam as she strolled past. She'd pause at the gate. Sean would be standing in the porch, one arm around Lucy, the other clasping Sam against his chest. Emily would be the first to see her. She'd let go of Lucy's hand and run towards her, laughing and shouting, 'Grandma, Grandma.'

She straightened her shoulders and quickened her pace. Wishful thinking would get her nowhere.

★   ★   ★

At least her quest for food was successful: no more than fifty yards away from the end of Lucy's road she had found a Leisure Centre with a bustling snack bar.

She was feeling stronger now, after a plateful of hot, floury chips with their slightly greasy coating sharpened by vinegar: comfort food. This was as good a place as any to begin her search. From where she was seated, she had a clear view through a plate glass window down to a vast pool. It was seething with children, from toddlers paddling around the curved, gently sloping 'beach' end, to teenagers screaming down water chutes and clambering onto a small island that flaunted a plastic palm tree and a life-size Long John Silver.

As she scanned the crowds below and beside her, alert for any child between the ages of three and eight years old, it was becoming increasingly clear that she'd need a more structured approach. She could conduct a survey, for instance. It shouldn't be beyond her new-found powers of invention to come up with a reasonably plausible subject matter. She would find a stationer's first thing in the morning and buy a pad of paper and a clip-board. People doing market surveys always seemed to have clip-boards. She'd wait till a reasonably civilised hour — ten o'clock should be all right — and then walk up the path and knock confidently on Lucy's door.

Her voice would be the only recognisable thing about her. If she managed to alter it a little, speak ve-ry, ve-ry, slow-ly — or perhaps very-quickly-indeed and an octave higher.

Agnes felt another surge of adrenalin. Time to go and find somewhere to spend the night. Get a good night's sleep. As she pushed back her chair and began to rise, she heard a man's gruff voice from a nearby table. It sounded remarkably like Felix. Turning, she saw at once that there was no resemblance to the man she'd dragged from the brink of death that morning.

Felix. She shuddered suddenly. Thanks to her, he might sleep tonight and be alive the next morning. But what sort of state would he be in? She must ring that number he'd given her and check.

★ ★ ★

'Meddlesome do-good female,' muttered Felix as he shivered on the front step of the house next door to his, jabbing the bell with his thumb again and again, leaning his ear against the peeling paintwork, trying to detect a corresponding shrill ringing sound from somewhere inside the house. Bloody students! He could freeze to death out here while they slept away the hours of daylight.

At first, when he'd emerged from the station, dodged his way between nose-to-tail taxis and stepped out from the covered car-parking area onto the open pavement, he'd taken a perverse satisfaction in the slow, fat drops of rain splattering onto his head, sliding off his bush of hair and trickling down his neck. He'd looked up at the drooping grey sky that seemed to be straining at the seams with the massive weight of water, willing it to burst. 'Crack, Heavens!' he shouted, like Lear on the blasted heath, raising his fists, oblivious of the curious stares of the incoming taxi-drivers. The elements obeyed him: the sky disappeared from view as walls of water came crashing down like giant breakers.

After forty years of living in that house, he had never once had to walk home from New Street Station. Never been this far from home without at least the cost of a bus-fare in his pocket. Still, he knew the way, from a driver's point of view. Couldn't be more than, what — three miles?

Felix waded along Smallbrook Queensway, already soaked from water bouncing off the pavement and surging up to his knees, as well as cascading down all around him, with the occasional bucketful flung sideways by tyres of a passing car. The worst of the downpour lasted no more than five minutes. Then the solid sheets of rain split up into pelting stair-rods and gradually slowed to the steady drumming of endless millions of separate drops.

'Wet enough for you, mate?' called a cheery voice from the doorway of the Irish Harp as he turned down Hurst Street.

His initial fierce satisfaction at the way the storm had seemed an extension of his own despair, and the resulting burst of energy that had propelled him this far, abruptly drained away. He became aware once more of the physical reality of his body, and what he felt was not pleasant. He could not have been more drenched if he'd fallen fully clothed into the sea and been tumbled over and over by raging waves. At least if that had happened, he'd have had a decent chance of dying. But a person didn't die just because his sodden hair was plastered to his scalp and every item of clothing had become a sponge, absorbing a hundred times its weight in water. His cords had been heavy enough to start with. Now they clung to his knees with the crippling strength of nightmares.

Perhaps he had died, after all. Perhaps this was hell. Felix expelled the idea with a snort of derision, but for that brief moment it had been both comforting and terrifying.

Not that he believed in its existence, but wasn't hell supposed to be somewhat hotter and drier than this? The world, which that damned woman had prevented him from escaping, was becoming increasingly cold as the rain gradually eased to a drizzle and a vicious little breeze sprang up. Well, he was stuck with it now — for the time being. Unless he dropped dead of hypothermia. Perhaps he could find a bit of wasteland, curl up behind a wall somewhere, fall asleep and never wake up. 'Those somewhat timorous folk — you know, close their eyes one night, drift off, never wake up.' That bloody woman again! What was her name? Agnes! Go away, Agnes! That pathetic childish society of hers.

Anyway, hypothermia was something that *happened* to a person, it wasn't reliable as a method in its own right, unless you stranded yourself on an ice floe somewhere, or half-way up Everest. With his current luck in the field of suicide he'd be 'rescued' by some little thugs intent on glue-sniffing, or worse, and then have to endure all the indignities inflicted on him by the well-meaning medical staff of the Birmingham General.

Methods! Now that was something he might usefully get some advice on, if Agnes did happen to contact him again. Not that she would. People like that didn't. All sweetness and light to your face, oozing concern for your well-being, then — out of sight, out of mind. Look at the way Ruby ... No, don't. Asking for trouble, that, turning the dull ache behind his breastbone into a sudden, twisting knife.

He quickened his pace for a moment. Agnes. Methods. And he could give her a bit of advice to add to her rule book. In case of failure. One: ensure you have sufficient money on your person to pay for a return bus or train fare. Two: put your front-door key in your pocket instead of leaving it on your kitchen table, next to your suicide note.

Yes, well, if she did contact him — and she bloody owed him, after all, interfering old bat — he certainly wouldn't risk the train method again. Not from a station, at any rate. Come to think of it — and how had he *not* come to think of it, to *really* think? — this would be no Monty Python caricature, jolly trumpet music with limbs flying, guts tumbling out, neat as a string of sausages. Those metal wheels would have sliced through real flesh, real bones. His. He felt his knees start to buckle. His head swam, and he stumbled forward, reaching out his hand towards a lamppost. He clung to it for a moment, resting his cold cheek against the icy metal, then he doubled up, retching until the last morsel of bile-covered chocolate croissant swirled away in the gutter.

As he squelched along the Pershore Road, he focussed all the attention his exhausted brain could muster onto the task of placing one foot in front of the other.

10

Somewhere to spend the night turned out to be a small hotel, ten minutes' walk away from Lucy's gate. Mainly travelling salesmen and other business people, thought Agnes, waiting for a response to the buzzer on the Formica-topped reception counter. She glanced around the square hallway where varnished pine panelling was topped by wallpaper of pink flowers sprawling up lime-green pillars. The carpet was a swirl of purple and red. Agnes was about to creep back out onto the street when a deep, cheerful voice, approaching from somewhere above called out, 'Sorry to keep you, I'm coming. I'm coming.' On the third, breathless 'I'm coming,' a pair of tartan slippers and black-stockinged legs appeared at the top of the carpeted stairs. The rest of the body, hidden at first by the archway, soon followed the legs down into the hall with a triumphant cry, 'Here I am!'

Agnes fixed her smile and took a step forward towards the apparition, whose ample bosom — no other words would do for this bulging expanse of hand-knitted, multico-loured stripes — rose and fell in rapid jerks.

Before Agnes could open her mouth, the other woman had managed to regain enough breath to launch herself into speech.

'It's the gas fire always makes me doze off of an evening,' she panted. 'That and the tele. So sorry to keep you waiting, dear. That buzzer's meant to sound in my room but it never does, and can I get anyone to fix it? Can I heck! Have to do everything myself, I do, or it never gets done.'

She paused for a moment while she bustled over to the reception desk. Before Agnes could collect her thoughts the woman was in full spate again. 'Don't get me wrong, this is a well-run establishment. Spotless, it is. Don't do dinners though. Just breakfast, these days. Full English, of course. And kettles in every room. Was it a single, dear? I get lots of singles here. No extra charge. Bad enough being on your own, isn't it, without having to pay more for it. You are on your own, aren't you? Got that sort of look, if you don't mind me saying. Me too. Was married once. Back in the dark ages, that was. Good riddance to bad rubbish, I said — '

This time, Agnes was ready for the momentary pause. She would politely make her escape, explain that she was looking for the nearest café. Feeling like a traffic policeman halting the oncoming rush of cars she thrust out her hand towards the woman, saying briskly, 'Good afternoon.' Her own thin, cool hand was immediately clasped in a hot soft palm. The words that emerged from her lips were not the ones she had intended. 'I would like a room for the night, please, if you have one available.' Immediately aware of what she had just said, she gave an involuntary glance from side to side. Henry? What are you playing at?

The woman's voice drew her back. 'Pleased to meet you. Molly Malone, at your service. It's Muriel, really. Then I went and married Pat Malone, and you know how it is, the way things stick. But that's enough of me. You'll be wanting your room. Let's see now . . . ' She drew out a large desk diary from under the counter and while she was finding the right page the stream of chatter continued to flow. 'My trouble is, I get carried away. 'Give it a rest, *Molly*,' Pat used to say, 'Customers don't like it. All they want is their morning call and their eggs cooked just right, not you clucking away like a yardful o' hens.' But that was him all over, old misery guts. So, just the one night is it? You can have your pick, then. My regulars have the best, Monday to Friday, but I never normally get trade on a Sunday.'

Agnes clutched vainly at this straw. 'I didn't realise you weren't open. It's perfectly all right, I can find somewhere else.'

But Molly bustled round from behind the counter and headed for the stairs, saying, 'I'll not hear of it! The day I turn anyone from my door is the day I shut up shop for good.'

When Molly had finally left her alone in a small bedroom — saved by the phone — Agnes heaved open the sash window to dilute the warm, stale air, and then bent down to fiddle with the knob of the bulky radiator. It reminded her of the vicarage, though there'd been no heating in those bedrooms apart from a rare blaze of coal in the small grate in times of illness, or one bar of an electric fire, scrupulously monitored by Henry. Lord only knew how much money Molly must be burning up!

Still hot, in spite of having opened the window, Agnes unzipped the tracksuit top and let it fall to the floor, then removed the cap and wig and eased the polo-necked jumper over her head. Suddenly overwhelmed by tiredness, she curled herself up on the bed. During the next couple of minutes her body temperature took a rapid dive as a cool breeze drifted across the back of her thin teeshirt. She struggled back from the edge of sleep and was about to crawl under the quilt when she realised with a start that she was still wearing her trainers. How quickly her standards were slipping! She was brushing a few dusty grains from the densely flowered cover when there was a knock at the door.

'Agnes, dearie? It's me, Molly. Thought you might like a nice cup of tea.'

'How kind! Give me just one minute, if you don't mind.'

Hurriedly, she pulled on the jumper, then retrieved the wig from the floor and peered into the square mirror tile above a small washbasin as she straightened the thick fringe and rearranged the short strands that curled against her cheeks.

She bent to pick up the jacket again, and was struggling to reach for the second armhole when Molly entered the room.

'Cold, are you dear?' She glanced across at the window, 'Well, no wonder. You don't want to let out all the nice warm air, now, do you? Tell you what,' she added, as she rattled the window down with a thud, 'if you've got no plans for this evening, why not come and join me in my little snug. I'll fix us a bite of supper, and we can have a good old chit-chat.'

'Er, that's very kind, but — '

'On the house, of course. Can't say fairer than that.' Her voice was jolly, but her eyes reminded Agnes of Jasper, Henry's old retriever that had outlived his master by five weeks. He'd spent that time moping outside the greenhouse, or on the rug by Henry's chair, whining softly and gazing pathetically at Agnes.

'I've got a bottle of port that I've had since Christmas. And some cream sherry, if you prefer,' Molly continued, her pleading eyes belying the bright smile. 'A little of what you fancy does you good, I always say.'

'Well, of course, I'd be delighted, if you're absolutely sure it won't be putting you to any trouble,' said Agnes.

Agnes was not accustomed to the role of confider — she was used to being the one who accepted the confidences of others. After Seb, Agnes had lost the knack of sharing. Except with Henry, she reproved herself; then, no, Henry, there was so much I could never share with you.

In Molly's cluttered, stuffy, upstairs sitting room, her tongue loosened by tiredness and several glasses of port, Agnes spoke freely for the first time about the effect on her of Henry's death. To her great surprise she found Molly an attentive listener. She appeared to be genuinely interested in Agnes's account of her grief and loneliness, her sadness at the loss of her grandchildren, her vain attempts to get on with Monica and her daughters, her disappointment at

Jack's uncaring attitude towards her.

Agnes paused, leaning forward to pick up her drink. 'To be truthful,' she went on, staring down at the little glass, 'I realise now that from the day I left the vicarage, I just gave up. I could have done more to try and get through to Hailey and Donna at least. Donna did try chatting to me occasionally. And Hailey . . . I let myself be put off by her appearance. Poor girl, she was probably badly disturbed when her own father left.' She paused again and sighed. 'I had all the time in the world to think things through, then. It's only now though, now I've been on the go for two whole days without stopping, that I'm actually using my brain for its proper purpose instead of . . . Yes, instead of wallowing in self-pity,' she finished in a rush, and drained her glass in two gulps.

'You mustn't feel like that, dear. I know he's your only son, but I think that Jack of yours has a lot to answer for. And that Monica woman. Cow! I'd give her a piece of my mind, right enough, if she showed her face round here.'

Agnes smiled, bending down to untie the laces of her trainers. 'One thing I can thank Monica for, she jolted me out of my Slough of Despond. When I first went to find out about the keep fit classes, I felt like a naughty schoolgirl playing truant. Henry would've been so shocked.'

'Husbands!' sniffed Molly, then added, 'Sorry, dear. I know your Henry was a real gem, but there isn't the man born that doesn't want to rule the roost, however much they might say otherwise.'

Agnes pushed her toes against the heel of one trainer until her foot slid out and the shoe thumped onto the carpet. She glanced at Molly enquiringly.

'Feel free,' said Molly, refilling her glass. 'Look at me in my scruffy old slippers. Comfy feet, comfy all over, I always say.'

Agnes kicked off the other shoe and curled her legs up onto the sofa. 'Funny!' She smiled. 'I'm beginning to feel like a girl again!' She swallowed two large mouthfuls of the sweet sticky liquid, and found that her glass was empty again. How ever many had she drunk already? She wondered vaguely where that bubbly giggle was coming from. It didn't look as though Molly was laughing.

'Just help yourself, dear,' said Molly, pushing the bottle across the low table towards her. 'Us girls can stay as young as we feel. No such thing as old age for some.'

'Well, perhaps just another teeny drop or two. I must say, it goes down very easily. Henry would be — '

'Yes dear, I can imagine,' said Molly. 'One thing I'll say for Pat, he never made a fuss over drink. Too much the other way, he was, if truth be told. So how old are you, in actual years, if you don't mind me asking?'

'So long as you don't mind me asking you!' Personal questions of strangers! thought Agnes. Whatever next?

Something was happening to the top of her head: part of her brain was slowly drifting upwards in a warm haze. This had the strange effect of allowing her to look down at her self from the outside — a carroty-haired woman of uncertain age in a turquoise tracksuit sprawled in an abandoned pose on the sofa, like a character from one of those 1960s American comedy shows.

'I've never been much good at guessing ages,' Molly was looking anxious. 'Oh dearie me! What can I say? You dress young, that's for sure. And all that hair! But from what you've told me, shunted off to an old folks home, well, surely they don't take people into those places till they're sixty-five, at least?'

Agnes laughed delightedly behind her palms, peering at Molly from over her fingertips, but she said nothing. Was it her own failing eyesight, or was that plump face really as unlined as it appeared? The jet black hair was dyed, certainly. It was parted in the middle

173

above a short fringe, and most of the rest was gathered into one thick plait that hung down between her shoulder blades. The remaining bits straggled out in loops and strands that Molly continually pushed behind her ears. Her face was round as a baby's, and had two chins, a smaller dimpled one nestling below the bright red mouth, and a larger, paler one that acted as cushioned cladding for her short neck. The only sharp lines were the two etched between nose and lips, and the plucked, painted eyebrows.

'Somewhere around — oh, I don't know, late forties?' ventured Agnes.

It was Molly's turn to laugh. 'Get along with you! I'll be sixty-one this July!'

Agnes needed little encouragement to pick up the threads of her story again. Whenever she paused for breath, or another drink, Molly urged her on, 'So *then* what happened?'

It was heady stuff, this storytelling. Seeing herself through Molly's eyes as protagonist in a series of adventures made her feel more than ever that she had entered into a world where Henry's Agnes could never have set foot.

It had been absorbing enough to find herself inventing the details of the Dangerous Sports Euthanasia Society for Felix. It was

174

even more exhilarating to let Molly into the secret of its non-existence.

'But of course it exists, dear,' insisted Molly.

'Molly, you don't seem to understand what I've just said. I invented the whole thing.'

'Yes, yes. I know that's what you *said*. You made it all up. But where did the idea come from in the first place? That's what I'd like to know. And now you've told this Felix person about it, it's real for him, isn't it? You can't un-invent something once it's got a life of its own. Live and let live, I always say.'

Later that night, having managed to get herself undressed and into bed without being wholly aware of doing so, Agnes felt as though her legs were rising gently into the air while her head span like a top on the pillow. Was it true, what Molly had said about an idea taking on a life of its own? And what about Felix? She certainly couldn't un-invent him. He'd have been happily dead by now if she hadn't pulled him back, literally, from the brink. *Happily* dead? There was no getting away from it, she had a responsibility towards this man.

Still, at least she had offered him her Idea as a way of keeping his mind off an immediate death, happy or otherwise. So in a way, Molly was right — the Dangerous

Sports Euthanasia Society was alive and kicking.

★ ★ ★

Agnes was sitting cross-legged on a vast, daisy-covered lawn, splitting long thin stems with her bright red fingernail, then threading each one through the next. On the grass beside her was a huge net, woven entirely from this rope of flowers. 'Keep going, Ma,' said five-year-old Jack. 'We'll catch Emmy and Sam with this.' Hot sun was beating down onto her head, making it throb. 'I don't know if I'll have time,' she said.

'It's gone nine, dear,' said a voice from somewhere above her head. 'Hope you don't mind me waking you. I've brought you a nice cup of tea.'

Agnes opened her eyes and sat upright with a start, looking at Molly in bemusement.

'I do hope I've done right, calling you,' she said anxiously. 'Only you did say you wanted to try and catch sight of your grandchildren this morning.'

'Yes. Yes of course. Thank you,' said Agnes, putting a hand up to her throbbing forehead, and gradually recalling the previous evening. 'I'm afraid I had a little too much of your splendid port.'

'There's plenty more where that came from,' laughed Molly. 'You're welcome to pop in for more tonight, if you want to stay on.'

'Tonight?' mumbled Agnes. This was Day Three. Based on the events of the past couple of days, there was no telling where she'd be tonight.

'Of course, if you'd rather not,' said Molly hastily. 'Just that I thought we were getting on famously and . . . '

Her voice trailed off and Agnes hurriedly added, 'I had a wonderful time, Molly. I don't know when I last enjoyed myself so much. It's only that I have no means of saying, yet . . . '

Molly's face brightened again. 'It was a good laugh, wasn't it? I'll keep the sheets on this bed, just in case. No bother. Now, what can I get you for breakfast?'

★ ★ ★

Half an hour later, Agnes was sitting at a table laid for one in a wide bay window overlooking a lawn of tufted grass and molehills, surrounded by straggling laurel bushes that kept the whole garden in shadow. Molly entered the room bearing a tray. 'There you are dear. A nice, lightly boiled egg and a little bit of toast. And I've made a fresh pot of tea. It's always best to line your stomach with a little food when you're feeling a teensy bit fragile, if you know what I mean.'

'Won't you join me?' asked Agnes.

'Don't mind if I do,' smiled Molly eagerly. 'I'll fetch myself a cup.'

When she was sitting down she asked, 'Where was it you said this Lucy lives? I'm meant to be popping over to keep an eye on my own grandchildren for a bit while Wendy pops along to the doctor's. If it's in the same direction, we can walk down together.'

'What a small world!' exclaimed Molly, when Agnes had told her. 'Number 56, you say? That'll be only a few doors up from Wendy's. What if you come round with me to Wendy's first? Chances are, she'll know Lucy.'

Agnes felt a rush of excitement. Molly was grandmother to children who could at this very moment be playing with Emily and Sam.

As she and Molly walked along the pavement, she pondered over a new problem: if she allowed Molly to introduce her to Wendy her cover would be blown. Lucy would be on the phone to Jack. He'd drive up immediately and take her back to the Harmony Home.

'No, dear,' protested Molly. 'Even if he tried to I don't expect they'd have you back. After all, you've set rather a bad example to the other inmates, haven't you? Running away like that!'

She stopped as laughter overtook her, and Agnes joined in, hugging herself, then punching Molly on the arm. 'Bad example! Oh dear, how shocking!' she gasped, and laughed even louder as Molly panted, tears streaming down her cheeks, 'Whatever would Henry say!'

A youthful looking postman, cycling past them on the opposite side of the quiet road, wobbled his front wheel violently and nearly fell into the gutter as he turned a startled face in the direction of this manic laughter. As he recovered himself and pedalled away at a greatly increased speed, the two women collapsed onto a conveniently low garden wall, Agnes clamping both hands across her mouth and Molly rocking backwards and forwards, hugging her stomach.

'Stop, stop,' she begged. 'I'll wet myself if I carry on a moment longer.'

Glad that she had only drunk half of her second cup of tea, Agnes managed to regain her composure. 'I just don't know what to do for the best, now,' she said. 'I mean, you could be right about the Home not wanting me back, though I rather think they need Jack's money. But still — '

'But still?'

'Well. One half of me wants to contact Jack immediately. Let him know that I'm perfectly well,' Agnes paused, 'But if he asks me directly where I am, I think I'd just blurt out the truth.'

'So it's obvious, then, isn't it? You can't trust yourself to speak to him, but I — '

'You mean you'd make the phone call for me?'

'I'll do it as soon as we get back. Dial 141 first, and he won't know where it's come from. And talking of keeping secrets,' she continued, levering herself up from the grey stone wall, 'perhaps I should introduce you to Wendy as Agnes Dale. We can drop the 'Borrow'. And 'Annie' might be better — Agnes is too unusual.'

'It's catching, isn't it? This storytelling!' giggled Agnes, 'What a dreadful influence I'm having.'

'For pity's sake, don't set me off again,' said Molly jumping back from the curb as she nearly stepped into the path of an oncoming car. 'And whatever you do, don't make me laugh like that in front of Wendy. She thinks I'm enough of a nutcase already. Lovely girl, Wendy, but she does tend to take herself a mite too seriously. We used to have such fun, the two of us, till she reached her teens.'

'Grown-up children! Jack's the same. One

minute they're lovely cuddly bundles of fun, and before you know it they're looking down at you from a great height saying, 'Pull yourself together, Ma'.'

Agnes did not feel in the least inclined to laugh as Molly rang Wendy's bell. Her headache had returned, and she felt her stomach turn over at the sound of children's voices on the other side of the front door.

'Gran, Gran,' shrieked the older girl, leaping at Molly, clasping her arms around her neck and her legs round as much of Molly's waist as they could reach. The younger child halted on the doorstep and stared solemnly at Agnes for a moment, then turned and trotted back through the hallway, calling, 'Mummy, Mummy. There's a funny lady.'

'Hi, Mum, what's upset Tara?' asked Wendy from the kitchen doorway, then stopped as she caught sight of Agnes. 'Er, hello? Don't I know you from somewhere?'

'Morning, love,' said Molly. 'This is my friend, Annie. She was stopping with me last night and I thought you wouldn't mind if she came to give me a hand with these two little monsters. Thought we might just pop down the park for a bit if it stays fine.'

'OK by me. Mind you remember to put their coats on first though. It's pretty nippy out there, and Tara's only just getting over that nasty cough.' Wendy looked at Agnes again. 'I know! You were here yesterday, weren't you? When Jodie fell off her bike. I never forget a face.'

'That's right. I was hoping to drop in on a friend of my — my daughter. But she was out.'

'Someone called Lucy, Wendy. D'you know her? Got two children, Emily and Sam?'

'Sam and Emmy's mum? Yes. Number 56, I think it is.'

Agnes could feel her heart beating so loudly she was sure the others would be able to hear it.

'Or rather, was,' continued Wendy, picking up a black leather jacket from the telephone seat and sliding her arms into it. 'I heard she's left. Friday, think it was. Took the kids with her. Got to dash now, Mum. Back about twelve, OK? I'll pick up a bit of shopping on the way back.'

'Just a moment, dear,' said Molly, seeing Agnes's stricken face. 'This Lucy — ?'

'Can't stop now. Sorry. Late already. Bye Jodie, love. Bye bye Tara. Be good for Grannie now.'

'But Wendy,' insisted Molly, following her to the front door, 'Can't you at least tell Annie where Lucy went?'

Wendy turned back a moment from the front gate. 'Honestly, I don't know. Some row with that man of hers, I think. You could try asking him. Think *he's* still there. Now I really must be off. Byee!'

*   *   *

The next hour and a half was like a tidal wave that carried Agnes forward in a daze. It lifted her through the chaos of collecting the children's coats, gloves, and bicycles, then swept their little group forward along the pavements, past the hubbub of Monday morning shops to the small playground next to the library. Here it bobbed them about from swings to roundabout, from seesaw to slide, laughing, chattering and patting eager spaniels and Labrador puppies. Agnes clutched small sticky hands, brushed wood chippings from woolly knees, pulled back the cold metal chains of swings and released each gleefully shrieking child forward into the sharp air.

Eventually she found herself sitting on a wooden slatted bench at the edge of the playground, watching Molly break into a lumbering jog, pulling the bar of the roundabout so that it span just fast enough for Jodie and Tara to scream with excitement.

As her gaze wandered around all the other small boys and girls who were not Emily and Sam, and the quietly chatting mothers and grandmothers, Agnes was overwhelmed by a feeling of isolation. She shut her eyes, and leaning forward a little she gripped her gloved hands over the edge of the seat as tightly as she could.

'You all right, Ag — er, Annie?'

Agnes sat up with a start.

Molly's light touch on her shoulder seemed to re-establish a link with the rest of humanity. 'I'm fine. Just fine,' she said brightly.

Molly looked relieved. 'This is one of Wendy's friends,' she said, gesturing to a woman beside her. 'Karen. She lives next door to Lucy.'

Agnes rose slowly to her feet as Karen smiled and held out her hand.

'Yeh,' she said. 'Gone to her mum's for a few days. Teach her bloke a lesson, I reckon. The word is, he's been playing around.'

'And the children? How are the children?'

'The kids?' Karen seemed surprised. 'Fine, I guess. Any road, the three of them went off happily enough. Friday night, just gone. He was out. What's his name? Sean. Yeh, well, I heard she just left him a note and scarpered.'

'So she's visiting her mother?' Agnes had first met Lucy's mother, Dianne, at Jack's wedding. She'd felt rather sorry for her at the time, an over-thin, nervous looking woman with huge, sad eyes, who smoked and drank too much and smiled too widely, but only with her mouth. Lucy's father had deserted them long before.

'Yep. 'S'what she said, anyway. Kids off school now for a coupla weeks. She's on holiday too, so why not let that Sean stew for a bit. Serve him right, lovely looking girl like her.'

'And, erm,' Agnes hesitated. Dianne had married again, a few years ago, she'd moved up to the Midlands somewhere. 'You wouldn't happen to have her mother's address, by any chance?'

'Nope. Sorry. Don't know Lucy that well myself.'

'A phone number, even? Perhaps she has one of these mobile things?'

'Urgent, is it?' asked Karen. 'My Dave sees Sean down the pub sometimes.'

'Not exactly. I was coming up this way and I promised my daughter I'd deliver a package to Lucy.' Her mind went blank, then suddenly a name surfaced, 'I think it was called Sutton Coldfield, where the mother lived.'

'That's part of Birmingham. Needle in a haystack job, tracking her down there. No point asking Sean either. I know for a fact that *he's* not saying anything. Lucy's ex was banging on the door just last night. Or was it Sat'day? Terrible state, he was in. Shouting something about losing his mother, and now his kids.'

Agnes felt her knees begin to tremble and she abruptly sat down again on the bench. *Jack!* He had driven all this way, trying to find her. So he did care, then. The sooner Molly managed to get the message through to him the better.

'Sorry I can't help,' Karen was saying. 'Still, I reckon she'll be back before long. If it was really urgent I could've asked Steve to find out more.'

Agnes barely heard her. Somewhere inside that rather selfish, balding man, that almost stranger, there might still be a trace of the boy she had once loved more than anyone else on earth.

She was still in a daze when she returned with Mollie to her hotel, and stood beside her in the hall while she picked up the phone.

'Ansaphone,' hissed Molly, one hand over the mouth piece.

'I am sorry. No one is available to come to the phone at the moment. If you would like to leave a message, please speak after the long tone.'

'Ah, Yes. Hello. I have a message for Jack Borrowdale from his mother, Agnes. She just wants me to tell him, er, to tell you, Jack, that she is well and will be back soon and you're not to worry and — what was that dear? — oh, and she's sorry if you were worried. and — and what, dear? — she's sorry not to speak to you herself and, and that's all. Goodbye.'

A little while later that same ansaphone, in Jack's house in Haywards Heath, relayed that same message to a very different caller.

'I am sorry. No one is available to come to the phone at the moment. If you would like to leave a message, please speak after the long tone.'

'Oh. Hi there! Donna. It's Craig. Hi! Er, well. I was just . . . Oh shit. Hate these damn things.'

'I am sorry. No one is available to come to the phone at the moment. If you would like to leave a message, please speak after the long tone.'

'Donna, 's'me again. Craig. Look. I'm SORRY! Geddit? An' I'll be at the usual place tonight so, well . . . I want you to be there so's I can explain prop'ly before I go, cos lotsa stuff I can't say on the phone so be there please eight o'clock. USUAL PLACE. OK? Right. Well. See ya. *Please*. OK?'

11

Agnes was sitting at Molly's kitchen table, scraping butter so thinly onto slices of hot toast that it melted and disappeared almost immediately.

'It's not on ration,' Molly laughed, putting down the pan of eggs she'd been stirring. As she scooped a huge wedge of butter onto the knife, she said, 'Are you sure you can't stay here a little longer?'

'You're very kind, Molly, but I've been so near to seeing the children, and it could be a whole week, or even more before they come back here. And of course, there's Felix too.'

'You must let me drive you to the station, at least. A good job you managed to remember her new married name — Lucy's mum.'

'Yes, but to think I was so close, just yesterday! Fancy not knowing that Sutton Coldfield was part of Birmingham!' Agnes pushed a little mound of egg onto her fork as she continued, 'I'd have found it hard to forget the name though. I mean, Lucy Lockett! That would've been a burden for Lucy if she'd had to grow up with it!'

'But you haven't got her actual address.'

'There can't be all that many Locketts in Sutton Coldfield. I'll just work my way through the list in the phone book and take it from there.'

Molly said wistfully, 'Shame I haven't got a Birmingham one here. You'd have been more than welcome to use my phone. And where will you stay? What about that Joe's house?'

'Joe's got his plate full at the moment, and he's got enough people around to help him out. Anyway, I've been lucky so far. Something'll turn up, I'm sure.'

'The devil looks after his own, Pat used to say,' laughed Molly. 'I do believe he'd have had a soft spot for you.'

★　★　★

Molly's off-white, rusty Ford Escort lurched to a halt outside the station, barely an inch from the bumper of the taxi in front. 'Well, this is it, then. Parting of the ways. Have to say I'll miss you, Agnes. Feels like we've been friends for years.' She fumbled in her sleeve, drew out a pink cotton handkerchief and dabbed at her eyes. Regaining her composure, she said, 'Don't mind me. I've always been the world's worst at saying goodbye.'

'I — I've enjoyed meeting you, Molly,'

began Agnes, surprised and touched by this show of emotion. 'Thank you for everything. And I will be seeing you again very soon, I'm sure.' She opened the door and placed her feet on the ground, ready to haul herself out of the car, but Molly carried on regardless.

'I'll be doing my best to see what else I can find out. I'll cook up an excuse to call round on that man of Lucy's. Once I set foot inside his house there'll be no stopping me. So just you make sure you ring me to check out how I'm getting on, and let me know if you get any leads. And that poor Felix too — I'll be on tenterhooks waiting for the latest on him. And another thing — '

Agnes never discovered what this other thing was. 'You gonna be here all day, ladies?' called a man's voice from a taxi that had drawn up behind them. 'This is taxis only, case you never noticed the signs.'

After Molly had driven off, waving her handkerchief at Agnes and blowing kisses at the taxi drivers, Agnes walked briskly through the entrance and looked around to get her bearings. Although she was alone again, she felt more confident about this journey. There was something comforting about the knowledge that she now had a friend in the town she was leaving and, if not friends exactly, then at least people she knew in the city to which she was returning.

She located the right monitor for the information about her train. Only ten minutes to wait. Ample time to buy her ticket and get herself onto the correct platform without having to rush. Should have bought a return first time. Could even pop into the ladies.

As she rounded a corner, following signs to the ladies, her heart gave a sudden leap, and she stepped quickly to one side behind a handy pillar. Her tongue seemed to have turned itself to Velcro against the dry roof of her mouth. Had he spotted her, that policeman, looking straight at her and then averting his eyes, talking into his radio?

Fool! Of course they'd be searching for her! She hadn't given the matter a thought since her escape from the Harmony Home. Even when she'd realised that Jack had come looking for her at Lucy's, the idea of police being involved hadn't entered her head. Thank goodness Molly had left that message on Jack's ansaphone, or she could have been in trouble for wasting police time. How pathetic she'd been, not daring to make that phone call herself on Sunday afternoon!

And what excuse could she give for not asking Molly to do it on Sunday evening? None! She'd been enjoying herself too much, hearing the sound of her own voice, an admiring audience, rather too much of that sweet, comforting port. 'Agnes, you will have to learn to be more attentive to the needs of others.' Her father's words. That sick feeling, like the taste of bitter aloes on her fingernails. Failing, again.

She hadn't failed, though. Her message would be picked up soon and they could all stop worrying about her.

But meanwhile, she most certainly did not want to be found, before she could speak to Lucy at the very least. She ventured another look. The man's head was bowed now, but he was still communicating with someone on his radio. She'd have to pass him in order to reach the ladies. Never mind, there'd be one on the train. Better dodge back round the corner again, buy her ticket, and slink off to her platform.

★ ★ ★

It wasn't until the rhythmic motion of the train had calmed her breathing again that the panic began to ebb away, making room for more rational viewpoints. One: if the police were in fact looking for her, and that was by no means certain, they'd have been given a description of the old Agnes. They'd not look twice at her, the way she was now. Two: What reason would they have for connecting her with Nottingham station? Even if Jack had begged them to start a nation-wide search, he'd have been unlikely to do that before he'd come looking for her at Lucy's. That was only yesterday evening, and it wasn't half past one yet. It probably took them a good deal longer than that to get going. Three: Agnes Borrowdale was not the centre of the universe! Hundreds of far more urgent cases would be clamouring for attention every day.

The train was hurtling through a tunnel, and the sight of her reflection in the window jolted her back to her immediate situation: every minute was bringing her closer to Birmingham and the possibility of a wild goose chase. There could be pages of Locketts in the phone book, and what if Dianne was exdirectory? Even if Agnes did manage to track her down, what, precisely, would she do next?

Then there was Felix.

Granted, without her action, he would almost certainly be dead. But what sort of life would he have to endure? And what was to stop him bringing it to an abrupt close this very week?

It was one thing to invent a mythical society, but was she going to have to take up pot-holing or parachuting in order to sustain her invention and carry it forward to the next logical step? She shuddered. 'The Lord gave us two feet with the clear intention that we'd keep at least one of them in contact with terra firma at all times.' That was one of Henry's sayings she would not dispute.

Ridiculous to be thrown into a panic at the sight of a policeman who wouldn't really have been in the least bit interested in her. She'd wasted more than four pounds, too, buying another single, instead of getting a Super Saver Return, just because she'd been in such a state that she hadn't wanted to rummage in her back-pack for her secret bundle of twenty-pound notes.

Rummage in her *back-pack*? Agnes raised her hands to cover her face as a vivid picture of her handbag and its contents flashed into her mind. Pushed right down to the bottom of the wrong side of the lining, through a small tear in the seam of the inside zip pocket, was a neat roll of twenty-pound notes.

The temperature in the train compartment suddenly plummeted. Her hands were trembling so much she was having difficulty in extracting her purse from her pocket and undoing the clasp. She spilled out the contents onto the seat beside her. One ticket from Nottingham to Birmingham. Six pound coins. Two fifty-pence pieces, and another ninety seven pence in coppers and small silver. Right at the bottom, under a couple of screwed up receipts, an equally crumpled small blue-green bank note.

Icy cold now, she replaced the money in the purse and hauled the back-pack onto her lap. Once, twice, three times over, she examined every single item, while her brain raced to her room at the Harmony Home, reliving each moment of preparation for the journey to Nottingham.

As she pictured herself standing at her dressing table, rolling up the notes into a tight bundle barely thicker than a fountain pen, she could almost feel the pressure of that crisp purple and white paper against her fingertips. Next step, secure it with a strong elastic band, over and over. Then the silky texture of the lining of the inside zip compartment, and the fine threads where the corner had frayed into a small hole. Push gently, another push, and the precious bundle drops to the solid, secret base of the handbag.

Now she was in the little copse near the bus stop, removing all she needed from that same handbag before storing it in the hole in the oak tree. She could smell the layers of dried leaves that she'd kicked across the steaming little patch of urine, and the mustiness as she'd peered into the cavity in the trunk. She felt, as well as saw, each object as she removed it from the handbag and placed it in the back-pack. She could not conjure up any image of herself fiddling with the lining and attempting to manoeuvre that tightly rolled bundle out through the hole in the seam.

'A stitch in time saves nine.'

'Oh, shut up, Henry,' she said fiercely. A bald head craned round from behind a seat further along the aisle on the opposite side, and quickly drew back.

But Henry would not shut up. 'My dear, there really is only one sensible course of action now.'

He was right. There was no longer any choice, she would have to acknowledge defeat: phone Jack as soon as she reached New Street, ask him to come and get her.

She leant back against the seat and closed her eyes. For a few moments she allowed a feeling of relief to seep through her. It was all right. She could let go now. In a few hours' time she'd be in Jack's car. Taken care of. Once her actions had been explained, and Jack and Phyllis Mapperley had had their say, it would be as if all the events of the last three days had never happened. The lives of all the

196

people she had met would carry on as if . . .

No! Agnes jerked forward, eyes wide open. She caught sight of the bald-headed man staring again and as she turned her face to the window the train entered another tunnel. The woman frowning back at her was not Jack's compliant, grey-haired mother, Henry's grieving widow. This was the outrageous storyteller, the inventor of the Dangerous Sports Euthanasia Society. She could not abandon its first recruit.

★   ★   ★

Birthdays! Bah, Humbug! He shouldn't have had to endure another. The way he felt now, he might not live to see the end of this one — if it was Monday still.

How long had he been sleeping? Ruby had made him drink something hot a while back. Soup? She'd never given him tomato soup before. She'd never sat on his bed before. Ruby's hands were as big as a man's. 'Sit up a bit, mate. You need to get something down you.' John the Baptist, with locusts and honey.

Ruby came and went. His bed was a furnace. Her icy cold tongue as big as a cow's was licking his forehead, his cheeks. 'Oh Ruby! That's nice. I'm so glad you came back in time. Don't go.'

He slept again. And woke. Slept. Woke. John the Baptist was staring down at him. 'Christ you look fucking awful! I'll get a doctor.'

Felix didn't want a doctor. He was huddled in a snowdrift. Tired. So very, very tired. Go back to sleep and never wake.

⋆ ⋆ ⋆

Agnes was relieved to find that Sutton Coldfield was only a couple of stops further down the line from Erdington — almost familiar territory. No time, though, to get a ticket at New Street or she might miss the connection. How silly not to have bought one straight through from Nottingham. There'd been no need to panic at the sudden sight of that policeman! She was still the law-abiding citizen she had been all her life.

There was no phone book in the booth at Sutton Coldfield, but the young man at the ticket office was very helpful. 'Sutton, you said? This is the one you want then, Birmingham North, Residential,' and he handed over a surprisingly thin book. 'People are always pinching them, ever since they split them into these separate books.'

When he added mournfully, 'Can't trust

anyone these days, can you?' she quickly looked away. Too late now to try and pay for that ticket. Once she got home, she'd make a suitable contribution to the Railway Workers Benevolent Fund, or some such. When she got home? Where *was* home, now? She pushed that thought away.

There were seven Locketts in the entire book, and only one of those had a Sutton Coldfield address.

'Radford Road? No, not all that far,' the young man answered when Agnes returned the book. 'Not much more'n half a mile, I reckon. 'Fraid I don't know about the buses, though.'

Agnes welcomed the idea of a walk. It didn't sound too complicated a route, and when she left the station the sun was shining. That lad had given her useful landmarks to watch out for. 'Cross over near the church, keeping it on your right, then first left, and on past the hospital.'

But Dianne Lockett's house looked as deserted as Lucy's had the day before. Agnes listened with growing dismay as the door-bell's tinny music echoed over and over from somewhere beyond the locked porch and solid front door.

After the final note from the third attempt had died away, she glanced back at the empty street and the next-door houses. Twenty past four, and no one around. She walked to the right of the house and peered through a wrought iron side gate at an immaculate garden. Expecting it to be locked she was surprised when the handle responded to her touch and the gate swung open.

Next moment she was peering through a gap in the full-length curtains behind the solid glass of the wide patio doors. At the near end of the long room was a Regency style dining table with six matching chairs, and a silver candelabra on a lace mat in the middle of the glossy surface. At the far end, a huge, powder-blue three-piece suite. A matching pale blue fitted carpet. Not a room that had recently contained young children, surely?

'Oh, Lucy,' sighed Agnes.

She noticed a highly varnished garden bench against the wall of the house and sat for a few moments, breathing in the scent of the recently cut lawn, edged by neat rows of multi-coloured primulas.

There was no one in the Midlands currently expecting her arrival. No one would be saying, 'I wonder where Agnes has got to, she should be here by now.' Her immediate future was a blank.

It took a few moments for the full

implications of this to sink in: no deadlines; no hurry; no panic.

She leant back, resting her head against the wall, and closed her eyes. There was not a breath of wind in this sheltered garden; the spring sunshine was hot on her face and soon it was boring through her clothes to the surface of her skin. Birds were chirping and trilling nearby, their clear notes echoing back from neighbouring gardens. She let her arms hang loose, palms upward on the bench beside her. It was like floating on air. She was a free spirit, at one with her own body as it absorbed the sun's rays.

With her eyes closed, Agnes had no warning of the approaching dark cloud that abruptly obscured the source of this warmth. As she tumbled back to earth, her stomach lurched. She could not just sit there until after dark in the hope that Dianne Lockett would return and offer her a bed for the night. The house could remain empty for a week. She could lie down on the bench and fall asleep and no one in the whole of this enormous conurbation would be any the wiser if she never woke again.

Floating on air was all very well, but she was not a bird. She needed people, human contact. Any human. Even the boy at the ticket office would be better than nothing.

Agnes breathed out again. It was all quite simple, she was used to train journeys now. Sutton Coldfield to New Street, New Street to Nottingham.

New Street! Felix! If she had felt so isolated at this brief lack of human contact, what might he be feeling at this very moment?

Agnes rose to her feet. Before doing anything else, she had to find a phone box. She had walked past the top end of a pedestrian shopping area on her way here. There were bound to be public telephones there. Once she'd spoken to Felix, she could decide what to do next. She really didn't want to return to Nottingham before she'd managed to find Lucy. She could try this house again a bit later. It was only twenty to five.

At twenty past five, Agnes put the phone down. Typical of Felix, not to have an ansaphone, even. She'd let the phone ring itself out four times. He must be out somewhere. That, at least, would be a good thing. So long as he wasn't teetering on the edge of a platform waiting for a high speed train. If he was in the house, then either he was deliberately not answering, or — he'd swallowed a bottle of sleeping pills. And she hadn't even got his address.

She was reaching out her hand to open the door when she remembered the other use for a phone book: addresses, of course! How else would she have known that the only Lockett in Sutton Coldfield lived at 62, Radford Road?

There was more than half a column of Biddles. It took several minutes to check and double check each phone number against the one Felix had given her. None of them matched. He must be ex-directory.

That was it, then. She really would have to do the sensible thing and go back to Molly's tonight. The phone number was on the glossy leaflet Molly had given her: Home from Home Hotel, Proprietor — Mrs M Malone. Replacing the phone book on the shelf, she remembered what that nice young man had said about them 'always getting pinched now since they split them up.' And 'Sutton? You'll need Birmingham North, Residential.'

Birmingham South, Residential, with Felix Biddle's address inside it, had been lying on the floor in a corner all this time, a few inches away from her feet.

Molly, and comfort? The security of the known?

Or Felix, uncertainty, discomfort, possible dangers of wandering around a vast, strange city as it grew dark, trying to locate the home of a suicidal man who might already be lying dead in his bed?

There was no way of telling how long it would take her to get to Felix's, and no saying that he'd be there or, if he was, that he'd let her in. What was the point in chasing off miles away just now, when Dianne might be back at any minute?

Her thoughts went round in circles. She would wait for Dianne to return. No, she should catch the train back to Nottingham before it got too late. But Felix? If she found somewhere nearby to spend the night, she could go and hammer on his door first thing in the morning.

'Do be sensible, Lambkin. Even if you could find somewhere suitable with your £12.97, you'd have nothing left over for bus or train fares, or even telephone calls.'

She couldn't just run back to Molly's without making sure that Felix was all right. She'd manage somehow. Hide in the ladies in a shop somewhere. Or that place near Joe's — whole streets of empty houses she could sleep in, if the worst came to the worst.

★ ★ ★

'Hi, Shaz, 's me. Hailey. OK to talk for a bit? I mean, no one snooping round your end, is there?'

'Na, all out still. So, what's up, then? Not

finally pulled Danny Whatsit?'

'Him! You're joking! He's gross! No, it's Donna.'

'Bit young for her, i'n't he? Thought she was screwing that Craig.'

'Just listen, will you? I'm trying to tell you. You know how Donna went and ruined my chances with Dez, Sat'day?'

'God! Isn't he just wicked, that Dez!'

'Exactly. And Donna went and let on that I'm only fourteen and he never said a word to me the whole night after.'

'So?'

'So I said I'd pay her. An' now I have. Craig phoned earlier. Left her a message. I was sat right by the phone and nearly puked. Then I wiped the whole tape clean, didn't I? An' he'll be waiting for her, eight o'clock an' she won't show! And the best of it is, he's off on holiday tomorrow, first thing. That'll teach her not to mess.'

12

Agnes walked briskly towards the wide frontage of Marks and Spencer's. Looking hesitant was the quickest the way of drawing unwanted attention. Perhaps she'd be able to curl up in the changing rooms for the night, secrete herself in the middle of a stand of floor-length dressing gowns until all the staff had gone home. But as she reached the nearest set of glass doors an assistant was turning a key in the lock. It was gone half past five already.

She walked on, glancing at the shop fronts as she passed them. They were all closed, or closing. She turned up a walkway on the right, past a camping shop on the corner. A fleece jacket would have come in handy. But even if the shop had been open still, she'd have had no spare money to spend.

Now she was in a covered arcade. At least she'd be out of any wind and rain here. Still walking, though at a slower pace, she scanned to right and left for any sign of an alcove to hide in. W H Smith's, Clarks, Mothercare, all with dim, shadowy interiors but with harshly-lit window displays behind impenetrable plate glass. The few people still in evidence had the purposeful stride of workers on their way home.

Agnes appeared to be the only loiterer.

A burly man in uniform was bearing down on her. She quickened her pace and bent her head to avoid any possibility of eye contact. Of course there'd be security guards patrolling a place like this; they'd not want hoards of teenagers bringing their transistors and holding all-night parties, not to speak of drug-taking. She shuddered as she remembered those uncouth young men in the sports car. How representative were they of their own generation?

Marks and Spencer's came into view again, the rear entrance, backing onto a wide square at the far corner of which metal chairs and round glass-topped tables were clustered outside one of those coffee shops that seemed so popular now. Mmmm! A large, steaming mug with that chocolate-sprinkled white froth — she could almost feel the warmth sliding down her throat, and her stomach becoming its own hot-water bottle. But a young man with spiky blond hair and a white jacket was starting to pile the chairs on top of each other and drag them in through the doorway.

It was nearly six o'clock now, and a long time since Molly's scrambled eggs on toast

— a long way from Molly's cluttered, cosy kitchen. The phantom warmth of the imaginary drink turned to a sudden chill. How much longer would the daylight last? She had to make a decision very soon. Another wide walkway led past British Home Stores, and back onto the High Street with the phone boxes.

Trying not to let herself expect an answer, Agnes held the ringing phone against her ear. If only there was a way of knowing for certain that Dianne would not be walking in through her front door the minute she replaced the receiver! But she couldn't stay in this phone booth all night. The later it grew, the more conspicuous she felt. There were none of the casual shoppers left, the young women in jeans, with dozing toddlers in push chairs and small children dragging their feet, the older women with tight grey curls and shapeless woollen coats, the frail old men in tired suits. These had all, long since, returned to their own warm homes.

After a few more vain attempts, alternating between Dianne's number and Felix's, Agnes was startled by a tapping on the glass of the door. A girl of about Donna's age was mouthing something at her, and then gesturing to her watch. Three more girls were giggling nearby and five or six others were crammed into and spilling out of the phone booth next to hers. Agnes nodded at the girl, put her change into her purse and stepped out onto the pavement. Still undecided about her next course of action, she found herself walking back towards the station.

Approaching the car park at the entrance to Station Road, she saw the words Clothes Bank printed in dark grey on the biscuit-coloured metal of a huge container, and noticed several bulging black plastic bags heaped around its base. She was used to Bottle Banks. There was one on the outskirts of Brighton near the enormous D.I.Y. store that Henry used to make forays into from time to time, emerging with bargain packs of fifteen assorted screwdrivers, or a dozen paint-brushes. It was her job to sort out their bottles and jars into brown, green and clear, and push each one through the correct small round hole. Even though she couldn't actually see the hard fat bellies smash open into jagged shards, the vicarious vandalism of this cracking, crashing din always gave her a tingle of delight.

Recycled glass. Recycled clothes. That wouldn't be stealing. Once the idea had entered her head it refused to go away. There'll be no harm in just having a look.

She strolled into the car park, glancing

nonchalantly around her, then she stooped to take hold of one of the bags and dragged it round to the far side of the container, out of sight of the street.

Six bags and several sneezes later, she paused to examine her findings: a man's bottle green fleece jacket with broken zip; a baggy pale grey Shetland polo neck jumper with badly darned elbows; a pair of lady's black ski pants, perfect condition but about four sizes too large; four assorted thick woollen socks with holes in toes or heels. It was the final item that pleased her most — a double-bed sized, fluffy pure wool blanket.

Three of the bags she had discarded as soon as she'd untied them, wrinkling her nose against the stench of stale sweat, or worse. Although everything she did select had the musty smell of fabric stored for weeks in a cellar or garage, it all looked and felt reasonably clean.

The air temperature was dropping fast. She wriggled into the fleece jacket and rolled up the dangling sleeve-ends, then crammed the other clothes into the back-pack and rummaged in one of the cleaner black bags for a good strong plastic carrier to hold the blanket.

This time, she was able to buy her ticket for the short journey. Only a couple of stops between here and Erdington. She'd have to stay alert.

'D'you promise there aren't any wolves left in England now, Seb? Not even in Cornwall? Cross your heart and hope to die?'

Agnes opened her eyes, blinked and shook her head. It was too warm in this carriage, making her drift off like that. This was no time for dreaming. Nor could she let her mind race ahead to her night's resting place. That made her heart begin to jump and flutter and her palms grow clammy.

That dream just now. A real event, but she and Seb had been in no danger then, at eleven years old. They'd packed more biscuits, fruit and sandwiches then they could eat, and too much bedding for a warm summer night. Still, it had cushioned their thin bodies from all but the most angular bumps on the hard floor of their secret cave. Barely two miles from home and with the full moon to light their way, they could have returned safely at any time they chose and climbed in through Seb's window by their usual route.

'My dear, it is excusable for young children to create challenging situations for themselves in the name of adventure. But an elderly person, a week away from her seventy-fifth birthday!

This was no time to be listening to Henry. Anyway, it was probably too late already to catch a train back to Nottingham.

'Reflect a little on what you're doing, my dear. Just think of the danger.'

Dangerous sports! Agnes smiled as the thought of Felix and her Euthanasia Society triggered a burst of adrenalin.

★　★　★

This energy propelled her legs away from the station, across the traffic lights at the main road and up to another crossroads with a fire station on the corner. That was a landmark she remembered from her journey to the station with Joe on Sunday morning, three days ago. It must be nearly a mile from here to Joe's road. If she had got her bearings correctly, the run-down estate she was heading for was quite a way ahead and then to her left, perhaps the same distance away.

A few hundred yards to her right she could see shops. Would there be a café or something still open? Perhaps one of those McDonald places?

She crossed the road and then hesitated a moment before continuing on straight ahead. First things first — finding a safe place to spend the night was a priority. Leave her baggage there, and then go out looking for somewhere to eat. After another twenty minutes of walking, she saw boarded-up windows and tangled front gardens along a road to her left.

Up till that moment, her mind had been focussed on the finding of this estate. She'd kept up the momentum of her brisk pace by humming the tune Seb used to whistle if she started to lag behind on their rambles over the moors. 'I love to go a-wander-ing, a knapsack on my back . . . '

As she looked more closely at the boards and corrugated iron that had been hammered securely across the doors and window frames Agnes realised that it might be harder than she'd thought to break an entry. She scurried up a cracked concrete path and pushed her way past a straggling privet hedge to the secluded back garden, where last year's soggy remains of Michaelmas daisies and long brown seed heads of golden rod were splayed across the matted yellowing grass of what had once been a lawn.

At first glance the back door and windows appeared impenetrable. Agnes looked down along the length of the narrow garden to see if there was a wide enough gap in the broken-down fence for her to clamber through to next door. She smiled at the sight

213

of brassy daffodils clustered at the edge of weed-covered paving slabs, and her eye was caught by what looked like a long, stout stick.

It was heavier than she'd expected and she shrank for a moment from the chill of metal against her palm. She had to tug it free from the white roots of couch grass, and saw that the other end was blunt and slightly curved, like the claw of a hammer. A crowbar?

No matter what this object was called, it certainly came in handy. After five minutes of levering and splintering, she had removed several planks and revealed an almost glass-free, rusting metal frame. She rested the crowbar against the wall and stood for a moment, warm from her exertions and panting a little, a broad smile on her face. It was when she peered into the gloomy depths of the bare-boarded room that she realised she was going to find it difficult to clamber up onto the chest-high sill.

Agnes turned and looked around for something to stand on, her sense of achievement draining away as quickly as the daylight was seeping from the garden. She felt suddenly cold, seeing herself through Henry's eyes. Totally irresponsible. Vandal. What did she think she was playing at?

Agnes was surprising herself. One part of her brain was still in touch with what she was increasingly thinking of as Henry's world — the world she had inhabited happily enough for two thirds of her life. Jack was part of that world, and the Harmony Home. But once she had scrambled down the drainpipe and out through the back gate, another Agnes seemed to be taking over, one who shocked and frightened her, but who also gave her moments of exhilaration and amazing clarity and calm.

As a child, Agnes had developed her own technique for dealing with the disturbing dreams that used to invade her nights when she was convalescing from rheumatic fever. Somehow, she was usually aware of the fact that she was not awake but caught up in a dream, and she used to smack her right hand sharply onto the back of her left wrist, and wake to find it stinging under her fingers. The knowledge that she could wake when she chose to gave her the courage to stay in the dream just to see what would happen next.

Now, she had set herself this task of spending the night in an empty house rather than run back to the safety of Molly's in Nottingham. She'd dared herself to complete this adventure. I've started, so I'll finish, as that *Mastermind* person used to say. If she didn't let herself go as far as she dared, how would she find out, at this late stage in her life, what she was capable of, for good or ill?

After a fruitless search of her immediate surroundings for a suitable object to help her climb in through the window, Agnes peered across the broken fence and caught sight of something white protruding from behind a low bush a few feet from the neighbouring house. Closer inspection revealed a moulded plastic chair, speckled with grey and black, but still as solid as the day it left the factory.

It was even light enough for her to be able to haul it up into the room after her, a minimum security precaution.

The room she was in was already thick with shadow; she could barely make out the furthest corners. Anything could be lurking there. And as for the rest of the house, how was she to know what lay beyond the closed door? Come to think of it, what about toilet facilities? There'd be no water, and even if there was still a lavatory, she wouldn't be able to flush it.

Agnes picked up the back-pack from where she'd flung it before clambering into the room. She took it over to the window, where pale grey light was still filtering in across the dusty floorboards. A sharp little breeze was also blustering its way in and she shivered as she knelt down and emptied out the contents of the bag, wondering which item of clothing she should put on next. At least she'd had the foresight to pick up a few discarded newspapers before she'd left the train.

Perhaps she'd be able to find a few more papers lying around in litter bins when she ventured out for food. Fish and chips would go down nicely. And a mug of tea. Places like that might well sell matches too. Was this house old enough to have a proper fire grate still? She could use some of the broken bits of board and light a fire — or at least twist some of the newspaper into a spill and explore the house a little.

She'd leave everything here and walk back to where she'd seen the shops. If she had to spend a few pence of her dwindling money supply on a broadsheet newspaper or two, it would be worth it. Some could be spread out on the floor, and other pages could be screwed up and stuffed inside a couple of socks for a pillow, even pushed down into the ski-pants and then under the grey jumper. Very good insulation, newspaper. She and Seb used it to line their Wellington boots when it snowed.

Half-excited now by the thought of improvising a cosy nest for the night, Agnes lowered the plastic chair out of the window again and clambered down into the darkened garden.

Those street lights which had not yet been used as target practice for stone-throwers shed puddles of harsh white light over the uneven pavements. The nearest unbroken light was still more than a bus-length away when Agnes heard raucous shouts and screams of laughter approaching from the darkness beyond it.

She stepped back against a hedge and pressed herself into the mass of scratchy twigs, holding her breath as she watched a group of youths clustering around the lamppost. They began to throw what looked like empty beer cans up at the light, and when something fell down onto the head of one of them, he gave a loud yell and hit out at the lad nearest to him. Soon all five or six of them were thumping each other, their loud obscenities interspersed with high pitched giggles.

They're only playing, she told herself. Not all young people will be like the ones in that car. But her heart was thudding so fast in her tightening chest she could scarcely breathe. She looked across at the opposite pavement. All the lights on that side had been broken. Those noisy youngsters wouldn't even notice her. She flexed her leg muscles, ready to dash across the road. 'One, two, three,' she whispered. But the word 'go' remained stuck in her throat.

Perhaps if she just waited a couple of minutes? And then what? Find them cavorting towards her, pushing and shoving each other, bumping into her. And even if this little group did eventually amble away in the opposite direction, what other threats might be lurking in these dark streets?

The idea of food had lost its appeal. Bile seared her throat and a cold, acidic liquid was slopping around in her stomach.

★ ★ ★

A fox must feel like this when it goes to earth, thought Agnes as she clambered back into what had become her room, her house. Even that grimy plastic chair was hers, and the comforting crowbar that she had retrieved from the garden with the help of the rising moon. She smiled as she found herself welcoming the back-pack like a long-lost friend.

But the hunger returned once she had rolled herself up in the doubled-over blanket, wearing every single item of clothing, layered with precious newsprint, and with a few remaining pages screwed up in the back-pack for a pillow.

She hadn't realised how thin she was until the nerve endings in the skin of her hipbone and her shoulder were pressing down against the wooden boards. With difficulty she rolled herself in her cocoon onto her other side, until that, too, felt bruised. As she lay on her back with feet flat on the floor and knees bent, sleep washed over her for minutes at a time, bringing such vivid dreams that she lost the power of knowing whether she was awake or asleep.

13

'Do try to stop worrying, Jackie. It's doing no good to anyone, least of all you,' sighed Monica. 'I mean, it's got to be more than just a coincidence, hasn't it, them both disappearing at once? I bet they've been plotting and planning for weeks. All I can say is, it's a pity Agnes didn't see fit to tell you before you'd paid up for the whole quarter in advance for that place.' She yawned and stretched her arms, sliding her legs along the bed so that the magazine she'd been flicking through fell with a dull thud onto the floor. Jack was slumped, head in hands, on the edge of the mattress, and her feet under the quilt caressed his thigh.

He wriggled a couple of inches further towards the end of the bed, still staring down at the carpet. 'Can't quite see that happening,' he said morosely. 'Ma and Lucy were never exactly close. I'm pretty sure there's been no contact between them for ages.'

'Look, sweetheart, it's perfectly natural, you being worried at first. You mustn't think I don't understand. But for God's sake, what more can you do? Driving off to Nottingham like that, more or less straight from your prison cell, barely stopping here for a bite to eat — you were absolutely knackered by the time you got home last night. And then traipsing round all those tea-rooms in Reigate and Guildford today. No wonder you're exhausted.'

Jack folded his arms more tightly across his chest. 'Somebody had to do something. Police aren't exactly busting a gut, are they?'

'I did try to tell you you'd be wasting your time — but a man's gotta do what a man's gotta do, as my dad always says. And you do it, no matter what. I sincerely admire that in you, Jack, really I do.'

Jack held his breath, waiting for the 'but'.

'But — ' Monica paused as Jack gave a derisory grunt. 'What's that for?' she demanded.

'Nothing. Go on, 'but'?'

'Well, what I mean is, you have to look on the bright side. No news is good news, so they say. It's only a mystery if you won't even look at anything else. For starters, why should Agnes choose to disappear?'

'Meaning?'

'Meaning, what if she was trying to punish you? Done it all on purpose to cause us the maximum worry and expense.'

'But why on earth — ?'

'Your dear mother has always tried to control you, hasn't she? Never was exactly loving towards you as child, from what you've told me, sending you off to that awful school. Then trying to keep you at her beck and call even after you'd left home. Probably turned Lucy against you from the start. Well known fact, isn't it, mothers of only sons get dead jealous of any other woman.'

'But Ma wasn't like that. She . . . she . . . ' Jack stopped, trying in vain to recall when his mother had last shown him any sign of affection. 'Well, why on earth would she want to go off with Lucy, then?' he said at last.

'Oh, Jackie, darling!' laughed Monica. 'You just don't get it, do you?'

Jack unfolded his arms and pressed his knuckles into the mattress. 'You needn't be so damned patronising, just because I can't follow your twisted logic.'

Monica knelt forward and put her hand on his arm. 'Don't be like that,' she coaxed. 'What I mean is, men are so much nicer than us women. Hell hath no fury, and all that. Agnes obviously didn't appreciate the trouble you went to, finding that lovely place for her. And Lucy, well, she'll be resenting your success. Specially as she can't squeeze any extra money out of you. I mean, look at how well you've done these last couple of years.

They'll be making you a director soon, I shouldn't wonder.' She was kneeling behind him now, and tension eased from his neck and shoulders under her supple fingers. 'Lucy wouldn't have been exactly thrilled when I appeared on the scene, either. Didn't want you herself, but didn't want anyone else having you. Stands to reason she'd jump at the chance of causing us both as much trouble as possible.'

'I suppose — ' began Jack, and then, 'Mmmm, that's *nice*, Puss-cat! Don't stop.'

'Who said anything about stopping?' she murmured, nuzzling his ear.

*   *   *

When the alarm clock broke through his sleep at seven the next day, Jack kept his eyes firmly shut and fumbled his hand around on top of the bedside table till his fingers located the off button. He was slipping seamlessly back into his dream of floating on a huge lilo in the middle of a warm blue lake, with a naked woman sprawling against him, when Monica's voice startled him. 'No, Jack, not now. You've got to get up and go to work.'

The woman in his dream had not been Monica, but the Lucy of ten years ago. Not surprising, really, he thought, remembering the previous night's conversation. It did make a kind of sense, even now, in daylight. Ma was bound to be off somewhere with Lucy and the kids. Mustn't let himself worry so much about her. He'd feel pretty silly when he got a phone call or postcard from the Lake District, or Cornwall — even Spain, perhaps. *Having a lovely time with Lucy and the little ones.*

It wasn't as though he was short of things to worry about — the job, for a start. Monica didn't know the half of it. Director, indeed! Fat chance of that. It was becoming increasingly clear that he was being shoved sideways. Should be looking for something else before that could happen. And then there was this drunk driving charge. Case likely to come up in a week or so, Piers had said. Could get away with a hefty fine and more points on the licence, it'd all depend on which magistrate he got. Luck of the draw.

By eight o'clock that Tuesday morning Jack was waiting his turn to edge into the stream of cars on the main road at the end of the estate. He'd persuaded Monica to ring in his apologies the day before: too ill to come to the phone himself, been sick all night, perhaps something he'd eaten. They ought to be impressed by his valiant effort in struggling back to work today. No need to say anything to anyone about Ma's disappearance, and still less about where he'd spent the night that Sunday.

★ ★ ★

A few miles away, in a neat 1950s semi on the outskirts of Crawley, Constable Timothy Dolan was still in his boxer shorts and teeshirt, indulging in the luxury of breakfast in bed. Having been on duty the whole weekend, and Monday, too, he intended to enjoy the next couple of days off. No Sergeant to lick the boots of. No Team to have to fit in with, tread on eggshells around. No one to please but himself. Apart from his mum, of course. He'd have got more pleasure from the leisurely meal of Rice Crispies, a lightly boiled egg, and two pieces of thin white toast with Golden Shred marmalade, if she hadn't been hovering in the doorway, watching him swallow every mouthful.

'That nice, dear, was it? Shall I take your tray now?'

'Very nice, thanks, Mum,' he said, handing her the tray and sliding his bare legs over the edge of the bed.

'You not going to stay there, then — read the paper for a bit?' she asked in surprise, taking the tray in one hand, and reaching towards the hook on the door for his towelling dressing gown with the other.

'Not today. Got a few things to follow up. You know that bloke I told you about, Sunday? The one with the mother just moved into the Home over Horsham way?'

'Ooh, yes! She not been found yet, then?'

'Disappeared. Completely vanished. Not a trace of her. Something very funny going on there.'

'What does your Sergeant think?'

'Nothing, really. None of them seem to be taking any notice. Just lecture me if I raise the subject. 'She's on our books. We got our systems. Can't go sniffing round all day like a dog in a rabbit warren.' Mostly, it's 'You wait till you've been around as long as we have, sunshine.' But I'm not going to just drop it. I think this could be the big one for me.'

'Oh, Timmy, dear, do be careful. You don't want to cause no trouble.'

'Don't worry, Mum. I've got my career to think of. I'll not be saying another word about it down the station. I'll just carry on off my own bat in my own spare time. Then when I've got something solid, actual proof, I'll work out the best way of letting them know about it without them ever — '

'Proof of what, dear? You don't think she's been — ? Oh! You do, don't you?' Mrs

Dolan's voice rose to a squeak, and she raised her open palms to her mouth. 'You think he's killed her. His own mother! Oh! It doesn't bear thinking of! The vicious brute!'

'Now, then, Mum,' said Timothy sternly, turning his head away to hide his sudden smile. 'It's still only a hunch at the moment. As a police constable I can't let myself jump to premature conclusions.'

'No, dear. Quite right. But I know you and those hunches of yours. And you've always got some good strong reasons, haven't you?'

'I like to think so. Though I have to admit to being wrong occasionally. But this time . . . For a start, the first thing that came into my mind when we pulled him over just outside the Home, well, you'll never guess.' He paused, and was proved right once more, Mrs Dolan could not guess.

'Macbeth!' he exclaimed at last. 'That bit when he's seeing Banquo's ghost and then pretending that everything's OK. You know, when I went to the theatre in Guildford with the school for my GCSEs. He had that exact same look on his face. The look of a calculating murderer. It's my belief he was on his way to dispose of the body, and we interrupted him.'

'Oh, Tim! Do you really think so?'

'Yes, I'm afraid I do. And what's more, I

think he's been doing the classic trick of trying to double bluff us. He was that insistent that something dreadful had happened to her. And he was back at the station again Sunday night, late. D'you know, he'd driven all the way up to Nottingham, to his ex-wife's place, to throw us off the scent, make us think he was actually searching for her. And there's something funny going on there, too. Says she's vanished as well. And the two little kids! But I'll get to the bottom of it all. Then they'll see who's just an ignorant lad.'

★　★　★

Agnes woke to an awareness of pressure against her closed eyelids: the soft, weightless dark had been invaded by seering rays of light. Morning at last! She and Seb could go home now, honour satisfied. The cave floor had been poking against her bones all night, so it was a surprise to find she'd actually managed to snatch a little sleep. Before opening her eyes she murmured, 'Seb! You awake?'

As she slowly took in her desolate surroundings Agnes felt as though she was bouncing on the end of a huge spring, or piece of elastic rope, like those people who jumped off bridges and so forth. Bungee jumping, that was the name of it. But it was decades of time, not yards or metres of space, through which she was hurtling back and forth, finally coming to rest in this unwelcome present where everything worth having was long gone.

She closed her eyes and tugged the blanket up over her head, as though sleep, too, could be pulled back again like that. Never to wake.

But a human body can't just shut down. All those internal workings have their own momentum. Her leg muscles were tensed for action, refusing to relax, her stomach grumbled, and something sharp was pressing against her bladder.

'First things first,' she muttered, wriggling free of the blanket and staggering across to the window. Little twinges of pain shot through each separate joint in her limbs and shoulders, neck and spine as they rebelled against the enforced movement. Her knees nearly buckled beneath her as she clambered out onto the chair, and down into the sodden garden. Shivering with cold and exhaustion she stood for a moment, leaning her back against the wall. Her lower half was in shadow, but the pale sun was already projecting a lukewarm glow against the rough brickwork. Agnes knew that she needed to keep on the move and stretch her body in some of those warm up exercises that always preceded the keep fit sessions. But she also had to cross her legs and clench her pelvic muscles as she glanced around her for a suitable place to relieve herself.

When she had hauled herself up from her squatting position on the trampled grass at the edge of the paving slabs she found that she was smiling. Relieving oneself! What an accurate description of the ease with which that unpleasant pain could be banished.

Before climbing back into the room to retrieve her belongings, Agnes spent a few minutes bending, stretching and jogging on the spot until, if not warm exactly, then at least she was no longer shivering, and only the tips of her fingers were still numb.

The main physical sensations for Agnes now were the dry throat, the stale, furry layer coating her tongue and the queasy hollow of her stomach. But as she sat on the crumpled newspaper on the wooden floorboards and struggled out of the ski pants without removing her trainers, she found that the tiredness had vanished as effectively as though she'd been sound asleep the whole night long. In place of that debilitating fatigue, tiny bursts of excitement were welling up like bubbles from an underground spring. She had done it! She'd survived the night alone! Cold, discomfort, hunger, fear. She could face anything now.

A wash would be nice. And food and drink, of course. Leave most of the clothes-bank stuff here, with the bits of newspaper. Pile them in a corner away from the window, just in case she had to come back for another night. Hide the chair under a bush. Shame about the smashed boards, room open to the elements. But the house was due for demolition anyway, so Joe had said.

Joe. He'd have his mother-in-law there now, looking after him and Scott. The feel of Scott's warm, firm skin, his soft damp curls. So many months since she'd nuzzled her own dry cheek against Sam's podgy stomach and blown raspberries on his navel till he squealed with laughter.

'Right, woman!' she said out loud. 'Work to do. Get hold of Lucy's mother. Felix, too. Check he's alive and doesn't really need anything from me. Then . . . ' Then nothing! She'd know what to do next when the time came. And the very first thing was to re-fuel herself before her batteries ran down.

★　★　★

It took her longer than she'd expected to reach the High Street. She'd been tempted to rest for a while on a low wall at the edge of a car park, but she could see the shops just a few hundred yards ahead and hunger got the better of fatigue. She noticed the public library on her left and made a mental note of this potentially useful resting place. The first shops she passed were all firmly shut, and the wide pedestrian area appeared to be deserted. There would surely be a newsagent, at least. A chocolate bar and a can of drink would be better than nothing. No, more like a feast!

Five to nine. A thundering clatter a little ahead on her right made her quicken her pace, and she saw two young men dragging open a pair of enormous metal shutters from across the entrance of an indoor market. A quick glance showed the stalls in front were still covered by drapery or plastic blinds.

Agnes felt her head suddenly seem to expand and fill up with a thick mist. Oh God! What was happening to her? In a panic, she looked around for somewhere to sit. On her left, a raised flower-bed, a wooden bench, hunched figure at the far end. She managed to collapse onto the seat before a wave of nausea swept over her.

'You orright bab?' A man's voice reached through the fog. She did not move a muscle, concentrating all her efforts on remaining upright on the seat. Then a blast of alcohol fumes and stale sweat hit her nostrils and she opened her eyes with a start.

'Orright, bab?' the man repeated. His gruff voice sounded anxious. 'Get some of this down you, aye?'

In a daze, Agnes put out her cold hand to take the proffered bottle, and let the man help her lift it towards her lips. It was fortunate that he'd retained his hold, or she would have dropped it as the bitter liquid burned its way down her throat.

When she'd recovered from her choking fit, Agnes found that her head was clear again. 'Thank you so much,' she said, smiling up at the man who was now on his feet, bending towards her. 'I don't know what got into me just then,' she continued. 'A sudden dizzy spell. I'm right as rain now.'

'Never fails, drop of the hard stuff,' the man laughed, bending lower and expelling another blast of reeking breath. 'Another little drop?'

Agnes swallowed hard, and tried not breath in. 'You're very kind. But, no. I, em, I have to be getting along now. Shopping, and so on.'

'You take care now, bab,' said the man, staring at Agnes with a mixture of curiosity and concern. 'None of my business what you doing here, but you ain't one of us. Not yet you ain't.'

'Oi, Mick,' called the younger of the two men who'd been opening the market. 'Got yourself a girlfriend at last, then?'

Mick straightened his back. 'Watch your manners, lad.' To Agnes he said, 'If it's food shopping you're after, you'll find the Co-op better'n the market. You can help yourself more easy there, know what I mean? Look. Just opening now.'

Agnes followed his gesturing hand and saw a couple of women disappearing into the entrance. Aware again of how ravenous she felt, she stood up, thanked Mick once more, and headed for the supermarket.

★　★　★

'Milk's the best value,' she muttered, making for the dairy stand after she'd surveyed the range of soft drinks available. She smiled wryly as she remembered the unkempt but gentle man, one of Henry's regulars, who'd given her that tip, years ago. 'Get it off doorsteps, mostly,' the man had said. 'But if I ever have to buy sommat meself, I never go for all that pop and stuff.' Agnes was about to put the half-litre, plastic container into the wire basket when she was overwhelmed by the dryness in her mouth and throat. She ran her tongue around her teeth and gums, trying to stimulate a trickle of saliva. Nothing. Surely it would be all right to take a few mouthfuls, here and now. After all, she'd still have the container to show at the checkout. Glancing up and down the deserted aisle, she placed the basket on the floor, removed the red seal and unscrewed the lid. *Nectar!* Once the first mouthful had gushed down her throat, she was unable to stop the flow. It was like lock-gates being opened. All she could do was swallow, swallow, snatch a gasp of breath, swallow again . . .

'Haven't you forgotten something, Missis?' The deep voice, and the hand on her shoulder, struck in unison — one second later a splutter of milk was trickling down a dark trouser leg and splashing onto a huge black toecap.

'Oh, I do beg your pardon!' exclaimed Agnes, catching her breath and craning her neck to look up, and up, past the broad expanse of suit jacket up to the jutting chin, the clamped mouth, thick frowning eyebrows above tiny eyes peering down at her in a startled squint. 'Oh dear!' she went on, surveying the trouser leg. 'I'm afraid you rather made me jump. That's not really any excuse for guzzling so greedily in the first place, but . . . '

The man took a step back but not before

reaching out his enormous hand and removing the almost empty container. 'Too right it's no excuse,' he said sternly. 'This is evidence, this is. Consuming goods before paying for them, that's theft.'

'But you don't understand . . . I can explain . . . '

'That's what they always says. Women's the worst — all them sob stories. Now then, if you'd just like to step this way,' and the hand came down on her shoulder once more. 'You can explain as much as you like when we get to the office.'

Her mind in turmoil, Agnes allowed herself to be propelled along the aisle, past a hundred different flavours of yoghurt, then shelf after shelf of cheese. At all costs she had to prevent the police being summoned to the scene.

Perhaps she could kick him on the shin, then make a run for it. Her heart was pummelling against her rib cage as she looked down at her feet, calculating distances, and the timing of her steps against the man's. Surprise would be her only asset. He would release his light grip on her shoulder, she'd be out of the store before he'd managed to gather his wits. But then what? How far would she get? Where could she go?

No. It would only make matters worse. The

only thing was to remain calm. She simply needed to exert her natural authority.

'Keep moving. Keep moving,' said the security guard as Agnes's pace slowed almost to a halt. They'd reached the end of the aisle and the weight of the large hand shifted a little on her shoulder, steering her to the right. The smell of in-store baking rushed at her like a physical blow, jolting her back into the reality of her situation. Not only was she exhausted and ravenous, but she suddenly became aware of her appearance: it would not be likely to inspire respect in a store manager engaged in constant battles against shop-lifters. Her face and hands would be grimy from a night spent on the dirty floor. Her clothes too. Was her cap on straight, and her wig? The overlarge fleece jacket and grey jumper had helped keep out the cold, but they were not exactly smart, and underneath them her turquoise tracksuit trousers must look very odd indeed.

For the first time since spewing that mouthful of milk down the man's leg, Agnes became aware of the curious glances of other shoppers. The fact that there were so few of them this early in the day made her feel even more conspicuous. Three shopping trolleys just a few yards ahead near Cakes and Biscuits slowly collided in a tangle of wheels as their temporary owners stared at the strange looking little woman being marched towards them by the huge security guard.

A small child clutching a packet of biscuits in each hand turned his attention from the scene of the crash to find out what they were all so interested in. He stood still for a moment, mouth and eyes wide open, then he looked up at the woman by his side and said, 'Nanny Edie, why is that man being horrid to Aunty Ness?'

★　★　★

Agnes stared in amazement as Edie bustled forward, Scott at her side, and stood, arms folded, glaring at the burly uniformed man. 'You should be ashamed of yourself, my lad. Call yourself a security guard, do you? Making trouble for this poor harmless lady, when there's all them young thugs getting away with murder!'

As the man attempted to explain the situation, Edie interrupted with a derisive snort. 'Milk!' she exclaimed, 'A few mouthfuls of milk! There's still the checkout to go through, in't there? Still a perfectly visible container to pay for, in't there? What gives you the right to say that this respectable person was trying to leave the store without paying for every last mouthful?'

'It's company policy, Madam. Zero tolerance, that's what we call it.'

'Zero, queero. Mumbo jumbo. That's what
we call it. In't that right?' she continued,
turning to the small group of shoppers
hovering nearby.

''S'right,' responded a large middle-aged
woman, 'Leave the poor soul alone, she ain't
done nothing, have you, bab?'

'Looks real poorly an' all,' added another.

'How long you been in this job, anyways?
Di'n't they teach you nothing?' continued
Edie, punctuating each word with a stab of
her pointing forefinger. 'You're not s'posed to
lay a finger on 'em till they're through the
checkout. Harassment, that's what it is.'

This display of solidarity was too much for
Agnes. To her dismay she felt her eyes welling
up with tears. As she drew in a deep breath in
an effort to calm herself, an audible sob
escaped, quickly followed by another and
another. A moment later, Scott was clasping
her legs and resting his cheek against her
thigh, and then Edie was at her side, an arm
around her shoulder, firmly leading her
towards the checkout.

14

Timothy Dolan switched off the ignition and inched up the handbrake lever of his red Ford Fiesta till he was sure it was at its tightest setting, then he put his foot on the clutch and slid the gear stick from neutral into first. Only a very gentle slope, but you couldn't be too careful where cars were concerned. Next, the crook lock. This was a nice area. Very nice indeed. But he wasn't ever going to be one of those cops that dashed off without even checking their car door was properly shut, let alone locked!

Be living somewhere like this himself, one of these days. Chief Inspector Dolan, drinks bar in the lounge, master bedroom with its own en-suite, huge sunken bath, foaming with bubbles, beautiful young wife. Was she blonde, this time, or a red-head?

Enough of that, better stick to the present for now. That kind of daydream was best kept for later, after the mission-accomplished stage.

Timothy enjoyed his own company. Having people around all the time put a block on his creative side. Vivid imagination, that was one of his more outstanding qualities. They'd said so at school. Well, Miss Allen, the English teacher did. Gave him top marks for his stories. Encouraged him to join the drama club. Got him into writing plays too. Still liked doing that, creating heroic roles for himself, though he didn't bother with pen and paper these days.

★　★　★

SCENE:
An executive estate situated in the most exclusive area of Haywards Heath.
TIME:
Almost eleven of the clock on a dull April morning.
DRAMATIS PERSONAE:
Timothy Ignatius Dolan, a dedicated young police constable. Good looking, without being flash. Perceptive, resourceful and courageous.
ACTION:
Timothy opens the door of his expensive sports car and nonchalantly steps out onto the pavement of the quiet cul-de-sac around the corner from Saxon Meadow. If anyone is watching him from behind the immaculately shining windows of the luxurious four-bedroomed detached dwellings, they would

never guess that beneath that coolly sophisticated exterior, the strong young heart is beginning to beat like a powerful drum. Timothy knows he is risking his job by this unorthodox undertaking, but his passion for justice spurs him on . . .

★ ★ ★

A policeman's lot is not a happy one, not when that policeman's superiors do their best to stifle any initiative. But there was more than one way of skinning a cat, as his mum was fond of telling him. He'd chosen his clothes with care. Important to look smart. Nice, but casual. His black anorak was new, and without its zip-on hood it could pass for a jacket, but did anyone wear ties these days except at work or a posh do? The navy, ribbed polo-neck jumper would solve that problem. Christmas present from his cousin Sharon in London. Always trying to change his image, as she called it. 'Matches your eyes lovely,' Mum said. 'And brings out the blond in your hair.' But it scratched his neck so he'd hardly worn it yet. And that wasn't the only reason. As he marched along Saxon Meadow he felt that same mixture of excitement and revulsion he always did at the thought of Sharon, ever since she'd tried to push her tongue in his mouth and her hand down his trousers at his eighteenth birthday party. And she was four years older and already married at the time.

There were only two houses between the road sign on the corner and number eleven. Timothy paused, and reaching into the side zip pocket drew out the white envelope before venturing across the herring-bone patterned brick driveway to the Grecian columns that flanked the front door of number seven. The bell chimes were answered by a woman of at least forty, with long blonde hair waving around her shoulders and a very low-cut creamy-coloured jumper that showed a lot of bare rather freckly brown skin above the glimpse of paler, smoother flesh and a gold chain that dropped straight down towards the cleavage, enticing his eyes to follow it. She was laughing and he felt his face go all hot as she said, 'Well, hello, there!' in a voice like that of Cilla Black.

Glad of an excuse not to have to look directly at her, he fumbled with the envelope and held out a coloured photo of a black and white cat sunning itself on a garden wall. His garden, his cat, Blackie, buried two years ago under their little vegetable patch round the back by the shed where he kept his collection of empty biscuit tins.

'No, Lovey, can't say as I have seen him anywhere round here. But then again,' she added, taking the photo and studying it more closely, 'I might have. Perhaps I'll be able to remember a bit better if you come inside for a little drink and tell me more about him.'

'I, em,' he gulped, cheeks hotter than ever. Then he straightened his back, picturing himself in his uniform, and declared in a rush, 'I am sorry to have bothered you, Madam. I have to be getting along now. Other calls, you know. If you wouldn't mind . . . ' and he held out his hand for the photo.

To his relief, the door of number nine remained firmly shut. He waited on the pavement a full minute, making sure that his heartbeat had returned to normal before trying number eleven.

Someone was in. Music, if you could call it that, whining and screeching from the back of the house. Would anyone be able to hear the bell above that din? A moment later the noise halted and he pressed his finger hard against the button again. Through the frosted glass panel he could see a figure slowly approaching. Then the door opened as far as the short chain would allow and a girl's voice demanded, 'Whadyer want?'

Timothy approved of the chain, but

245

although the questioner was absolutely right to be suspicious of a total stranger at the door, there was no need to sound quite so aggressive. 'I'm trying to trace my cat, Blackie. He's been missing more than two weeks. Can I just pass this photo through to you?'

An eye and half a face appeared in the gap, and then the door slammed shut. For a moment, Timothy thought that he had lost his chance, but there was a clank and a rattle and the door was flung wide open. 'Go on then, give it me,' said the girl.

With practised eye he swiftly took in details of her appearance as he calculated the most effective approach. Fifteen, sixteen years old. Tricky age that, on the border between legal and strictly out of bounds. Clearly a bit of a rebel — all that metal work and the blood-red hair with black streaks and a style that could have been the result of an hour in front of a mirror or a night in bed and not been combed yet. Good figure. Petite, but nice shaped what's-its under the skimpy pink top. Low-cut jeans revealing a jewelled ring in her navel. Turned his stomach a bit, that, so he had to compose his face before speaking.

'Relief to find someone normal in this road,' he said at last, and was rewarded by a start of surprise followed by a quick smile that quite transformed the fine-boned face before the sullen look re-appeared.

'You taking the piss, or what?'

'Sorry,' he said, putting on the apologetic expression he reserved for Members of the Public when his uniform failed to intimidate them. 'Quite out of order, running down your neighbours like that. I'm sure they're all very nice people really, but . . . ' he gave his boyish laugh. 'Look, I'm in danger of digging myself in deeper here. I'll leave you in peace, if you wouldn't mind just taking a quick look at this photo first?'

''S'orright,' said the girl. 'I don't belong round here. Effing deadsville, this is. Say what you like about it. Can't be as bad as what I feel.'

★　★　★

After that, it was easy. Timothy was sitting in the kitchen, munching on his fourth chocolate digestive and watching Hailey put on the kettle for a second mug of tea. Same old broken-home story. Same old eagerness to spill it all out. Must be something about his face — couldn't put it down to the uniform this time — the way that seemed to provoke an excess of either hostility or trust. Minor details altered, but the basic whinge didn't

247

— poor me, unhappy childhood. So, same difference: parents divorced when the girl was eight. Sounded like it was the mother who'd strayed first. Taken the two daughters to live with a wealthier man. He'd got bored after a couple of years, or perhaps it was her. Another home to get used to, another school. Money very tight. Older sister the favourite. Hailey always in trouble. Just beginning to get on better and make friends at school and along comes yet another man making up to her mum. Pretty disgusting, at their age, wasn't it? Enough to put a girl right off it. And here she was, landed in this fucking dump. Well, no, she hadn't actually had to change schools this time, but she might just as well of, for all the good it did her. Living bloody miles from all her mates now.

'So what's he like, then, this Jack?' asked Timothy as Hailey sat down again.

'Booor-ring! Can't see what Mum ever saw in him. 'Cept his money, of course. Not her usual type. Not like my real dad.' She was silent for a moment and Timothy waited, watching the way she pressed her lips together as if trying not to cry. 'Well anyway,' she continued, 'just when I'm getting round Mum and Jack to let me have the room at the back — it's kind of separate, and more like a sort of flat — well, next thing that happens is,

Jack's own mum has to move in too, and bang goes my chance of my own bedsit.'

'Poor you,' murmured Timothy, and then, with a deliberate glance behind him at the open door, 'So she's here now, is she? What'll she say if she sees you entertaining a total stranger?'

'She won't say nothing, cos A, it's never been none of her business what I do. And B, she's not here any more. Her loving son stuck her in one of those dumps for old fogies. I felt almost sorry for the old bag. Wasn't like it was her choice to come and live here. Anyway, for a coupla weeks it looked like I was getting the room after all, even with Donna playing her face as usual, then suddenly, bang! It's all up in the air again.'

'Bang?' said Timothy. 'Was there an accident?'

'You mean did she finally flip and go an' shoot herself? Na, nothing like that. Well, not exactly . . . ' Hailey paused dramatically and fixed her eyes on Timothy's face.

He did not have to pretend an interest. He leant forward across the table, sliding a hand towards her, then thought the better of it, letting his fingers perform a little dance back along the grain of the wood as he prompted, 'What, then? What exactly?'

'She went and vanished, didn't she?'

Timothy allowed her to tell him what he already knew about the old woman's disappearance on the previous Saturday.

'So what do you think's happened to her?' he asked. 'I mean, you're a sharp kid — young lady, I mean,' he amended, noticing her sudden frown. 'I bet there's not much goes on that you don't find out about.'

Had he gone too far with the flattery? She'd lowered her head and was peering up at him through half-closed eyes, chewing on one side of her lower lip. 'Thought you was meant to be looking for your cat,' she said at last.

For a moment he couldn't think what she was talking about. He quickly recovered himself and laughed. 'Whoops! Doesn't look too good, does it? Concerned pet owner so easily distracted. That's me all over! Always more interested in people than animals. To be perfectly honest, it's my mum's cat.'

To his relief, this admission evidently made her feel more relaxed. 'That's actually nice,' she said, putting her elbows on the table and cupping her face in her hands. 'I mean, not many blokes could be arsed to do something like that for their mum.'

'Oh, I don't know!' he murmured, in genuine awkwardness at this undeserved praise.

'Well I do know, so there!' she laughed. 'Lots of men don't give a sod. Can't wait for 'em to drop dead, matter of fact. Just so's they can lay their hands on the money.'

Careful, now, Timothy said to himself. Don't go and blow things just when you're getting somewhere. He cleared his throat. 'So. This new man of your mum's. I take it you think he could've shown a bit more feeling for his own mother?'

'Too right he could! I mean, I know I wasn't that cool about having her here, but I didn't have nothing against her really. Fact is, she wasn't that bad. Didn't actually cause me no bother. Only for the room. I was dead shocked when I found out he was sending her off to that place. An' trying to blame it all on my mum when she was the one who'd been looking after her.'

'Mmm. Sounds a bit of a dodgy character to me.'

'You don't know the half of it,' she responded, straightening her back and clasping her hands in front of her. Her eyes were shining now. Tears, perhaps? Or was it excitement? Either way, he'd managed to press the right button. Over the next few minutes the whole sordid story flooded out in a rush, as though he was the first, the only, person to have heard it.

It was worse even than he'd feared. Or rather, if he allowed himself to admit it, more than he'd hoped for. As he strode towards his car he was smiling broadly. He could just picture the scene at the station when he, Timothy Dolan, the ignorant youngster, wet-behind-the-ears, casually informed the sergeant exactly why he ought to be bringing that Jack Borrowdale in for questioning.

He lived the scene for a brief moment, hugging himself in delight. Shame it could never come out like that, though. Not with all those stupid, stifling rules. Never allowed to use your brains and follow your own instincts, like they do on the tele. Bloody ridiculous — the fact that he could actually lose his job for being cleverer than that dozy bunch.

But this wasn't the end of it. Oh, no! Still the rest of today, and the whole of Wednesday and all before he was due back at work. Now that he knew, beyond a shadow of a doubt, that he was on the right tracks, he'd surely be able find some concrete evidence to prove it. And once he'd found that, it'd be a piece of cake, working out a suitable way of explaining how.

★　★　★

'What you been up to now, Hailey?' demanded Donna a little later, leaning against the kitchen door frame, arms folded.

Hailey stifled a shriek of surprise. She'd been so wrapped in her own thoughts she hadn't even heard the front door open and close. Five minutes earlier, and Donna would have interrupted her in the middle of the tale she'd been spinning. Strange bloke. Couldn't work him out. Nor her own feelings neither. First sight, he was just an anorak trying to look trendy by leaving off his tie and specs. A real geek. Seriously boring mousy hair and that old-mannish way of speaking. Bit like a teacher. One of those eager new student ones that got theirselves gobbled alive. She'd only let him in for a laugh. But when you saw him close up, his eyes were kinda . . . well . . . she'd never gone for blue eyes before, just that his weren't the pale bulging sort, they were real dark and sort of drew you in, so you forgot about his pointy nose and his much-too-small chin. The way he'd looked at her! Like she was real interesting and important, not just a kid. Especially when she made up all that stuff about Jack.

Hailey frowned at Donna, pushed back her chair and stood up without saying a word. She was beginning to feel a little uneasy now. What if he'd taken her so seriously that he felt he ought to do something? Like go to the cops! Poor old Jack had already spent one night inside. Pr'haps he was already on their wanted list.

'I said, what you been up to? Why's there two mugs on the table?'

'Wouldn't you like to know?' she jeered. Typical Donna, making her feel guilty. No harm done. Nothing to worry about. It was that ansaphone was making her feel so jumpy near Donna now. Wiping off Craig's message. That's what it was. Her eyes were still looking puffy. Like she'd been crying all night.

'Who was it? Who's been here?' insisted Donna.

For a moment Hailey was tempted to confess everything. Timothy wouldn't have looked so admiringly at her if he'd known what she'd done to her sister, however justified it might have been. And Donna had been punished enough, waiting in all last night just in case Craig rang to make it up with her before he went off to Florida with his mum and dad for two whole weeks. Craig might be a right wimp, but . . . It wasn't exactly making her feel good about herself, thinking of how he must have been hanging around all evening, waiting for Donna to show.

Still, too late now. And it would just be asking for trouble, saying anything. She must be mental, even thinking of it. Going soft, just cos some bloke had paid her a bit of attention! Donna would hold it against her for fucking ever. Mum and Jack would go on and on about telling lies — she'd sworn blind there'd been no messages on the machine.

'You turning into a detective or what? Two cups don't have to mean two people. Actually, I've been chatting away to Prince bloody Charming while you've been down the shops. Or perhaps I just didn't bother to clear away my first mug before I came down for another.'

'OK, OK,' sighed Donna, walking over to the kettle. 'Silly of me to show any interest in you. D'you know where Mum is?'

'It's Tuesday, innit?' said Hailey, shuffling out of the room. Then she turned and added in a softer tone, 'I mean, I 'spect she's at work this morning. Should be back one-ish.' Turning back into the hall, she nearly tripped over the corgi as it waddled towards the kitchen, trailing the leather lead. 'Didn't realise you'd taken Queenie out too,' she said. 'That'll please Mum, anyway.'

She'd not even noticed that the dog hadn't burst out with its usual yapping when the door bell had rung.

It was Hailey's turn to sigh as she put her hand on the banister and paused with one foot on the bottom step, staring at the telephone. What a mess everything was. She almost wished it was still term time and she had school to go to. What if there'd been another message on the machine before those two of Craig's? She'd pressed rewind and gone right back to the start, to make sure she deleted everything. Thinking about it now, she sort of remembered seeing a flashing number three. But if there had been anything important, whoever it was would be bound to try again.

15

Agnes lay submerged in a rising tide of hot water, clouds of steam curling themselves around her face and shoulders. As every pore in her body opened to greet the warmth that lapped against her, it felt as though nothing else in life had ever matched the luxury of this experience in Edie's small bathroom with its grey lino tiles, cork mat and chipped enamel bath.

What an amazing woman Edie is, she thought.

During the ten minute walk to her house, Edie had not asked a single question, and she had easily deflected the few that Scott had fired at Agnes. He'd been quite happy to chatter away about his new baby sister: 'Mummy's in hospital. And Baby is. Nana's gone to see Mummy and Baby.'

Agnes had managed to murmur responses in the right places as her legs kept pace with Edie's measured steps, her arm linked to Edie's coat sleeve, fingers clutching at the black and mauve bobbles of wool. Scott had taken hold of Edie's other hand, and Agnes experienced the strange, but not unwelcome sensation of being just another one of Edie's little charges.

Still feeling like a child, Agnes let herself be led into Edie's kitchen and sat down at the small Formica topped table. 'Be with you in two shakes, dear,' said Edie, pouring squash into a mug for Scott and reaching up for a biscuit tin.

American voices and a background of jingle jangle music blared through from the front room, and were muffled as Edie shut the kitchen door behind her. 'No, don't try and talk yet,' she said. 'Get this down you first.' She placed a bowl of milk-softened Weetabix on the table. Agnes watched in silence as two heaped spoonfuls of sugar were absorbed by the liquid. Her mother had never allowed her to sweeten her cereal, and although Henry was very liberal with the sugar for himself, she'd never acquired the taste. But now! It was the most delicious food she had ever eaten.

'Just shows how much you needed it,' laughed Edie, watching like an indulgent parent as she scraped the last morsel from the bowl.

With her energy levels temporarily restored, Agnes found that she could not stop the words tumbling from her mouth. In the course of the next half hour or so, pausing only to sip from the mug of strong sweet tea, Agnes found herself telling Edie the whole story. Jack's divorce, Henry's death, Lucy's move to the Midlands, Monica, the Harmony Home, and all that had happened since she'd climbed down that drainpipe.

Edie listened in rapt attention, punctuating the tale with little shrieks and laughs and, 'Well, I never did!' or, 'Ooh, you are a one!'

'And now I really had better get going,' said Agnes. 'See if Lucy's mother is at home now, and then go and check on Felix.'

'You're not going nowhere yet, and that's that. No arguing, mind,' Edie scolded. 'You can stay put for today. Have a nice hot bath and then a bit of shut-eye while I have a go at washing and drying them clothes you've been in since Sat'day. Bit ripe, they are, if you don't mind me saying.'

'But Felix!' exclaimed Agnes, 'Dianne! I've got to — '

'Got to nothing. You've got the phone numbers, haven't you? And I've got a phone. I won't have you set foot outside this house. Not till you're feeling stronger.'

Agnes meekly followed her out into the narrow hallway towards a small, spindly-legged oak table. The telephone squatting on the lace mat took up almost its entire surface. It seemed to be challenging Agnes to summon up the energy to dial.

She clenched her lips tightly as she waited for the ringing tones on Dianne's phone to come to an end. 'Not in,' she breathed. It took a huge effort of will to try the next call. Felix, too was not responding. 'I'll try again later, if that's all right, Edie.'

'I'll look out one of my nighties for you and you can pop yourself straight into bed after your bath. Get some sleep. Best medicine, isn't it? You're looking right poorly, and no mistake.'

★   ★   ★

Edie's bedroom was spotless — the small double bed with its gleaming brass knobs and railings was covered with a cream-coloured crochet bedspread tucked under in a neat line along the edge of the pillows.

'The sheets were clean on yesterday,' she said, 'You're welcome to get right in under the covers if you don't mind.'

'You're so kind!' said Agnes, smiling with anticipation. 'Sheer luxury. You can't imagine . . . '

'Now that you've cleaned yourself up, that is,' added Edie with a laugh. 'Wouldn't want you bringing all them bugs and germs into my bed!'

Agnes walked slowly across the small room to a kidney-shaped dressing table and let her fingertips stroke the ivory-backed brushes and hand mirror. This set was almost identical to the one she'd taken with her from the vicarage. It was a mere three weeks ago that she'd placed it on the ugly yellow varnish of the bedside table in her room at the Harmony Home. Would it still be there now, awaiting her return? Or would all her belongings have been carted off to be recycled in a charity shop?

'So I'll be taking Scottie round to Joe's later, when Pauline gets back from the hospital,' Edie was saying as she pulled back the bedspread and plumped the pillows. 'So if I'm not here when you wake, just make yourself a cup of tea and I'll be back again in two shakes.'

As if in a dream, Agnes allowed herself to be tucked into bed. Her head was dissolving into a feathery cloud while her heavy limbs pulled her down, down, down into soft warm darkness.

★　★　★

My dear Ruby,
When you receive this, I shall be dead. I am sorry if this causes you grief, though I see

261

no reason why it should since you will never return to England, and I never had the slightest intention of boarding an aeroplane to Tobago.

I would like to thank you for your kindness and forbearance towards me over these last few years. I have greatly enjoyed our little Sunday outings, and I venture to express my belief that the pleasure was not entirely one-sided. However, all that is now a closed book.

Since this is the last time I shall address you, I must tell you that I have misgivings about your Errol. I fear he will let you down, as he has in the past. I have taken the liberty of arranging my affairs to include a bequest for you in my will, so that whatever happens there will always be a small annual income for your sole use. You will be hearing shortly from my solicitor.

I am tired now, but perfectly calm. My life has not been wholly without enjoyment. However, I see no reason to prolong it. My body and mind are still in working order, but my spirit, or whatever it is that makes me the person I am, has had enough.

Goodbye, Ruby,
Yours very sincerely,
Felix Biddle.

'What utter tosh,' muttered Felix as he reached the end, crumpling the letter and flinging it towards the bin by the sink

He pushed back his chair, shuffled across the kitchen and switched on the kettle, then rummaged in the cupboard for a sachet of instant soup. Damn! No tomato. Perhaps that student had used it all up, the one who'd been looking after him through the worst of his fever. Have to be chicken noodle, then. Not a clean mug in sight though. Students! Probably even worse since Philip's day. Positive aversion to washing up, as Sylvia used to say after their visits to their son's student flat in Bristol.

Felix sniffed and shivered slightly as he put the steaming mug of soup on a tray, together with half a packet of Jacobs crackers — no bread, of course — a tin of sardines and a glass of water. Plenty of liquid, that was the thing. And get himself out of this freezing kitchen. Gas fire in the front room was the quickest way to get warm.

He was scraping the last of the noodles from the bottom of the mug when he heard the phone. 'Go away, whoever you are,' he growled, reaching for the sardine tin. His grip must have been weakened by his illness, because he tugged awkwardly at the ring pull, spilling some of the strongly smelling oil onto the sleeve of his jumper.

'Damn and blast it!' he shouted, placing the tray on the footstool before rising to his feet. 'Bloody phone! You won't stop, will you?'

★   ★   ★

When Agnes woke, dim grey light was filtering through closed curtains. She lay still for a while, gradually surfacing to a recollection of where she was, and when. Tuesday. That was right, wasn't it? But she had no idea of the time.

She fumbled for the light switch and slid her legs over the edge of the bed, looking down at her bare feet. The trainers were waiting for her on the multi-coloured rag rug, but where were the rest of her clothes?

She wrapped herself in the beige quilted dressing gown that was draped over the bedrail and made her way downstairs.

No sign of Scott or Edie. The kitchen clock said twenty-five to six. Nearly the whole day gone!

She hurried into the hall and sat down on the cane-seated chair by the telephone.

Still no reply from Dianne's house. If only there was a way of telling if Lucy and the children were with her. Would she have to wait till tomorrow before venturing back to the house and pushing a note through her door?

And what about Felix? The least she could do was to try his phone again. She drew a deep breath as she dialled his number and counted ten ringing tones. Better let it ring a bit longer before she gave up. She nearly dropped the receiver when the ringing suddenly stopped and a gruff voice barked in her ear, 'Hello? Who's there?'

Before she could collect her thoughts he said, more fiercely, 'Whoever you are, stop playing silly buggers. Tell me what you want or get off the bloody line.'

Oh dear. This was even worse than she'd feared. What if she simply put the phone down? Coward! Even Henry wouldn't approve of that!

'Felix Biddle?' she said at last, and was annoyed to hear a quaver in her voice.

'Who is it?' he snapped.

She drew in a deep breath and said more steadily, 'This is Agnes. Agnes Borrowdale. I was just — '

'You! What the devil d'you want now, woman? Haven't you done enough damage already? Nearly caught my death of cold, having to walk all the way back home in the pouring rain! For chrissake, leave me in peace, can't you?'

Should have just let it ring, he scolded, making his way back to the fireside. Damned woman. He'd had to agree to let her phone again the next day, just to get her off the line.

'I shall turn up on your doorstep in person if I can't get through to you,' she had declared.

Confounded cheek! He would take himself out for the day. She certainly wasn't going to set foot over his threshold, that was for sure.

As he munched his way through the sardines, mashed on the plate with the back of a fork and then spread carefully onto six of the cracker biscuits, Felix found himself wondering again about Agnes and her Society. Perhaps he would allow the woman to visit him after all. Life was no more palatable to him than it had been on Sunday, but now he might have a greater range of choice regarding methods of departure.

What would Ruby make of Agnes? She had always been a good judge of people, women especially, but even Ruby might find this one hard to fathom. Her voice and mannerisms didn't quite match her appearance, and she spoke with the persuasive sincerity of that type of inveterate liar that Felix was accustomed to observing in court.

The more he thought about Agnes, the more convinced he became that he had detected a mystery. How Ruby loved mysteries! What fun they would have had, getting to the bottom of this one.

Felix felt a sudden sharp prickling in his nostrils and rummaged in his pocket, drawing out a large crumpled handkerchief just in time to catch the explosive sneeze.

'Bloody woman,' he muttered, sniffing and wiping his nose. That chill he'd caught on Sunday. Could have died on the doorstep before one of those idle students finally appeared, and agreed to let him through their house to his own back door. Lucky he'd left it unbolted.

Give them their due, though, those young men had been very kind, popping in every few hours with mugs of lumpy soup and plates of burnt toast and peanut butter. Apart from Ruby and the meter readers, those lads were the only people to have set foot inside his door for the past twenty years.

Not that there hadn't been plenty waiting around on the doorstep, in those early days. Local press. Then Sylvia's cronies, her work colleagues from school, and a few of his from chambers. None of them ever tried more than once. Philip's friends were the hardest to deal with: their red eyes and runny noses.; their pathetic cards and poems. What right had they to be alive, when his son — ? No. Enough of that!

He sneezed again. The damp handkerchief stung the raw skin around his nostrils. His throat felt like sandpaper, and he leant across to retrieve the glass of water from the tray before collapsing back into the chair.

What day was it? He'd lost all track of time, and of reality. Tuesday, more than likely. Of course Ruby hadn't been sitting on his bed, stroking her cool hand across his scorching face. Kissing him . . .

Ruby. The way she'd managed to break through to him, lighting up those last three years at Chambers! People must have wondered what such an elegant woman was doing with a scruffy old codger like him. Not the barristers, of course, with their prejudice and snobbery. How had he stuck it out for so long?

Their Head Clerk had a say in who got the juiciest cases, so they'd had to keep him sweet, but he should know his place, stick to the unwritten rules. It was permissible to flirt with office juniors and clerical assistants — but to treat them as equals, as friends! God forbid! Especially if they were from a different — what was that word? Ethnicity!

More than two years since he'd left that

place. Water under the bridge.

His face softened. Ruby had seemed to enjoy their ritual Sunday afternoon stroll along the canal, or around the art gallery, with tea and cake in the Edwardian Tea Room. Creole pork and rice at her flat. Smoked salmon and scrambled egg in front of the Antiques Roadshow here, in this room. A real English gentleman, she'd called him.

Then along comes her good-for-nothing, long-lost husband, snapping his gold-ringed fingers, and off she goes.

'You come too, Felix. Errol says to me he have biiig house — plenty room for all the three of us.'

'I don't think so, Ruby.'

* * *

There was a sudden a sharp cry from the street. Felix sat bolt upright, listening. Kids, larking about. A moment later something was thumping against the front door. He crossed the room to the wide bay window and peered out through a chink in the dusty velour curtain. At first he thought he had been imagining things: there was nobody there. But before he turned back into the room he heard it again. This time a scrabbling, tapping sound was coming from the base of the front door. Pressing his forehead against the cold window-pane, he could make out a large dark shape. A dog? No, that was more like a knuckle rapping. And then a groan. One of those students, probably. Drunk. Outside the wrong house.

Too bad. He was off to bed now.

'Go away,' he muttered, hesitating in the dimly lit hallway.

An unmistakably human voice, 'Please, Felix. Let me in! I'm bloody freezing.'

People! Should never let them near in the first place. Deflected you from your isolation. Especially once they'd discovered your name. That gave them power to drag you down. Anchor you, like guy ropes on the basket of a hot air balloon. Strange image to pop into his head like that! Something to do with the feeling of light-headedness induced by the recent fever? An urge to soar up and away into the sky. He shuddered. A is for abseiling, B for ballooning.

It was no good. He'd have to open the door.

Cold air rushed at his face and something heavy tumbled across the threshold knocking into his legs. He stepped back as the bundle shook itself and a head emerged.

'Whoops! Didn't think you'd heard me. Sorry. Lost me key. No one in. All buggered off home for Easter. I'm Gazza.'

Felix remained silent, peering down at the young man. There seemed to be only two possibilities for the young male scalp these days — no hair at all, or long matted locks. This uninvited guest was one of the hairy variety.

'Gazza,' repeated the figure on the doormat. 'The one that brought you over some toast earlier? Look, mate, I wouldn't have bothered you only I've gone and buggered up my ankle. I was trying to climb up the drainpipe, get in my window. Sodding thing gave way, didn't it? Ouch!' he concluded as he tried to stand.

Felix bent down and helped Gazza to hobble into the sitting room and collapse onto the sofa. 'Just rest yourself a minute till I can get that boot off and have a look at the damage,' he said. 'And I should think you'd like a drink. Might be able to dig out some brandy.'

'Ta. Not sure about brandy though. Got anything else?'

Felix paused at the doorway. 'Could be a bottle or two of stout lurking in the kitchen. Possibly some sherry. Sweet. Best thing for you right now.'

★ ★ ★

So much for peace and quiet and his own company. Felix had quickly established that the ankle was more likely to be badly sprained than broken, and would come to no further harm by waiting till morning for a professional medical opinion. He had always preferred the role of listener, and very soon knew far more than he wanted to about Gazza's life experiences to date. The one that disturbed him most was Gazza's matter of fact, almost comical account of waking in hospital on New Year's Day of the previous year while large quantities of paracetemol were being pumped from his stomach. 'Fucking awful, it was. Never risk that again. Make sure I make a proper fucking job of it next time.'

It was almost midnight before Felix finally hauled himself upstairs to his room, leaving Gazza on the sofa, snoring under a pile of blankets. Between them he and Gazza had consumed a third of a bottle of the Bristol Cream he kept for Ruby's visits, (mainly Gazza, becoming nostalgic about his gran), quarter of a bottle of Highland Gold ten-year-old Malt, (mainly Felix), two bottles of Guinness, (one each) and a few sips of foul-tasting six-year-old rhubarb wine. While Felix was ceremoniously pouring the remains of that bottle into the toilet bowl in the draughty cloakroom, Gazza suddenly remembered what he had been going out for in the first place when he had left his key behind.

'Fuck me!' he yelled. 'There's a six pack of Carling on my own fucking doorstep! How the fuck could I forget that?'

So Felix had fumbled around Gazza's tiny front garden in the drizzle until his eyes had become accustomed to the semi-darkness. They drained three cans each, time enough for Gazza to hear about Felix's wife and only son — killed twenty years ago in a light aircraft accident just days before Philip's twenty-first birthday. The pilot of the said aircraft had misjudged the height of Scafell Pike in a sudden mist.

'Jeezuz fucking Christ. You poor bastard,' sobbed Gazza. 'What a miserable sodding world this is. It's a wonder you didn't top yourself.'

Felix was silent for a while. Yes, in a way it was surprising that he'd managed to carry on. Perhaps, in the aftermath of real tragedy, a person finds the inner strength to cope. It is the relentless monotony of unchanging, aimless existence that ultimately wears one down. This young man's sympathy touched him, but in a strange way it also provoked irritation. No one else had the right to shed tears for Sylvia and Philip. Partly to deflect conversation back to the present, but also because he found that he wanted to contradict Gazza's depressed outlook on life, Felix told him about the events of that Sunday morning.

When he started to explain about the Dangerous Sports Euthanasia Society, Gazza's face lit up. 'Fucking brilliant!' he exclaimed. 'Hey, Mr Punch, d'you think I could join?'

'I very much doubt it,' Felix had retorted, his irritation surging back. Mr Punch, indeed. Whatever had possessed him to let on about that old nickname? 'You're far too young,' he said firmly. He was sure Agnes had mentioned something about over sixty-fives. He'd have to check that out. Wouldn't want cocky youngsters taking that over, like everything else these days.

* * *

When Felix woke next morning, his first reaction was puzzlement at finding his room bathed in daylight. He never normally slept later than six, and at this time of year it should still be dark. He sat up, and almost cried out at the sudden stabbing pain in his head. Very slowly and carefully he lowered it back down onto the pillow and closed his eyes.

Delayed shock, after the trauma of his failed suicide attempt? A sudden brain tumour that was about to do the job for him? This thought was surprisingly distressing. Before he could work out the logic of this he remembered the events of the night before: the student, Gazza, all that drink. A hangover! He immediately felt a little stronger: this was something he could cope with.

Half an hour later he was in the kitchen, downing a glass of cold water, and wondering if he dared risk a small piece of toast. All at once there was a loud thud from the front part of the house, followed by a series of curses and groans.

Holding his head between his hands to avoid any sudden neck movements he made his way along the passage and opened the sitting room door. Gazza, swaddled in a blanket, was struggling to heave himself back onto the sofa.

'Ghhh! I feel like shit. This fucking ankle. Hardly slept a wink.'

Felix bent to help him, and winced. 'Not feeling all that well myself,' he muttered, but managed to manoeuvre the young man back onto the seat.

Gazza groaned as Felix pulled back the blanket, and the swollen ankle came into view. 'Shit. Shit. Shit. I've gone and broke the fucking thing.'

Felix took the foot in both hands and very gently ran his fingers around the joint. After a moment he said, 'I think it's just a bad sprain. Nothing to worry about. I'll run you down to the doctor's in a bit.' Seeing Gaza's anxious face he laughed. 'No. I wasn't thinking of carrying you on my back! I've got my own vehicle in the garage down the end of the garden.'

'Yeh. Ta. That's cool. It's not that though. I just remembered Saturday. I've gone and fucked up good and proper there.'

'Er, Gazza,' said Felix, clambering slowly up from the floor and then, very gently, lowering himself down onto his armchair. 'If we are to continue our acquaintance for any length of time, do you think you might do me a favour?'

'You what?'

'A favour, Gazza. Call me an old fuddy duddy, but I have to say I don't really go in for all this language.'

'Language? Oh! Got it! Sorry mate. No offence. 'Spect I just felt at home here. Forgot, like.'

'That's all right. Carry on then. Saturday? You're in some kind of predicament there?' Felix leant his head against the back of the chair and allowed his eyelids to flicker and close.

'Too right. Half the uni's sponsored me, five hundred bleeding quid, more than. Cancer research. Meant to be abseiling a hundred feet off the roof of some hospital, aren't I? Broken or sprained makes no odds. You gotta have two feet for abseiling.'

Felix jerked his head forward and immediately regretted the sudden motion. Gazza hadn't noticed the grimace of pain, and carried on talking. Most of his mates had skived off home by now. No one to step in and take over for him. Only Kez, his mate at Nottingham uni. He'd be around for a bit longer. Been planning to hitch over to visit him this week anyway.

Felix was picturing his brain as a rough, spiky landscape, obscured by swirling grey fog. Every now and then words would emerge from the fog and float across his vision, but they were too blurred for him to read clearly — ah! What was this? 'A is for abseiling.'

'I'll do it,' he declared, and would have looked around to see who had spoken, if he'd not been afraid of experiencing more pain.

'Do what?' asked Gazza.

'Abseil. I'll do the abseil for you,' said Felix. Was the boy stupid? Should've been clear enough what the words had meant. Had to make a start somewhere, didn't he? With or without Agnes.

'You mean . . . ' said Gazza, pausing between each word, 'You mean you'll do the abseil for me?'

'Yes, Gazza,' said Felix. 'That is precisely what I mean.'

'Fuck me!' exclaimed the boy, then, 'Sorry mate! I mean, well, aren't you a bit, you know, getting on, rather?'

'Old, you mean? Past it, you mean? One foot in the jolly old grave, you mean?' Felix's voice was rising in pitch and volume with every question, his headache miraculously banished. 'How many feet did you say a body needs?' he went on, stamping one foot at a time. 'Nothing wrong with these, is there? Or these?' and he raised his clenched fists.

'OK! OK!' laughed Gazza, raising an arm to shield his face in mock horror at the outburst. 'You're going to stand in for me, Saturday, right?'

'Right. Now then, my lad, better get you along to the doctor.'

'By the way, Mr Punch,' said Gazza, hobbling down the garden, hanging on to arm of the older man, 'you ever done abseiling before?'

'There's always a first time for everything,'

he answered in a level voice.

Gazza expelled his breath in a slow whistle. 'Don't get me wrong,' he said, 'about age and all that. But what I must say is, hope I've got as much bottle when I get old.'

16

'Maybe they've all popped out to the shops,' said Edie as the final melodic peal from Dianne's doorbell faded into silence.

'Maybe so,' sighed Agnes. In spite of having slept till nearly ten that morning, she felt a wave of exhaustion wash over her. She shouldn't have stayed up so late, chatting to Edie over a tumbler of strong brown ale, followed by a mug of hot milk, honey and cooking brandy. When she'd helped Edie to make up the spare bed in the little back room, her mind was still buzzing: Jack. Emmy and Sam. Lucy. Molly. Felix. It had taken her hours to fall asleep.

Felix was her main worry now. Lucy and the children were bound to be with Dianne, wherever that was. She must leave a note for Dianne, asking her to get in touch.

Agnes was wondering how she could get hold of a pen and a scrap of paper when Edie tapped her forearm and hissed, 'We're being watched.'

At the same moment a woman's voice called out from the other side of the low dividing hedge. 'If it's Dianne and Barry you're after, you're out of luck. They've been in Tenerife since a week last Wednesday. Due back today. Early evening, I think.'

If Dianne had been away for a fortnight, and Lucy and the children had disappeared only last Friday, then — ! Agnes clutched at Edie's arm.

'Don't you fret, dear,' said Edie. 'I mean, at least they're not in no danger from that Sean now, are they?'

Agnes gave her head a shake and blinked back tears. She hadn't realised till that moment quite how much she had been longing to see her grandchildren. To hold them, safe and sound, in her arms again.

★ ★ ★

As soon as she got back to Edie's Agnes strode across the hall to the phone. Her hands trembled a little as she dialled Felix's number. She'd waited till nearly eleven that morning before phoning, but there'd been no answer, and he'd sounded so ill and depressed the previous evening when she'd finally got through. What state of mind would he be in now?

Her relief at hearing him sounding more buoyant quickly turned to horror. Abseiling! Perching himself on the edge of a hundred foot drop! On the great scale of things, would the fact that she'd saved him from death on their first meeting cancel out a death caused by her impetuous storytelling? Her lies!

★　★　★

'No, dear, you mustn't think like that,' came Molly's comforting voice a few minutes later. 'It doesn't have to mean, well, you know — '

'You have to admit it's a bit too neat, though, the coincidence.'

'But you've just said he was surprisingly cheerful.'

'Well, he would be, wouldn't he? If he thought he was going to get what he wanted.'

'Death, you mean? Agnes, dear, aren't you taking things a little too far? Crossing bridges, and all that. Why don't you come back here? Now I know your Lucy's not with her own mum, I'll ask around some more of Wendy's friends.'

'I'd better wait till Dianne gets home. She's bound to know something. And I have to set my mind at rest about Felix. See if I can dissuade him from that crazy scheme.'

Agnes became aware of Edie, hesitating in her kitchen doorway. 'Look, Molly, I'll ring you later, when I've heard from Dianne.'

'You got through to your new friend, then.

Everything all right, is it?' said Edie, as Agnes put down the receiver. Her voice was a little sharp as she added, 'I'spect you'll be wanting to leave me now.'

'Only if you want to get rid of me, Edie!' laughed Agnes, noticing her tone. 'I was rather hoping you might let me stay another night.'

'So you'll not be rushing off straight away, then?'

'To be honest, Edie, if you can put up with me for a bit longer, I could do without rushing anywhere today.' Agnes put her hand to her mouth, stifling a yawn. 'If you don't mind me using your phone again, I really ought to try to speak to my son at last.'

'Time for a nice cup of tea, I think,' said Edie more cheerfully. 'I'll put the kettle on while you do that.'

Jack. She didn't have his work number. Anyway, he didn't like being disturbed there. Wednesday. Where would Monica be at this time on a Wednesday? The girls would be at school, of course. No. It was the Easter holidays. Daft, to be so reluctant to phone. What was she afraid of? They couldn't bite her!

'The person you are calling knows you are waiting.'

What a temptation to put the phone down, there and then. Twice more, that same message, and then, to her immense relief, 'Please try later.'

'Yes,' said Agnes, to the brisk recorded voice of the woman. 'I'll try later.'

Probably Hailey or Donna, chatting to one of their friends. If so, the phone could be engaged for the next hour, at least. It might well be better to drop a card in the post. No need to actually *talk* to anyone from Back There, until she had sorted out what she was going to do next. Even if she could get Jack to understand why she'd run off in the first place, how could she even begin to explain about Felix?

'Tea's up,' called Edie from the kitchen doorway.

★　★　★

Agnes had guessed wrong about which member of the household at 11, Saxon Meadow had been engaging the telephone.

'Oh Dad! Thanks for ringing back. You won't believe what I'm going through at the moment! I just had to talk to someone I can trust. Someone who really cares about me.'

'Monica, sweetheart, don't cry. What's that Jack of yours been up to? If he's laid a finger

284

on my princess — '

'It's nothing like that. But I am worried about him. He's letting this business about his mother really get to him. His case comes up next week. You know, driving over the limit. The solicitor thinks he could lose his licence. Jack says his work won't stand for that. What will I do if he loses his job? I mean, you know what a struggle it's been for me, these last few years . . . '

'I do, Princess, I do. It's just not fair, what you've had to put up with. Lucky I've got a nice little nest egg put by for a rainy day.'

'Daddy, I wouldn't dream of it! That money's for you and mum.'

'Now then, Miss, I won't have my own daughter telling me what to do with my money.'

'No, Dad. Of course it's up to you. But I'm sure we'll pull through all right. I shouldn't be disturbing you with my little worries.'

'That's what fathers are for, Princess. I know people would call me old-fashioned, but a woman shouldn't have to worry about things like that. However hard times were, I made sure your mother never wanted for a new winter coat or party frocks, and if your Jack hasn't got it in him to look after his own woman, he sure as blazes can't stop me from seeing you right.'

'Oh Daddy. I do love you!'

'I know you do, sweetheart. Now then, when are you coming up to Lincoln? Your mum was hoping you'd be bringing the girls up for Easter.'

'Yes, yes. I'm sure that'll be all right. Look, there's someone at the door. Got to dash. I'll ring you later and let you know if we can make it.'

★   ★   ★

SCENE:
A small copse near to an Old Folks' Residential Home.
TIME:
Almost four of the clock on a damp afternoon in early April on the middle day of the week.
DRAMATIS PERSONAE:
Timothy Ignatius Dolan, the talented young police constable.
Various assorted small birds and a squirrel.
ACTION:
Against the wishes of his superiors, resourceful Timothy is using his days off to pursue a difficult and possibly dangerous case involving the mysterious disappearance of an elderly lady. After a tip-off from a tragic young girl which has led him to suspect foul

play, Timothy has been scrutinising every inch of ground around the bus stop. A subdued rustling in the undergrowth has alerted him to the presence of a grey squirrel. Closer inspection reveals a narrow track through the undergrowth. Undaunted by brambles, our brave constable proceeds with caution and emerges into a small clearing surrounded by trees, the most notable of which is an ancient oak. (Its genus deduced as such from the presence of acorns and appropriately shaped leaves on the ground.)

TIMOTHY:

Oh my God! This earth has been disturbed recently. That could be a footprint. And what's that? Bloody hell, I really am on to something! Christ! There's something — down in — can't quite reach. Yesss! Oh no! God! I don't believe it! I was right all along. It's her clothes! Oh God! That poor old woman! He has! He's done her in!

This was real. Not Shakespeare, or a cops and robbers drama. Timothy Dolan suddenly felt sick.

★　★　★

Monica looked up in surprise as Jack entered the room. Home already! Before the end of *Neighbours*!

Jack, too was surprised. This was an unaccustomedly domestic scene: Monica, in the middle of the sofa, with her left arm round Hailey's shoulder, and her right around Donna's.

'Hi, Jack. Any news on Aggie?' asked Hailey. Even more of a surprise, Hailey deigning to address a civil word to him.

'Not a dicky bird,' he responded, striding down towards the cocktail bar and pouring a large whisky. 'Want one, Mona?'

'Why not?' she said, withdrawing her arms from the girls and preparing to rise. 'Nice to see you so early, Jack. Everything all right?'

'All right as it can be, in the circumstances.' He drained the glass in one gulp, spluttered, and poured another. Hailey and Donna remained in their seats, staring at the bright, neat drama reaching its cliffhanger climax. Monica reached his side and pursed her lips to receive his abstracted kiss, as he murmured, 'I don't think I can stand this much longer.'

'This what?'

'Ma, of course. What else? This waiting. Not knowing. Can't concentrate on anything at work. Might as well not be there, for all the good I'm doing right now. Still no reply from that mother of Lucy's. Must be away. So is Lucy with her? And Ma, too? God! If only I knew! That turd, Sean. Says he hasn't a clue, but he must know something about Lucy and the kids. My kids! I feel like going up there and knocking the bloody daylights out of him — '

'Calm down, Jackie, love. It's doing you no good at all, getting all worked up like this.'

'And it's Easter this weekend,' he continued, thumping his fist against the bar. 'Meant to be my Sunday for Emmy and Sam. Lucy'd better be back by then, or I'll set the law on her. Piers is already trying to get me more access rights. Something's going on in that house, I'm sure of it. Ma was worried too. If only I'd taken the time to listen!'

'Never say die, as my dad always says. Everything will turn out all right in the end, I'm sure,' soothed Monica, filling her own glass, and then reaching along the bar to pour some more into Jack's. 'And talking of my dad — '

'Thought we were talking about my mother.'

'Well, yes, of course. But what can I say? You're doing all you can for the moment, you know you are, phoning people all day long — the police, Lucy, the Home etc. It's a wonder your work aren't saying something.'

'I'm there, aren't I? And it's only every hour or so I'm calling. Using my own mobile, too. Anyway, it's a bank holiday, Friday. I've got a meeting first thing tomorrow, but I'll take the afternoon off. Go up to Nottingham.'

'Will you be staying the night, then?'

'Well, there's not much point going all that way and running back home again before I find out anything, is there?

'So you could be there for the whole weekend?'

'No. Yes! I don't know. Monica, please. I can't take any hassle right now.'

'That's all right, sweetheart. You do what you have to do. I just wanted to make sure you wouldn't mind me going to see my mum and dad for Easter. Bring the girls, too, if they'll come.'

'What's that, Mum?' called Donna from the sofa.

'Easter, love. Granny and Granddad,' said Monica, making her way back to where the girls were sitting. She was about to flop down between them when she realised that Jack had left the room.

'So you couldn't have heard anything from her, anyway,' he was saying into the telephone when she stepped into the hall. 'Mmm. You could be right. Never let me down yet over one of my days for the kids. Well, I hope you feel better soon. You've got this number if you do hear anything? I'll leave you in peace then. Bye for now.'

Jack turned towards Monica as he replaced the receiver. 'That was Lucy's mum,' he explained. 'Just back from a fortnight in the Canaries. Feeling like death warmed up, she says. Some foreign tummy bug. Not heard a word from Lucy for at least a month. Didn't seem the slightest bit worried though. 'Oh, she'll just be taking a little break. It is the Easter holidays, after all'.'

'That's one less worry then, isn't it?' said Monica brightly. 'I mean, if Lucy's own mum isn't worried, why should you be? So, what did she say about Agnes, then?'

'Didn't ask her, did I?' snapped Jack. 'I mean, if Dianne's been gone a fortnight, and only just got back, she's not exactly going to be able to tell me much about what's been going on here in the last five days, is she?'

★　★　★

Thursday morning. Her sixth day! Agnes stared at the rain pattering against the window by her bed and hugged herself, snuggling down under the quilt as she tried to identify the jumbled feelings that were drifting across the edges of awareness: anticipation — yes, it would be lovely to see

Molly again; apprehension at the thought of meeting up with Felix. She shouldn't be feeling this irritation, though. Dianne had been very abrupt on the phone the previous night, but, to be fair, she wasn't at all well. 'I've just put the phone down on Jack. Don't know why you're all making such a fuss. Lucy'll be with one of her friends.'

Nor was there any reason for the lurking guilt that she was detecting: her postcard to Jack would arrive at Saxon Meadow any time now. *Am in good health. Will be in touch again very soon. All my love.* Agnes smiled ruefully as she remembered her hesitation at that point. How should she sign herself? She'd had no occasion to write to her son since his time at university, when she'd still used the Mummy and Daddy of his boarding school days. As for Jack, he never wrote letters. Mother would look too formal, written down. Mum was not her at all. To put Agnes could seem like a denial of their relationship. She had finally scrawled a flourishing capital M followed by a squiggle and finished off with a line of three x's.

How would she define her relationship with Felix? If he kept to his word, he would be turning up on Edie's doorstep before the morning was over, and try as she might, she could not persuade herself that she was looking forward to meeting him again.

When she'd finally managed to get through to him, late on Wednesday afternoon, he had been his usual surly self. 'What's all the fuss about, woman? I'm not sitting by my phone all day, just in case you take it into your head to ring me. And no, sorry, you can't come and see me tomorrow. I shan't be here.'

Fighting the temptation to put down the phone and sever any feeling of responsibility towards him, Agnes had managed to coax from Felix the destination and purpose of his journey. This was an opportunity she could not miss. 'So you're driving the young man to see his friend in Nottingham tomorrow?'

'Do you have to repeat everything I say? Yes. *I* am the one doing the abseil on Saturday because *Gazza* has sprained his ankle. When a person is hitch-hiking, a certain amount of walking is unavoidable, so I am told. Walking with a badly sprained ankle is not conducive to a speedy recovery from said injury, so — '

'What a coincidence!' interrupted Agnes, as politely as she could. 'I'm going back to Nottingham myself tomorrow. I don't suppose . . . '

'On the scrounge for a lift, are you?'

'I, er, I wouldn't quite put it . . . '

'Trying to save on expenses? Tut, tut! No

doubt you'll be charging your head office for the train fare, anyway.' Agnes seethed inwardly. *Insufferable man!* Still, at least his interruption was allowing her a few moments of deep breathing to steady her voice. 'Well, I suppose it could be worth my while to make a little detour to pick you up on the way,' he continued. 'After all, you've still not finished telling me about that crazy society of yours, and you owe me a laugh or two yet.'

★ ★ ★

Apart from Felix's erratic driving, the journey to Nottingham was turning out far better than she'd feared. The young man, Gazza, in spite of his somewhat dishevelled appearance and occasional use of crude adjectives for which he was constantly apologising, was friendly and courteous, and seemed to have exerted a civilising influence on Felix. Whatever the reason, the Felix who appeared at Edie's front door shortly before twelve o'clock that morning was barely recognisable as the man Agnes had last seen slouching along the platform at New Street Station the previous Sunday.

He had obviously visited a barber some-time during that week: the wild mass of silver hair had been trimmed and combed back behind his ears in a distinguished fashion. The jutting chin was clean shaven. But it was the wide smile, half-delight, half-mischief, which transformed his face as he looked down at Agnes and said, 'Why! You're only a little slip of a woman, after all! Strange what tricks the memory can play — I'd have stood up in a court of law and sworn you were a good six inches taller!'

What gives people the right to comment on a person's size? thought Agnes crossly. As a child, visitors always assumed that Seb was two or three years older than her, and once they'd discovered their error, would try to 'feed her up', remorselessly plying her with extra helpings and sound advice.

'I see your manners haven't improved at all, even if your appearance is a good deal smarter,' she retorted.

'Agnes!' he exclaimed, extending his hand so suddenly that she took a step back, 'I unreservedly apologise for any offence I may have caused you. Henceforth, I shall be a model of decorum.' He shook her hand vigorously and then turned and gestured towards the green Morris Traveller, parked a few yards along the street. 'Madam, your carriage awaits.'

★ ★ ★

What a two-edged sword her rashly-invented Dangerous Sports Euthanasia Society was turning out to be. On the one hand, it had succeeded in its original purpose of injecting a strong dose of curiosity into Felix's brain — enough to stimulate at least a temporary interest in staying alive. But on the other hand, he seemed absolutely set on flinging himself over the edge of a hundred foot drop and attempting to walk like a fly down a sheer brick wall.

'Honest, he won't actually be flinging himself,' laughed Gazza, joining in the conversation from where he was sitting behind Agnes, with his leg stretched out along the back seat. 'He'll be holding on to a rope.'

'As I understand it, I'll be strapped on in some way,' put in Felix. 'They aren't going to actually put people's lives at risk when they're trying to make money for charity, are they?'

'Yeh, it's dead safe,' agreed Gazza without a trace of irony.

Agnes was sitting bolt upright, her hands clasped tightly together in her lap.

'You're not much of an advocate for your society, are you?' Felix said. 'I do what you suggest, start with the letter A as a warm-up exercise, and then you try to talk me out of it. One might be tempted to imagine that you'd — '

'It's part of our rules, er, our techniques,' blurted Agnes. 'We're supposed to test out the serious intent of potential new members.' She shrank back into her seat as she sensed a looming object darkening the space on the other side of her window. It felt as though the lorry was only a couple of inches from her left shoulder, but a moment later it had overtaken them and was speeding ahead, leaving the inside lane mercifully free.

'I'd not have thought that one could show intent more serious than I displayed on Sunday,' said Felix, seemingly unaware of other road users.

'You on about this Euthanasia thingy?' asked Gazza eagerly. 'Sounds like a fun idea. Can anyone join?'

'We-ell,' started Agnes, 'er . . . '

'Certainly not,' declared Felix. 'It is strictly limited to people over sixty-five. Isn't that right, Agnes?'

'Bloody great lorry flashing up our arse, Felix,' said Gazza in an anxious voice. 'Feels a bit on the close side from where I'm sitting.'

'Lorry drivers!' snorted Felix, pulling over to the inside lane. 'Think they own the road.'

Agnes clamped her lips, remembering how it felt to be perched up in the cab, towering above a slow-moving little Metro, or some such. She looked across at the dashboard, trying to read the speedometer.

'Almost sixty,' Felix answered the unspoken question. 'More than fast enough, by my book. Whole world's in far too much of a rush these days.'

★　★　★

Agnes felt more relaxed once Felix had settled back onto the inside lane of the motorway, cruising along at fifty and keeping a good distance from the cars ahead, so she was happy to talk to him and Gazza about Edie and Joe and Scott and the new baby. She was just beginning to wonder which parts of her other life she could disclose without compromising her story about being a Trail Blazer for the Midlands region, when they reached the junction where the M42 joined the M1. The slow moving Morris Traveller seemed to be swept along like a stick in a torrent by the rush of cars and lorries that surrounded them on all sides. Even Gazza appeared to realise that their safety depended on Felix's total concentration.

When they finally left the motorway, heading for Nottingham along the A52, Gazza turned his questioning on Felix.

'Go on, then. I heard you blabbing away to this Ruby woman while I was mopping your fevered brow. Sounded like you'd got the hots for each other real bad. So what went wrong?'

'I assure you, it was not that kind of relationship.' His voice was level, but Agnes saw a faint flush rising on his pale cheek.

'Quit the crap, man. I heard you, remember! Or are you saying you're past it, can't get it up any more?'

'Must I remind you that there's a lady present, Gazza?'

Agnes was intrigued. Might this information lead to a way of deterring Felix from the abseiling? 'Thank you, Felix,' she said sweetly. 'You certainly are a model of decorum today. And your intimate relationships are obviously your own private business, but surely you can tell us something about your friend?'

He recounted a little about his life at Chambers. How lonely he'd been all those years since the accident that killed his wife and son, then his gradually deepening friendship with the glamorous, lively West Indian woman who, unaccountably, seemed to have taken a liking to him almost as soon as she appeared in the office as yet another clerical assistant.

'We were just, comfortable together. That's all.'

'And then she went and buggered off to Tobago? Whoops, sorry Agnes. Sorry Felix. I mean, she just *went*? You didn't have a row or nothing?'

'Certainly not. Her mother was taken poorly, and then her ex-husband from God knows how long ago — eight, ten years? — Well, Errol turned up on her doorstep the day after she'd got that news, and that was it.'

'She just up and went, without a word to you?'

'Well, she did invite me to go and live there with them, but . . . '

'Live there! Wow! That sounds like some invitation! And you turned it down and you've heard nothing from her since?'

Felix coughed and reddened. 'Actually, there was a letter just this morning.'

Ah ha! thought Agnes. That explains his change of mood. 'That's nice,' she said, 'and is she well?'

'What's she say, man? Bet she's asked you again, to go out there, I mean. You gonna go, this time?'

'No.'

'You mean, no, she didn't ask? Or no, you're not going?'

'If you want me to get you to your friend's house, Gazza, you'll have to start giving me directions. And if I'm going to have to turn left or right anywhere, make sure I get plenty of warning. I've never had an accident in all my years of driving, and I don't intend to have one today.'

★ ★ ★

Now that they had reached the main student district of Nottingham, Agnes became aware of an unexpected sensation of loss. This car journey seemed to have bound the three of them together, weaving words around them like silk threads that would snap when the doors were opened.

Not that she was going to be parting with Felix just yet. He'd agreed to drive her to Molly's, and, if Molly was not fully booked up, would take a room there for the night, so that he could drive Gazza back to Birmingham the next day.

'You coming to the abseiling Saturday, Agnes?' asked Gazza as he eased himself out of the car onto the narrow road, while Felix stood awkwardly holding the door, seeming unsure of whether or not to offer help.

'If Felix is still insisting on doing it, certainly I'll be there. But I rather hope you'll manage to persuade someone of a more suitable age to stand in for you.'

'Shame on you, Agnes,' laughed Felix. 'Is this the woman who spoke out so forcefully the other day about youngsters trying to do

301

things for the good of people of our generation?'

Felix seemed oblivious of the fact that he was totally blocking the road as he said, 'You going to be OK now, Gazza? Sure you don't need a hand up those steps?'

'Don't fuss, Grandpa,' said Gazza with a grin. 'Thanks for the lift, mate. I'll ring you at that Molly's place, shall I, when I'm about ready to be picked up?'

'When is it we're due at that place for the lesson you booked me onto?'

'Oh, yeh. The abseiling. Two-thirty, that was.'

'Right, then. Leave enough time to get back home first. Say, twelve o'clock?'

'Do my best to be up by then. Right. See ya. You too, Agnes. Nice meeting you. And don't you worry about Mr Punch,' he put up one hand to shield his mouth from Felix and said in a stage whisper, 'I'll fix up someone else instead. Bound to find *someone*.'

'Over my dead body, you cheeky young cub,' growled Felix.

17

Henry had been an over-cautious driver and Jack veered wildly towards the opposite end of the scale, but Felix somehow seemed to incorporate the most irritating and the most dangerous habits of both. By the time they reached Molly's road Agnes was beginning to wonder if each decision to slam his foot down on the brake pedal or the accelerator was based on a purely random choice.

As soon as the noise of the motor had stopped, Agnes fumbled for the door handle and almost fell out onto the pavement. She clung to the side of the door for a moment until her legs felt stronger, but her head was still throbbing and her stomach was tightening itself as if gathering the energy to eject its contents up towards her throat.

'Agnes, dear! You've arrived at last! You can't imagine how relieved I am to see you. I was beginning to despair of ever setting eyes on you again — thought you might have had a last minute change of plan, or Jack had managed to track you down, or even Lucy. Still not heard sight nor sound of her, though there's a chance my Wendy might be onto

303

something. Was the traffic absolutely awful, you poor dear? Did you stop off for lunch somewhere? I had a meal all ready for you, but no matter, let me get you inside, you look done in. And this must be Felix. Glad to meet you, I'm sure, come along in, come in, do, the pair of you.' Molly put an arm round Agnes's shoulder and bustled her across the pavement and up the two stone steps to the wide front door, while Felix, looking a little shell-shocked at the exuberant greeting, locked the car doors.

'Of course there's room for you, Felix,' beamed Molly, leading them through the garish hall along a narrow passage and into the kitchen. 'Any friend of Agnes is a friend of mine. Truth to tell, business is a little quiet right now, what with it being nearly Easter and all. Now then, you've eaten, did you say? Or could I tempt you to a teensy taste of home-made soup and a nice fresh roll or two?'

Agnes collapsed onto a chair and rested her elbow on the table as she looked around the room. The enticing smell of food appeared to be coming from a large saucepan that was steaming away on the Aga. The old waiting-room clock on the wall next to the cluttered Welsh dresser said twenty-five past three. It had taken them nearly two hours to find their zig-zag way across Nottingham, stopping at petrol stations for fuel or toilets, but mostly for directions, which Felix blamed Agnes for being unable to follow.

'Soup would be lovely, Molly,' she said in a weak voice. 'And then, if you don't mind, I think I'll just have a little nap before I do anything else.'

★   ★   ★

'Felix has gone off to fetch his young friend,' Molly said, a while later, placing the cup of tea on Agnes's bedside table without allowing a drop to spill over into the saucer.

Agnes sat up in surprise. 'But I thought Gazza was meant to be staying the night there?'

'Seems like the friend he was with had to dash off — some kind of emergency, so this Gazza phoned Felix. Not ten minutes gone. Wanted to shoot off back to Brum right away, but Felix and me, we've been getting on like a house on fire while you've been off in the land of Nod. So I said, why don't you bring the lad back here and make it more of a party, like? Well, there's that big lasagne I made for lunch that didn't get touched, and apple crumble too. There's no one else stopping right now. Place has been like a morgue all week.' Molly's voice came to an abrupt halt. She turned her face away and padded across to the window.

'Really must do something about the condensation in this place,' she muttered, then turned back with a forced smile and said, 'Everything sorts itself in the end. At least I've still got my own roof over my head.'

Before Agnes could venture a tentative question, Molly was in full flow again. 'I was that worried about you dear, till you rang yesterday,' she said, lowering herself onto the pink seat of a small chair near the dressing table. 'Shame about Lucy's mum, but to be honest I was really chuffed to have you coming back. Lucy'll be with a friend. Stands to reason. I mean, I know Wendy and me are closer than most but there's plenty of things she doesn't let on to me about. Rather spill it out to friends, like. Your Lucy'll be the same.'

Agnes stood up and moved across to the washbasin. 'I was thinking along those lines myself,' she said, straightening her wig in front of the mirror, not even registering the fact that her appearance now seemed perfectly normal to her. 'In fact, I was rather hoping Wendy might have found out something.'

'Nothing concrete yet, I'm afraid. Only that she's heard of someone who knows Lucy through the college she works at. She's trying to get that address for me.'

'That's encouraging,' said Agnes slowly, and then, 'I don't suppose she's back with Sean again by now, though? I mean, that's always a possibility, isn't it?'

'Well it is, and it isn't. What I mean is, I actually popped along there to have a peep myself, yesterday.'

'Oh, Molly, how kind you are!' said Agnes, sitting back down on the bed. 'And?'

'And nothing much, I'm afraid. There's an elderly couple on the one side, and they were just getting out of their car when I walked past. Lovely little kids, they said. Better'n watching tele, seeing them play in the back garden. But they've not seen sight nor sound of them for days.'

Agnes gave a sigh and stared down at her trainers. They had lost that startling brand new whiteness. 'I'm not doing very well, am I? I've upset a whole lot of people, and what have I actually achieved? I'm no nearer to finding Emily and Sam. I'm bound to have worried my son, not to speak of the people in that Home. Goodness knows what they'll all think of me now.'

Molly laughed. 'If they've got any sense at all, they'll realise that you're well able to take care of yourself, and that Jack of yours will spend the money on a nice little flat for you instead.'

'If only things were that simple,' sighed Agnes. 'The way we seem to rub each other up the wrong way, me putting my foot in it every time I open my mouth. He'll probably have me certified as absolutely off my rocker, a danger to myself and others.'

'Over my dead body,' said Molly, folding her arms across her chest, which was enveloped this time in a bright green jumper with fat appliqué lambs grazing around her stomach.

Agnes gave a wry smile. 'That brings me to the other thing I feel bad about. Felix. The abseiling.'

'Stuff and nonsense,' said Molly. 'Now I've met him for myself, I have to say he doesn't look in the least suicidal to me. So you ought to be congratulating yourself on your wonderful invention. Didn't I tell you your Dangerous Sports Society's taken on a life of its own?'

★ ★ ★

Rex Harrison's gravelly voice growled from the speakers on the sideboard in Molly's dining room, complaining that women were not like men.

'My sentiments entirely,' exclaimed Felix to Gazza.

'Apple crumble coming up,' said Molly, nudging a bowl across the wide oak table towards Agnes. Ignoring Felix, she gave an exaggerated sigh. 'I absolutely adored that film, didn't you? That Audrey Hepburn. So dainty. That lovely warm smile of hers.'

'Never smiled in real life, you know,' said Felix. 'Thought it would give her wrinkles.'

'What would you know about it?' scoffed Molly. 'Ten to one you never even saw *My Fair Lady*.'

'Matter of fact it was one of Ruby's favourites,' he retorted.

'Ruby!' exclaimed Molly, sensing a diversion. 'Who's Ruby?'

'Felix's girlfriend,' said Gazza, delighted at the chance to probe Felix further. 'Come on mate, you were going to tell us why you're still not accepting her invitation.'

'I'm all ears,' said Molly, spooning crumble into a bowl and passing it to Felix. 'The truth, now, Felix.'

'Yeh, the truth,' chipped in Gazza. 'Truth and Lies. That'd a be a good game for us.'

'Is that the sort of thing students amuse themselves with these days?' asked Felix. 'I thought they spent all their time in front of the television.'

'Don't try changing the subject now, Felix,' laughed Molly. 'Truth and Lies sounds like fun.'

'Come on, Felix. Spill the beans about Ruby. It's up to us to work out what's true and what's not.'

Felix hesitated, leaning forward over his bowl, spoon poised midway to his mouth. Agnes recognised that look of indecision — the desire for secrecy battling with an impulse to confide. Perhaps if he could be encouraged to really open up to this strange little group she could find a way of deterring him from his dangerous venture.

'What if we all go upstairs to Molly's cosy sitting room when we've cleared away the meal?' she suggested. 'I could do with snuggling down into an easy chair with a little sip more of this nice wine.'

★ ★ ★

'I don't know what you're all getting so excited about,' said Felix, leaning back in the armchair by Molly's gas fire and crossing one leg over the other. 'The truth about Ruby can't be the least bit of interest to anyone, and I don't see any point in telling lies.'

Gazza opened another can of beer. 'Cheers, all!' he said, raising it to his lips. 'Felix, you've been like a dog with two tails ever since you got that letter this morning. So go on, then. What's she said?'

'Only that her mother finally died last week after a long illness. That was one of the reasons she went back there in the first place.'

'And? What else did she say?' pressed Gazza.

'Nothing else. Apart from a friendly enquiry about my health. I did warn you it wasn't going to be very interesting. Over to you now, Gazza. Better still, what about you, Agnes? You owe me, don't you?'

Before Agnes could draw a breath and collect her thoughts, Gazza was shouting in triumph, 'Liar! Liar! You've got it coming now, Felix.'

'Gazza!' murmured Agnes, reaching across the sofa and lightly touching his arm. 'Isn't that taking things a little bit too far?'

''S'all right, Agnes. It's the rules, see. If one player doesn't believe the storyteller, then that person has to do a forfeit.'

Felix uncrossed his legs and picked up his wine glass from the low table, 'No need to get so worked up, lad,' he said. 'If you really want to be bored by the details, I'll give you the whole letter.'

He drained his glass in two large gulps and placed it on the table. Then he stretched out his right leg in front of him and reaching deep into his trouser pocket, drew out a folded envelope.

Agnes held her breath. Molly stared, eyes wide. Gazza frowned, and the tip of his tongue appeared at the corner of his mouth.

Felix looked at each of them in turn, as if relishing his moment of drama, then rummaged in his other pocket for a brown spectacle case, perched the half-moon glasses on his nose, cleared his throat and began, '*My dear Felix. My friend.*'

'Sounds promising,' murmured Gazza.

Felix coughed and began again, '*My Friend. I have to tell you that my beloved mother passed away on Sunday last. It is hard for me to speak of this, even though she is now at peace. Praise to God, in her last days she did not suffer pain the way she suffered all the time I was here.*'

He paused, and looked defiantly across at Gazza. 'There you are. As I told you, the main purpose of her letter was to let me know that her mother has died. At a time like that, women can say things they don't really mean.' He started folding the letter as if to put it away, and Agnes felt it would be too much of an intrusion to ask him to read any more.

Gazza displayed no such inhibitions. 'Hey,

man. Fair's fair. You can't go back on your word now.'

'I thought I might be boring you, that's all,' declared Felix. 'I wouldn't dream of disappointing anyone.' He unfolded the letter again and continued his reading. This time, it seemed to Agnes, his voice was lighter, taking on a hint of a sing-song lilt as he read:

'*I think of you often and often, so far away in England. Many a time I dream and it is not a good dream. I see you in the coffin, white as white and when I wake I think you dead. How is it that a mere dream can make me sad all through the day?*

'*Felix, I wonder what you do each day. I think maybe you have a new friend now? Here in Tobago there is no big art gallery but every turn in the road reveals to me a beautiful picture. You will not believe the colour of the sea.*

'*It is hard for me now. I have friends but I am much alone. Errol, he has no badness in his heart but he is more like a son to me than husband — restless all the time, not settling. Now he is in Trinidad. He has business there, and, I think, a woman also. He gave this house for me to live in. Maybe I will make a little business here — sell smart clothes to tourists.*

'*Will I return to England again? What can I*

313

do in that cold place? Here it is bright sun and sky so blue you would not think it possible. At six o'clock the day goes and the night rushes in as black as black, holding a million, billion stars like a great, glittering cloak. I think you will like to see this, Felix. Must you make a proud woman beg you to visit her? I know you to be proud but you are a kind man also. I have money from my dear mother — plenty enough to send you the plane ticket.

'Will you come?

'Your ever loving friend, Ruby.'

The hushed silence that followed was finally disrupted by a loud sniff from Molly, 'That's the most beautiful letter I've ever heard,' she quavered.

Agnes could not trust herself to utter a word, and was relieved when the spell was broken by Gazza as he gave a delighted laugh and exclaimed loudly, 'Jeezuz fucking Christ, Felix!' then clapped his hand to his mouth, muttering, 'Oh fuck! Swearing again! What I mean is, bloody hell, Felix. What you playing at, man? Catch me hanging around if I got a letter like that! I'd be away on the next plane out of here, no messing.'

Felix looked bemused, almost as though he'd not taken in the contents until he had

314

heard himself reading the words aloud. His mouth seemed unable to decide whether it wanted to smile or not.

'It sounds to me as though Ruby is very fond of you, Felix,' said Agnes. 'And what a lovely turn of phrase she has.'

'Ooh, you lucky man! I've always fancied the Caribbean,' said Molly. 'Never got further than Paris, me. Honeymoon, that was. My Pat's one romantic gesture. Or would've been, if he hadn't drunk himself silly on the ferry over and sicked up on my new outfit. Never been in a plane, neither. Not like my Wendy and her kids. Florida, it was, last year, when the divorce went through. Kids think no more of it than a coach trip to Blackpool these days, do they?'

'So when you going, then, Mr Punch?' asked Gazza, detaching another can of beer from the pack. 'That Ruby's all but asked you to set up a business with her. And who knows what else, hey?'

'Hold your horses, Gazza. I've been invited out there for a holiday. Nothing more than that.'

'Oh, pull the other one, man. 'I am wondering what you do all day, Felix, Have you got a new girl-friend yet?' And all that poetic stuff about the stars. It's on a plate for you, hot and steaming.'

'Your game is getting out of hand now,' snapped Felix.

'OK. That's cool. Someone else's turn now.' Gazza took a gulp of beer and let his eyes rest on Agnes. 'I guess Felix and me both want to hear about this Dangerous Sports Club of yours, Agnes.'

Felix relaxed into his chair, stretching his legs and resting his elbows on the broad arms, 'Got it in one, lad. Your turn, Agnes.'

'You really want the truth?'

'I don't think they do, dear,' said Molly.

'Truth! Truth! Truth or forfeit!' chanted Gazza.

'Very well then,' said Agnes, drawing her feet together and leaning forward a little, palms on her knees. 'For one thing, you've got the name wrong, Gazza. It's Society not Club. But in fact you are at liberty to call it what you choose, because the truth is, it's a lie.'

Gazza raised his eyebrows and let out his breath in a slow whistle. 'You played this game before, Agnes?' he asked. 'That's one of the advanced manoeuvres, that is, double-bluffing.'

'No, I haven't played it before. And no, I'm not bluffing. Tell them, Molly.'

'Well. Actually, it's not that easy, really,' faltered Molly.

'You're an absolute natural, Agnes. Double bluff, followed by a counter call. Classic stuff!'

'Gazza, dear,' said Agnes, 'game or no game, it really is time for me to tell the truth.'

At her solemn tone, the others fell silent. Agnes fixed her gaze on Felix. 'You have no idea what a relief it will be for me to tell you the whole story. I hope you won't mind hearing it again, Molly?'

'I'd love to,' she said with a smile.

'Very well, then,' said Agnes, and plunged straight into her account of the moment when she'd first suspected that Felix was intending to fling himself under a train.

Gazza managed to stifle his exclamations, limiting himself to gasps, and the occasional muttered aside. Felix looked grim as Agnes described the way her invention had unfolded bit by bit, as though it was telling itself.

'Making a fool of me, weren't you?' he growled, but Agnes carried on, weaving her way back to the moment of her escape from the Harmony Home, and then to a brief account of life at Saxon Meadow after Henry's death.

'So that's a wig you've got on, is it?' said Gazza, as Agnes came to a halt. 'That's great, that is. And the cap. I'd love to see your son's face when he catches sight of you in this gear.

Still an' all, it's a bit disappointing, your society. I was all set to join it myself!'

'Too young, I've told you. Anyway, plenty of stuff for the young already. This is for the over sixty-fives,' said Felix.

'Over sixties, you mean,' said Molly. 'You're not keeping me out. The way I've been feeling recently, it's just what I need.'

'What's up?' asked Gazza in concern. 'You seem so — y'know, such a *jolly* person. Jolly Molly, in fact!'

'You're not the first to call me that,' she laughed. 'Though I do have to put some effort into it sometimes. That's why I like the idea of Agnes's Society. Bit of a challenge when you're feeling down, does you the world of good.'

'It's not supposed to be fun and games, you know,' said Felix. 'It's deadly serious.'

Agnes had been listening in bewilderment. At last she burst out, 'But you're all talking about it as if it's real! Don't any of you understand? It's a total lie. I made the whole thing up, from start to finish.'

'It's too late, Agnes. It's not up to you to say if it's real or not,' said Felix.

'Molly?' Agnes turned to her friend. 'Tell Felix, please. It doesn't exist. It never has and never will. And he doesn't have to risk his life with this abseiling nonsense.'

318

Molly hesitated, looking at Felix's determined expression, and then at Agnes's equally determined face. 'I'm sorry, Agnes. I know it's an invention, but it served its purpose with Felix. I mean, just look at him — got back the will to live, hasn't he? He'll soon be winging his way across the sea to meet up with Ruby.'

'Molly, I don't wish to be rude, but you don't understand. I still intend to exit life in my own way, at my own time. Like it or not, Agnes has given me the idea of exploring more novel means to that end. I admit, it's been rather a disappointment, discovering that the infrastructure is not yet in place, but — '

Gazza could contain himself no longer. 'Too right, Felix. And that's where I come in. I've got lots of contacts in all sorts of dangerous sports. There's clubs for just about everything at uni. I think you'll find me very useful.'

'Hmm. Well. We'll see. As for me and Ruby, that's really nobody's business but mine.'

'Truth, truth, truth or forfeit,' giggled Molly.

'I've finished my turn. All I'll say is, I'm not flying out there, and that's that,' he growled, then he cleared his throat and said, almost apologetically, 'What about you, Molly? What is it that's been making you feel low?'

'Oh, me! You don't want to hear about me. It's nothing, really.'

Agnes looked at Molly in silence, confident that Gazza would drag her story from her. Sure enough, he said, 'Sorry, Molly. 'Nothing, really' is not allowed. Come on, spit it out. What's been bothering you?'

Molly sighed, and her chins quivered a little. At last she said, making a wide gesture with her right hand. 'I love this place. It's kept me going, hustle and bustle, day and night. My customers — travelling gentlemen, mostly — they've been more like friends over the years, but now . . . ' She felt in her sleeve for a handkerchief and dabbed at her eyes with the little piece of mauve, lace-edged cotton.

'Go on,' prompted Felix in a tone of surprising gentleness. 'Now?'

'Ever since the summer, business has been going down and down. It's always quiet over the Christmas, but it usually picks up again, after. Not this year, though. Ones and twos still, and April already. Don't know how much longer I can keep it going. It'll break my heart to sell this place.'

'Have to diversify,' said Felix, 'find a new client base. Advertise in the right magazines, and so on.'

'Different sort of customer? Well, yes. But who? What sorts of people want to stay in small hotels these days? Except on holiday. And you need something like the seaside or moors and mountains for that.'

'Oh, I dunno,' said Gazza. 'There's that cool water sports centre near here, isn't there? Holmepierpoint? I guess windsurfing could be classed as a dangerous sport, at a stretch. Specially if you tried to cross the Channel. People have to learn in the first place, don't they?'

'What are you rambling on about, Gazza? We've moved on from Agnes's society, in case you hadn't noticed. We're trying to solve Molly's problem for her.'

'I wasn't ignoring you, Molly,' said Gazza with a grin. 'It's just, well, my Nan used to say, set one problem to solve another.'

Agnes was staring straight ahead, a smile slowly lighting up her face. 'You mean, if two or three people have problems they need to solve, they can weave them all into the one story, and somehow, an answer — *finds* itself?'

'You've got it, Agnes!' said Gazza.

'Are you all right, Agnes, dear?' asked Molly.

Felix said impatiently, 'Got what, Agnes?'

'Got the answer. Several answers,' she

replied serenely. 'At least, I think I have. But I've learned my lesson about jumping in too quickly. I'll need to sleep on it. If it still seems to make some kind of sense, I can tell you all about it at breakfast.'

'And if not?' asked Gazza.

'If not, as is more likely, she can tell us anyway. It's good to start the day off with a laugh,' said Felix.

18

Thursday was fast becoming the worst day in Jack's entire life — up there in black letters alongside his first day at boarding school and the day Lucy told him she was leaving.

It wasn't so much having Piers phone him at the office to inform him the police were pressing charges of drink-driving and his case was coming up next week straight after the bank holiday and, 'be prepared to lose your licence, old chap,' though Piers would do his jolly old utmost to plead extenuating circumstances because of his mother's strange disappearance, 'though on second thoughts, perhaps the least said about that the better.'

Nor was it the fact that Jack's phone was on the wrong switch at the time, so bloody Stenlack, who was in the office with him at that very moment snooping for info. about the Matlock account, was able to sit there smirking, listening to every word.

It wasn't even those coppers turning up an hour later and asking to see him because someone had found a carrier bag stuffed into a hole in a tree, and that bag contained the clothes his mother was wearing when she'd disappeared, and would Mr Borrowdale mind accompanying them to the station, to help with their enquiries? Nor was it the prickling feeling between his shoulder blades as he was virtually marched from the premises.

It was the way his guts turned to pulp when he saw the clothes. 'Recognise these, then, do you?'

Jack was slouched in the interview room with Piers at his side, opposite the two coppers, the older one stern but kindly, the younger, self-righteous one, glaring at him, baby-blue eyes nearly popping out of his head as he shook out the contents of the carrier onto the table.

The faint smell of her lavender soap when he held the soft, stubbly tweed of the jacket against his cheek! Eleven years old. 'Don't leave me here, Mummy. Don't leave me.'

With the logic of dreams, he was also the father, depositing a troublesome child in the pink-carpeted bedroom of an old people's home. As he burrowed his nose into the smooth jacket lining, breathing in the scent of her, Jack saw her face in a way he'd not let himself see it at the time: the jaw clamped tight, mouth immobile, eyes dark with — fear, was it? Or pleading? A moment later, she'd lowered the lids and opened them again to reveal — nothing. Then she'd turned towards the window, saying brightly, 'You'd better be getting along now Jack, before the traffic starts building up on the A23.'

'What've I done? What have I done?' The words seemed to be wrenched from somewhere deep inside him. He'd hardly been aware of speaking them aloud until the younger one smirked,

'Perhaps you'd like to tell us that, Mr Borrowdale.'

As Jack stared blindly at the clothing on the table, he was only peripherally aware of their voices: never, in all his life until this moment, had he ever stopped to wonder about what Ma herself might have suffered at that separation from her beloved child. Yes, beloved. She had loved him, once.

This time, Jack felt no relief when he was finally allowed to stagger out of the police station and into his own car. What did it matter if they did suspect him of foul play, hadn't charged him with anything yet because they were building up their case? That was kids' stuff, compared with the torture he was inflicting on himself: lurid pictures of his mother, huddled in a torn and dirty blanket, shivering with cold and terror in the dark cellar of a deserted house — worse still, her naked, mutilated, lifeless body.

'Utter nonsense,' Piers had attempted to reassure him. 'You heard what they said, too much of a coincidence, your ex-wife vanishing at the same time. Trust me, Jack, they'll be safe together somewhere.'

★ ★ ★

Monica took a similar line, once he had managed to spill out the whole story. That had taken a while. It was a good twenty minutes and several whiskies before he'd been able to speak coherently enough for her to understand what had happened.

'You mean, all her clothes? And her handbag? In a tree?'

'Everything. The skirt and jacket, thick tights. Shoes. Shoved into a hole in a tree near the bus stop. And nothing missing from her room.'

'Must've changed into other clothes. Deliberately run away.' She stared at his stricken face as he slowly shook his head. 'Jackie, you can't really think she's been . . .'

'I don't know. I just don't know. I tell you this, if she is alive, if she's OK, I'll never let her out of my sight again. I don't care what you think. She's my mother and I love her and I'm going to . . . I'm going to . . . ' He raised both hands to his mouth, stifling the gulped sob.

Monica was patting him awkwardly on the shoulder when Hailey came into the room. She took one look at the two figures on the sofa and stopped in her tracks.

'Jack's been at the police station,' Monica said carefully. 'Agnes's clothes have been found and Jack thinks the police think he's . . . '

'Omygod! Oh Jack, that's awful!' A moment later Hailey was kneeling on the sofa on Jack's other side, and had flung her arms around his neck, sobbing into the lapel of his dark grey suit.

Jack's hand hovered just above her right shoulder blade. With the caution he might have used on a sleeping tiger or a newborn baby, he lowered his open palm onto the cerise cotton sweat shirt and gave it a few tentative pats before wriggling a little in his seat and reaching into his pocket for a handkerchief. 'Come on now, Hailey. Your mum only said some clothes have been found. You know Agnes — always got a trick or two up her sleeve. I'm sure she's alive and well and causing mayhem somewhere.'

Hailey raised her head, sniffing loudly, and accepted the handkerchief. 'You think she's OK then?'

'Sure of it,' he said, and was surprised to find that he half believed his own words. 'I expect she was finding the regime in that place was cramping her style. She'll have taken herself off somewhere with Lucy, or be visiting an old friend. Turn up right as rain any time now.'

'Yeh. I reckon. Can't blame her, can you? I mean, must've been a bit boring in there, cooped up with all those sad old bags. Isn't that right, Donna?' she added as her sister entered the room.

'You what?' said Donna, flopping down into the armchair near the log gas fire. When Monica, with several interruptions from Hailey, had filled her in on the latest news, Donna asked, 'So what're you going to do now, Jack?'

'Do! Not much he can do, is there?' said Monica.

'You've got to do something!' burst out Hailey. 'I mean, poor Aggie!'

'Hailey, dear, you've just agreed with Jack. She's obviously planned this well in advance. Lucy could have driven down with a change of clothes and — '

'But we can't be sure, can we?' persisted Hailey.

' 'S'right,' put in Donna. 'You'd think she'd have rung you, at least. I mean, grown-ups don't just go off and not even leave a message, do they? Not ones like Aggie. Not real grown-ups.'

Hailey gulped and put her hand to her mouth. Monica leant across Jack's lap to pat her wrist. 'Don't look so worried, sweetheart. Everything's going to be just fine. I think we're all letting ourselves get a little panicky now, and I'm sure there's no need.'

'Hailey, I do appreciate your concern, and yours, Donna,' said Jack warmly.

'We're all concerned, Jackie darling,' interrupted Monica. 'I hope you don't think I'm not, just because — '

'I can't drive anywhere this evening, not with what I've had to drink,' continued Jack 'But first thing tomorrow I'll be off to Nottingham, I'll leave no stone unturned. I'll . . . '

'Of course, if you think that's best. But mightn't it be better to stay here, in case she does ring, or just turns up. Or if the police . . . '

'We'll be here, though, won't we, Dons?'

'But we're all going to Lincoln tomorrow,' exclaimed Monica. 'You both said you'd come. Granny and Granddad haven't seen you for ages and they're so looking forward — '

'You're not still going, Mum?' Donna

sounded shocked. 'Not with all this?'

Monica gave a weak laugh, and then a little cough, 'If Jack really thinks I should stay here while he chases off to Nottingham to find Lucy and, er, Agnes, then no, of course I won't go. I'm as concerned as you are about Agnes. It's just, well, Lucy has always kept to the arrangement for your Sundays, Jack, hasn't she? If she's not intending to be there I'm sure she'll let you know.'

'What's that got to do with it?' demanded Hailey. 'It's Aggie we're talking about, not Lucy. And I'm not leaving this house till we hear something.'

Monica gave a long sigh. 'No one seems to understand what I'm trying to say,' she protested. 'I care very deeply about Agnes. I always did my best for her, when you two weren't exactly showing much interest. Not that I blamed you in any way,' she added, seeing Donna open her mouth to speak. 'But still, I really believe Agnes is safe with Lucy somewhere. They'll both be back in Nottingham before Sunday, and if the ansaphone's left on, Jack can check it from where he is and . . .'

'You're probably right, Monica,' said Jack. His voice was flat and tired. 'But still, I need to go and tackle that Sean face to face. If I get no joy from him, or from the neighbours then

I'll go and see Lucy's mum. She did say she'll phone if she hears anything, and Lucy's bound to get in touch with her sooner or later. One thing's for sure, I can't just sit around here all weekend.'

Monica sighed again, then she withdrew her hand from Jack's thigh and rose to her feet.

'What you doing, Mum?' asked Hailey.

'I'm going to phone Dad and ask him to break the news gently to Mum for me.' She gave a little sniff and patted her finger tips at the corner of each eye. 'She'll have been shopping and baking all day, knowing her. She always does, especially when you girls are coming too.'

'Of course you must go,' said Jack wearily. 'No point in upsetting your parents.'

''S'orright, Jack,' put in Hailey. 'I'll be here, I told you. It'd be just too awful if she turned up on the door step and no one — '

'I'm not having you staying in the house on your own, young lady,' said Monica firmly, adding in a gentler tone, 'It's very sweet of you, darling, but you heard what Jack said. And really, apart from disappointing Granny and Granddad, I just wouldn't have a moment's peace, thinking of you here, alone.'

'She won't be alone,' said Donna. 'Sorry, Mum. And I'm sorry about Gran an' all. But

I agree with Hailey. I'm staying put till we get some news.'

'I need a drink,' quavered Monica, turning towards the bar. 'Want another whisky, Jack?'

Jack was gazing with half-open mouth from Donna to Hailey. 'What was that, Monica?' he said, then, 'No, thanks. I've had enough for the moment. Be better off with a cup of tea.'

'What you gawping at me like that for, Haize?' said Donna. 'If you don't want to be here with me, you can go off with Mum now, can't you?'

Hailey bit her lower lip to stop it trembling. 'No. I mean, yes, I do want to be here. It's just . . . like, thanks, Dons. That's all. Thanks.' Then, as Jack drew his feet together, preparing to stand, Hailey jumped up and said, ' 'S'orright. I'll make you a cuppa, Jack.'

Later that night, Jack lay awake in the dark listening to the ragged whistling sound of Monica's exhaled breaths. His thoughts felt as jumbled as the Saturday morning washing swirling and tumbling against the circular glass door. The way Hailey and Donna . . . What a surprise that had been! Made him feel quite ashamed of his past impatience. Ma. Ma. Where are you? Please God! Please God pleasegod pleasegod pleasegod. Yes, of course she would be OK. Monica was right, and she'd be even more anxious to do right by her own parents wouldn't she, in the circumstances? Didn't mean at all that she didn't care. Yes, she was right, someone had to keep a steady head. No good to him if she panicked too. No, and hadn't she just shown yet again and oh so *mmm* how much she did care for him so why this feeling of self-disgust immediately after?

★   ★   ★

Timothy Dolan enjoyed a good night's sleep as much as the next man, but periods of wakefulness never bothered him too much either. He could replay his day-time dramas over and over behind his flickering eyelids. Director, Producer and Star, he could cut out anything that was less than flattering — zoom in, close up, on the best bits.

That Jack Borrowdale, his face when he saw his poor mother's clothes. Guilty as hell. Not a shred of doubt.

Then they went and let him go! After all his brilliant detective work. That solicitor was a right crook coming up with that story about the ex-wife. Had to wonder if his Sarge wasn't bent too. 'Look lad, I admit you done well enough finding that stuff, but you can lay off now, right? There's ways of keeping a quiet eye, and we'll be doing that, thank you. If the old girl doesn't like being stuck in a Home — wants to sneak off with her daughter-in-law — that's her business. Anyways, it's none of yours, that's for sure.'

Well, they didn't know what he knew about Mr Jack Borrowdale. All that would come out later. In court. The girl, Hailey, she'd tell them all soon enough what type of a man he really was.

More than one way of skinning a cat. Get Mum to phone in, first thing. Been sick all night, or whatever. Park down the road from that pervert's house. He'd never notice the red Ford Fiesta, tailing him wherever he went.

★   ★   ★

'Lazy bastard. Nearly half one and not even up yet,' muttered Jack, removing his forefinger from the brass bell button. Either that, or Sean had gone away, leaving all the curtains drawn.

Jack wasn't going to give up at the first hurdle. He hadn't driven all this way through torrential rain and Easter holiday traffic for the fun of it. Managed to get round the M25 OK even though he'd overslept and not got away till gone nine, but the M1 had been a nightmare: the usual lines of superfluous traffic cones, miles-long jams, flashing police lights around heaps of crumpled metal skewed onto the hard shoulder, and no wonder, in this god-awful weather, road surface like a sodding swimming pool.

When he finally drew up at the curb outside Lucy's, he sat for a while with the engine still running and the wipers going whirrr-slosh, whirrr-slosh pushing back the sheets of water streaming down the wind-screen. These days, water on glass would often spirit him back twelve years to that first meeting with Lucy. Brighton seafront in pouring rain like this. Would they still be together now if it hadn't been for that bastard? And Ma . . . There'd have been plenty of room for Ma in the Lewes house, with Emily and Sam. Lucy wouldn't have minded at all.

Couldn't sit here all day! He switched off the ignition, reached over to the back seat and pulled his raincoat towards him. It was tented over his head as he fumbled with the latch on the gates and splashed across the driveway and along the path to the porch.

Jack was about to venture out into the rain again and scurry round to the back of the house for more clues when the door suddenly opened. At first he didn't recognise the man standing there in grubby teeshirt and jeans, with bare feet and dirt-encrusted toenails.

'You? Jack? What the hell d'you want?' came Sean's voice from the cracked lips of the stranger. One eye was bloodshot, and there were dark rings under both. Two days of stubble covered the lower half of his face. His formerly thick black curls that had made him look ridiculously and unfairly youthful were now more like matted vegetation from the bottom of a compost heap. Jack wrinkled his nose as he took an involuntary step back from the threshold.

The hostile phrases that he'd been refining and rehearsing during the worst of the traffic jams simply vanished. 'You er, you all right, mate?' was the only possible thing to say.

Which was how he found himself sitting at the littered table in his ex-wife's partner's breakfast room while the ex-wife's partner was fumbling around the galley-kitchen, making them each a mug of strong black coffee.

'Sorry, no milk. Touch of flu — not been out for a coupla days,' muttered Sean after a brief fit of coughing, as Jack pushed aside cereal boxes, half-empty baked beans tins and heaps of dirty crockery to make a space on the table. 'We could go in the other room if y'like,' continued Sean, as if only now becoming aware of the mess.

'Might be more comfortable,' agreed Jack.

His relief was short lived: more dirty crockery, empty beer cans and assorted items of crumpled clothing were strewn all over the sitting room. Still, at least he could choose a more comfortable chair, and one that kept a great distance between them.

It was patently obvious that his mother was not here, and Jack didn't need Sean to tell him that Lucy and the children hadn't set foot in the house for several days.

'Left a week ago,' confirmed Sean morosely. There was a long silence as he stared down into the mug, clasped in both hands on his lap.

'You mean — *left* left? Not just away for a bit?' asked Jack at last, bemused by the sudden flow of fellow-feeling for the man he'd hated so vigorously these last two years.

'Left me. Gone. Scarpered. Well, she did say it was just to give her thinking time, but I'm not blind. Writing on the wall in foot-high letters. Thought she'd gone back to you, matter of fact.'

'Me!' Jack's head was reeling.

'Well, not in that way, perhaps. But back down south, any road. Let the kids be near their dad, like.'

'But, I thought — I mean, she's never

seemed that bothered. Thought you'd stepped into my shoes with them as well. First my wife, then my kids.' Anger surged back again, 'I could've fucking killed you, what you've done to us all, and looks like you couldn't even get that right.'

If they'd both been standing at that moment, Jack's fist would have smashed itself against Sean's unshaven jaw. The deep armchair and the full mug held in his right hand caused enough of a pause to curb the full force of the impulse. Instead, it was words that exploded from him. 'So what the fuck've you been up to? If you've laid a finger on — '

'Steady on, man,' Sean's laugh betrayed his nervousness. 'It's not like that at all. I'm an easy-going guy. Bit too easy, have to admit. Fact is, well, women seem to like me. You know how it is.'

'You been cheating on her, you bastard, after all she's given up for you?'

'Oh, come on! You're not so squeaky clean. Had your own bit of totty lined up and ready, didn't you? I only — '

Jack's voice was smooth as a knife. 'I may not have been the perfect husband. Might have let my eyes wander occasionally. Only natural. But I never *did* anything. Not once in ten years. But you, you slime-ball!'

'Perfect husband! *Not!* There's more to it

than keeping your dick on a leash, y'know. I worshipped Lucy. Did everything for her, and the kids. Some nights we'd be awake till two in the morning, Luce an me, just *talking*. Conversations. That's what women really want. How often did *you* listen to *her?* Really listen.'

I don't need to sit here and take this, thought Jack, But he couldn't just get up and walk out yet. 'So what exactly did she say when she left? Where *is* she?'

'Cut a long story short, I honestly don't know. There was this supply teacher at school. Just a quick fling. Lucy found out. I get back late from work Friday, and there's this note and half her clothes gone.' Sean leant forwards and shifted a couple of plates from a heap of papers. After rummaging through them he extracted a folded sheet. Jack stood up and with one stride bent down to take it from Sean's hand, then walked over towards the French window where the rain was still lashing down, obscuring the view of the small garden.

Would those blotches on the page be Lucy's tears, or Sean's?

Darling Sean, Darling! That didn't sound very final. *I'm going away for a bit. I think I still love you, but it's becoming just too painful, not being able to trust you, not* knowing who you're with when you're supposedly working late. In fact I'm not sure if I really know what love means any more, if it exists at all, outside the 'in-love' bit. I need some time away from you to think things through. I've got to regain some kind of control over myself. And that's another thing I'm not sure about any more, the kind of person I seem to be turning into, a horrid nagging suspicious wimp. And where have you disappeared to, Sean? We seem to do nothing but row these days. That's no good for either of us, and it's certainly not good for Emily and Sam. I hate doing this, but I've got to.

I can't let you get in touch with me till I've sorted my head out. I might be back for Easter Sunday. That's Jack's day with Emmy and Sam. At the moment it doesn't feel very likely, but I honestly have no idea how I'll be feeling by then. Don't worry about Jack (as if you would!) I'll let him know about Easter as soon as I know myself.

Take care of yourself, Sean. Please try to understand. I love you.

Lucy.

Jack read the letter through again, almost guiltily. Eavesdroppers hear no good of themselves. All that powerful emotion, love and regret, was directed at the sorry looking figure slumped on the sofa.

Lucy had barely mentioned his name. The short reference at the end had made him sound like a mere acquaintance. It caused a sharp pang, seeing himself as the irrelevant third party, even though he'd accepted the situation more than a year ago. His new life was with Monica. There was nothing between him and Lucy but the children. So where were they? And where was Ma?

Jack perched himself on the arm of the sofa and stared at the brown carpet. Those creatures were fluttering in his stomach again. Lucy's letter had the stamp of truth on every line. She was entirely focussed on her own problems. There was no hint of any plot to team up with Ma. If Lucy wasn't staying with her own mother, she'd be with one of her women friends. So where was Ma? Who was looking after Ma? Or *not* looking after —

'See what I mean?' Sean's voice made him jump. Lucy was OK, even if she was a bit cut up, and she'd be getting in touch with him. He'd be seeing the children on Sunday, as planned. All his fears now had just the one focus, and it was overwhelming.

'About Lucy,' continued Sean. 'Sounds like she's already made her mind up, doesn't it?'

'What? Oh, yes. Does sound a bit dodgy. But still, you never know with women. Maybe she just needed a break.'

'You really think so,' Sean enquired eagerly. 'You think she'll come back?'

Humour him, thought Jack. Move him on a bit. 'Yeh, could well do. But she'll walk straight out the door again if she sees this mess!'

'Right. Yes! I was about to make a start on it. Oh my God! It is in a state isn't it?' Sean glanced around the room and sprang to his feet, as though he'd had a dose of adrenalin injected into his veins. 'Better get cracking then.'

'Er, there is just one more thing, Sean,' began Jack.

Sean straightened up from gathering socks and teeshirts from the carpet. 'What's that then?'

'You know I was up here on Sunday evening?'

'Were you?'

'You remember! You told me then that Lucy was away with a friend for the weekend.'

'Oh yeh. Sorry! Everything's been a bit of a blur since then. Something about your mother, wasn't it?'

Jack filled him in on the story, and without much hope of any answer he finished off, 'Don't suppose you've heard anything at all from her? No phone calls asking for Lucy? Nothing of that sort?'

Sean thought for a minute. 'She has been phoning recently. Quite a few times over the last few weeks. Tell the truth it bugged me rather. Felt it unsettled Luce, having too much contact with down south. I suppose they've not gone off somewhere together?'

'That's what I was hoping. Look, I'd better be going now. But if you do hear anything at all d'you think you could give me a ring? Here's my mobile number.' Jack took a pen from his pocket and scribbled on the back of Lucy's letter. 'And my home. You could leave a message there too. I'm sure that my mother will be trying to make contact with Lucy. She's been fretting after the children for weeks. Who knows, she could be wandering round West Bridgford this very minute.'

'Perhaps you should stay here for a bit then,' said Sean, and added half-jokingly, 'I could do with a hand in getting this place in order. I'm still not over this damned flu yet.'

'Pass,' laughed Jack. 'Thanks all the same. Thought I'd knock on a few doors and see if anyone here might have some clue about where Lucy is.'

'You'll be lucky. These damned women are all thick as thieves. Whatever they do know, they sure as hell aren't telling. D'you think I haven't tried that myself? My bet's on her own mum. Just back from holiday this week and pretends she hasn't a clue. I'd thought of camping out on her doorstep, but I don't think it would do my case much good.'

'You're right about that. Lucy's made her wishes pretty clear. Look, we'll keep in touch, shall we? If you hear anything about my mother, you'll let me know, and . . . ' Jack paused. When Lucy did get in touch with him, whose side was he on? Not Sean's, that was for sure.

Sean didn't seem to notice the hesitation. 'It's a deal, mate,' he said, shifting the bundle of clothes and holding out his hand.

At least the rain eased off a bit while Jack was trudging up and down Lucy's road. Sean had been right. Even the women who admitted to knowing who Lucy was denied all knowledge of her whereabouts. Some of them might have been telling the truth, but there was one particular woman, two little girls at her side, she'd flushed at the mention of Lucy's name. Seemed very agitated when the older child had begun to speak. 'That's Emmy and Sam's mum. Everyone's asking 'bout her. They've gone away on holiday.'

'Run along into the kitchen with Tara now, Jodie. You can get down the biscuit tin. Just two each, mind, there's a love.'

'You a copper, or what?' she demanded, as the little girls ran off down the hall. Then, peering at him more closely, 'I've seen you before. You're the dad, aren't you? Come up Sundays.'

'That's right. Actually, I'm looking for my mother. She disappeared last Saturday and I've heard nothing.' It was his turn to study her expression. 'You know something! She's been here, hasn't she? For God's sake, tell me she's all right!'

But the woman had stared blankly at him, 'Don't know what you're talking about. Sorry. Got to go now.' And the door was shut in his face.

Back in his car again, Jack slumped forward against the steering wheel, trying to control the thoughts that were thudding round his skull like squash balls. At last he sat up and took out his mobile.

'Hi, Jack. Yeh, we're fine. I've done pizza and beans for our tea and Hailey's made chocolate crispies.'

'No news, then?'

''Fraid not. You found out anything?'

'Drawn a complete blank. No one seems to know anything. I just can't understand why she's not been in touch.'

'Er, Jack. Hailey wants a quick word.'

'Hello? Hailey? Whatever's the matter?

345

Don't cry, sweetheart!'

'Stop being so nice, Jack. I've done something really awful. I wiped off messages from Donna's boyfriend, Monday night and I just never thought there might've been one from Agnes and then later I sort of remembered seeing a number three and I think only two of those was Craig but I couldn't be sure and then I didn't dare tell you and — oh I'm so sorry.'

So this is what a drowning man feels like, when he's given a few straws to clutch! thought Jack as he rang off.

Hailey had seemed amazed at his reaction, obviously having expected a lecture at the very least. 'Bless you, Hailey. Bless you for telling me now.' Of course, it was only a slight hope. The third message could have been anyone, but that had to include Ma. Before he'd rung the girls, he was ninety-nine percent convinced that his mother was either dead, or seriously injured. Now there was a fighting chance that she was alive and well.

No reply from Dianne Lockett, though. Never mind. He'd drive over to Sutton Coldfield straight away. No point spending any more time round here. Dianne was really his best hope, for Lucy, at least, if not for Ma.

If he couldn't get hold of Dianne, he'd give his mate Charlie a ring, one of his few remaining friends from university days. He and his wife had moved to Birmingham a few years ago. They'd give him a bed for the night if need be.

Before leaving West Bridgford he stopped at the off licence and bought a couple of reasonably decent bottles of claret. Too soon to buy champagne, yet.

19

That Friday morning, with rain as dark as shutters at the window, Molly's hotel felt to Agnes like an ark, cut adrift from the rest of the world. Or a large tent, perhaps.

Whatever made her think of tents? She'd never been under canvas as a child. Her night adventures with Seb had only taken them to their cave on the moor, or the makeshift shelter of branches in the woods.

Switzerland. Of course! Setting out from the huge house by the lake. The three-day hiking trip. The early autumn storms. Her distant cousins, the young Wyatts, and the rest of the lively house party, had gradually absorbed her, the shy outsider, into their group. There'd been one in particular, a fighter pilot, like Seb. But unlike Seb, he'd come back alive. The relief of talking, for the first time in nearly two years, about the death of her twin! And the way this man had seemed to find her, not just pretty, but intelligent and interesting, a person in her own right. Till Mother had taken ill and Father needed her back home.

'No, Henry my dear. You were not second

348

best. I never let myself think that. I never will.'

*   *   *

Breakfast was a casual affair that started late and continued intermittently all morning between desultory conversations triggered by leafing through back copies of the *National Geographic* and *Good Housekeeping*, and listening to Molly's collection of Broadway musicals. Molly even managed to get Felix, and Agnes herself, to join in with *Oh What a Beautiful Morning*, as the three of them stood at the window watching the rain battering against the steamed-up glass.

Agnes was relieved that no one seemed to have the energy for serious, problem-solving conversations. She needed more time to examine the idea that had sprung into her head the previous evening. It was hard to focus on any future beyond the next day's abseiling event, and she allowed herself the comforting illusion that if it was not discussed, it would not actually happen.

This illusion lasted until nearly two o'clock, when Gazza and Felix were finally ready to leave. 'Too late for my abseiling lesson now, thanks to you, Gazza,' grumbled Felix, as Molly opened the front door.

'Stop hassling me, man,' said Gazza with a grin. 'You're the one who wanted the last minute fry-up. Anyway, if it's been like this in Brum, I reckon they'll have cancelled. I think the climbing wall is outdoors.'

'What if it's pouring with rain tomorrow?' asked Agnes.

'Forget it, Ags. Rain or shine, that'll go ahead. Too much cash involved. Felix'll just get a good soaking.' Seeing Agnes's face he continued. 'Take it easy. They'll show him what to do. Don't worry. He'll be fine.'

★   ★   ★

'Nice man, really, underneath it all, isn't he?' said Molly as the Morris Traveller jerked away in a cloud of exhaust.

'Crying shame about his poor wife and son,' she continued, when Agnes followed her through to the kitchen. 'Small wonder he's felt so guilty all these years.' The rest of what she said was drowned by the sound of water drumming into the big flat-bottomed kettle, which she placed on the hob.

Agnes drew out a chair. 'Guilty? I know it was a terrible tragedy, but surely . . . why should he have to feel guilty?'

Molly looked surprised, 'Well — I mean, it was his fault, in a way. If he hadn't been

350

so . . . ' she paused, seeing Agnes's puzzled face. 'Oh, he didn't tell you the full story?'

'Just that they'd been in a light aircraft that crashed.' Agnes felt an unexpected twinge of jealousy, Felix was *her* find! Why should he confide in Molly?

As if reading her thoughts, Molly continued. 'Don't forget, you went off for a nap yesterday afternoon. Felix and I had time for a good old chin wag before young Gazza rang.' She poured the tea, then added, 'Evacuated at the age of five. Wales.'

'Wales?'

Molly laughed at Agnes's puzzled face. 'Felix, dear. It wasn't just the London kids got sent away, was it? But getting back to the tragedy. It seems his wife, Sylvia, was a real livewire. Everyone loved her. Taught drama at some private girls' school. Well, as you know, Felix had this one son, Philip, couldn't have any more, something to do with complications at the birth. Bit like what you told me the other night, your problems after Jack.'

'Mmm,' said Agnes abstractedly, 'So this Philip?'

'Of course, Philip! Dreadful, it was. Quite dreadful. No wonder, really, he tried to . . . I mean, more surprising, in a way, that he didn't do it years back.'

'But I understood it was an accident. Nobody's fault.'

'It was an accident, yes, but, well, Philip, see, it was his twenty-first birthday, and coming up to their twenty-fifth wedding anniversary. They'd planned a joint do for the three of them with all their friends and relations, though Felix hadn't got much family left. Own mother dead. Father and two much older brothers killed in the war.'

'So Sylvia was planning a party?' prompted Agnes. She reached for the fat brown teapot and refilled her mug. Molly's was almost untouched.

'A party wasn't going to be enough. Sylvia was dead set on arranging a separate little celebration for the three of them on their own. She booked them all into a hotel in the Lake District for the weekend before, and she'd also booked a private balloon flight for the Sunday.'

'Balloon!' exclaimed Agnes. 'I thought it was a plane crash.'

'That's the whole point,' said Molly grimly. 'It was. You see, years back, Sylvia had wanted to take up gliding and her father was going to pay for lessons, but Felix was terribly against the idea, and then she'd found out she was pregnant so she agreed not to do it.

She thought a balloon would be a compromise, something gentle and safe that Felix would enjoy too, but he'd refused to take part. Said he wasn't going to let himself be suspended by a bag of hot air, hundreds of feet above the ground and he wasn't at all happy about her or Philip doing it either, and there was a row and she'd said, 'OK, then. We'll use something with a nice reliable engine.' And she'd driven off to an airfield and got someone to take her and Philip for a flight over the peaks in some tiny little plane, and you know the rest. Sudden thick mist. Crashed into the side of a mountain. All killed — her and Philip and the pilot. All dead.'

Molly fell silent. Agnes felt something sharp swelling in her throat. The ticking of the large clock on the wall grew louder and louder. All — dead. All — dead. All — dead.

Oh poor Felix. Poor Felix. What he must have gone through. No wonder he'd tried to take his own life at last. She'd thought herself so clever, coming up with that stupid, stupid story, the Dangerous Sports Euthanasia Society. It would all have seemed to fit, for Felix. She'd given him the words, hadn't she? A is for abseiling, B for ballooning. A is for aeroplane, too. It was because he'd not dared the ballooning that Sylvia and Philip had been in that fated aeroplane. And now, he was going back to the start of the alphabet too. The start, and perhaps the finish.

★ ★ ★

'One of my many talents, hairdressing,' laughed Molly. 'Trust me!'

Agnes was sitting on the padded, flowery lid of the laundry box in the middle of Molly's pink-tiled bathroom. The seat was too low for her to see her reflection in the mirror above the washbasin. Probably just as well. She'd become so accustomed to the appearance of her face framed by the orange wig that her own grey hair had begun to feel as though it didn't belong. Now, hanging in rats tails around her shoulders, water seeping into the thick purple towel that Molly had draped on top of her tracksuit jacket, it was a sight she had no desire to behold.

'Lovely and thick, still, isn't it?' said Molly, combing through a long strand, holding it up from the crown, then reaching across to the vanity unit for a large pair of scissors.

Agnes gulped and pressed her open palm against her breastbone. 'Aren't you going to dry it a little bit more first?'

'Cut wet, blow dry,' said Molly. 'Anyway, we're going to put the colour in, soon as I've taken most of the length off. I'll be styling it properly after that.' She let go of the hair and stepped forward, bending to peer into Agnes's face. 'You're not changing your mind are you? I mean, just say if you are, I don't want — '

'No,' said Agnes firmly. 'We've been through all that.'

'I refuse to lift a finger until I'm sure you're absolutely sure yourself.'

'Very well, then,' laughed Agnes. 'One, I've got used to the colour. I like it. Two, the wig gets hot and uncomfortable over all this hair. Three, it's time for a permanent change, now I know I'll never go back to the Harmony Home — '

'And four, Madam will suit a modern style, slightly spiky, with a feathery fringe,' said Molly, in a prim voice.

'So what are you waiting for? We don't really want to spend the entire evening in your bathroom, delightful though it may be.'

As Molly lifted the strand of hair again, Agnes mused, 'Do you know what? This feels like a coming-of-age ceremony, the way, years ago, a young girl might have her hair bobbed. I wasn't allowed to do that, the most I could do was pin my plaits up across the top of my head!'

She closed her eyes, relishing the gentle tugging on her scalp as the separate strands were lifted from her shoulders, and then the crunch-click of the scissors before each shortened lock dropped softly back against her head.

Hours later, Agnes was sitting at the dressing table in her bedroom, using the three mirrors to examine her reflection from all angles. 'A cross between Julie Andrews and Mia Farrow,' Molly had said, standing back to admire her handiwork. 'The colour's a bit more carroty than it showed on the packet, but you can get away with it. The style really suits you, that pixie kind of look.'

For the twentieth time that evening, Agnes raised her hand to the back of her neck, and ran her fingers through the inch-long hair before smoothing it back onto her exposed nape. Then she patted the short orange tufts on her crown, and leaning forward, lifted the jagged strands of the fringe and let them fall again, half covering her eyebrows and obscuring the deep furrow that made her look as if she was frowning. 'Oh, Lambkin,' said Henry. 'It is not very becoming, my dear.'

Agnes smiled shyly at herself. She'd got used to the orange wig quickly enough. She'd soon become accustomed to this new look. As for 'becoming', what did that really mean? The only 'becoming' she wanted, was to become herself at last.

The thought of Henry reminded her forcibly of Jack. Since dropping the postcard into the letter box on Wednesday, she'd scarcely given him a thought, she'd been so involved in other people's lives. She owed him more than a scribbled message on the back of a multi-view of Beautiful Birmingham. He'd have paid up money in advance for that un-homely Home, and now she'd decided, finally, never to return, she really ought to let him know as soon as possible.

Remembering his impassive face when he had first left her in that room, her throat tightened. What kind of a mother had she actually been to him, that he could have so little feeling for her now?

When she finally crept into bed, she lay for a long time staring up at the wedges of light spreading across the ceiling from passing cars. Soon her mind was wandering back to happier days. Little Jack's purple fingers and lips as he scoured the hedgerows with her, gathering blackberries for jam. Frogspawn in the carefully rinsed out sandcastle bucket. The toddler, Jack, smelling of Coal-tar soap, snuggling on her lap and turning the pages for her as she read Peter Rabbit, or Jemima Puddleduck. Then it was Emily asking for 'Just one more, Grandma, one more story.'

Suddenly Agnes herself was drifting down, down into the bottomless rabbit hole, and woke with a start as Felix hurtled past her like a stone . . .

Felix! Molly had tried her best to convince her that he was definitely not in a suicidal mood — 'just glad to be given the chance to prove something to himself, laying a ghost, so to speak.' Agnes had pretended to agree, but she couldn't help thinking that Felix's cheerfulness had a different cause. It seemed far more likely that he was planning to join his wife and son in a way that would link his death more closely to theirs. All she could do was to make sure that she and Molly arrived at the abseiling in plenty of time. Felix's descent was timetabled for 11.30. She must get there well before that, and warn the organisers, make them prevent the impending tragic 'accident'.

★　★　★

Not easy, driving through Saturday holiday traffic in blinding spring sunshine when you've got miniature road-drills banging away in your head, and your stomach juices are sloshing up into your gullet.

'Cool it, Mr Punch,' Gazza had said at half past nine that morning when Felix had stumbled down the stairs in response to the hammering on his front door. 'It'll soon be over and then we can all go out and celebrate.'

For a brief moment Felix was tempted to shut the door again and stagger back to bed. 'Bit of a rough night. I'll be OK when I've had a wash and shave,' he mumbled. Couldn't let the boy down at this stage, could he? No need to let him know he'd been vomiting and shivering most of the night. Curries didn't usually affect him like that, but Gazza had insisted on taking him to a place he'd never been to before.

'Wicked food, 'n dead cheap,' had seemed like a particularly accurate description as he retched up most of it into the toilet bowl.

By the time they'd found their way across the city and out on the Express Way to the north side, through Erdington to Sutton Coldfield, Felix was sweating as he gripped the steering wheel, and wondering how much longer he could keep going before he collapsed. Gazza obviously attributed his silence to nervousness about the approaching ordeal, and spent most of his time giving directions and stretching forward awkwardly over the back of the passenger seat to fiddle with the radio controls, trying to find a channel that offered something other than crackling and hissing, opera, or a gabble of French.

Even the car park at the hospital was a challenge. Row on gleaming row of cars packed like sardines. After driving round and round the acre or two of tarmac, Felix spotted a couple of disabled parking bays. 'You're disabled, even if I'm not.' Under his breath he added, 'and I bloody well am! Be a miracle if I make it to the toilets in time.'

For a few yards he was able to let Gazza rest some of his weight against his arm, but all of a sudden he had to let go. 'Sorry, lad,' he called over his shoulder as he quickened his pace towards the nearest entrance. 'You go on. I'll catch up with you later.'

Through a pair of double doors, and round a corner, he nearly bumped into a lad in a green cotton coat, pushing an empty wheelchair. 'Quick. Nearest toilet!' he gasped. He must have looked pretty ropy because the young man, instead of giving lengthy directions, bundled him into the wheelchair and ran the full length of what seemed like a mile-long corridor.

Sitting in agony as a thousand knives stabbed into his guts and a scorching stream of some noxious substance exploded from his rear end, all Felix wanted to do was to curl up and die.

Agnes felt her heart begin to speed up in time to the music blaring from a tannoy stationed somewhere among the cluster of buildings that made up Good Hope Hospital. She'd persuaded Molly not to waste time driving round and round the car park, trying to find a space. Instead they'd turned back to the exit and ventured down a no-through road opposite the hospital.

'Perfectly safe,' Molly assured her, parking on an unbroken yellow line near a patch of open ground. 'No one's going to bother on a Saturday.'

'Ooh, this is fun,' she exclaimed a little breathlessly a few minutes later as the music quickened to a frenzied beat and they followed a straggling stream of young families along a maze of paths between the hospital blocks. 'Like a fairground or a circus,' she added as they emerged into an open space where a hundred or more chattering, laughing people were milling around on the tarmac near an organisers' trestle table, a First Aid tent and stalls selling cups of tea and candy floss. Some youngsters were sprawled on their opened anoraks on a grassy bank, and Agnes scanned the little group, half expecting to see Gazza with a beer can to his lips. Then she turned back towards the building behind her, following their gaze up, up . . .

Molly had just bustled through the crowd to her side and Agnes clutched her arm. 'Oh Molly!' her voice came out as a whimper. 'Look! Look!'

Two tiny figures were beginning their descent over the edge of the flat roof. They were leaning right back into space with their feet against the sheer wall, each clutching what must be, surely, a good strong rope that dangled down between their outstretched legs swaying and jerking, down, down, down to where a couple of men in helmets were craning up at them. One hundred feet! So that was what a hundred feet looked like.

'Oh my goodness!' exclaimed Molly. 'It is a bit high, isn't it?'

Agnes swallowed hard. 'A bit,' she managed to say, then began to make her way towards the long table where posters proclaiming 'Abseil for Cancer Research' stirred in the light breeze.

★ ★ ★

Sunlight punched Felix in the eyes as he staggered out from the shadow of the building into the congested open space.

Deafening drums throbbed in his skull. Or were they coming from somewhere outside his head? He peaked both hands across his forehead and squinted at the throng of people.

A few yards to his right, leaning against a mobile tea-bar with his back towards him, was a young man with long matted locks and a denim jacket. The youth turned, scanning the crowd and then his eyes lit on the solitary figure near the doorway. 'Felix!' he exclaimed, then, more loudly, 'Fuck!' as he put down his right foot. He transferred his weight immediately, grabbing at the counter top with both hands.

Felix smiled grimly: there was no way that Gazza could change his mind and attempt the descent. Stomach cramps, nausea, dizziness, shivering — no matter what, somehow or other he still had to go through with it.

'Watcha, Mr Punch. You OK?' asked Gazza, hobbling over to him.

'Touch of the runs,' he gasped. 'I'll be fine. Where do we go now?'

'Signing in's over there. I better come with you and explain about the change. Probably have to sign something myself too.'

It was not merely the warm spring sun in the confined space that brought beads of sweat to Felix's face and made his shirt cling to his back under the heavy jersey. Nor was it the pressure of Gazza's hand on his shoulder as he hopped along by his side. There was no getting away from it, his temperature was way above normal.

'Hot, innit?' said Gazza, looking at him anxiously. 'You wanna take off that sweater?'

★　★　★

Agnes had reached fourth place in the queue when she became aware of a commotion a few yards behind her.

'Some old bloke's fainted back there,' giggled one young woman to another. Agnes stepped from the line and saw Gazza, bending over a figure on the ground. An eager St John's Ambulance man was hurrying towards the little group who were clustering around.

'Stand back now. Back, please,' he said as Agnes reached them.

Felix had regained consciousness and was struggling to sit up. 'Look here, I'm going to be late for my abseil, meant to be signed up by now,' he insisted as the man laid a restraining hand on his shoulder and gently touched his forehead with the other.

'Not with that fever, you're not,' he said. 'Better come along to our tent for a check up.

Sorry, mate, there won't be no abseiling for you today.'

'But I — ' protested Felix.

'Look, it's not the end of the world,' said Gazza. 'I'll just have to give the sponsor money back and that's that. I'll try again next year.'

'It's all right, Felix. Don't worry, Gazza. I shall be doing it now,' said Agnes, stepping forward. She hadn't been aware of the meaning of what she was saying until she heard the words emerging from her mouth.

'Agnes?' said Gazza, taking in her newly-cropped hair, an even brighter orange than before.

'Agnes! Trust you to turn up where there's trouble!' muttered Felix.

Several people who'd been standing around wondering how they should react to this little drama broke into spontaneous applause for the sprightly looking woman in her bright turquoise tracksuit, trainers, and trendy hair-cut — clearly a fit old bird, and not so old, neither. Hard to guess what age she'd be. Sixty, at least. Nice to know people that age could still do stuff like that.

'What's going on?' asked Molly, bustling up with two polystyrene mugs of tea. 'Whatever's the matter with Felix?'

'Just something I ate,' he growled, as the

ambulance man tried to lead him away. 'Lot of fuss about nothing. I'm absolutely fine, now.' He shook his arm from the man's grasp, took a couple of strides towards Molly, then stumbled and would have fallen against her, spilling hot tea down them both, if Agnes had not stepped forward to steady him.

He glared at her as the ambulance man reached him and placed an arm round his shoulders, but then a spasm of pain crossed his face and he clutched his stomach.

'Come on, Mr Punch,' said Gazza. 'Looks like a mercy dash to the toilet again.'

'Here, let me go with him, what with your ankle,' said Molly, handing the two cups to Gazza. 'See you in a bit, Agnes.' And Felix allowed himself to be led away.

Agnes had slipped in at the front of the queue, smiling benignly at the young couple behind her. 'Thank you so much for keeping my place,' she said, ignoring the baffled expression on the young man's face. 'My friend back there has just been taken ill, and I'm already a bit late for signing in.'

'Name?' asked a stout, bearded man, looking up at her from his seat behind the table.

'Agnes Borrowdale,' she said, her heart beginning to beat faster. Had to get this registration business over before anyone tried to stop her.

'What time was you due?' asked the man, scanning the list on his clipboard. 'Don't see no Agnes Borrowdale here.'

'Oh, silly me!' she exclaimed, her mind racing. 'I'm standing in for a young friend of mine who has injured his ankle.' Was Gazza a real name, or short for something else? 'Gazza, he's called. Down for eleven-thirty.'

'Gary Patterson,' said a voice behind her. 'But she's not — ' he stopped abruptly as Agnes swung round and fixed him with her most imperious stare.

'Ah! My tea at last. How kind,' she said, reaching out for one of the cups, and then in a low voice added, 'Just agree for now, please Gazza. We can talk about it in a minute. Trust me.'

The man at the table was keen to get on with his job, and happy to accept Gazza's assurance that this woman was a perfectly suitable substitute.

'So how much have you managed to raise?' he asked Gazza. 'You got it all here, have you?'

Gazza hesitated, glancing at Agnes.

'He's done really well,' she announced, 'Over £500, wasn't it?'

'£523,' said Gazza, reaching into the pocket of his denim jacket and drawing out a crumpled envelope.

'Excellent! What a splendid contribution,' smiled the man as he counted it out. 'Thank you!'

When Agnes had signed an acknowledgement that she was undertaking the abseil at her own risk, and agreed to follow all instructions to the letter, the man said, 'Wait over there, by those double doors. See that man in a helmet chatting to those youngsters? He'll be taking you all up in the lift to the roof, six at a time. Won't have to wait more than a couple of minutes at most. You'll be shown exactly what to do when you get up there. Good luck!' And he turned towards the next name on the list.

Gazza gulped the last of his tea and threw the cup into a box of rubbish by the table, then hobbled painfully after Agnes. 'Hang on a sec,' he called. She paused and waited till he reached her. 'Where d'you think you're going? You're never thinking of — not really!'

'Gazza,' she said, surprised at how calm she felt. 'Have you seen any of your own friends here?'

'Wasn't expecting to. Most of my mates have gone off home for Easter.'

'So there isn't anyone here you could ask to stand in?'

'No, but I've already said, there's always next year.'

'And how are you going to manage to give all that money back? I mean, that's what you'll have to do, isn't it?'

' "Trust me!' you said. 'We'll talk about it', you said. You're definitely worse than my Nan. Should've guessed, shouldn't I? What's Molly going to say? And Felix'll kill me!'

'Molly'll take it in her stride. She's spent long enough trying to convince me that Felix wouldn't be in any danger, and as for Felix . . . ' she stopped as her eyes rested on the helmeted man who was staring over in the direction of the organisers' table

'Just waiting for the sixth,' he explained to two young woman in jeans, who were clinging to each other and giggling nervously.

'Here I am,' said Agnes calmly. Inside her head another Agnes looked on amazed, wondering how much longer this dream-like bravado could last.

★　★　★

'Can we go to the fair, Mummy?' piped a small boy of about four years old, grabbing his mother's hand and trying to pull her towards the garden gate. 'We better be quick. It's nearly all finished.'

'What fair?' she asked. 'Oh, you mean that noisy music! I don't think that's a fair,

369

Sammy, love. D'you know what's going on, Mum?' She turned towards the porch, where a woman with an amber tan and white-blonde hair in a French pleat was watering pots of blue and pink hyacinths.

Dianne Lockett put down the small watering can and eased the yellow rubber gloves from her hands before stepping out to join her daughter and grandson on the drive. 'Charity abseil. On all day today. Bit much, really, isn't it, all that din? Still, in a good cause, I suppose. Why don't you take Emmy and Sam along?'

I've only been here five minutes and she's trying to get rid of me! thought Lucy. 'I'll go in a bit,' she said. 'Will you come too?'

Dianne seemed to wince. 'Not really my cup of tea, darling. Anyway, I need to get on with a few little jobs inside while Barry's off at the golf club — away from under my feet.'

★　★　★

Lucy sat on the bench in the sunshine, watching Sam tumbling around on the back lawn, all legs and arms as he tried to copy his sister's handstands and cartwheels. They both looked as carefree as lambs. They hadn't mentioned Sean once since arriving at her friend Sarah's house. But then, why would they? They had Sarah's children to play with, and new people and places to get used to.

Lucy sighed and closed her eyes, clamping her lips together to prevent them from trembling. Then she shook her head and blinked. Silly cow. Was she still looking for the perfect Mr Right, who'd take care of her, cherish her, never let her down? She laughed, then waved at Emmy. 'Yes, darling. That was a brilliant cartwheel. Do me another.'

Better go in and see if she could lend Mum a hand. All those years of letting dust settle unnoticed for weeks on end, cluttered corners, a haven for every spider in the neighbourhood, those empty glass bottles bulging out of plastic carriers all over the kitchen floor, and now look at her, almost too far in the other direction! How long would Mum be able to put up with smeary fingerprints on the varnished table and the glass-paned doors — traces of mud on the carpet and scuff marks on the skirting? Her patience had never yet been tried for more than a couple of days.

Still, it was great that she seemed so much happier now, more like she'd been twenty years ago, before Dad left home. Barry might not be the world's cleverest, in terms of conversation, anyway — hardly uttered a word on anything other than golf, cars, or his latest business deal — but he couldn't do enough for Mum. A kind man, really, under the self-important bluster. What a huge relief not to have to worry about her any more.

'Grass stains are the very devil! You'll never get them out, you know.'

'You made me jump!' Lucy turned to see her mother leaning against the open patio door, arms folded, frowning a little as she watched the children sprawling on the lawn. Or was she merely squinting against the strong sunlight? 'I was just going to come in and give you a hand,' Lucy added, half guiltily.

'Nothing left to do, now. For the moment.' Dianne stepped out onto the patio. 'Of course, I've had a good dose of sun already this year. Actually able to feel the benefit of it, now I'm just about over that dreadful tummy bug.'

'But you had a good time in Tenerife, though?' began Lucy. 'And how was Barry's — ?' she broke off abruptly as a piercing scream rang out. A moment later she was at the far end of the lawn, calmly reassuring Sam that nothing had been broken when he'd slipped off the swing. 'I think it's time we all went to take a look at where that noisy music is coming from, don't you?' she finished off.

'Are you coming too, Nana?' asked Emily

as they reached the house.

Dianne hesitated, and Lucy was surprised to see her face soften into a smile as Emily continued, 'We haven't seen you for ages and ages and you're our only grandma now, even though you don't look like a proper granny.'

'What does a proper granny look like then?' she asked, reaching out her hand and letting it rest for a moment on the child's silky brown hair.

Emily glanced up at her mother. Lucy felt a pang at the slight hesitation in her face as she said, 'Our Grandma from Before. She isn't in heaven with Granddad but we never do see her now. She looks like a little old lady. You don't look hardly old at all, Nana.'

'That's nice of you to say so, dear,' she laughed. 'I would very much like to come with you, for a little while, at least, but . . . now then, why don't you all trot into the kitchen and get yourselves a drink while I have a quick word with Mummy?'

'What's up, Mum?' asked Lucy, following her mother in through the patio doors, while the children ran round the side of the house to the kitchen.

'Nothing's up, exactly. Just that I haven't yet managed to tell you. I had Jack on the phone yesterday evening. Told him you'd be here today. He's staying the night with friends in Harborne, and he'll be round this morning sometime.'

'Jack! Oh, well. I was going to have to ring him about tomorrow anyway. But what was he phoning you for?'

'Well, apart from going frantic, wondering where you and the kids had got to — '

'He's got no right to worry about us. I don't have to tell him my movements.'

'It's Agnes. He was looking for Agnes. He thought she'd been abducted or something.'

'Agnes?' exclaimed Lucy, 'You mean — Agnes?'

'The very same. Granny from Before. You know, the one who isn't dead but the children never see. The little-old-lady one who — '

'Stop it! Stop trying to make me feel guilty,' Lucy burst out. She turned and walked back towards the patio door and stood for a moment, staring down the garden. Those phone calls. 'Could I speak to Emily, Please? Sammy then? Perhaps I could come and stay?' Oh God! What a bitch you are, Lucy. What a thoughtless cow, wrapped up in your own problems, and that poor harmless old woman . . .

Dianne was at her side as Lucy turned to her, tears in her eyes, 'You said thought. Jack 'thought'. So that means she is all right?'

'I assume she is,' said Dianne with a brisk

laugh. 'Had her on the phone just after Jack rang me — when was it? Wednesday, yes, I'd not been back an hour. Didn't know then that he'd been looking for her. You can imagine what he felt last night when I told him! Laughing and crying like a madman.'

'Oh, poor Jack!' Lucy was surprised by the wave of warmth she felt towards him. What he must have gone through!

'I got the impression she's been chasing all over the place trying to find you,' Dianne said. 'Shouldn't be in the least surprised if she doesn't show up here as well for a fine old family gathering of the Borrowdales! Better check the state of my freezer, just in case I need to send Barry off to the shops this afternoon.'

20

SCENE:

A quiet side street in one of the better residential districts of Birmingham.

TIME:

Ten of the clock on a fine April Saturday.

DRAMATIS PERSONAE:

Undercover police constable, the brave and resourceful Timothy Dolan.

ACTION:

Timothy yawns and stretches. Ouch! He has banged his right elbow against the steamed-up window of his vehicle. Is that bloody man going to stay in that house all day? God! He's dying for a nice hot mug of tea. And a slash. Not going to risk losing his prey now though, not after camping out all bleeding night in this not-so-roomy car.

Timothy wound down the window and glanced up and down the street. No one around. He opened the door and edged himself out onto the pavement, wincing as he straightened his legs.

Nice thick laurel hedge by that driveway. He unzipped and aimed a steady yellow arc at the glossy leaves, sighing with relief — never mind the odd splash bouncing back onto the leg of his jeans.

'Back you go now, Johnny,' he muttered, then jerked his head round at the sound of approaching footsteps. Damn! Zip jammed in y-fronts, and there's Jack Borrowdale, striding towards his Volvo.

★ ★ ★

Jack braked hard as he realised he'd nearly overshot the turning on his left. Radford Road. That was it. He drove more slowly now, looking for number sixty-two. Why had he been in such a tearing hurry to get here? He wasn't seriously expecting to see Ma, was he?

Calm down. Calm down. You know she's all right. Not only had she phoned Dianne on Wednesday, but there was that postcard, arrived at Saxon Meadow this very morning.

Hailey had sounded over the moon. 'So she's got to be OK hasn't she? I mean, actually writing like that. Makes it seem even more, you know, definite. When you see her, make sure an' tell her we've missed her.'

Extraordinary, mused Jack, smiling. Those girls had come up trumps. Of course, Monica couldn't let her own parents down. When was it she'd last visited? Mmm. Even more reason to go now, then, really. But he'd never

thought that Donna, and Hailey, especially
. . . He'd make more of an effort with them
from now on.

Number forty-four, fifty, fifty-six. Quite a
nice road, this. Dianne was sorted now. Lucky
for Lucy. And what if Ma was here? What on
earth would he say to her? What kind of state
would she be in? Let her be here. Please,
God, whoever you are, let her be all right.

★   ★   ★

'Sorry, Jack,' said Dianne as he stepped into
the hall. 'Not a peep since that phone call.
Still, she's bound to call again to find out
about Lucy.'

'How is Lucy? How are the kids? Has she
said anything to you about leaving Sean?' The
four most important people in his life. No
wonder his feelings were in such a jumble,
trying to prioritise his levels of anxiety. *Four*
people? Ma, of course. Sam and Emmy, of
course. But not Lucy. Not any longer. He
suddenly became aware that Dianne was
speaking again.

'You know as much as I do, Jack. She's
hardly said anything since she got here. That
was only an hour ago, and now they've
dashed over to watch the abseiling. But then,
she's never been one to confide. So she's left

that Sean, you say?'

''S'what he thinks, anyway. Me, I haven't a clue. If these last few days have taught me anything, it's that all women are a total mystery. I mean, my own mother! I ask you!'

Dianne laughed. 'So — you going over to join them? Kids'll be pleased to see their dad.'

'I . . . Yes, I'll see if I can find them.'

'They've not been gone more'n five minutes. I'll stay here though, in case Agnes rings before Barry gets home. See you later, Jack.'

★   ★   ★

What on earth induces people to do things like that? Jack was elbowing his way through the crowd, glancing from time to time at the towering wall and the tiny figures slowly descending. Leaning back over a sheer drop, trusting their lives to one little rope! Didn't life provide enough hardships for the average person without them making more? He saw a throng of people clustered around an ice-cream van, several children among them. And a tall, slim woman. Long straight hair between her shoulder blades. Jeans hugging the neat little bum. Lucy? He half hoped not. Somehow it'd seem worse to be ogling his ex-wife than a total stranger. More disloyal to Monica.

But it was Lucy. Emmy and Sam were pushing through the ragged queue towards her, their still-wrapped ice lollies held high. Emmy was the first to catch sight of him.

'Daddy, Daddy,' she shrieked and a moment later she was in his arms, legs round his waist and something cold pressed against his left ear. Soon Sam was tugging at his trouser leg, wanting his turn, and Lucy was hovering almost shyly at his side.

'Hello, Lucy.'

'Hi, Jack. I was so sorry to hear about Agnes. It must've been a dreadful worry for you. Any more news yet?'

A small, stooped old woman next to them, holding the hand of a red-haired little boy, suddenly jerked her head in their direction and stared from Jack to Lucy to the two children, then back to Lucy again. Lucy caught her eye and gave her a questioning look, but the woman turned away as though she'd noticed nothing.

'I wonder where that funny old Felix has got to. And Auntie Ness,' she said to the child.

A young man on her other side glanced at her briefly, then fixed his gaze back on the little family group.

'So that's the ex-wife,' murmured Timothy Dolan, his smiling lips hidden by a steaming polystyrene cup. All his hard work was beginning to pay off. If the old woman wasn't in hiding with her ex-daughter-in-law, where was she? What would that dozy lot back at base make of it all now?

★　★　★

Still in a dream-like state, Agnes emerged from the lift and followed the others along a dim, corridor, through a set of heavy double doors and out into the glare of sunlight once more.

All the way up in the lift she'd forgotten about the music, but it had burst through as soon as those doors were opened. There was always background music in films, a constant reminder that events were taking place in front of a camera. No one ever actually died, or got hurt in any way.

Agnes peered past her companions to where four people in blue or orange helmets and straps around their waists were chatting and laughing with two men in army camouflage gear. A few yards beyond them, near the low wall at the edge of the roof, was a short wooden ladder leading to a platform that had clearly been specially constructed for the event. There was no time to take in exactly what was happening on the platform because the leader of their own group had stepped forward, blocking her view.

'Here we are then,' said the man. 'We'll just hang on a mo till those army guys there get you all kitted out. While you're waiting, have a little read of these guidelines.'

Agnes studied her leaflet as if reading instructions for an activity she would never undertake herself, assembling a flat-pack of furniture, for instance. So that was the harness that you'd be suspended in, and there was a big metal clip that attached you to the rope. The rope itself was on a pulley, reminding her of the wooden clothes-drier that could be pulled up almost to the ceiling in the vicarage kitchen. Wet sheets must weigh a fair amount, and there'd never been any problem with that pulley going wrong, or the rope fraying.

So far, so, more or less, good.

'I guess you've done abseiling before,' said one of the young women in jeans. 'It must be OK then, I mean, if you're still up to it.' Seeing Agnes's puzzled frown she added, 'Oh! Didn't mean to sound rude. It's only 'cos I'm shit scared, myself. First time, see. And you're not bothered in the least. Didn't mean to suggest you were too, you know . . . '

'Too old?' smiled Agnes, wondering what age she thought her. 'Actually, I . . . ' she stopped. No, it might make the girl feel even worse if she admitted that this was her first time too. 'Actually, there's nothing to it, once you've started. You just keep going down, like it shows here, look.' And she pointed to the diagram of a figure leaning out with straight legs at right angles to a wall. 'See, it says to take small steps and plant your feet flat against the brickwork.'

The girl still looked doubtful, but her friend chipped in. 'Don't worry, Nita. They'll tell us exactly what to do before we start. Look, if that dippy Lisa Dodds can do it, we certainly can. No sweat.'

'OK, send 'em over, mate,' called one of the young soldiers, and Agnes followed the two girls and three young men onto the centre of the roof.

'Right, ladies and gents. I'm Dave, and he's Andy. Now then, any of yous had a stab at this before?'

Agnes looked down at her trainers, hoping that Nita would keep quiet. A vain hope.

'Yeh, this lady here,' said the girl.

'OK. Let's have you up front, Ma'am. And you Sir, you with the nice red Gortex there. Now then, all. Me and Andy's going to give you each a helmet, and a pair of gauntlets, and then you'll all get strapped into one these, see,' here he held up a harness. 'Keep you nice and safe, so if ever you did let go the rope there's no way you could fall. Safe as houses, isn't that right, Missis?'

Agnes nodded. Safe as houses. Of course it was. How silly to have been so worried about Felix. She looked over to the wall on her right. From where she was, in the middle of the roof, all she could see was blue sky and a distant spread of buildings somewhere far off, towards the centre of Birmingham. There were patches of green too, and splodges of pink and white from flowering cherry and magnolia in gardens or parks. She felt absolutely safe here. No hint of vertigo, surrounded by solid brick wall a good four foot high. The trick was not to look down once she got to the edge. She felt a little thrill of pride run through her. Calm as the cream on top of the milk, while young Nita still needed the comfort of her friend's words, 'Worth it, to have that Dave's hands round your waist, hey? Well fit, he is.'

'Blue or orange?' asked the one called Andy.

'No preference,' said Agnes. 'Oh! Very well, then, orange.' It had been a lucky colour so far. But the orange helmet came down over her eyes and rested on her nose. The blue was a better fit. She suppressed a giggle as she stepped into the harness and drew it up round her waist for Andy to check the buckle. Having those loose straps between her legs and round her thighs felt a little like wearing a nappy.

She heard Nita whisper, 'Does my bum look big in this?' as she wriggled into her own harness and both girls shrieked with laughter.

'OK then,' smiled Andy. 'Ready for the off?'

Probably better to be one of the first. No time to get too worried. 'Good Luck,' called Nita as Agnes stepped towards the platform.

⋆   ⋆   ⋆

Molly was not taking this news in her stride, thought Gazza. Far from it. Trust Agnes to get that wrong.

'How could you, Gazza? I turn my back for a matter of minutes, and you — Do you realise what age she is?'

Gazza nodded dumbly. Older than his nan was when she died. In those last few months, Nan had been old. Sometimes she'd not known who he was. Thought he was his dad, or even his granddad. But Aggie didn't seem old, so it was easy to forget. Even if you did remember her actual age, it didn't sink in.

'Seventy-five on Tuesday! And you let her sign up for — for that!' Molly pointed to the roof of the building and her chins trembled.

'What's going on?' called Felix in a querulous voice from where he was lying stretched out on a camp bed inside the First Aid tent. 'Molly! Gazza! What is it?'

'Better not tell him,' muttered Molly. 'It'll bring on another fainting fit.'

'What will?' said a weak voice behind them. Felix had hauled himself to his feet and was tottering towards them. Molly was by his side in a trice, offering her arm, while Gazza placed a small wooden folding chair near the entrance, in the shade of the awning.

'Well, go and stop her, you daft 'ap'orth!' he snapped at Gazza, once the situation had been explained.

Gazza tensed himself, ready to run, then remembered that he could only hobble. Where would he run to, anyway?

'You, then. You Molly. Go to the registering place — they're bound to be in walkie-talkie contact with the fellows on the roof. They'll get a message through.'

'Yeh, I know they're in contact, cos they already agreed to announce Agnes when she's about to do it. They've done that already about some groups from firms and clubs, so I thought Aggie deserved a mention.'

Molly was already breaking into a trot when the music was halted in mid-shriek, and the tannoy coughed and spluttered into speech.

Jack could not believe what he was hearing. Nor could Lucy. Emily and Sam did not make the connection between 'brave seventy-five-year-old Agnes Borrowdale, standing in for her young friend,' and their own Grandma from Before.

Scott had no inkling that this was Auntie Ness, but Edie gave a loud squeal and turned in horror to gaze at the couple at her side. The man, Jack, had gone white. He was gripping Lucy's hand and whispering, 'No! No! It can't be.' Then he raised his hand to cover his open mouth. Tears were running unchecked down his cheek.

Timothy Dolan let his cup, half full of tea, drop like a stone onto his right foot. He didn't even notice the wet brown liquid seeping through the canvas of his shoe.

It was the wooden platform that did it — four feet above the flat roof. There were cracks between the boards. Like on Brighton pier. She'd been an adult then but infected by

Jack's fear. 'Mummy!' he'd shrieked in pure terror, 'I'm going to drown!' and he'd flung himself onto the wooden floor, refusing to take another step.

'Don't look down,' Seb used to say, when he helped her climb out of the bedroom window and onto the handy branch of the nearby oak. But now, the short drop to the gravelled surface of the roof was enough to start that fluttering in her stomach. Quick, focus on something else. Sam and Emmy. The adventure playground near their house in Lewes, nice safe wood chippings on the ground.

'All right, bab?' asked another youth in play-time camouflage as he clipped a huge metal ring onto the waistband of the harness. 'Remember now, once your feet are on the wall, legs straight, small steps, no hurry. And don't go gripping the rope too tight. Let it slide through your hands, nice an' easy. That's what these great gloves are for, see? It's this rope here, the one I've just clipped to your belt, this is the one that'll stopping you from falling. See. It's attached to that good sturdy winch here, just behind me. Solid it is. You got all that?'

Agnes nodded. Better not try to speak.

'Good girl. Now, take a step back there, and another, balls of your feet balanced on the edge, heels sticking over. They always say this bit's the worst. After that, it's a piece of cake, believe me.'

Listen, thought Agnes, desperately. You've got to listen to what he says. A hollow numbness had crept into every part of her body and was now invading her brain. No. Numbness was not the right word . . .

'So, when you're ready, you're going to bend at the hips, keeping the legs dead straight, and let yourself lean right back over the edge. When your legs are parallel with the ground, and you've dropped your heels right down against the side of the wall, that's when you start walking. OK? Shall I repeat?'

The background music stopped abruptly. Help me, Seb! This was no film set. It was real. Real as drinking lukewarm tea from a polystyrene cup, real as needing the loo and not being near one. A moment from now, she'd be leaning backwards into space, a hundred feet above the concrete paving. She could hear the wind slapping and tugging at a banner on a pole near the doorway they'd come through, a lifetime ago. The crunch of gravel as another abseiler shuffled towards the platform to wait her turn. Thudding of blood in the channels of her ears.

The tannoy was crackling now and a gravelly voice making some announcement.

389

'And the oldest person yet to undertake this daring act. So let's all give a big cheer for Agnes Borrowdale, and I'm sure we all wish her the very best for her seventy-fifth birthday on Tuesday.'

The youngster looked at her in horror. Probably thinking of his own grandmother. Then he composed his face, 'That you, is it? Agnes? Well, happy birthday, then.'

She nodded, almost grateful for the momentary distraction. But it was a very brief moment. She knew what that word was now. Not numbness. Not fear. Something much darker, older, more pervasive. Something she had never, ever, experienced before. Absolute terror. Utter dread.

Another second or two of hesitation and she'd not have done it. Her knees would have crumpled.

Suddenly, above the blaring music, loud and clear, Seb's voice, 'Ready, Steady. Go!'

Agnes leaned back against the empty air.

It was true — the worst was over — she was doing it! Seven or eight feet down already. Amazing how comforting it was to see the pattern of bricks in front of her face. And the way her feet felt almost secure, flat against the wall. One step, two step, a couple of inches at a time, almost shuffling down. Legs still nice and straight. Rope sliding slowly, slowly through the thick, clumsy gauntlets.

She glanced along the building a few yards to her left where Red Gortex had been. Only the rope visible. He'd probably nearly reached the ground by now. That was fine. She was in no hurry. She'd never felt so buzzing with life since — since never! The jazz medley of *Happy Birthday* was still belting out from the tannoy. In her honour! Agnes Borrowdale, abseiler!

She was speeding up now, her steps getting longer. Watch it! Too late, the right foot wasn't making contact with the wall. The left foot fell away. She was kicking the air as she spun round on the rope.

★　★　★

Even above the noise of the music, Lucy could hear the sudden intake of breath all around her. Jack took a few steps forward, dragging her with him, her hand still tightly clutched in his.

'Sorry, mate. No public beyond this barrier. Not safe,' said one of the helmeted stewards.

'That's my mother up there! Can't you do something!'

'It's all right,' soothed the man. 'No danger, honest. Happens all the time. She's

391

managing fine, got one foot back on the wall again, look.'

'Well done, Agnes! Not that far now,' called a plump woman in a hand-knitted multi-coloured jumper, leaning forward across the barrier of red and white plastic tape.

'Watcha, Aggie! You're a star!' shouted a young man at her side.

People seem to be taking a really personal interest, thought Lucy. Well, well. Good old Agnes! She loosened her hand from Jack's grasp, flexing her squashed fingers before automatically linking her arm through his. 'She's nearly made it, look. She's OK, Jack. She's OK.'

'Thank God! Oh, thank God!' Jack disentangled his arm from Lucy's and was over the barrier and reaching up towards his mother's foot. He was hauled back just in time to prevent Agnes inadvertently kicking out at his head.

★   ★   ★

Solid ground again! Almost tempting to fall down and kiss it, the way a pope did when he came down the steps of an aeroplane. That last part hadn't been such fun, she had to admit. Not frightening — more embarrassing, really, losing her footing like that after doing so well. If her knees hadn't started trembling as soon as she'd reached the ground, she'd have felt like going back up and having another go.

Someone was standing in front of her, helping to remove the helmet. Someone else had put an arm across her back, steadying her. There was Molly, a few feet away. And Gazza, one hand on her shoulder, grinning like the Cheshire cat. And there was dear Edie, and little Scott. Before Agnes could take a step towards them, someone else was blocking the way. *Lucy?* Lucy! And the children! Emily with long hair now, and that must be Sam, staring up at her, bemused. Remembering the state of her own hair, Agnes slowly raised one hand to the nape of her neck. They wouldn't recognise her.

The man on her other side still had his arm around her shoulder, preventing her from stepping forward. She glanced up at his face, saying, 'I'm all right, now, thank — ' The flow of words halted abruptly when she recognised the features of that face, and read the expression in his eyes. He had never before looked at her with such . . . such *tenderness*.

'Ma,' he said in a choked voice. 'Ma.' and she was lifted off her feet in a fierce bear hug while claps and cheers and cat-calls rang out from the crowd.

★ ★ ★

Because of Felix, the little group gravitated towards the First Aid tent. For the next few minutes the churning thoughts and emotions of ten very different people were whizzing around as giddily as waltzers in a fairground. Joy, excitement, laughter. Love, of course, and twinges of jealousy. Curiosity, guilt.

'How did *you* get here?'

'What about you?'

'How long have you known Agnes?'

'When?'

'But *why?*'

'So who is . . . ?'

'But she's *my* Auntie Ness!'

'She's not, she's my grandma.'

There were silences too as they clustered under the awning, some finding chairs to sit on, some standing, shuffling from foot to foot, each trying to sort out the other's connection to the woman who was the pivot of their attention. It felt to Agnes as if her face would split in two if she didn't manage to stop herself from smiling quite so broadly.

'Grandma's swallowed smiley medicine,' whispered Sam to his sister, as Edie called out, 'Look, here's Joe!' and the introductions began all over again.

'So *you're* Jack!' muttered Joe, glaring at

him suspiciously. 'Your mother's told me about you.'

'I understand you've been very good to her,' said Jack in a hesitant voice. 'I can't begin to tell you how grateful I am . . . '

'Agnes is a real lady and I think we're friends, the both of us, so grateful doesn't come into it,' replied Joe before turning away.

In a couple of strides he was standing on the other side of Agnes, bending down towards her. He planted a light kiss on her cheek and said in a low voice, 'I got the shock of my life back there, hearing that tannoy. Can't stop now, though. On a visit to Sally-Ann. She'll be home Monday. Only came over to fetch Scott and Edie to see her.'

'So she's all right now? I'm so glad!'

'You will come and see us all again, won't you?'

'Try and stop me!' she laughed. 'Once I've sorted out my next movements, I'll give you a ring. You're high on my list, you and Scott, and Edie of course. But look at all these people I've got to please!' Agnes made a sweeping gesture with her hand.

She hadn't stopped smiling since Joe had first caught sight of her, sitting like some TV celebrity under the awning, surrounded by people eager to talk to her. Now it seemed that her smile was stretching wider still.

Smiles are like yawns, the way they spread from person to person, thought Joe as he looked around at Agnes's friends and relations. Even that Jack was smiling.

★ ★ ★

SCENE:
The main road outside a large hospital. A red Fiesta is parked dangerously close to the entrance.
ACTION:
Timothy Dolan, the exhausted young police constable, breaks down in tears of frustration at the sight of the parking ticket on his windscreen.

21

The relentless music hammered on. More and more people were milling around on the tarmac and almost every spare inch of grass had disappeared beneath sprawling bodies. The St John's Ambulance men and women were busier now with minor injuries: scalds from spilt tea; young children with grazed knees; an old woman in a thick winter coat who'd collapsed in the unexpected heat.

'Time to get moving, I think,' said Jack, clambering up from the groundsheet and stepping out onto an unclaimed square of grass with Sam still clinging to his neck.

'Suits me,' said Felix, rising slowly from his chair. 'That racket is getting to me now. What d'you think, Gazza, lad? Should we be making tracks?'

Agnes wanted nothing more than to spend the rest of the day with her son and grandchildren. Lucy as well, since that would please Emily and Sam. But there were all the others to consider too. 'Aren't you meant to be going home to your father for Easter, Gazza?' she asked.

'What, me? Na. Suit myself, really. Dad's

gone off with his new woman and her kids. Newquay. Could've gone too, only for the abseiling, but I'm not bothered. I'll keep an eye on Mr Punch, make sure he don't get up to anything.'

'But how are you going to get back?' pursued Agnes. 'I don't think Felix should be driving.'

'And I don't think you should've been dangling a hundred foot up from the end of a rope, Mrs Busybody.' His words were softened by the hint of a smile at the corner of his mouth. 'Anyway, don't want to speak too soon, but I'm feeling almost like a human again, a living one, not a week-old corpse.'

Lucy had been standing a little apart from the group, as if unsure of her role among these new friends of Agnes. She'd been sneaking little glances at her — those casual clothes, the trainers and tracksuit, that extraordinary hair! There was more to it than that, though, a deeper change. Lucy had never seen her looking so relaxed and bubbly. So at home with herself.

She took a few steps towards Agnes as she made to rise from her chair, and in a low voice said, 'I'm sure Mum and Barry wouldn't mind if you all come back to the house for a while. I mean, if you think people would like that? Relax in the garden for a bit while everyone decides what to do next.'

It really was too bad of Lucy. She could've asked first, before suggesting it to the World and his Wife. Put her in a very difficult position, this did, having them all trouping in through the front gate. Couldn't exactly say, 'Sorry, no, you'd better all clear off out again.' Where would she draw the line, anyway? Jack, she'd more or less invited already. Agnes? Of course she'd have to welcome Agnes. They might be ex, but you can't just write people off like that, can you? Anyway, no telling what might be brewing in Lucy's head. So, relations and exes only? And that Felix person who'd been so unwell, still looking like death warmed up, she could certainly sympathise with him. Then there was that scruffy young friend of Agnes's, he'd only just managed to hobble along to her house. And as for the woman with such dubious taste in knitwear, once she'd opened her mouth there was no way of escaping that flood of words.

'Ooh! This is really kind of you, inviting me into your lovely home, when you don't know me from Adam, or Eve, I should say, and I've only just made the acquaintance of your daughter and grandchildren, but of course, I felt a bond with them right from the start since I've been helping Agnes try to track them down all week, and you too, in a manner of speaking. So here we all are then, quite a little crowd, and seeing as it's such a lovely day you might prefer we all went straight round the back into your garden. I don't expect you want all these hundreds of shoes tramping through your house.'

That final sentence redeemed her. Molly could talk the hind legs off a whole herd of donkeys, but at least she'd shown some consideration.

Might not be too much of a disaster after all, if she could keep them outside. How many was it, five, six adults? Plus her and Barry and the two kids. It was gone 12.30 already so why not go the whole hog and give them all lunch? Barry would jump at the chance of getting out the new barbecue, big as a kitchen range, with more fancy knobs and settings than she'd ever want to fathom.

He could stop off at Sainsbury's on the way home. Easy way of feeding the kids too, and save her from doing a big meal tonight.

★　★　★

Half past three, and the sun was hotter than ever in this sheltered garden — like mid-June, and still only the first week in April. The party was beginning to break up. Felix decamped to the bottom of the lawn and the speckled shade of the huge copper beech, where Agnes soon joined him, hugging an armful of cushions which she placed on Dianne's tartan travel rug.

Molly was making herself useful in the kitchen with Barry, while Dianne was relaxing on the bench, absorbing the sunshine with Lucy. Jack was rolling around on the grass with his son, while Gazza surprised them all by his endless patience in combing Emily's hair into tens of stringy little plaits as she sat cross-legged at his feet, giggling and squealing when he tugged a little too hard.

'He's getting extra time today, isn't he? Jack, I mean, with the kids. Nice for them, too.'

'Mmm,' responded Lucy, as Jack rolled over onto his hands and knees and Sam struggled to climb astride his back.

'Like a great kid himself. But then, aren't they all?'

Lucy remained silent, her face unreadable. After a minute, Dianne ventured, 'Is he planning to stay with those friends of his again tonight, d'you think? I could make up a bed for him here, if you'd like, since it's his real day for the kids tomorrow. Agnes too, now he's found her again.'

'What you playing at, Mum? You've only got four bedrooms, and I'm certainly not sharing with him.'

'That's unfair, Lucy,' Dianne retorted. 'You know I've never interfered in your life. I'm just trying to plan ahead for the weekend, that's all. Anyway, if you must know, there's a Z-bed I could make up in the study if necessary.'

'Sorry,' sighed Lucy. 'Bit of a touchy subject. It's not that I want Jack back again. Far from it. Anyway, he's got that Monica now. And Sean's still . . . Oh, I don't know! It's just . . . seeing Jack with the kids, and how they are with him.' She sighed more deeply. 'Why does life have to be so complicated?'

'It'll all come out in the wash, at the end of the day. Look at me and Barry! I'd never have thought — '

'Yes, Mum,' interrupted Lucy, tapping her fingers on the arm of the bench. OK, so it wasn't Mum's fault. Dad was the one who'd left them. But her second marriage so late in life wasn't exactly going to solve things for Emmy and Sam.

As if on cue both children appeared at Lucy's side, Emmy with her miniature dreadlocks, each fastened with a different coloured plastic tag from a box of freezer-bags, and Sam tugging her hand and saying,

'Come 'long Mummy. We're all going to the park with Daddy.'

Lucy hesitated, glancing at Jack who was standing, arms folded, shifting his weight from one foot to the other and staring with exaggerated interest at the mass of flowering currant and forsythia against the fence beyond the kitchen window.

'There's that nice little playground in Rectory Park, just across the road. You won't have to be out long,' said Dianne. 'I'm going to take myself inside and see what that Molly's up to with my husband!'

⋆ ⋆ ⋆

No leaves out yet. Not on the lower levels at any rate. Agnes gazed up past the smooth, thick boughs, up and up through the criss-cross pattern of thinner branches to a denser scribble of twigs against flickers of blue. A long way off — but not as high as the roof she'd balanced on a few short hours ago, paralysed with cold, sick dread.

A smile seeped back across her face as she savoured again the delight of breaking through that barrier of fear into a world where she was light and powerful as the wind, where she could do anything she chose.

A sudden snort was followed by a deep

grumble of breath from Felix, stretched out fast asleep on the edge of the rug. Another, louder snort, and he sat bolt upright, looking around in bemusement.

'What? Agnes? Oh! I must've dropped off there for a second.'

Agnes smiled. 'How are you now, Felix? Can I fetch you a drink or anything?'

'No. No thank you. Er, Agnes, I don't want you thinking. I mean, I do seem to be all right now, but . . . '

'Felix, a blind man could've seen you were in no fit state for anything. Anyway,' she laughed, 'you might find this hard to believe, but I got a such huge amount of satisfaction! I still feel . . . how can I put it? I think the expression these days is high. High as a kite!'

Felix sighed. 'I couldn't even get that right. All keyed up to do it, this time, and then look at me!'

'Yeh, look at you!' Felix and Agnes started in surprise at Gazza's voice. He had hobbled down the lawn towards them, supported by Molly's arm. 'Skiver. And that's not short for sky-diver, is it?' Gazza was still laughing as he lowered himself carefully onto the rug. 'Call yourself a member of the Dangerous Sports thingy? Real earth-worm, you are. The only sport you'll be fit for is pot-holing, I reckon.'

Molly knelt down, then sat back on her

heels. 'Thanks dear,' she said, as Agnes passed her a couple of cushions. 'Now, then, stop bullying poor Felix, you horrid boy! He really has been very unwell.'

'Well,' said Gazza, 'he's the one who was dead set on carrying on with this Dangerous Sports idea. Needs to put his money where his mouth is. Don't you, Mr Punch?'

'Gazza, dear,' said Agnes sweetly, 'If you're trying to tell Felix something, I think you're going to have to dispense with subtlety and come straight to the point.'

'Oh! OK then, Aggie,' he laughed.

'Perhaps you'll pay me the courtesy of allowing me to speak, now?' said Felix, picking up a spare cushion and positioning it on a broad tree root, before settling himself comfortably, resting his hands on his knees and leaning forward to address the little group.

Enjoys theatricals, smiled Agnes to herself.

Felix coughed. 'Friends,' he began, 'Fellow members of the Dangerous Sports Euthanasia Society. I have an announcement to make. As you all know, I owe a debt of gratitude to this incorrigible troublemaker here, Agnes Borrowdale. I am of course referring to Agnes's invention. It has set in motion a train of thought — '

'Train! That's a good one!'

'Thank you, Gazza. May I continue? So, a train of thought, one way or another, which has led me to contemplate other forms of transport — '

'You never are!' interrupted Gazza. 'I mean, I know we discussed it last night, but I thought it was just the drink talking. You mean you're really going to?'

'Let the man speak, for pity's sake, Gazza!' exclaimed Molly, completely mystified.

Agnes remained silent. He *was* going to. He *was*. And yes, it would be down to her, in a way. She clapped her hands together, and beamed at the three of them.

'*In vino, veritas,* Gazza. You'd do well to remember that. Yes, I am really going to,' said Felix solemnly, 'but since my fear of flying has in no way diminished, the only way I can be sure of getting on that plane is if Agnes will to agree to come with me, breathing fire and brimstone at my back.'

'But where to, Felix?' wailed Molly. 'Where is it you're — Oh!' she shrieked, light dawning, 'It's Ruby! You're going to visit Ruby! Oh Felix! Agnes! I think that's quite the most romantic thing I've ever heard,' and she reached out her hands to clasp Agnes's in her right, and Gazza's in her left.

Agnes smiled at Molly, then turned her head. 'A very wise decision, Felix! I'm sure you won't regret it, not from what I gathered about Ruby in that lovely letter. But I'm afraid you'll have to travel on your own. Or not with me, at any rate.'

'And why not?' he barked. Then his frown lifted and he said in a mischievous tone, 'I thought it was part of your job, supporting new members. Isn't that what you told me last Sunday, back in New Street Station?'

'Felix! You know it was all a fabric of lies!' exclaimed Agnes. 'The fact is, it would be a little beyond my budget. But I do I feel honoured to be asked. Very honoured.'

'Honoured, my foot! You're the only person I could rely on to be bossy enough to prevent me from backing out of it at the last minute. As for your budget, it's your birthday on Tuesday, isn't it?'

'Ye — es?'

'And it was mine, if you remember, last Monday, the day after you — well, you know.'

'Ye — es.'

'So, I could say you owe me a birthday present, and letting me pay for you would be a most acceptable present. Or I could say, I owe you — well, quite a lot, as it happens, and I'd like to give you this as a present. So which is to be? Will you give, or receive?'

'Smart move, Mr Punch,' exclaimed Gazza.

'Give, or receive! Try and get out of that one, Aggie!'

'Agnes, dear, you can't possibly refuse. Not when he's asking you so nicely.'

'But . . . but . . . ' faltered Agnes.

'If there's one thing I've learned from you, Agnes, it's that people *can* do things — if they want to enough. Why do you suppose I agreed to step in for Gazza with the abseiling?'

'I thought, well, you can imagine! Yes, I did think it was all because of my silly Dangerous Sports idea.'

'Precisely! That was what set me thinking. Not very happy thoughts to start with, I admit. Sylvia and Philip — my part in that. But I'd be letting them down even more badly if I turn down Ruby's offer. Not that I'm saying she feels what you all seem to think, but she must feel something, offering to pay for my flight out there.'

'Phew!' sighed Gazza, wiping his brow in an exaggerated gesture, 'You've actually managed to twig that!'

'So you see,' continued Felix, ignoring Gazza's interruption, 'the abseiling was an ideal opportunity to push myself, conquer my fear, all that corny stuff. Make me more likely to fly, wouldn't it? So that's where you come in, Agnes. If you'll agree.'

'But . . . It's just . . . I'd like a bit of time to think things through. For a start, it can't be cheap, flying all the way out there and back. I don't honestly see how I could let — '

'Give me strength!' groaned Felix. 'I'm certainly not going into details about my financial affairs. What I will say is, there's a sizeable sum of insurance money that's been sitting untouched in a building society for twenty years, and I owe it to Sylvie and Pip to start spending it. You can't insult their memory by refusing, can you Agnes?'

There was a long silence as three pairs of eyes were fixed on her solemn face. It was taking all her concentration to prevent the bubbles of laughter from rising too quickly. Of course she couldn't refuse! Not after all she'd been through this last week. She'd never dreamed that she was the sort of person who'd hitch a lift in a lorry, or break into an empty house for the night, and as for abseiling!

'So when do we go, Felix?' she said, as her smile broke surface.

* * *

Jack was pacing up and down on the path just outside the kitchen window, glaring towards the little group sprawled under the tree at the

409

bottom of the garden. What had they got to be so merry about — all that cheering and clapping? His own mother, giggling like a schoolgirl.

Of course he'd been relieved to see her alive and well. Amazingly well. Never so relieved about anything in all his life. But now the reaction was setting in — had she any idea at all of what she'd put him through, this last week?

All right, there'd been a message on the ansaphone, and a postcard that arrived only this morning. But what about the sheer thoughtlessness of running away in the first place, as though it had been some kid's game, dressing up for the part. And now look at her, that outrageous coloured hair, as bad as Hailey! Be getting herself a nose ring or a tattoo next.

'She's some woman, your mother,' Barry had said, offering him another helping of sausages and charred pork. 'Whatever made her choose to go and live in an old folks' home? Never be the kind of place for her, however old she gets. No wonder she took herself off pretty sharpish.'

Agnes hadn't been able to prevent her friends from boasting about her exploits as they sat around in the sunshine devouring the food as fast as Barry could cook it — apart from Felix, who was sipping cold lime juice, and toying with a plain bread-roll. Emily and Sam had listened with their eyes on stalks as Molly and Felix and Gazza filled in the details of her week's adventures.

She's got more friends than I have, right now, thought Jack morosely, as he watched Emily skipping down the lawn towards them, Lucy following more hesitantly a few yards behind. Barry and Dianne had taken Sam off for a final trip to the supermarket. 'Better have too much than not enough,' Dianne had said.

Jack himself might just as well be back in Saxon Meadow for all anyone here would care. Only there'd be no one there, either, apart from that smelly little dog of Monica's. Hailey and Donna were out when he'd rung them from the hospital grounds, his voice bubbling over with excitement when he left the message on the ansaphone. There'd been no one in at Monica's parents' house either. He'd felt cheated, having to transmit his wonderful news to another machine.

Yes. It was wonderful news. It still was. Face it, Jack, it's not Ma that's the real problem, is it?

Jack stopped his pacing and stared at the mass of yellow flowers on the shrub in front of him. Past their best now. He could see that, close up. If he reached out and shook that branch, they'd tumble to the ground.

He turned and slouched towards the bench against the wall of the house. It was still in full sun, and the bricks behind his head were radiating warmth. From where he was sitting he could see Emily, snuggled up against her grandmother, and Lucy, sitting cross-legged on the grass, clearly joining in the animated conversation.

Lucy.

What a mess. It wasn't just his cock that was responding to her presence. If only it was as simple as that. Or the fact that she was younger and prettier and cleverer than Monica. Jack, you're a real shit, even thinking it! Totally out of order, comparing people like that. He owed a lot to Monica, he really did. Without her, he could well have sunk into a serious depression.

But Lucy. There was no getting away from the fact that she was the mother of his children. Their children. For a few brief minutes they'd been a family again, the four of them. There'd been this . . . this . . . something he couldn't find a word for. Love was the nearest he could get to it. But it was more even than that. It was a completeness, the way they all fitted with each other, hands reaching out so naturally as they crossed the road together, Lucy and Sam, Sam and Jack, Jack and Emmy.

It lasted all the way down the short road to the open ground, cricket field on the right, copse of oak trees on the left. As one body they'd turned towards the trees. The children had scattered, darting backwards and forwards, giggling and squealing, playing tag round and round the gnarled trunks, deeper and deeper into the little copse until suddenly they'd reached an open field on the other side. Neither Jack nor Lucy had uttered a word. Had Lucy, too, been afraid of breaking the spell?

Then Sam had run back to them panting and smiling as he took Lucy's hand and said, 'Now we've got our other Grandma back, can we go and live in the House-Before with you and Daddy?'

Emily was standing a few feet away, looking down at her feet. Her hands were clenched at her sides. She seemed to be holding her breath.

Jack realised that he, too was holding his.

Lucy said gently, 'We can't do that, Sammy. Other people are living in that house now.'

'But if we said we want it back, could we?'

'Things don't work like that, I'm afraid. When you've given something away, you can't expect a person to give it back again. Remember when Emmy gave you her bike last year — '

'I was only pretending to want that back,' said Emily fiercely. 'It was much too small. I was only teasing.'

'I know that, sweetheart. I was just trying to explain to Sammy — '

'It's not very nice, teasing people, is it?' muttered Emily, digging at the grass with her heel.

Jack caught Lucy's eye.

'You're absolutely right, Sugar Plum,' he laughed, striding towards his daughter and hoisting her round onto his back. She clutched his shoulders and he galloped off into the field calling loudly, 'Come on Lu, come on Sammy, catch us if you can!'

★ ★ ★

It had been a different sort of silence on the way back to Dianne's house, broken, eventually, by snatches of strained conversation. Yes, wasn't Agnes extraordinary. Lucy could scarcely believe, even now, that she had really done that abseiling. Yes, what a strange little bunch of friends she'd accumulated along the way. Fallen on her feet, really. Where was she likely to want to go next?

414

'Back to Saxon Meadow, I expect,' Jack had said. 'Though I'm not sure she wouldn't prefer to be in a little flat somewhere. I should have realised that from the start.'

'We all make mistakes,' Lucy had said, as she pushed open the gate.

Before she'd rejoined the others Jack said hurriedly, 'Look, we need to talk, later, when they're in bed, the kids. Sean, and everything. Of course it's your business what you do, but at the same time . . . '

'You're right. We'll have to talk. Not that I've finally decided anything.'

And that was it. He'd been almost glad to have to postpone any real conversation. What could he say, anyway?

★　★　★

Lucy looked across at Emily, preening herself as she and Agnes compared hairstyles. She seemed to have recovered from that little upset, thank goodness. That was the hardest thing about all this. The effect on the children.

'Are you really going on holiday with that man, Grandma?' she heard Emily ask. 'Is he your boyfriend, then?' As everyone around her collapsed into helpless laughter, Emily frowned and asked, 'What's so funny? There's

415

lots of much older people on *EastEnders* and *Coronation Street*. Some of them kiss each other when they aren't married. None of them would dare do that climbing thing that Grandma did.'

Gazza was the first to regain the power of speech. 'You're absolutely right, Emily. Old people do behave very shockingly these days. And then they have the cheek to complain about the young! We're only laughing because Felix already has a girlfriend, and your Grandma is going with him because he's scared of flying.'

'Oh,' she said, and thought for a minute before looking straight at Felix and adding kindly, 'I used to be scared of flying, but me and Mummy and Sean and Sam went to Spain last year, and actually, it's not scary a bit. In fact, it's exactly like being in a train, only you see clouds instead of fields and stuff.'

The conversation turned to West Bridgford for a while, with Lucy and Molly working out what acquaintances or shops they had in common.

Molly was explaining the exact whereabouts of her little hotel when Gazza chipped in. 'That reminds me! Agnes, you said you'd got an idea for Molly, and you were going to tell us at breakfast the next day, only you never did.'

Agnes caught Molly's eye and she nodded.

'Tell them,' Molly said.

'We were only talking,' began Agnes.

'And now for something we couldn't have guessed,' laughed Felix.

'If you'll allow me to finish,' said Agnes, 'It was only the start of a possible idea.'

'It would be so lovely if we could do something along those lines,' said Molly. 'Felix, you were talking about attracting a different sort of customer, and then there's Agnes's own problem of where she's going to live. There must be lots of other people who don't want sit around in an old folks' home just waiting to die — '

'When there's a hundred and one interesting ways of finishing yourself off, you mean?' put in Gazza excitedly.

'Exactly. So what we could do is, combine everything together, and open up my hotel to people who want to try out exciting things they've never dared to do before.'

'They don't actually have to want to die, though,' said Agnes sternly. 'In fact, that's not the aim at all. The whole point is to squeeze some excitement out of their last few years, and be among other like-minded people who won't forever be telling them they're too old to try out new ventures.'

'And you're fully qualified now, Aggie.

Living proof!' said Gazza. 'I'll get on to my mate at Nottingham about his uni's sporting activities. And hey, Mr Punch, what about a Brum branch? You've got plenty of space in your house, haven't you?'

'Hold your horses, Gazza, lad,' laughed Felix.

'There's a lot to think through first,' said Agnes. 'It's just an idea, remember!'

'An ace idea, though,' said Gazza.

'My Grandma!' said Emily proudly. 'Did you say Grandma has a problem about where to live, Molly? Did you?'

'Er, in a way, yes,' said Molly.

'Well it's my turn for ideas. Grandma can come and live with me and mummy and Sam. And Sean, if he promises not to shout any more. Though not Daddy, cos Daddy has another family now,' she added sadly.

'That's a lovely idea,' smiled Lucy. 'Grandma and I will talk about it later.'

'Oh! Later! That means no, then. Sorry Grandma,' said Emily resignedly. 'When I grow up you can come and live with me if you want to.'

'Thank you, Emily. I should like that very much indeed,' said Agnes, fumbling in her sleeve for a handkerchief.

'What I meant was,' said Lucy, 'I'm not sure about how Sean would take it, darling.

He's been a bit, you know, busy at work, stressed. I was thinking it might be a good idea if we leave him alone for a little longer. Find somewhere else to stay for a while when we go back to Nottingham.'

'Oh! cool!' said Emily, perking up again. 'We can stay in Molly's hotel then. Can we Molly? Say yes! Please, please *please* say yes! And then Grandma can stay too cos she's your friend. I've only ever stayed in a hotel once and that was in Spain. But I never have in England. Not ever. Can we, Mummy? You've got to say yes this time.'

★　★　★

Yet another different bed. How many did that make? Fancy counting beds instead of sheep! Not that Agnes was in any real hurry to get to sleep. Her thoughts were too exciting. How wonderful to be kept awake by exciting thoughts! How nice it was, being old. The freedom of it!

Selfish, perhaps. But realistic, too. An individual could only shoulder full responsibility for one life, with its own particular set of mistakes. All she could hope to do was try to rectify her own, and be on hand to offer help where it was wanted.

Jack, for instance. His court case this

coming Tuesday. Molly had wanted to arrange a little birthday party for her, with Felix and Gazza, but that would have to wait a few days. The least she could do for Jack was to be there with him. Even though her presence was unlikely to influence any magistrate, she couldn't not be there. Plenty of time for parties later.

Dear Jack. He was thrashing about like a fish on a line. Two lines, Lucy and Monica. Three even, counting the children. Or four, with his new-found sense of responsibility towards her. He'd work out what to do for the best, in the end, and be the stronger for it. She'd been surprised and touched to hear him talk with genuine concern about Monica and the two girls — how much they relied on him now, what he felt he owed to Monica. She could have tried harder with Monica herself, if she hadn't been so wrapped up in her own misery.

Life was much more difficult for married people these days. It wasn't for her to pass judgement on them. Clearly, Lucy had needed something that Jack had been unable or unwilling to give her. Something she'd found in Sean. Or thought she had. Where had that need come from in the first place?

The more she thought about everything — Lucy and her parents, Jack and Henry, herself and Seb in that chilly stone house with its rigid rules — the more confusing it all seemed. Random images drifted across her mind's eye: Father's tight face as he ripped open that telegram, his scorn at her tears, she should be proud of her brother — a hero's death; Henry in the pulpit proclaiming the straight and narrow way to salvation; Henry's dog, Jasper, on the back lawn on a summer Sunday evening circling round and round and round, snapping in vain at his own defiant tail.

Everything suddenly clicked into a single certainty: she could be sure of nothing, she knew nothing. Was this the ultimate wisdom, a realisation of one's own ignorance?

'If I can't be a shining example, at least I can be a dreadful warning.' Where was it she'd read that? Certainly, she was no shining example. How much else might she have achieved in her life, if only —

No. There was one thing she could be sure of: if she was ever going to write a constitution for this society that Molly and Felix and Gazza refused to let her bury, then that phrase would be banned for a start: *if only*.

Her society would be dedicated to the principle of better late than never.

Everyone should have the chance of

experiencing, at least once in a lifetime, that exhilaration she had felt this morning when she'd forced herself to lean out over the abyss and discovered what had seemed at the time like the secret meaning of life: the beautiful simplicity of letting go of fear.